A Star for Mrs. Blake

Center Point
Large Print

**This Large Print Book carries the
Seal of Approval of N.A.V.H.**

A Star for
Mrs. Blake

APRIL SMITH

CENTER POINT LARGE PRINT
THORNDIKE, MAINE

This Center Point Large Print edition is published in the
year 2014 by arrangement with Alfred A. Knopf,
an imprint of The Knopf Doubleday Publishing Group,
a division of Random House, LLC.

The text of this Large Print edition is unabridged.
In other aspects, this book may vary
from the original edition.
Printed in the United States of America
on permanent paper.
Set in 16-point Times New Roman type.

ISBN: 978-1-62899-036-2

Library of Congress Cataloging-in-Publication Data

Smith, April, 1949–
A star for Mrs. Blake / April Smith. — Center Point Large Print edition.
pages ; cm
ISBN 978-1-62899-036-2 (library binding : alk. paper)
1. Mothers and sons—Fiction. 2. Parental grief—Fiction.
   3. United States—History—1919–1933—Fiction.
   4. World War, 1914–1918—Fiction.
   5. Cemeteries—France—Verdun—Fiction. 6. Large type books.
   I. Title.
PS3569.M467S73 2014b
813′.54—dc23
                                                    2013046236

For those who have served

In 1929, Congress enacted legislation that authorized the secretary of war to arrange for pilgrimages to the European cemeteries "by mothers and widows of members of military and naval forces of the United States who died in the service at any time between April 5, 1917, and July 1, 1921, and whose remains are now interred in such cemeteries." Congress later extended eligibility for pilgrimages to mothers and widows of men who died and were buried at sea or who died at sea or overseas and whose places of burial were unknown. The Office of the Quartermaster General determined that 17,389 women were eligible. By October 31, 1933, when the project ended, 6,693 women had made the pilgrimage.

—NATIONAL ARCHIVES

This is a work of fiction.

A Star for Mrs. Blake

DEER ISLE, MAINE

1931

1

February

C ora Blake was certainly not planning on going to Paris that spring. Or ever in her lifetime. She was the librarian in a small town on the tip of an island off the coast of Maine, which didn't mean she'd never traveled. She did spend two years at Colby College in Waterville and visited family in Portland, went to Arizona once, and if you counted yachting, knew most of the New England coast. Her mother had been the great adventurer, married to a sea captain who'd taken her all around the world. Cora was born off the coast of Rio de Janeiro, which might account for her venturesome spirit, but now she roamed only in books. Summer people from North Carolina and Boston would stop by the quaint old library building to chat, and wonder how she could stand to live in such a tiny place with those terrible winters.

"I have everything I want right on the island," she'd say. "We're so off the beaten path, you've got to be satisfied with the way it is."

Since the crash of 'twenty-nine the county had stopped paying her salary, but Cora kept on librarying anyway, two days and one morning a week, for free. She did it for the sociability and out of duty to her readers, but she was as hard up for cash as anybody. That's why when the whistle started blowing at the break of dawn out at Healy's cannery, it sounded to Cora Blake like Gabriel himself swinging out on the horn.

It was 5:00 a.m. in the pit of February. The cannery had been silent for more than two weeks, but now the whistle was loud and clear, piercing the bleat of the foghorn. *Wake up!* it shrilled. *There's work!* and throughout the village women rose up out of warm beds wondering how much work there would be and how long they might be gone doing it. The length of the job depended on the catch. Clams, as long as they're watered down at night, will be fine until the next day—but fish has to be put up right away or it will spoil. They could end up packing twenty-four hours straight, which nobody would moan about at a time when the Great Depression had taken away so many jobs, but they had just thirty minutes to dress and put out food for the family before the second whistle started up, scolding them to get out the door. By then the worker-transportation bus would be leaving from in front of the post office, and if you missed it, well, good night and good luck.

In the top bedroom of one of the old stone-cutter's cottages facing the harbor—mustard-yellow, with squares for windows like a child would draw—Cora was rapidly calculating four meals ahead. Life had changed since she'd left Tide's End Farm, a hundred acres that had been in the family since 1759. Five years ago, her mother, Luella, and older sister, Avis, had passed from cholera, and Cora moved to town in order to look after her nieces, Sarah, fourteen, Laura, twelve, and Kathleen, ten. Now the farm lay derelict and far from her mind. There were the three girls plus her brother-in-law to cook for, and all she had in quantity was beans.

Most people can't tell the difference between one bean and another. Most don't give a hoot. Down East anyway, a lot of folks were making it through hard times on the Marafax beans supplied by the federal government, chewy amber-colored little things that prudent types cooked only with salt. Cora had gone up to the city and gotten some, along with margarine you had to mix by hand with yellow coloring, so it didn't look like dental wax. They still had turnips and squash in the cellar hay mow.

She woke Sarah, who was sprawled beside her in a dead pile under the quilts, and gave her the lowdown. Aunt Cora was going on a pay streak and, as the oldest, Sarah would be in charge of the household, most of which was laid up with flu. Sarah didn't move. She wasn't sick, but her eyes remained shut on principle.

"Can I make biscuits?" she asked.

"I don't want to see a speck of wasted flour

when I get home," Cora warned. "And no cigarettes. Don't think I won't know, because I can smell them on you."

The girl uttered something befitting a half-asleep adolescent, but Cora was already across the frigid bedroom. It was impossible to keep warm without coal. Her brother-in-law, Big Ole Uncle Percy, had started cutting wood off someone else's parcel, but what could you do? Rags stuffed under the doors did nothing to stop the glacial drafts that swept down from Nova Scotia. She looked to the window to gauge the day; the glass was scrolled with the roseate frost of dawn. Outside the snow was fresh and it was well below freezing, but Cora was cheered to see there would be sun.

She pulled a pair of large woolen stockings from the cedar chest. They had been patched up so often they had acquired the combined character of the three generations who had worn them, which meant they belonged to nobody, and were seen by Cora not with sentiment, but as a handy something to be pulled on top of her shoes, followed by galoshes that had been resewn where the rubber split.

Entering the icy kitchen, Cora was grateful for the millionth time to her pragmatic mother. She had sailed through the Panama Canal as Captain Frederick Harding's wife on the windjammer *Lara Leigh*, delivering molasses and timber and sometimes chartered for the pleasure of wealthy businessmen in Florida, but it was hardly as glamorous as it sounded. Her duties were to cook, sew, and clean the cabin, and to be pleasant company for the wives at the yacht clubs where they moored. When they returned to Tide's End Farm, Luella raised Cora and her sister with the self-reliance she'd learned at sea. She taught them, for example, that no matter if you were tired and falling off your feet, you always got the stove ready before you went to bed. Mostly it was an island tradition for the man of the house to lay the fire, but Captain Harding would be gone on voyages for months, and so it became a mother-daughter ritual every night to whittle sticks of winter pine into clean-smelling curls.

"No need for kerosene a'tall," her mother would say with satisfaction.

When she was little, it was Cora's job to stack the kindling neatly in the fire box, a thing she loved to do, because once the iron door was latched, the day would come to a quiet close with the reassuring knowledge that Mother had taken care of today, tonight, and tomorrow. Every night she did the same for her nieces, using the sharp old jackknife to turn out perfect spirals before their captivated eyes. It still gave her a feeling of being in safekeeping. And in the morning the stove always lit with just one match.

She got the kettle steaming and this she poured into another kettle of those reliable beans. She lit a lantern on the oilcloth-covered table. The light fell on the lush jacket illustration of *Treasure Island*, which was sitting on top of the pile she'd brought home for the kids who were sick in bed. One thing about librarying is you can take home whatever you please off the shelves, and since she was the only one keeping the place open, Cora felt perfectly in the right doing so. *Treasure Island* was one of her favorites. She dragged her fingertips over the book as if to take it all in, even the feel of the type. She knew the story by heart— her father had read it out loud to her, she'd read it to her son, Sammy, and later on he'd read it back to Grandpa Harding—about young Jim Hawkins and his indomitable mother, who runs the Admiral Benbow Inn. One day a mysterious old sailor named Pew shows up to end his days in peace by the sea, but he's given the terrible "black spot," a warning that means death, and sure enough, the pirates attack the inn, and Jim and his mother barely escape—

The second whistle startled her back to life, and she hastily swallowed a last bite of corn bread. What had she been dreaming of? She checked to be sure the beans were simmering nicely, took her mackinaw from its peg, and closed the kitchen door firmly against the wind.

Her eyes watered as the cold hit. It wasn't just the cold, but the blinding attack of whiteness that mirrored off the ice-encrusted snow. Navigating the granite slope from the doorstep to Main Street was perilous, especially buffeted by a screaming northeast wind. She caught hold of a clothesline and edged down. Rows of whitecaps marched across the harbor. Icicles hung off the pier, sharp as staves. The frost-blue sky wheeled above, hard in the light of a heatless sun. Her nose ran and teeth ached from the bitter temperature. Nothing moved in the village except snow-smoke billowing off the roofs of the chain of severe wooden cottages implausibly anchored to a finger of rock. Their closed white faces took the pummeling directly off the ocean and said nothing. It was as if everything had frozen into a crystal of itself and Cora Blake was the only warm and living thing.

Then she saw that she had missed the bus. Because there was certainly no bright red little puffer waiting in front of the post office; no black exhaust stains on the snow, or tire tracks, either, had she been composed enough to notice. Cora almost cried. Being late, she had just thrown away a dollar and a half, tossed it to the breeze. Marooned at the snowbound post office with no way to get out to the factory, she raged at her dawdling over a child's book, numb fingers clenched inside the pockets of the plaid mackinaw so worn it might have come from the Scottish Highlands with her forebears.

Hell, she would walk.

The shore road was open to rolling gusts off the harbor that pierced the poor wool of the ancient mackinaw and swept clouds of dry snow off the wooden sidewalk ahead. A skiff had broken loose, tossed up and smashed against the wharf. But the square-built lobster boats rode the twenty-foot waves like smart-aleck tough guys, chins out. Cora put one foot in front of the other, eyes fixed on the crest of Peaks Hill, methodically getting past the hooded shapes of the variety store, barbershop, the notions and yard goods store—all shuttered with snow—the sawmill, the Odd Fellows Hall out on the bend, until the village was at her back and the wind died wailing in the spruce.

It would be deep snowfall all the way to the point. Cora was hoping for an easy trek on the tire tracks left by the bus, but there were none—erased by whirling devils of ice particles? Or had she gotten off the road entirely? She took in the silence, unafraid. It went with a certain hum in her head that was always there, a nameless sense of direction that seemed to come from the earth up through the soles of her feet. She became aware of jaybirds. Evergreens standing in unspoiled snow up to their skirts. She noticed a patch of shadows, dug up by something, possibly moose. Closer, she saw they were shoe prints, multiple tracks heading east. Cora thrashed forward, snow sliding down the galoshes. At the top of Peaks Hill she saw a small group of cannery workers trudging through the endless white like anxious refugees. By the time she'd reached them, she was sweating in the woolens and couldn't feel her toes.

They were women dressed as she was, in heavy dark skirts down to their ankles and hodgepodge layers of tattered coats.

"Where is the bus?" Cora asked, breathless.

"Ain't no bus. Not no more," snapped Essie Jordan. With her long bland face sticking out beneath a cap that was crocheted with green filigree, she resembled a bunch of celery.

"What happened to it?"

"Mr. Healy says gasoline's too expensive. So we walk."

"We walk," echoed Cora, grateful to join the march of plain-featured, hardworking ladies in homespun clothes that smelled of cow dung and pine pitch, ages twelve to sixty, trooping along in the snow to do the filthy factory work of the republic—slow, resolute, keeping in a tight group to buffer the wind, the young ones breaking trail for the rest.

It was another mile to where the continental bedrock ends, a rocky ledge that slopes into the water, the cannery looking like it was about to slide off the tip. She thought about a cup of tea with sugar when the sandwich man came. It was just a distraction of mind. She wouldn't spend two cents on herself for a cup of tea.

After a while the sun bowed out behind a bank of fog and the air grew dense and bitter cold. Nearer to the ocean, the drifts thinned away, showing outcrops of basalt lying sideways in the empty fields where they'd been dumped a millennium ago, and soon there was more road than snow beneath their feet. When the shape of a somber little chapel appeared in the mist, they knew they had reached the farthest crossroads, and from there it was just half a mile to go along a cobble beach before they caught sight of the smokestack and double roof of the cannery.

Cora was to cut the heads and tails off sardines with a scissors. It was a job she had done since childhood, and her nieces would have been there too, if they weren't home sick. The first thing she did was to tape her fingers because you had to press hard against the scissors in order to make two strong cuts that severed the spine. More than two cuts would make Mr. Healy mad. The fish flipped around dangerously, suffocating on air. The heads were used for bait and went into one bucket, the bodies another. The buckets were tended by the littlest girls. This was how one day at the cannery Cora's older sister, Avis, nearly cut off a thumb when she was eight, chasing a dying sardine. Their mother, Luella, was on the labeling machine down the other end, and Mr. Healy wanted her to stay put, so he said nothing about the accident, shoving Avis out the door and telling her to run home, halfway bleeding to death.

Luella was incensed when she found out, and told Mrs. Healy what her husband had done. The next day he showed up with a bag of peppermints for Avis, but it was only because Luella was a fast packer and saved him money in the long run. Cora had inherited the knack. When the racks holding trays of cooked sardines started coming out of the ovens on that February day, Mr. Healy moved Cora Blake to the canning line. She could do fifty cans in half an hour despite the stench and the rivers of gurry—gray sludge of wasted fish heads and entrails—they were forced to stand in. For every tray you finished you put a wooden token in the jar. Cora wasn't sorry to put those scissors down; her sleeves were already all stiffened up with the juices and lifeblood.

The cannery shook with the impact of waves breaking just below. Spume off the whitecaps spit right through gaps in the rotted wood. Inside it was cold as an icebox, except for scalding fits of steam when the oven doors were opened. Despite the treacherous conditions, Mr. Healy enforced the regulation that employees must wear aprons and coverings over their hair. None were provided, so women brought their own— bandannas and boudoir caps would do—resulting in some odd costumes. Cora kept the mackinaw on, along with a sunbonnet tied beneath her chin, so the ribbons wouldn't get caught in the machinery.

It was just her luck to be on the assembly line across from Mrs. Celery Face, Essie Jordan, president of the Martha Washington Benevolent Society. Martha Washington was a temperance society, which meant a hodgepodge of angry wives who were fed up with living with drunken men. The men wouldn't listen to them, so they turned to other women, in the hope that collective female power would get them to behave. Some, like Essie Jordan, seemed mad as hell at just about everything. Her small cunning blue eyes said, *I'm still here and don't you forget it!*

"I'm telling you for your own good," Essie said. She had to shout above the clatter. "Your brother-in-law is askin' for it, right out flouting the law."

"Just what are you referring to?"

With Big Ole Uncle Percy there were always possibilities: stealing wood, stealing lobster traps, spitting, shooting at the racket boys from Portland—

"I'm *referring,*" Essie said archly, "to importing illegal alcohol. As if you didn't know."

Ah yes, that too. But Big Ole Uncle Percy was only getting his small draft of the spoils of Prohibition, brisk business on the craggy coast of Maine. You could hide a Canadian steamer loaded with booze in those coves, where bootleggers had radio stations to warn the ships, and armored cars to deliver the goods to upstanding Republicans at private clubs in Bangor. Percy was just the chump in the rowboat.

"Everybody knows," Cora said mildly.

"Don't mean we have to stand for it."

A secondary conveyer belt was grinding into action, moving rows of flashing cans. The edges were razor sharp. Cora would not give Essie Jordan the satisfaction of drawing blood and kept her eyes on her work.

"Essie, it's no shame that your own husband was arrested for disturbing the peace. He's not the only man who likes to take a drink."

The blue eyes fired. "That's not true."

"Nobody cares, Essie."

"Men are weak. That's why *decent* women fight against the devil alcohol. You think it don't affect you because you ain't married."

"You know full well my husband died. It was a long time ago," Cora added with a twist of bitterness. "Maybe so long you don't remember."

"I know you *was* married," Essie sneered. "The point is, now you ain't."

It was afternoon and the sandwich man did not come. Mr. Healy patrolled the tables in the rubber apron he always wore, tweed cap on his swelled head. Cora's neck ached and she was thirsty. There were no good memories in this reeking place. Even in fair weather, even while their mother was alive, the cannery yard was cluttered with mountains of decaying vegetable matter and clamshells fought over by swarming birds. Mr. Healy counted the ocean as his garbage dump and the tide as his street sweeper, but nature didn't always oblige, and the facility was usually surrounded by scarlet pools of fish gore. This was the summer playground for the village kids, where they threw rocks at wild cats and raccoons.

The trays of fish kept coming. The cans kept flashing past. Essie's snide little jab had been aimed at Cora's friendship with Linwood Moody, a sweet-tempered soil scientist she'd known since high school, who'd recently lost his wife in a car accident. They'd been seen around town together, so what? You call bean supper in the church basement a tryst? Still, Cora's stomach clenched at the unprovoked attack. How could a person be so put off all the time? It was like Essie Jordan ate mustard for breakfast. There was only one way to put the poor lonely woman out of her misery.

"Essie?" Cora shouted. "How's your rugging coming?"

Essie was an expert in the art of making rag rugs. Her coils were pulled so tight it was like she turned old bedsheets into steel cables.

"Comin' fine, I guess."

"Mrs. Grimble said you're making braided chair seats for the spring fair."

"That's right. Round ones."

"What kinds of colors?"

"Blues, mostly. Got some nice bright purple from a housedress that belonged to Aunt Dot."

"Memories in every braid, isn't that the truth?"

"I suppose."

"I find it calms the heart." With no response from Essie, Cora plunged ahead: "Say, did you know I'm going to be chairman of the July Fourth church fair?"

"Ain't you always?"

Cora bit her lip and let it pass. "I'm thinking we could use some help," she went on. "How would you like to take over on the crafts committee?"

Essie blinked several times. Her eyes scanned the room with suspicion.

"You're asking me to run it?"

"Nobody knows more about rugging and weaving than you. I'll bet you could draw in some good people. What do you say?"

Essie took her time in answering. Something like this—although she'd never admit it—she wanted to keep close to her chest as long as possible; prolong the warmth and softness before it bolted off like one of her black cats. Just then, the steamy room was filled with daylight. Everyone looked up in surprise. The big door had been slid open and the town postmaster, Eli Grimble, stood in the wide space. He'd come on his horse and sleigh, and the stomping of the thick-coated animal and the ringing of its harness were like silent pictures as the clanking of the machinery overtook all other sounds.

Mr. Healy strode up and shook his hand, expecting a bundle of mail, but Eli Grimble kept peering into the dimness and gesturing until he sighted Cora Blake. No doubt he found her easily. She had been staring right at him as if with some kind of second sense. After a moment Mr. Healy motioned that she step forward and the eyes of all the other packers followed. Now she was outside in the cold fresh air and the drifts of snow were tinged with sunset.

"Went by your house—" Eli began.

"What's wrong? Are the children all right?"

"Yes, not to worry, your niece said you were out here, so I thought to come. You have a letter. From the U.S. government."

He held out an official envelope with her name neatly typed.

"The government? Whatever for?"

Mr. Healy leaned over her shoulder. "Paid your taxes, Mrs. Blake?"

"Of course I paid my taxes!" Cora said.

When she realized the letter was from the War Department she had an unnerving sensation, as if the ground was tilting under her feet. It was just the same as thirteen years ago, when the envelope had contained a handwritten note in pencil from someone named Harris in the Adjunct General's Office saying that Samuel Blake, her only child, had been killed in action in Montfaucon, France. The letter had been delivered by Eli Grimble, with this same horse and a two-wheeled buggy. There'd been no snow yet, as it was October, near the end of the war. Eli Grimble had come all the way out to Tide's End Farm to deliver the news, along with the minister and Doc Newcomb.

"What's going on?" Mr. Healy asked.

The postmaster shrugged. "Seems important."

Cora tore the envelope open and made them wait while she took her time reading it. Then she read it again, just to be sure. Finally she looked up from the letter and smiled broadly, maybe the first time she'd ever looked happy in that place.

"I won't be needing work this spring, Mr. Healy."

"Pleased to know that, Mrs. Blake. Meanwhile, you got plenty of work today," he said, and walked toward the factory.

"Don't you care to know the reason why?"

Eli Grimble leaned close. "You can tell *me*," he offered, the biggest gossip in town.

"Mr. Healy!" she called with exuberance she'd never dared before.

"What?"

"There's a *reason* why."

The boss dug his boots into the slush and turned with exaggerated patience.

"I guess you're going to tell me whether I like it or not. All right. Why?"

"I'm going on a trip."

A group of curious packers had gathered in the doorway. Cora said it loud enough that all of them could hear. Especially Essie Jordan.

"I'm going to Paris," she announced. "On an ocean liner. First-class."

2

March

There was never any question in Cora's mind that she would be on that boat. The War Department had pledged to send any mother or widow whose loved one was killed in military service during the war and buried overseas on a pilgrimage to visit their graves in the American cemeteries in Europe. How could she not stand up and be counted? No matter what the hardship might be in leaving the island, it was the right thing to do. She had a duty to Sammy as well as to the country. She knew it, clear as day.

The decision had come a lot easier than the wrenching choice she'd been forced to make thirteen years before, when her grief was still fresh—whether to have Sammy's body shipped back home or permanently interred in France. Everyone in town had a different opinion. Some said yes—let their final resting place be overseas, to show America's commitment to her European allies. Some thought hell no, bring the boys back home, where they belonged, because we never should have gone to war in the first place. The rest of the country was fervidly divided as well. In the end, the War Department left the choice to the families.

Cora didn't even know how to think about it. She wanted Sammy close, but what was best for the country? He had left home to serve—was she being selfish to want to bring him back? She yearned to ask her father's advice, but Grandpa Harding had died the spring just before Sammy enlisted, and so she heeded the words of the biggest daddy of them all, Theodore Roosevelt. He and his wife had decided that their son Quentin should be buried over there, and strongly urged other parents to do the same.

"Mrs. Roosevelt and I have always believed that where the tree falls, there let it lay," he wrote.

It was a poetic image that appealed to Cora's good sense—things die and go back to nature. But was it too much to ask for yet another sacrifice, after losing Sammy in the first place, not to have his marker in the town cemetery next to her parents and sister in the Harding family plot, along with the Higgins, Noyes, Spofford, Pressey, and Haskell clans that had inhabited the island since the Revolutionary War? Not to be able to stop by for a visit anytime she pleased?

A decision was called for, and she'd have to make it on her own. It was a fair day in March 1919, four months after Armistice. A kindly sun and stiff breeze had dried the linens by noon. There was chop in the harbor out to the bay. Cora had been walking north on Eaton Road, over to Elizabeth Pascoe's to buy her scrumptious homemade maple sausage. She had received two cards from the Graves Registration Service. The first gave the location of Sammy's temporary burial. It was a place in rural France called Chaudron Farm, map reference 78.6-02.4, although of course she didn't have a map. He was in grave number 72, identified by his dog tags, which were apparently nailed to a stake. The second card asked that she state her relationship to the deceased and answer yes or no to the question "Do you desire that the remains be brought to the United States?"

In the spent garden of the last house before a stretch of woods, she came upon the odor of geraniums. Geraniums always smell as if they're dying anyway, that turpentiney scent, which even when they're bright with flowers can bring a melancholy mood. These were nothing but a browned-out tangle along with last year's yarrow and veronica. Cora kept walking, but what was on her mind and in her heart were two different things. Instead of going straight to Elizabeth's she took a right at the Cross Road, which led to the town cemetery.

Sarah Bently, Elizabeth's mother, had been walking in the road as well, but the poor thing didn't know where she was. She wore a housedress and slippers and her knobby fingers worked desperately to keep her cardigan closed. Cora stopped and buttoned it for her, speaking calmly about ordinary things. Battered blue veins showed through the thin skin at the old woman's temples, as if the endurance it took to stay alive had become visible. Sarah said she was going to the hospital. She meant that she was going to die, as she was walking toward the cemetery also. Cora waved at Elizabeth, who was running after her mother.

A hundred-foot sycamore marked the entrance in the rock wall around the graveyard. Even bare, its network of zigzag twigs seemed to fill the sky. Although the sun was shining, it could not penetrate the chill that rose from the creek at the bottom of the hill on which the family plots were laid. Nothing moved in this timeless place but shadows. Cora strolled between the stones, familiar as the houses on her street, calmed by a porous quiet that let in just birdsong. *"Lost at sea, November 3, 1845." "Drowned in Havana, June 15, 1893."* Many of the inscriptions were too worn to be read.

As if a veil had been lifted, Cora began to accept the possibility that Sammy might not be buried here. It was not his place. He was a young man just making his way. He was part of the future, not some distant past. Behind that veil was a parade of patriotic ideals, each more rousing than the next, a drumbeat of Americanism that finally solidified the image in her mind: *He deserved to be in the field of honor in France. He made the world safe for democracy and he should be part of that future—the future of a peaceful world. He was truly an American hero, loyal to his friends, never hesitating to fight for what was right— Good Lord, he'd always been like that, even when he was nine years old.*

It must have been around eight o'clock at night. Cora had been at her sewing table in the parlor of the farmhouse and looked up to see a double pair of headlights. They had no phone service and no electricity, only a generator that ran on kerosene. It was pitch-black out there, deep country dark, the nearest neighbor a quarter mile away. Seeing those headlights made her heart beat like mad. There were only two cars on the island; one belonged to the doctor and the other to the sheriff. Both were on their way to her door.

Sammy had been warned about saltwater ice. The danger of it was drilled into every local child. If you fell through the ice on the Lily Pond, you had a reasonable chance of staying put, but when the harbor froze, even if it was two feet thick, there would still be strong ocean currents raging underneath. You'd get dragged under and swept all the way to China.

An Irish family with five rough boys had moved next door to the yellow stonecutter's cottage where Avis lived. She was up in Ellsworth, leaving the door unlocked as she always did in case someone needed to come in from the cold, and, in fact, Sammy had stopped by. The newcomers were from Boston and therefore smarter than Sammy and his friends and with more tricks, too. That day it had been fifteen below. The harbor had congealed into a solid glacier all the way out to Isle au Haut. The temptation to walk across from end to end was like a free bowl of jelly beans. The boys from Boston challenged the locals to a race. No sleds, no skates. Boots only. Nine went out, seven returned—slipping and falling, snot running down their bright red faces, screaming for help. One of the outsiders, a ten-year-old named Patrick, stumbled into a hole halfway across and was stuck with his butt in freezing water and his feet up on the ice, arms flailing, unable to move. The other was lying on his belly, on liquefying frost a couple of feet away, trying to reach him with a flung-out scarf. That was Sammy.

The cars stopped by the side door of the farmhouse and the headlights cut out. Sheriff Lundt and Doc Newcomb trooped him inside like a prisoner, wrapped in a blanket, tiny ice particles in his hair and shaking with cold. Cora slid halfway across the floor on her knees to get him safely inside her arms, and Sammy held on. His poor ear was like a block of ice against her cheek and his lips were thin and blue.

"I'm sorry, Mama."

She soothed him—"Don't worry, as long as you're safe"—and ran for another blanket, then propped him up at the kitchen table while she got the kettle on and hot water bottles going.

She poured the men big shots of whiskey. Both were riled in the way that comes from a near disaster. They said Sammy deserved a whipping, like the other kids who were being punished by *their* parents, for even stepping foot on saltwater ice. A double whipping, because when they shouted at him to get the hell out of there he refused to budge, stubbornly attempting to reach the boy with the hopelessly wet scarf. They'd had to make a human chain from shore and rescue *two* boys, as by that time Sammy could barely stand up on his own, about to succumb to the frigid air. And why he'd risk his life for a mick, Sheriff Lundt couldn't comprehend, going on about "people from away" coming into their waters and stealing traps, shooting at local fishermen.

"They don't belong here," he said.

Nine-year-old Sammy couldn't stop shivering, but his intense blue eyes were defiant and his fists clenched.

"Patrick's my buddy," he told the authorities,

right to their skeptical faces. "You always go back for your buddy."

"He's your buddy?" mocked the sheriff. "What about your mama? What about the heartache you caused her?"

Cora straightened her back. "I'm proud of what he did," she said. "I think he showed fast thinking for a boy his age."

Sammy didn't look at her, but she had her hand on his shoulder and could tell that he was glad she'd said it.

The doctor advised warm liquids and bed rest. They got up to leave and at the door he said, in a sympathetic way, "It's not your fault, Cora. A boy needs a man around to discipline him." It left her with a sick feeling, as if it really were her fault, going all the way back to the choice she'd made, against everyone's expectations, to raise the boy with her parents and sister—without the husband, who obviously wasn't here to give her son the whipping he deserved.

Sammy didn't understand all that, but he did feel the rebuke aimed at his mama.

"I hate them," he murmured, his eyes drooping with fatigue. "I'm leaving and never coming back."

Cora told him that was fine, after he had a hot bath.

The shadows moved. Her knuckles ached from the dampness of the creek bed, and she realized it was late afternoon. Leaving the cemetery, she resolved to have him buried overseas, but not without a sharp stab of doubt that she had betrayed something else, deep within. She'd have nothing in her hands of him. This was truly the "final sacrifice," as the papers called it. She'd given up the baby that had come from her body, and the yearning to protect him and keep him close, no matter what. She couldn't have said such a thing out loud without embarrassment for both her and her son—and yet, she felt she had surrendered something in favor of what was more important. Important to whom? To the country, she told herself emphatically.

She went back to Eaton Road. Elizabeth had the sausages all wrapped, plus a nice chunk of cranberry bread. Her mother was at the table, slowly picking at crumbs. Cora hurried back to town. Not the sort of person who liked to waste time, she went directly to the post office and sent a telegram to the War Department, giving them permission to inter Sammy in an American military cemetery overseas.

When she was done, she stepped outside the post office and took long calming breaths of salt air. A man wearing a hunter's cap came out of the grocery and stopped to read the notices posted in the window. Seagulls cried and a lady went by on an old-fashioned bicycle with wooden wheels. Cora took in the untouched rhythm of the village, safe from harm because of young men like Sammy. She felt almost giddy with relief; righteous and blessed. Blessed by Teddy Roosevelt.

Now that she'd sent the official notice, gears and levers went into action in Washington, D.C. Orders conveying Mrs. Blake's wishes were telegraphed to the colonel in command of the Graves Registration Service in France, which several months after the war was still recovering bodies. They sent back the Record of Disinterment and Reburial that had gone into Sammy's folder. It listed the nature of the original burial ("Earthen grave"), condition of the body upon disinterment ("Decomposed, unrecognizable"), and means of identification ("Identity tag attached to cross"). Also noted were "Teeth 14 and 29 missing before death."

A few weeks later Cora received a form letter titled Disposition of Body, which gave the location of Sammy's new permanent grave: Plot C, Row 44, Grave 16, Meuse-Argonne American Cemetery, Romagne-sous-Montfaucon, Meuse.

She'd felt an ironic liberation from knowing exactly where he was.

In that same folder, in a cabinet of folders, in a storeroom in the Adjunct General's Office in Washington, D.C., was a carbon copy of Cora's application to join the American Gold Star Mothers, a national organization that had been chartered by Congress the previous year. It was open to mothers of sons or daughters who served in the Allied Forces during the World War and died as the result of that service. Cora had typed her answers to their questions on the library Remington: natural father of veteran ("Curtis Blake, deceased"); cause of death of veteran ("Killed in action"); remarks ("Meuse-Argonne, France. Cited for gallantry in action and especially meritorious service. The local post is named in memory of him").

When President Herbert Hoover signed the Pilgrimage Bill in 1930, assigning five million dollars for the government-sponsored pilgrimages, those folders were opened once again, and the status of the mothers and wives of American soldiers buried overseas was reexamined. Cora Blake was found eligible to go. In February 1931 came the confirmed date of her trip—June 2, 1931—in the letter she had been so thrilled to receive in the dead of winter at Healy's cannery.

At that point it was no longer grief that pushed her, it was pride, and she was surprised by the force of it. She supposed that she had reconciled those feelings long ago, but they must have been slowly uncurling in her mind, like those coils of dry kindling in the kitchen stove, because with one hot breath they burst into a ball of fire.

The moment she read that letter—that she was really going!—she'd felt deep kinship with thousands of women she'd never met. They were from different parts of the country and all walks of life, but what they had in common was this: they had each gone to the front window and taken down the banner that showed a blue star set in a field of white surrounded by red borders. The blue star symbolized hope and pride, one star for every family member in military service. Most likely they'd hung it up in private and taken it down in private; most likely they'd made it themselves, of cotton or felt, or crocheted it, maybe with tassels and colored cords. Then one day they accepted the lonely task of replacing the blue star with one of gold. Gold meant sacrifice to the cause of liberty and freedom. It meant they were now Gold Star Mothers. They hadn't asked for this, nor did they have any say in how it happened, but they been given to bear the most violent and dark cost of the nation's war. Each one shouldered this responsibility without protest, as stoically as her child had rested a rifle against his chest. More than 100,000 American mothers lost their cherished sons. Each had been alone; but they were alone no longer.

Cora had straightaway written to the president of the New England chapter of the American Gold Star Mothers, offering to help. She was experienced in running things, she'd said earnestly. Aside from recruiting high school girls ("—and you know how lazy they can be") to clean

41

out the library from top to bottom, she was president of the Student Health Council, where parents volunteer to keep the records for school physicals and vaccinations. Even when she no longer had a child in school, she emphasized, to show her dedication, she'd kept the position to this day. (Unsure if they would consider this a plus or a minus, she did not add that she was unable to get anyone to test the urine samples, and so she did them herself.)

The answer she'd received was a surprise.

The reply had come from Mrs. Genevieve Olsen of Cambridge, Massachusetts. It was written in midnight-blue ink on ivory Crane's stationery embossed with *Olsen Railroad & Co.*, making no secret of the fact that she was *that* Mrs. Olsen, granddaughter of the tycoon who made his fortune in railroads and the fur trade. She had married a cousin, Franklin Olsen, and when he died, she was left one of the wealthiest philanthropists in America. She had built a wing of a hospital in Boston and served on the boards of museums and charities. She was known to give exclusive dinner parties that drew all sorts of smart people, at which she wore unabashedly eye-popping jewels.

But the war had leveled certain things. Like Cora, Genevieve Olsen was a widow who had lost her only child. Dr. Henry Olsen, a surgeon, had been killed in a German attack on a dressing station during the Meuse-Argonne Offensive, the same battle that had taken Sammy. He, too, had been in the Twenty-sixth Infantry, or Yankee Division, which included all the New England states, and from which their group, Party A, would be drawn. Such is the democracy of death that a plainspoken librarian and a sophisticated socialite could become warm correspondents and eventually close friends.

"I look forward to you joining our pilgrimage to France," Mrs. Olsen had written to Cora. *"You write of the difficult decision about Samuel's final resting place. For us it was simple, as Henry had been a student in France when he was an undergraduate at Harvard, and we spoke French at table. Have no fears—I am certain that when you enter that beautiful field of honor peace will come to you.*

"Remember our purpose. We go not only to be reunited with our hero sons, but to promote peace and goodwill among nations. We must continue to press Congress for increased monetary compensation, so no Gold Star parent will ever be without a roof over his or her head, nor without food for sustenance, nor be an object of charity. In the words of our charter, which always bear repeating: 'To unite with loyalty, sympathy and love for each other, mothers whose sons or daughters had made the supreme sacrifice.'"

In response to Cora's imploring letters, Mrs. Olsen finally offered her the position of member coordinator for Party A—a job that she'd made up specially to accommodate this "determined gal from Maine," as she remarked to her niece at dinner. The organization needed more staunchly devoted members like Cora Blake.

3

April

Late evening in early spring. The tide was out, the harbor calm under a cold mist. The shops were closed. In the stillness every sound was magnified. You could hear a ham-handed guitar and bursts of male laughter coming from Lester King's shop at the end of the wharf, where lobstermen gathered to trade insults and give Prohibition a kick in the pants. Up in the village there was just the ticking of the rain.

The only light still burning on Main Street was in the library. It was past closing time but Cora was still at work. The library was her second home; she knew every creak in the planks. It was a cottage of white clapboard with a sweet wraparound porch built by a reverend and his wife a century ago. Most recently it had served as a millinery shop with a dentist's office on the top floor, where the children's reading area was now. The rooms were tiny, every surface worn to smoothness like a good old rowboat that's seen its day.

From the high librarian's desk Cora commanded the front door, which opened with a pleasant tinkle meaning, *Here comes someone to talk to.* She'd look up with an eager smile that launched a thousand conversations—on wholesome and intellectual topics, no doubt, but shot through with satisfying gossip like fat through bacon. She liked that, being in the center of things; it was an antidote to the aloneness. She made it a point to notice what everyone liked and she read a lot herself, even stuff she didn't care for, so she could find the right book for the right person. If all the other responsibilities she took on for the church and school weren't enough to fill the need, there would always be someone stopping by to ask about a book.

Tonight she wasn't there on library business. Yes, she was hoping Linwood Moody would drop by. He was a lot of fun to be with, and had promised to bring materials for his talk that weekend, "Precious Stones of Maine"—she'd set out the easel and arranged the chairs—but mostly she wanted her mind to be clear in order to figure out what to do about the letter from Mrs. Minnie Seibert.

Mrs. Seibert was one of her Gold Star Mothers in Party A. Cora had to put the letter off because the storm kept bringing people into the library, but what it said had worried her. Minnie Seibert desperately wanted to make the trip to France—but her husband wasn't letting her go.

Cora was orderly. That's the way you solved a problem. She'd made three neat stacks of envelopes and tied them off with ribbons—red, white, and blue. Red was for official correspondence from the government, white for the general public, and blue for the ladies in her group. Aside from Mrs. Olsen's only Minnie Seibert's letter was in the blue. Although she'd gone to the post office every day, neither of the other two—Mrs. Katie McConnell of Dorchester, Massachusetts, nor Mrs. Wilhelmina Russell of Prouts Neck, Maine—had replied to her cheery note of welcome.

Minnie Seibert had made up for it with three pages of remorse for the way her life had turned out—having to flee for her life from the Russian pogroms, her tyrannical husband, Abraham, and the loss of her son, Isaac. *"My only light."* They were educated people who moved from a small Jewish neighborhood in Bangor to the rural countryside in order to become chicken farmers, of all things. Minnie explained that since Jews couldn't own land in Russia, her husband was overjoyed at the opportunity. They wouldn't need anybody else, he said—not the synagogue, not the state—which Cora thought was a bunch of hooey. Having grown up on a farm, she was pretty sure you couldn't get along without neighborly kindness, but it seemed this Abraham would have none of it. He refused to take even a bag of beans from "the capitalists," which had left Minnie and the children (two older girls plus the youngest, a boy) isolated and poor. He sounded like all he wanted was to tear everything down.

"Abraham is on the difficult side," Mrs. Seibert wrote. *"I'm his wife, I know what he's like. I have to be on my best behavior. Isaac always stood up to him. My husband forbade him to join the army, but Isaac said,* I am an American, *and he joined. It's been very hard for me."*

Rain beat down on the library. Cora picked up a pen. She wanted to tell Mrs. Seibert that she understood—it had been the same with Sammy. It broke your heart but what could you do? They were already men. Sadness overcame her, and without knowing it she put the pen down, rested her cheek in her hand, and stared at a blur of bookshelves in the dark pool of the room. It was the way Sammy had left without a word. Maybe he'd known that if he'd come back to say goodbye she would have broken down. Then he might have, too, because he was a feelingful boy, a son who was not ashamed to love his mother, just as she was openly devoted to him. What if he couldn't face her tears and backed out on the promise he'd made to his buddies? The other boys must have been just as scared, because one night they had all gotten stinko and gone up to Portland, and by morning they were in.

Cora had almost lost her mind with worry. It wasn't until three days later that she received a postcard: *"Dear Ma, I joined the Army to fight the Germans. Don't worry, I'll be back soon. Your son, Sammy."* He was sixteen and lied about his age in order to enlist. But things didn't really seem that bad. It was late in the war. Everyone thought it would be over by Christmas. Sammy was an excellent shot. As a boy he could bring down a deer that would last them the winter. He became a marksman assigned to clear a French village, but his scouting party was ambushed by German machine guns hidden in the trees. It was October 22, 1918, a scant month before Armistice. He was the only island son who died in the war.

The whole town mourned. There were two separate services that filled the Opera House on Main Street—one official, one religious. They named the American Legion Post after him. In the Fourth of July parade, the oldest member carried a flag in honor of Samuel Blake. His spirit, what he stood for, carried on. In the tawny light of the library lamp, Cora gripped the pen and bent closer to the papers on her desk, looking for words to convince a perfect stranger to defy her husband and come with people she'd never met to a far-off place that nobody could pronounce.

"These boys couldn't have been heroes if their mothers lacked courage," she began.

The wooden door to Lester King's shop swung open and Linwood Moody stepped out smartly. Very smartly, so he wouldn't fall. He made sure to shut the door firmly, so they wouldn't be shouting about losing the heat. He had the chart for "Precious Stones of Maine" wrapped in newsprint under one arm, and he was grinning like an idiot, happily full of rum and Cokes, as he ambled down the wharf in the rain toward the darkened town. He could still hear the stomping of boots behind him, and a deep-chested chorus:

> Walkin' down Canal Street
> Knockin' at the door
> Couldn't find her anyplace
> When I finally found her
> She was mighty thin
> Goddamn sonofabitch!
> Couldn't get it in—

He started laughing all by himself. The policy at Lester King's was men only allowed. No woman in her right mind would go there, anyway. It was hot as a sauna and stank of cigars and smoke from the woodstove. The walls were covered with naked pinups along with citations for fishing violations that Lester King proudly ignored. The floor was covered with nets, buoys, coils of rope, traps stacked up to be repaired. A half dozen lobstermen would squeeze themselves inside, chewing tobacco and enjoying their cocktails. They wore blue jeans with splatters of paint and tar and ripped sweaters and soiled caps over greasy hair. Their beards were hoary and wild. Most of the older men were overweight, some hard of hearing due to the roar of the diesel engines, and many faces were veined and red and spotted with cancers.

Big Ole Uncle Percy was in his usual spot, perched on a spool of wire, slapping the strings of a beat-up guitar. He had meaty shoulders and legs like wooden pilings. He could palm a twenty-inch round buoy in one hand. Even if he shaved, there'd always be a residue of dark scruff so he scarcely bothered. He got up in the dark and came back in the dark, never taking off the black wool cap pulled down over curly black hair, making him look like a curly black bear. He ate like a bear. When she cooked for him, Cora cooked enough for three. He'd pretty much abandoned family life after his wife, Avis, died, except to provide money, disappearing into small-fry illegal enterprises and surfacing when the law got too close. Like his nephew, Sammy, Big Ole Uncle Percy skated on thin ice.

Tonight he was the star of the show, having just pulled up a haul from one of his traps that was worth a lot more than lobsters—a dozen bottles of Canadian booze. A week ago he'd placed an order in an empty bottle in the trap, and here was the prize. He was in cahoots with an uncle up in Nova Scotia who had a second sense when it came to the coast guard. His boat could outrun them anyway. The stuff he sold was first-rate—the proof being that nobody had died from alcohol poisoning so far.

Linwood Moody was feeling nothing but warm sloppy love for the horny old horn blowers. He'd been singing and clomping along with the rest, his clean L. L. Bean hunting shoes in cadence with their filthy rubber waders the size of kayaks. He was as strong as they were, every inch an outdoorsman, but his sandy hair was clipped and he favored slacks and Fair Isle vests, because he was a professional soil scientist, and in this company there was no need to pretend otherwise. He was not like these men, but he was of them—comfortably so—because his father had been a mariner and he'd grown up on the island, graduating from high school a year ahead of Cora Blake.

Still, he had not become a regular until after his wife, Grace, had died and they'd made an effort to bring him in, because a man who found himself suddenly alone like that needed friends and encouragement if he ever hoped to get back on the horse. It took two years before Linwood could step foot inside and even then he felt like an impostor—not at Lester's, but in life. Grace had been a passenger in a cousin's car going from Ellsworth to Augusta to visit her aunt when they hit a patch of black ice and went off the road and head-on into a tree. She had a good job with the phone company, which was just then expanding service throughout the state; he mapped soils for the government and taught geology at the University of Maine at Orono. Hundreds and hundreds of miles on the road between them, and one patch of ice trips everything up.

He drank. He slept. He hurt. He worked. He felt nothing. He went hunting with his brothers. It didn't make sense, but a voice kept saying, *Go home,* so one Saturday the previous fall he took a drive to the island, crossing the reach on the ferry scow. He'd stopped for a hot dog at the top of Caterpillar Hill. Sitting alone at a picnic table with a good view of the cranberry bogs, auburn and russet, he could feel the colors starting to change inside himself, too.

He wasn't overthinking everything like he always did, running the accident like punishment in his brain; he was just an ordinary Joe, following the road where it wanted to go, through a couple of townships with neatly clustered communities until it ended at the harbor, and that felt right, the sea ahead of him dotted with far-off islands, everything opening up. He sat for a long time on a stray block of granite at the entrance to the wharf, not yet ready to walk the streets of his childhood, go up to the Lily Pond and the quarry, and a couple of fishermen happened along and they talked for a while—"Come out to Lester's sometime, don't be shy"—and when they were gone he turned away from the waterfront and happened to look across the street, and there was the library.

Not in any hurry, he wandered over and went inside, three steps up and across the porch. He wanted just to warm himself, but a pretty woman smiled at him from a high-up old-fashioned desk and said, "Hello"—and it was Cora Blake from high school, hadn't seen her since Grace's funeral, didn't know that she was working there, a miracle the place is open, hard times, glad to see you back.

A patch of ice.

Three steps up.

That had been eighteen months ago. Now he was sauntering along the wharf on a wet April night, the music growing faint behind him until, by the time he reached Main Street, the only sound was rain resonating in all directions, on shingled roofs and slick granite embankments, trash cans and wooden sidewalks, tapping on leaves and running in drains. The newspaper around his chart was getting wet and starting to wilt. He could see the light ahead, and Cora Blake framed in amber glow as she peered out the window—was she watching for him? She wore a thick rust-colored sweater with an orange scarf at the neck. Her golden-brown hair was parted in the middle and pinned back loosely in a knot, the clean oval of her face mottled by raindrops sliding down the pane. She looked like brandy in a glass. Not able to make him out in the shadows, she folded her arms impatiently and turned her back on the rain.

Three steps up.

The doorbell tinkled and Cora nearly jumped from the desk. "Good Lord, you scared me!"

"I guess I'm the scary type."

"Terrifying."

She turned on the stool, reluctantly drawn away from her letter to Minnie Seibert, and watched as he slowly took off the slicker. He did things in a deliberate way that could be exasperating when you had something else on your mind.

"You've been at Lester King's," she said.

"Can't deny it."

"What are they up to over there?"

"Singing. I learned a new song from Big Ole Uncle Percy."

"Does he know you were off to see me?"

"Are you joking? I value my private parts. Want to hear it?"

"No."

But he started anyway: " 'Walkin' down Canal Street / Knockin' at the door—' "

"I can imagine where that leads."

"Dirty girl."

"You actually have a decent voice if you would use it properly," Cora teased him.

"I have another talent."

"Is that so?"

He stood the chart on the easel and drew the wet newspaper away. "What do you think?"

She nodded with approval. "Looks good."

"I made it myself."

"You did not."

"True. I stole it from the college."

Cora was pleased to see that the chart was colorful enough to hold the attention of the eleven-in-the-morning ladies, and that the letters were large enough for them to read. Specimens of precious stones were glued to the cardboard under drawings that showed their origins: volcanoes, soil, or sand.

"It's nice that you can touch the rocks."

"Minerals."

Linwood's glasses were all fogged up. He wiped them off.

"We've got a spell of weather," he observed, offering a flask. "There's a big tree down in the village. Had to take the Pressy Road."

"Whereabouts?" she asked, taking a pull.

"Just before you get to the old schoolhouse."

"Next to the Pickerings?"

"Other side. Sellers."

"Anybody hurt?"

"No."

"That'll be a mess."

55

"Nothing for it now."

"They've got flares, I hope."

Linwood nodded.

They listened to the rain. He saw the letters on the desk.

"What are you doing?"

"Tending to my flock in Party A."

"If you want a job with the army, why don't you enlist?"

"Oh, they wouldn't want me. I'm too mean."

"Yes, you are."

"It's not a big job, anyway. Only five of us in the party."

"Hardly seems worth the trouble."

"They have to keep the parties small because there aren't any big hotels where we're going, to the little French towns."

"With little French men on the prowl?" Linwood asked.

"Ha! They treat us like a bunch of school-children. We're supposed to be chaperoned by an army officer and a nurse."

"A nurse? Is she pretty?" Cora gave him a hard stare and Linwood added quickly, "Not as pretty as you."

"Right answer." She smiled.

He jammed his hip against hers and squeezed beside her on the stool.

"Go away," she told him, laughing. "You smell like a brewery."

Instead he leaned in closer, pretending to study the letters on her desk.

"What's the game?"

"Well, I'm called the member coordinator for Party A. My commanding officer is Mrs. Olsen, the one I told you about—"

"The rich Cambridge lady."

"She sends piles of instructions and I pass them on. Still haven't heard from two of them."

"Forget it."

"They might need my help. Like this one." She tapped Minnie Seibert's letter. "I feel bad for her. The poor thing wants to go, but she's too afraid."

"Maybe she should just stay home."

Cora made a wry smile. Sometimes she couldn't tell if Linwood was joking or just being his practical self. Sometimes they were the same.

"It's her husband."

Linwood looked confused. "Why? Does *he* want to go?"

"No! And he doesn't want her to, either."

"Why can't he go?" Linwood wondered, tipping the flask.

"Because he's not a mother or a widow."

"So what? It's his kid."

Cora took the flask again. "Women only. You don't like it, write to Congress."

He laughed. "I know how far that would get me. It's too bad."

"What's too bad?"

"Never mind."

"What were you going to say?"

He shrugged. "Do you sometimes wish Curtis was still around?"

"My husband, Curtis?" she asked, surprised.

"I was thinking, at a time like this."

She shook her head. "Nothing to do with him," she replied sharply.

"Sorry. Too much to drink. Just tell me to shut up."

Cora was feeling a sick reaction in her stomach. She didn't like to talk about Curtis, she didn't like to type his name on the forms or hear it spoken out loud. He was like poison on her tongue; the poison of a lifetime of lies, layered and molding in a trunk that was closed once and should never be opened. It brought to mind the trunk with Sammy's baby clothes she'd stashed in the cupola on the barn after he'd outgrown them; after she'd left college and come home with an infant son and without a husband.

"It was a long time ago, Lin," she said, softening toward him. "Sammy wasn't even one when Curtis died. He didn't know his son and he had no share in raising him. Don't say sorry. It was God's will," she added.

More poison on the tongue. She could almost feel a blister rise every time she told that lie.

"At least Sammy didn't get cholera," she went on, horribly. "That's the way I have to look at it. I had sixteen good years with him."

How low could she get, to use Sammy in order to duck the truth? *It's better for everyone this way,* is what she always told herself.

Linwood said, "I understand."

"I know you do," she said, thinking about Grace.

He realized that he was stone-cold sober. The booze had abandoned him. He'd come to a dead stop.

"No use to talk about sad times," he said.

Linwood put his slicker back on and went to the door. He wasn't being pensive or rude. It was customary in that region that when conversation comes to its natural end you simply leave, just the way he'd left without saying a word at Lester King's. No goodbyes or apologies are necessary; no future plans need to be made. It was understood the parties would naturally run into each other soon enough. It was an island, after all.

If Cora hadn't gotten up and kissed him, Linwood would have walked into the rain. If he hadn't put his hand on her breast, she might have found it easier to let him go. Instead she reached behind them and turned off the lamp. The room went black. With the twist of a switch the cottage, porch, the library and all its books, the unfinished letter to Minnie Seibert, and the man and woman in a strengthening embrace disappeared in the dark.

4

June

Cora barely recognized Linwood Moody's Chevrolet pickup as it rolled down Main Street. The blue truck, a squat workhorse usually covered with mud, had been transformed into the bluest truck she'd ever seen—robin's egg blue—and so shined up, you could watch the clouds float by on the polished fenders. It pulled up and parked beside the wooden sidewalk at the bottom of the hill, looking swank against the weathered bait shacks that fronted the harbor. *Aren't* you *pleased with yourself?* Cora thought of the stubby old thing.

Linwood hopped out. He'd put on a pressed shirt and bow tie along with his summer fedora. Cora watched from the porch, suitcases at her feet, as Linwood went through his hello ritual: took off the hat to smooth his hair, checked his keys, patted his wallet, and lit a cigarette, before even turning to wave. He was taking so long! Her fingers drummed the railing. She wanted to fly right off the porch.

The train for New York City with a stop in Boston would leave Bangor that afternoon at 2:46 p.m., and three days later the ocean liner

S.S. *Harding* would debark for Le Havre, France. Before she knew it, she would be standing on a street in Paris! And from there—she couldn't think. The past month had been a whirlwind. Once her name had appeared in the paper on the list of pilgrims leaving from Maine, she'd heard as far away as Somerset from others who were unable to make the trip, and the white-ribboned pile began to grow, as they asked her to bring back a bag of French soil, lay rocks and read poems, sing Johnny's favorite song, say a prayer, write a travelogue, go on the radio.

She even got a send-off by the Martha Washington Benevolent Society at the Odd Fellows Hall. They gave her a bouquet of pink carnations and multicolored gladioluses from Mrs. Healy's garden, plus a travel bag filled with toilet articles and accessories, handkerchiefs, and a sewing kit—presented by Essie Jordan herself. Punch and angel cake were served.

She had already said goodbye to Big Ole Uncle Percy the day before. He'd been going over to Sunset to put in windows for some summer people. Yes, they were both glad of the cash. When he raised a hand in farewell and started down the road for the twelve-mile hike to the job, Cora realized that despite his bulk and outlaw reputation, Big Ole Uncle Percy was shy. It made her smile. He hadn't come back that night, which she half expected.

The morning of her departure she cooked rolled oats for breakfast with the last of the sugar—her going-away treat for the girls. School would soon be out for the summer—that was a load off her mind. All they had to do was not drown in the Lily Pond or fall out of a tree. Once again she'd gone over her list of warnings and instructions.

"Now, your dad will be working over in Sunset, which means sometimes he might not get back in time for supper—"

"*Sometimes?*" Sarah said, with an emphatic eye roll.

"But he still has to be fed, so remember to leave a covered dish. And if he doesn't come back for a couple of days, it's because he's up north fishing," she'd said, hoping they hadn't heard otherwise. "Even if your dad's not around, a dozen people know to look out for you, but if you're *really* worried about him, go down to the shop and ask Lester King his whereabouts—"

Laura patted her wrist. "It's okay, Aunt Cora."

Kathleen, the little one, nodded solemnly. "We can handle our dad."

Cora held back a smile. "Good."

There was no help for it. They'd have to fend for themselves. As she stood on the porch watching them scramble down the rocks clutching their books, she knew—in that place in her gut where she knew what she knew—that her girls would be all right.

"Aunt Cora! Come down, you got to see!" they were calling, but suddenly she felt weepy and strangely paralyzed. A moment ago she'd been elated. Now her feet would not move toward the steps. Linwood and his truck all gleaming down on Main Street meant that she was really leaving home.

"You come up here, Lin!" she called instead.

The stonecutter's cottages were built up high, with no access from the street, but Linwood strode easily over the granite outcrops and patches of chickweed, surefooted despite his size, from climbing over stone walls and across fields. He'd recently been promoted to the head of a survey crew assigned to map the soils in Penobscot County, which entitled him to transportation. The blue truck belonged to the government, but government workers had to go by a strict gas allowance, which would not have covered the trip to Bangor. A collection was begun to get Cora Blake to the train station, but it had come up short—and Linwood Moody had to make some inventive arrangements in order to make up the difference.

"You look smart," he said when he'd reached the porch.

"Liar," she mocked gently. "Haven't gotten any sleep in a week."

She was wearing the dress she'd sewn for the trip. It was soft and feminine, made of light heather-gray wool that fell to the ankle, with a natural waist and a scalloped collar of white eyelet. Cora was afraid it was too fancy, but everybody said that's what they're wearing in Paris—certainly not a housedress! She'd also been given a burgundy silk chemise on loan from a neighbor, and a navy suit Doc Newcomb's wife had worn to their daughter's high school graduation six or seven years ago.

That morning she'd put on the entire traveling ensemble for the first time—including the new black pumps and claret-red beret. The rising sun on its way to summer solstice struck a new angle, saturating the bedroom in light. She saw every cobweb and stain in the old paint (money for spring wallpaper had gone for the pumps)—but in the mirror there was a surprisingly young and eager face with inquisitive blue eyes. Her figure was nowhere near the slim silhouettes they were showing in the magazines, but she looked well proportioned in the dress. The beret was . . . questionable, but what the heck. If she was trying too hard, it was for Sammy. She wanted to look good for Sammy. She wanted him to be proud of his mother.

Cora was not the only member of Party A concerned with what to wear. The letter she had finally received from Mrs. Katie McConnell, the maid from Dorchester, Massachusetts, made her sure of that: *"I changed places and I guess you maybe couldn't find me here, but I am glad to have your lovely letter. I work for a lady who is a good lady but I got plenty to do I cannot be Idle. I want to know if France is cold as Ireland and how we are to wash clothes. I am sorry that I do not have my mother's pearls for the occasion as I had to sell them for passage."*

But the chatty tone of their exchange had ended when Katie later wrote that the pilgrimage would be doubly hard for her because she'd lost two sons in the war. *"Tim and Dolan. Fifteen months apart, but so different. One was Night and one was Day, but they were bound to be together. Killed a week apart. My heart was broken twice."*

When they received their official pilgrimage badges, Cora had written first to Mrs. McConnell. From a bronze bar engraved CORA BLAKE, MAINE hung a red, white, and blue ribbon, at the end of which was a heavy bronze medallion with a gold star and the words *Pilgrimage of Mothers and Widows*. The medallion was elaborately decorated with crossed American flags and an eagle surrounded by oak and laurel leaves. *"Isn't it wonderful?"* Cora wrote, hoping to cheer her up. *"Never mind pearls, we have the most beautiful jewel in the world! The War Department says we must wear this badge in a conspicuous place at all times while on the pilgrimage, so that everybody knows who we are and why we're over there, and we should be treated special."*

Mrs. McConnell replied, *"I cried when I saw it. I Promise I will never take it off. I am sure now that our Darling sons are in heaven."*

Earlier that morning Cora had reverently taken the badge from its velvet box. Considering what was meant by "a conspicuous place," she smiled to herself and jauntily pinned the badge over her left breast.

Linwood's reaction was somber. "That's very handsome. I'm proud of you, Cora."

She blushed. "We'll see."

He stood beside her as they lingered on the porch. It was always hard to give up the view of the harbor, especially on such a rare day of warm sun and high, carefree clouds. The lobster boats were coming in; farther out a double-masted schooner passed under full sail. Cora squeezed his hand.

"What's the matter?"

"Butterflies," she said.

"It's the excitement. When you get back it'll be high season. I'll take you out to Great Spruce Island and we'll have some fun."

The suggestion meant more than a pleasant half day's sail, a picnic of macaroni salad and ham sandwiches. Great Spruce Island was where they'd secretly first made love—away from the eyes of scandalmongers who would disapprove of a widow lady shacking up with a man who had just lost his wife. Free at last, Cora had peeled off her clothes and run shrieking through the icy wavelets, plunging into the tide. When she surfaced, a dozen yards from shore, a dark head had poked out of the water just an arm stroke away.

"There's a seal!" she called.

He went in wearing his undershorts. The frigid water nearly stopped his heart, and his privates withdrew like a stunned quahog, but sixty seconds later their bodies were straining together on the heat of a smooth boulder, like the first humans after the tectonic plates crashed, and land rose out of the sea, and the ice retreated a couple of millennia ago. They would live forever on wild blueberries. Nothing else existed in the world but the tide grating over pebbles and her fingertips grazing his thighs. They rested naked on worn towels, a warm breeze crisscrossing their skins, small green crabs bright as silver dollars, living and dying in a hollow of basalt.

"Yes," said Cora as they stood on the porch. "We'll go back to Great Spruce Island."

In her pocket was a velvet pouch containing a handful of tiny shells she intended to bring to France. She'd collected some from the island and others at Kydd Cove, where she and Sammy used to go clamming. All you needed was a clam hoe and a strong back, and you could make twelve dollars in a day. How old was he when they stopped going to the cove together? When he'd go instead with his friends and she would be at home, slicing potatoes and stewing onions in pork fat for the chowder, and the door would slam open and Sammy would dash inside—dump the heavy burlap bags because the guys were waiting—*Here's your clams, Ma*—and was gone. At what age did he start skipping school and hanging out at the wharf, picking up information for the life he could already see for himself, becoming a sea captain like his grandfather?

When Sammy was twelve, Grandpa Harding had come home from the sea. Those were the good years, when Cora was relieved of the guilt she felt for bringing up her son without male influence. If there was mischief in town, he was the one who caused it. His best trick was the time he and his friends stole a toilet house and put it on the principal's porch. The thing he loved best, besides being a nuisance, was to go fast. Once, sliding down the steepest hill in Hancock County, he had crashed his cape racer and was knocked out cold. Sammy and his grandfather became inseparable, and he calmed down from being a kid who seemed born to make trouble.

Grandpa Harding had skills a boy could respect. Sammy, the guy who hated to memorize spelling words, became a meticulous knots man. He seemed to crave the discipline of sterning for his grandfather on their lobster boat. The captain could talk sense to anyone—child or man—and he could build anything. Touch any part of his body and it was like iron. His thumbnails were at least an inch across. He could speak Spanish. He'd escaped pirates off Africa and transported English royalty. He knew how to roast a pig. He liked whiskey as well as his wife's fudge. It was unthinkable that this conqueror would lie down one night on their marriage bed when he was fifty-seven and wake up unable to speak or move his right side. Sammy quit hanging around and smoking in the bait shops to come home and read to his grandpa, and feed him and help him to the bathroom, trying his best to keep him here for one more day. Six months after he was dead, Sammy enlisted in the army.

". . . I'll have the boat ready when you get back . . ." Linwood was saying, halfway down with the suitcases. The granite quarry on Crotch Island had started up, the piercing shrieks of the jaw crushers reverberating across the harbor. A white sheaf of seagulls shot up in protest. Cora patted the shells in her pocket and then picked her way after Linwood. The new black pumps were a catastrophe on the rocks.

The nieces had gathered around, ogling the open bed of the truck. It was a short bed, maybe four feet deep—which was taken up with the carcass of a slaughtered animal. A porcine leg poked through the neck of a burlap sack, stained with brown blood and leaking fresh. The nieces were making faces and pretending to gag.

"What on earth is that?" Cora asked.

Linwood said, "Eli Grimble's hog."

"Why?"

Cora's eyes grew wary as she stared at Linwood. Her eyes were usually the radiant sky-blue of turquoise—and he deeply regretted the way they were darkening.

"To be honest," he said, "it's half of Eli's hog. He's keeping the other half."

"What's it doing in your truck?"

"He wants to get it to the market in Bangor."

"We're taking a hog to Bangor?"

"I said I would drive it for three dollars."

Laura giggled and danced. "Aunt Cora's going to France with a pig!"

Cora couldn't take the nervous tension one more minute.

"Stop fooling around!" she snapped.

"Say goodbye to your aunt. Quickly," Linwood advised.

They dutifully clung to Cora's arms and tried to climb up her body, moaning with sorrow.

"For heaven's sake!" she said. "Get off my dress. I'll be back in three weeks. Longer, if you don't behave. Go to school. And don't forget to soak those beans before you cook them!"

When the girls had finally gone off—running backward and blowing kisses—Linwood drew closer and lowered his voice.

"Don't be sore, sweetheart. A lot of folks pitched

in . . . Everybody did their best . . . But . . . this'll make the gas money to get you to the train," he finished lamely.

"I shouldn't have let you talk me out of taking the steamboat."

"I wanted you to go in style."

"Well, you sure managed that," Cora said, eyeing a hairy hoof.

Linwood shook hands with it and said, "Shall we dance?"

Cora laughed in spite of herself. "Stop it."

Then he did a little jig with the pig and sang,

"Why don't you go
Where fashion sits? Puttin' on the Ritz—"

Cora shoved him. "Will you *stop?* Where am I supposed to put my suitcases? They're not even mine, they're borrowed."

"I'll put them inside."

"They'll never fit!"

"Watch."

Cora held on to her red tartan travel bag while Linwood gallantly grabbed the handles of the suitcases and swept them off the ground, despite a queasy sense that his cheapness had spoiled it. Why hadn't he sprung for the three bucks and left the damn hog at home? Only one of the cases fit up front; the other had to be tied to the roof. By then it was as hot as noon and Cora was moaning that they might miss the train, and that would ruin everything! She'd made a firm arrangement with Mrs. Katie McConnell, who lived on the outskirts of Boston, to meet in the women's waiting room in South Station when Cora's train got in. They were to catch (*"Catch!"* It made them sound so stylish!) the 7:45 p.m. express to New York City. If they missed each other in Boston it would be a calamity and start the whole thing off on the wrong foot.

Once she was in, Linwood closed the door and tapped her window two times for no good reason. He got around to his side and slid into the seat that welcomed his six-foot frame and lanky legs, molded from driving hundreds of county roads, recording in a notebook the locations of houses, streams, and boundaries in miles, tenths, and hundredths of a mile. Measuring things brought him peace of mind; and he knew he was about to plunge into uncharted territory.

They drove in silence. The woods were at the peak of growth, treetops meeting in a green canopy over the sunlit road. They passed through pine forests and crossed a placid river. Summer had brought out roadside attractions like gnats. The hand-lettered signs advertised *"Crafters," "Pies," "Collectibles and Unusuals," "Cold Ice Cream," "Used Books," "Country Cookin'," "Mulch and Hay for Sale,"* and there was the Half Moon Inn with red awnings, famous for its cold potato soup.

"I know I shouldn't be nervous," Cora said finally.

If everything went smoothly and she met Katie McConnell at the station, the rest of Party A should take care of itself. Minnie Seibert, heeding Cora's advice, had gotten her two grown daughters to gang up on their father and convince him to let their mother go. Mrs. Olsen was coming down from Cambridge by limousine. She had business in New York City, and would meet them on the boat. The only one Cora hadn't heard from at all was Mrs. Russell, and Mrs. Olsen had just the Prouts Neck address for her. In any case, there was nothing Cora could do about Mrs. Russell now.

"They'll show up one way or another," she said out loud.

"Well then," Linwood replied. "You'll be swell."

Still, she fretted. "It's not like I've never traveled before."

"It's not like a picnic at Orchard Beach," he said, trying to lighten the atmosphere.

"No, it's not like anywhere you've ever been," she agreed.

They took a curve. The hog slid heavily across the truck bed.

". . . I guess that's why they say it's a pilgrimage," Cora said.

She worked the word in her mouth like a cherry

73

pit, seeking the essence. The more everyone made a fuss, the more she wondered. They said the pilgrimages were "good for the morale of the country," but how would Mrs. Cora Blake's going to France make anyone forget about bread lines and folks who'd lost their jobs living in tents? For herself, she didn't need a row of crosses to know that Sammy was gone. She knew it every time she passed the girls' room and instead of her boy there was little Kathleen fast asleep, with the covers thrown off and the cat perched on her rump. Sometimes Cora had to sternly remind herself that she loved her nieces.

"How's the time?" she asked.

The only way to get off the island was to cross the bar and then take the car ferry. The causeway was banked with stones, but high tide could leave you stranded.

Linwood glanced at his watch. "Tide's out. We'll be fine," he said and took a sudden left off the main road.

"Where are you going? You missed the turn!"

"Don't you worry," Linwood said with a tight grin. "I've got a little something up my sleeve."

Cora hoped it wasn't whoopee. Then they'd truly miss the train.

"Lin—"

"Just be patient . . . give it a minute . . ."

They cruised through a village and crossed the bay and soon they were on the shore road.

"What are you doing?" she asked, not a little annoyed. "Can we please go back?"

And then she saw where he was taking her.

"Linwood! Don't go down that road!"

But he pulled into the driveway of Tide's End, her family's old farm, now deserted. They drove past the familiar quartet of maple trees until he finally brought the car to a stop between the house and barn. At one time they were painted bright white with black gambrel roofs and red doors, but both were showing age and disrepair, most dramatically in the disintegrated front porch and missing shingles from the west-facing side of the barn. It was distressing to see the broken pump, the lonely birdbath, the rusted pulleys where clotheslines once told the story of the family in long johns and pillowcases, and the flagpole, empty.

"Thought you'd like a look," Linwood said.

"For God's sake, why now?"

Her voice sounded so strangled that he had to get out of the car. The fields were mostly fallow except for the one Big Ole Uncle Percy kept up in order to sell off hay. When Cora was a child they'd had five milking cows, chickens, sheep, vegetable gardens, and oxen to plow the fields. There were seven small upstairs bedrooms and during the summers her mother would take in boarders, providing three full meals a day. The girls had to clean rooms, wait on tables, pick corn, and forage for berries. Cora learned early about hard work and endurance; she hated the hens but collected the eggs. That was her job, so she did it.

Summer nights the neighbor kids came over and they cranked ice cream and played Red Light, Green Light between the buildings. They'd get lost in the dark and scare each other with flashlights. And although they weren't allowed, they'd sneak into the barn and climb the perilous spiral staircase to the top of the cupola, which Grandpa Harding had built between travels, with a sailing ship for a weather vane. The vista up there was unobstructed from the bay to the mountains, and he'd installed a compass to instruct the children how to find the most important land-marks. But now the cupola meant the opposite for Cora—the place where she'd escape when Sammy was an infant, to be alone with her shame, until her mother called that it was time to nurse. The place she'd hidden the trunk of memories, and their secrets.

Cora swung out of the car. The harbor breeze had been fresh; just eleven miles away the country air was pollen-filled and mild. Linwood stood in the overgrown grass, fiddling with a daisy.

"Do you think about coming back here?" he asked.

"The soil's not good. Mainly clay, isn't that what you said?"

He nodded. "You'd need help to get it running."

"And where would that help come from?"

"I could do a soil analysis at the university. See what else it's good for. You could hire out the work and keep on librarying." He twirled the stem in his hand. "It's no secret that we get along," he said out of nowhere.

"What do you mean?" she asked, alarmed. "Who else knows about us? Not Big Ole Uncle Percy—oh my Lord—"

"Nobody, Cora, nobody. I'm talking just between you and me—you know it and I know it."

"Yes. Okay. We get along," she said, not seeing the point. "Unless you make me miss that train."

"A shame to leave the place idle."

"I think my farming days are past."

"It could be our future."

"What are you getting at?"

"Why don't we get married?"

For a long moment Cora lost her words. "What about Grace?" she managed.

"I could ask you the same. Would you hold back because of Curtis?"

"I might."

"I don't believe it. I've never heard you say one good thing about that fellow. Grace would tell me to go ahead and live another life. I firmly believe that. Curtis would, too, if he cared about you at all."

Cora took a few confused steps in the direction of the barn. Linwood's romantic idea to bring her here had boomeranged in ways she didn't have the means to say, but it was there before them in the rust and weeds. Much had been lost over the last decade, leaving her hollowed out, almost seeking isolation so as not to stir the eddy of desire with its lacerating bits and pieces of the past. She didn't have it in her. The parts that had capacity for hope had all scarred over and shut down. When two people cherished each other, deeply and steadfastly, it also meant that they were prepared to carry on. Not for one's own sake, but because of an unspoken promise to the other: *We are joined in life as well as death.* She didn't have the strength of character to love Linwood Moody the way he deserved to be loved. He was too much of a trusting soul to grasp the truth: she wasn't good enough for him; her heart was not that big.

"You're a wonderful man—"

"Just say yes."

Linwood gave her the daisy. He'd tied the stem in a loop like a ring, like they did when they were kids.

"Look!" he said with a hopeful smile. "We even have a witness!" Meaning the dead pig.

Cora didn't know whether to laugh or cry. Instead, she touched his cheek.

"You've been giving this some thought."

"Little bit."

They looked into each other's eyes and saw the questions there.

"Can we just go?" she asked quietly.

"Sure. Sure we can," Linwood said, and they went back to the car and down the short gravel driveway to the main road. He drove through the quiet village, shoulders tense and staring straight ahead, until the blue truck broke from the archway of trees and hit the causeway, Eggemoggin Reach fanning out in all directions.

They were miles past the farm by then, with no further conversation on the subject of marriage. The windows were all the way down and Cora had been engrossed by the marshy breeze blowing straight through. As Linwood said, the tide was out, unrolling before them unexpected distances of sea and sky. The busy shipyards on the far shore of Sedgwick looked like a blurry brown pencil sketch. Closer, almost under their wheels, wide mudflats were steadily exposed by the receding water. The image had come to Cora of Sammy and his friends, maybe six years old, playing in Blue Hill Harbor with the tide way out like this, poking around with driftwood in mud up to their hips. The gulls went insane for mussels, fighting on all sides of them in a mad barrage of wings and snapping beaks, while the mothers watched from a grassy rise, gossiping and knitting, never thinking that the mud of faraway France might someday swallow their sturdy bare-chested little boys. At that point the memory vanished and Cora was left with terrifying fear—

had she left the special international Gold Star Mothers passport in a dresser drawer?

At the same moment, Linwood was seeing underwater volcanoes and gray-white granite plutons going all the way down to the center of the earth, a scientific reality that might have been reassuring if it hadn't brought to mind the chilling fact he faced every day in his work with rocks and minerals, that the origins of the universe were unintelligible. He appeared to be the man in charge of things, wearing a man's hat, skimming a truck along a body of water with both hands on the big leather wheel, but he was hamstrung by an awareness that he believed few outside the field of geology could grasp, of five hundred million years of time, and the pointlessness of any destination; even the convergence of the road ahead, allegedly leading to the ferry ramp, was an optical illusion. In an accidental universe that had been in flux for millennia, what was the point of holding back? Why not make a stand?

"I have some news," he finally said. "They offered me a new job."

Cora had been frantically rummaging in the tartan tweed travel bag on her lap, tomato-red and brown with leather handles that Grandpa Harding had brought back from Australia. The size was more suited to a man, but it was practically unworn except for the smell of cologne and clove cigarettes that lingered in the silk lining, and that's what she loved; it was like taking her father along on another globe-trotting journey. She prayed to him to please let the passport be inside.

She dug past wallet, comb, hairpins, itinerary, the bundle of letters from Party A, travel diary, and the new Willa Cather novel, *Shadows on the Rock*, which had just come into the library.

"Who offered you a job?" she asked distractedly.

"The fellow I'm working with on the Penobscot County survey. He asked if I'd like to move over to the Soil Conservation Service and I told him I would consider it."

"But you never said anything."

"It's civil service, you have to apply. I just got the letter that I made it."

"That's wonderful," Cora said with relief. She'd found the passport underneath the snack she'd brought for the train—homemade bread and butter and an apple, wrapped in a handkerchief. *Thank you, Papa.*

She closed the bag. "When do you start?"

"We're supposed to report the end of July. The in-service training starts in August."

"That'll work out fine. Just when I get back! We'll go out to Great Spruce Island and celebrate," she said, thinking that would please him.

"I was kind of hoping it would be an engagement celebration."

"Lin—"

"Hear me out. I don't want to put any pressure on, but I have to tell them yes or no."

"Tell them yes. It's an opportunity."

He couldn't seem to look at her. "The job's in Massachusetts."

"Massachusetts?"

"Pittsfield, Mass. Western side of the state. It would mean a big jump in salary," he went on, almost apologetically. "Forty-two hundred a year. That's a thirty-three-percent increase over what the University of Maine is offering."

"Do you want this job?"

"I'm happy where I am. The thing is, I'd be a lot happier with you."

She folded her arms. "I'm not moving to Massachusetts, if that's what you're asking."

"Listen, I don't want to leave the island, either."

His profile was steady and he drove with great concentration, as if they were navigating a wind-whipped lightning storm instead of rolling along on a mild day.

"We could make the farm work, Cora. If you wanted to. That's what I've been trying to get across." He threw her a sideways look. "I thought you had affection for that place."

"Of course I do. Tide's End will never leave this family. I just can't manage it right now."

"Great!" He bounced one hand off the wheel with mocking cheeriness. "I'm glad you feel that way! Now I have an excuse to turn down the Conservation Service!"

"I didn't say yes," Cora put in quickly.

They passed the gatehouse and rolled down the ramp, where the ferryman was impatiently waving them forward. There was a passenger car behind them and one already on the scow, which could only carry two vehicles. They were lucky to make it and not have to wait.

"Linwood?" she said anxiously. "Did you hear?"

"Yes," he said, somber now. "I heard exactly what you didn't say. I heard it loud and clear."

They bumped over the boards and stopped behind the first car. Linwood turned the engine off and they waited uncertainly for the other to get out first. It was quiet except for birds screeching and water sloshing heavily against the shifting platform of the ferry.

"You deserve some happiness," Linwood said.

BOSTON

5

It might have taken a whole town and half a hog to get Cora Blake to the train, but once she was on board, Uncle Sam was footing the bills and no expense was to be spared. It was true: the official pilgrimage badge with the red, white, and blue ribbon was like a magic charm that transformed Cora Blake from a humble traveler to a VIP. When she got out of the truck at Union Station in Bangor, her suitcases were whisked away and a senior trainman with a gray mustache, wearing a dark uniform with epaulets, respectfully asked if he might escort her to her seat.

"Lin?" she called. "Aren't you coming inside?"

Linwood stayed where he was.

"I'd better get Mr. Pig to where he's going. He's becoming an embarrassment," he added, with a glance toward a beat cop who was eyeing the bloodstained sack.

"Don't go," she begged. "Keep me company. We still have time."

Linwood shrugged and gave Cora a halfhearted smile. She could see that her indecision was hurting him.

"No point, really," he told her.

"It's—it's hard times," Cora said helplessly.

"I know you have a lot to think about. A lot ahead of you."

She found his wounded eyes in the shadow of the fedora.

"But I am coming back," she said deliberately.

He nodded, and for a moment they felt the reassuring island connection that had attracted them in the first place. They'd grown up together; they knew each other in ways no outsider ever would.

"Will you give some thought to what I said?" he asked.

"Of course," she promised. "I'll think about it every day. And I'll write."

"Send me a postcard of the Eiffel Tower."

Linwood flung those last words over his shoulder, walked around to the driver's side, got in, turned the engine over, and, as if to show her the frustration words couldn't tell, jumped the truck right over the trolley tracks and careened into downtown traffic. The trainman, who had been discreetly holding back, stepped forward and offered Cora his arm. They paraded through the station and across the main foyer, turning heads. When they reached the tracks he confided that it was a personal privilege to escort a Gold Star Mother, because his nephew had served on the Western Front, and if anything had happened to him, his poor sister would have lost her mind, so he knew exactly what she'd gone through.

He bowed slightly and helped her step into a car marked *First Class*. Cora was baffled by his behavior but before she could thank him the conductor was there to show her to her seat. "Let me know if you need anything," he told her. "Anything at all. God bless you."

The walls were paneled in mahogany and the seats covered in violet-colored velvet, set in groups of two-facing-two so you had a private alcove with a curtained window. There was a fold-down table and a rack full of magazines just for her, but Cora could only sit there, stiff as an arrow, with the tartan bag on her lap, stunned to find herself alone and in this new world of outlandish luxury. After some time other passengers came on board, there were distant shouts and whistles, and the train began to move. A black porter in a white uniform leaned over and said, "An honor to have you with us, ma'am," and set up her table, then returned with complimentary lemonade in a frosty glass. That wasn't all. He'd placed beside it with great care a dish of sugared almonds, and a napkin that was embroidered *Olsen Railroad & Co.*, just like the writing on Mrs. Genevieve Olsen's ivory stationery! It was thrilling. There were several train lines that met in Bangor, and Cora hadn't thought a whit about which one she would be on, but as they left the station, she became keenly aware of the money and power behind the railroad set to which Mrs. Olsen belonged, *and Cora knew her!* As they crossed a drawbridge over a quiet inlet she caught sight of herself in the window and thought, *Cora, close your mouth, you look like a kid on Christmas morning.*

Union Station was like an illustration from a child's book, made of buff-colored brick with brown edging, two peaked façades, and a clock tower in between that wore a conical roof like a hat; a fairy-tale place that promised any train you boarded here would provide a safe and pleasant journey. As they slipped away, past icehouses that once shipped Penobscot River ice all over the world, lumberyards that had given way to paper mills shuttered because of the Depression, Cora was departing a world of simple equations and screwed-down values that she had always taken for granted. The porter came by again to refill her lemonade and leave a saucer with a celery stick and olives and a packet of oyster crackers, which she ate one after the other until they were gone. She was too excited to think. There were three hours and twenty-two minutes to Boston and she could not contain the delicious anticipation of meeting Katie McConnell. Making contact with a stranger. In a washroom. In a train station. It was right out of one of the spy novels that flew off the shelves in the library. Cora pulled out the letters from Party A tied with the blue ribbon and reread the one she'd just received from Katie:

"Dear Mrs. Blake—I will be in the Lounge at 6:15 in the Evening as we said. I have been liven for the day. And here is Good News! I am bringing the Family to. My Husband wants to see us off. He is so very carefull of me. You will meet our little Son, Damian. He is Four years old. Your friend, Mrs. Katie McConnell."

It was comforting to know that Katie would be in South Station as planned, but there was something about the letter that always stuck. It was that Katie said she had a little boy. Every time she read it, Cora flushed with jealousy. Sometimes when she saw a child with a young mother she felt hunger so strong she believed she was capable of stealing it away. Even though Katie McConnell had endured the unimaginable loss of two sons, Cora envied her for having the softness and beauty of childhood so close to her again. And for having been given another chance at the happiness of motherhood.

The porter offered to reserve a table in the first-class dining car, but Cora declined. She'd had a look on the way to the restroom and it was horrifying: white tablecloths and rattling silver, well-dressed couples silently picking at shrimp over ice. Then, he suggested, perhaps a seat at the bar? Even worse. Nothing could have dragged her into that smoke-filled den of hard-looking men with flowers in their lapels sitting at circular tables painted black and white like shooting targets, fawning over women with loud red mouths.

Her little alcove was just fine. She devoured the bread-and-butter, ate the apple down to the seeds, wrapped the seeds in a napkin so the porter wouldn't see, took off her pumps and put her feet up on the automatic footrest, and fell asleep. When she awoke, the small farms that had been regularly dividing the countryside into paddocks and fields had vanished, and all you could see for several miles were grimy shoe factories and textile mills, as if the train ride that had begun at the station in Bangor had passed through time to the pragmatism of present day; as if, where the tracks ended at South Station, Boston was the culmination of a century of progress.

Cora stepped off the train into humid summer air and the smell of coal fire. The steel mass of a dozen engines idling in the open-roofed depot made her feel slight, as if she could be swept away like a leaf under the polished heels of well-dressed commuters striding along the bays, casting impatient shadows on ashen squares of daylight. She followed the crowd through a gate that led to a vast arcade, where high arched windows brought in the evening sun. You'd think, from all the light everywhere, that Boston was a city made of gold.

South Station was the largest manmade structure she had ever been inside. You could hear the rumble of the trains below, but there was also a hush that came from the echoes of voices and hurried footfalls dissipating in the great marble hall. It was just past six o'clock as she hurried through a maze of kiosks selling newspapers and sundries, saltwater taffy and chocolate caramels, people streaming in and out in all directions, until she saw a sign for the women's waiting room and made a beeline for it, eager to avoid the rows of benches where unsavory derelicts and large immigrant families had spread themselves out.

But the entrance to the women's waiting room was blocked by a large woman hovering in the doorway, holding on to the molding to support her considerable weight.

"Are you all right?" Cora asked.

"I'm wonderin' where I might sit down."

Her voice was soft with a southern inflection. She wore a worn brown cloth coat and a turban-style hat with a veil. The hat was bright purple and seemed to have nothing to do with the coat. Her legs were bowed and her stockings rolled down, the ankles all swollen up. This woman was somebody's grandma. She had the right to sit down.

"Why, you can rest inside," Cora said. "You'll be comfortable there. It's for ladies only," she added encouragingly.

The woman's rheumy eyes moved over Cora with pity, as if she were the slowest-minded idiot in the world.

"Those kinda ladies don't want me in there. Don't you worry yourself," she added with a bitter edge.

The only Negro people Cora ever had anything to do with were the porters on the train and the seasonal workers who came up to Maine from Jamaica for employment on the potato farms. They had made an impression. She remembered being five or six years old and seeing a poorly dressed mother and her children walking down the middle of Main Street, as if they didn't think they were allowed to use the sidewalk. They wore head scarves made of potato sacks. Cora was frightened and held on to her mother's hand, but Luella took them right up to those people and said, "That's not how we do it in our town. You're welcome here, like any other."

"It's okay to go inside," Cora told the grandma in the doorway.

"Really?" She made a mocking look. "Young lady, you got a lot to learn."

She mopped the perspiration on her neck and lifted a wicker suitcase. Cora caught sight of a bronze badge on a red, white, and blue ribbon pinned to her stout bosom.

"Wait!" Cora said. "You're a Gold Star Mother."

"Don't make no difference to some people."

"So am I!" Cora pointed to hers.

The woman's reddened eyes slowly softened. "Where'd you lose your boy?"

"France."

"Mine, too." She rocked back and peered at Cora. Her dark brown face was all chubby cheeks that crowded her eyes into crescents when she smiled. "Looks like we both going to the same place."

"New York City? The Hotel Commodore?"

"That's right."

"And then are you going on to Paris?" Cora asked.

"So they tell me. If I stay on my feet."

When she finally followed Cora into the women's waiting room, nobody paid attention to the colored woman in the purple hat; everyone was in too much of a rush. There was no "waiting" in this cosmopolitan crossroads, where a flood of women from all walks of life, loaded down with shopping bags and children, went in and out at a fabulous rate. The place was more elegant than the clientele, done up like a feminine palace in pink and gold, with round mirrors and clusters of crystalline electric lamps floating from the ceiling as if conjured by a magician. An attendant in a black uniform was handing towels to each patron, and most of them tossed some pennies in a dish.

"I can't hardly afford to even pee in here," the grandmother observed.

Cora left her to search for Katie McConnell, even asking strangers if they went by that name, but Katie had not arrived. It was 6:45 p.m.

The elderly black lady had found a seat on a pink settee and invited Cora to sit down. Cora settled beside her, eyes on the door.

"Lookin' out for someone?"

"A member of my party. We're supposed to meet and take the train to New York. Her name is Mrs. McConnell," Cora added, as if saying it would make her appear.

"What's your name, young lady?" the grandma asked.

"Mrs. Blake. What is yours?"

"Mrs. Russell."

Cora turned to her and gasped. "Mrs. Russell? You're in my party, too. Party A?"

Mrs. Russell fumbled with her purse, put on her glasses, and came up with a letter that had the familiar seal of the War Department. "Party A. There you be! Mrs. Blake, member something—"

"Coordinator."

"Let's see. There's a couple of other names . . . and at the bottom it says Mr. Thomas Hammond and Miss Lily Barnett, R.N."

"That's the army officer and the nurse assigned to our group. Oh, good Lord!" Cora continued in a rush. "What a stroke of luck for us to run into each other! Well," she decided, "this was meant to be! I've been waiting and waiting to hear back from you. Didn't you get my letters?"

"No, ma'am."

"Don't you live in Prouts Neck?"

"Whose neck?"

Cora threw up her hands. "Oh, never mind! The army must have sent the wrong address. I understand there will be more than four hundred of us going on that ship. You can't really blame them."

Mrs. Russell objected vigorously. "That exactly what the army *do*. I ain't hardly got any letters from my son, Elmore. And those I did receive did not arrive until a whole year after he died."

"What a shame. Did Elmore fight in a place called Meuse-Argonne, do you know?"

"Yes, indeed."

"Sammy, too. He was in the Twenty-sixth Infantry, the Yankee Division."

"Elmore was in the Ninety-third Division, Service of Supply," Mrs. Russell said proudly.

"Good for him," Cora echoed, with no idea what that meant.

But it must have meant something, because Mrs. Russell was still nodding to herself with pleasure.

"He was a hard worker and a good son. The Germans killed him with a bombshell. You just can't keep the devil in the hole. I know that for a fact."

Sitting down was doing Mrs. Russell good. Her wide forehead was no longer prickled with sweat. She'd accepted a glass of water and seemed to perk up. Now she was looking around with satisfaction at the grand marble columns and the mural of a lady with a whippet dog that covered an entire wall.

"This is fine," she said.

Cora learned her companion had come north from Georgia at the age of twenty-eight when Elmore was a baby and still sewed ladies' wraps and underwear for a manufacturer in the textile district of Boston. She was sixty-two years old and lived with her daughter and grandchildren. She said that she was glad when her son joined the army because she thought it would improve his education, and the pastor of her church preached that it was important for black people to stand up and show their patriotism. Cora had been listening with one eye on the clock and the other on the door. It was 7:10 p.m. and Katie McConnell hadn't showed.

"I'm getting worried about Mrs. McConnell," Cora said.

"She comin' or she ain't," Mrs. Russell pronounced. "Meanwhile, we best get on that train. Now, what are those two up to? Sellin' Hershey bars?"

Two teenage girls, almost identical, with long blond hair and dressed in green plaid school uniforms with pleated skirts, had burst into the waiting room and were scrambling about, tapping shoulders, stopping people at the sinks, cornering them before they walked out the door, and generally disrupting everybody's business. The attendant shooed them out but instead of leaving they formed their hands like megaphones and screamed at the top of their lungs:

"Mrs. Blake? Is anyone here named Mrs. Blake?"

"I am!" Cora said, springing to her feet.

They rushed over. "Mrs. Blake? Katie McConnell said to tell you that she's looking for ya!"

"Who are you?"

"Come on! She's our aunt!"

"This is Mrs. Russell," Cora said, pulling back. "She's also in your aunt's party—"

"You go on," Mrs. Russell said. "It'll take me a minute."

"Are you sure? You can get to the train all right?"

"I'll be fine."

"We won't leave without you," Cora promised, grabbing the tartan bag. To the girls: "Where is Mrs. McConnell? Is she here?"

"Hurry up. She's waitin' outside."

"Why outside—?"

They marshaled Cora out the door and across the main hall to where a group of people had formed an island in the midst of the flux. They were more like a tribe. The men kept guard with feet planted and arms folded, casting suspicious glances at passersby. The women huddled in threes and fours, chatting a mile a minute while their children practiced sliding across the marble floor. Except for a couple of uniformed cops, they were dressed in battered shoes and poor working clothes. Some were compact and swarthy, some thin and fair; they resembled each other in attitude more than looks. In short, *"We own this place."* It reminded Cora of fishermen guarding their traps.

The girls broke through the outer circle shouting, "Here she is!" and Cora was somehow sucked into the center, where a tall woman wearing black was holding a struggling little boy.

"Oh!" she exclaimed. "Would you be Mrs. Blake?"

"Yes!" Cora answered breathlessly. "Mrs. McConnell? Happy to meet you at last!"

They tried to shake hands but the boy got in the way with all his squirming. Katie McConnell was not at all the way Cora had pictured her, dressed in a smart store-bought wool shirtwaist with the Gold Star Mothers badge on the lapel. Carrot-red hair showed beneath a black cloche hat with a rhinestone buckle. Her fair skin was lightly freckled and her front teeth stuck out just enough to give her an air of girlish abandonment.

"Say hello to Damian."

Her little boy was a moon-faced bruiser with dark chopped-off bangs. He refused to look at Cora, burying his face in his mother's neck. Katie laughed apologetically.

"He doesn't want to let me go."

She spoke with a Gaelic intonation that made everything a statement and a question at the same time. The boy kept tugging on Katie's ear until she gave him her attention. Cora disapproved of the way she continued to hold him. He was four years old, not a baby. If she'd just put him down, he would settle. And then she did.

"Here we go," Katie said finally. "Give Mama a rest, why don'tcha?"

The boy had a withered leg. One of the relatives produced a pair of crutches. He greedily took hold of them and crab-walked over to the other kids.

"Polio," Katie explained. "He got sick when he was nine months old and spent a year in Children's Hospital in an iron lung. He's well cured, but people are afraid they might catch the disease. We've been chased from public rest-rooms more than once, which is why I don't dare go inside."

Damian tried to slide on the floor like his cousins, fell down, and was picked up by an older boy.

"He seems to get on," Cora said cheerfully.

One of the policemen interrupted. "Better get on that train, ladies," he said in a kindly manner. He spoke with the rough clang of a born Irishman. He was a large man with a jowly face and sad downturned eyes.

"This is my husband, Sergeant Ian McConnell,"

Katie said. "I was just tellin' Mrs. Blake about Damian."

"He's a fighter." The father smiled and put an arm around his wife. "But she's the brave one. She does the whole family honor by going on this pilgrimage. It's far away and we'll miss her, but I said right off it's our sacred duty and she should do it. We're all proud of her."

Mr. and Mrs. McConnell kissed, and Cora remembered that Linwood had said the very same thing to her before leaving the house, while they'd stayed on the porch for a last glimpse of the harbor. *"I'm proud of you."* It softened her heart toward him and made her regret leaving every-thing so unsettled. She knew Linwood wasn't going to take the job in Massachusetts, it was just something he'd used to try to urge her along. He'd lost his wife in a terrible way, a single instant of a car going out of control—maybe he was afraid that if he pushed too hard, Cora would go spinning off as well. Leaving the island took her out of his territory; going to France, she was well off the map. But there was no harm done, not really. They'd left things open, hadn't they? And you could say a lot on a postcard. She steadied herself by remembering that her mother and father had crossed oceans and come back. It was in her blood: the fear of it, and the thrill of going, just the same.

The entire clan accompanied them on the long

walk downstairs to the track: Ian's brother, Jack; Margaret, his wife; William and Sean, their grown sons; cousins Michael, Devora, and Allie; another Jack who was someone's uncle; and his children, Eddie, Steve, Brooke, and Lane. Ian carried the little boy and Katie took his crutches along with her carpetbag. When they got to the first-class car, Cora looked up to see Mrs. Russell knocking on the glass, already settled in a window seat. She waved back. Party A was here!

They wouldn't let Cora go without goodbye hugs and safe wishes from each of the McConnells. Damian was back in Katie's arms and he was crying.

"I'll be back before ye know it," she said, smoothing his bangs. "What's the matter, darlin'?"

"Mama—are you going away to heaven?"

"Oh, God, no," said Katie. "What gave you that idea?"

But the child could not be soothed, and in the end had to be forcefully pulled away. Katie steeled herself and got on board without looking back. She'd left her mother in Ireland; she could leave her boy for a couple of weeks. Damian was handed off to the two teenage girls, who jostled him and carried him along to see the big locomotive at the front of the train. The crying ceased and he stared over their shoulders at the place where his mother had disappeared. Cora watched with stinging eyes as the somber little face became smaller and smaller, borne off to the darkness of the tunnel.

The members of Party A had been given their own compartment. Here the velvet seats were patterned with businesslike checks and the glass doors finished in walnut. A painting of an English landscape was nailed to the wall. When Cora climbed in, Kate and Mrs. Russell had already introduced themselves and were commiserating over Damian.

Despite her resolve, Katie's eyes were red and she was blowing her nose into a handkerchief. "I don't know what came into my head to bring him."

"Shame about the polio," Mrs. Russell clucked. "We got a lot of that down South."

"We count it a blessing."

"That so?"

Katie folded her hands in her lap. "He'll never go to war."

The train continued to move through the tunnel a long time before breaking daylight. The summer sun was going down over the church steeples and triple-deckers of South Boston when the conductor who had boarded them opened the door to the compartment and smiled at the three unlikely occupants—a grandma from the South, black like he was; a mom from the big Irish family with the crippled boy; a nice lady on a through ticket from Bangor, Maine—who already seemed to have much more in common with one another than just their Gold Star badges.

"Welcome to the *Mayflower* line, Boston to New York City," he said.

They smiled back pleasantly enough. Of course they didn't know it, and the conductor was not about to tell, but there had been some trouble with the lady from down South. He'd had to call in the supervisor to override objections by certain passengers about her sitting up front with the whites. Negroes were not usually seen in first class, except if they were famous entertainers, but it irked him that her being a war mother and the fact that her son gave his life for this country didn't make such a thing automatic. The supervisor settled it the smart way. He said as long as Mrs. Russell had a government-issued ticket with her name on it, she was entitled to be there.

"What can I do for you, ladies?"

Cora spoke up confidently. "A table for three in the dining car, please."

"It will be my pleasure," the conductor said.

NEW YORK CITY

6

General Reginald Perkins had taken over the grand ballroom of the Hotel Commodore, which was just across from Grand Central Terminal on Forty-second Street, and turned it into a war room. A fashionable location for society weddings had been converted into a command center, alive with urgency and pinpoint purpose. Beneath the tiered chandeliers were thirty-six metal desks manned by ranks of secretaries, and the vaulted ceilings echoed twelve hours a day with typewriters clacking out reports in sextuplet. Army officers in olive green uniforms strode to and fro, pushing tackboards with maps of the European battlefields. Telephones rang. Orders were issued. The only remnant of civilian life was a grand piano in the center of it all, incongruously poised on a platform draped with blue silk.

General Reginald Perkins was fifty-six years old, a big-shouldered Kentuckian with thick silver hair and bushy, theatrical eyebrows. He had the set mouth and perfect posture of a horseman. Just like clearing a jump, he used to say, the trick in life was to use your heels and keep your eyes fixed on where you wanted to go. He came from a lineage that proved it. His father had fought in the Mexican War. His grandfather was a general in the Confederate army. Young Perkins abandoned the family tobacco business to attend Virginia Military Institute, where he was trained as an engineer. He served five years in the Philippines before commanding the 104th in the Meuse-Argonne Offensive of 1918, for which he received the Distinguished Service Medal.

Back in the States, he was assigned to the Quartermaster Corps, which combat types might deride as a bunch of glorified supply sergeants, but it suited Perkins's acerbic blend of meticulousness and hunger for power. Small victories could build a career. He'd revamped the Graves Registration Service and received high marks for coming in on budget for the construction of depots and army hospitals. Two years before, when Congress passed the American War Mothers Act, which inaugurated the Gold Star Mothers' tours, Reginald Perkins was the obvious choice to tackle the logistical mess of transporting, accommodating, feeding, and medicating almost seven thousand mothers and widows from all over America to and from Europe—many of them over the age of fifty and therefore, by the army's calculation, in a state of physical exhaustion. But now, from a balcony above the grand ballroom where he had built the perfect machine, General Perkins looked down at his creation and thought, *Balls!*

He'd known from the beginning the project

would be a nut-cruncher, but if he pulled it off, he'd be first in line for an appointment by President Hoover as quartermaster general. Congress was watching. The press was watching.

And one of the mothers was missing.

While Cora Blake and Katie McConnell had been getting to know their new friend in South Station, Boston, an alert had been issued in New York City that a war mother named Mrs. Wilhelmina Russell from Prouts Neck, Maine, was lost. She had allegedly arrived the day before, but somehow, between Grand Central Terminal and the Hotel Commodore across the street, she had vanished.

Thirty feet above the parquet floor, General Perkins chewed his pipe and looked for someone to blame. He was furious. The S.S. *Harding* sailed for Europe in two days, a massive undertaking involving more than four hundred pilgrims, and the departures were always heavily covered by the news services. Sooner or later some local yokel reporter would realize that one of his hometown gals was nowhere to be found to give him a juicy quote on the quality of the laundry service, and start asking awkward questions. Perkins scanned the war room, hectic as usual, and wondered with a jolt of anxiety whether this Russell incident would become the first crack in his personal *Titanic*. Then his eyes fell on Second Lieutenant Thomas Hammond, chugging purposefully up the steps to where Perkins stood on the balcony. He was carrying a clipboard and looking grim. Maybe the kid knew something.

Hammond saluted with bravado. He was twenty-three years old and in tip-top shape, having survived the rigorous demands of West Point. He had lush brown hair that was almost black, a patrician nose, large wide-set intelligent brown eyes, and polished manners. Perkins's forebears were dirt farmers and mountain sharpshooters; Hammond had been raised in upper-class Washington, D.C., with a military pedigree that rivaled the general's, going back to the Civil War. His father, Thomas West Hammond, had commanded troops in France during the war, retired from the army as a colonel, and was now a commissioner of New York City appointed by Mayor La Guardia.

The younger Hammond's grades were excellent, and he was captain of the baseball team at Western High School in Georgetown, which made it a smooth transition to Shadman's Preparatory School, where, after just a few months, he was admitted to West Point by presidential appointment—and certainly not without his father's influence—at the early age of eighteen. Once he was there, he earned a reputation for toughness. A competitive athlete, Hammond stood out at the academy where stars were made: on the playing fields. Sport was the proving ground for courage and teamwork, and great individual plays became the kind of lore invoked throughout careers and even in eulogies. Hammond was a three-sport athlete—baseball, basketball, and football—and again captained the baseball team, which, along with an open and easygoing personality, made him a leader. It followed that on graduation he would land the plum job of one of the liaison officers for the Gold Star Mothers' pilgrimages, supervising Party A on its sojourn across the ocean to the American cemetery in Meuse-Argonne, France.

Perkins stared resentfully at the young man, seeing instead his four daughters, skinny silly little girls in frilly white dresses with ribbons in their hair. No sons. None of *his* progeny would soldier on. But he was smart enough to see an opportunity. Word would get back to Colonel Hammond on how Perkins treated his son, which would count when it came to a promotion. Coddling would not do. The old man would appreciate rigor, Perkins decided, and therefore he would bring this newly minted hotshot down to size.

Hammond was looking down at the war room with satisfaction.

"Looks like we're preparing to take Berlin, sir."

He meant it as a compliment but Perkins seemed annoyed.

"Glad you approve."

"Sorry, sir, I didn't mean to presume—"

Perkins cut him off. "What about that missing woman?"

"She's not exactly missing, sir. We just haven't located her."

"What's the report from the New York police?"

"Negative. Nothing to report, sir. They're out there . . . on patrol."

Hammond hoped that covered it. He had no idea how the police were proceeding, as the surly detective had given him no clue, scribbled two words in a notebook (*"woman missing"*), and vanished into the hotel bar. He could see that Perkins wasn't buying. He'd stuck the pipe into the corner of his mouth and bitten down so hard it bobbled up and down as he spit out two years' worth of exasperation in the young officer's face.

"You have no idea what it's taken to get this thing to float."

"I understand, sir."

"Do you? I have personally met with every Mickey Mouse agency commissioner in the navel lint of France. Why, of course they're allies in the trenches tried and true, but try convincing some pompous little bureaucrat to give a centime off the price of admission to the Galeries Nationales, or a place to put your goddamn bus. Remember our orders!" he snapped, as if Hammond were responsible for blowing up a bridge to stop the Germans from taking Paris. "The quartermaster wants us to conduct this business with as little

114

interruption to the way of life of these pilgrims as possible. It's all about *details*. Wherever American pilgrims go, a U.S.-style breakfast will be served. And who do you think was *responsible* for getting the rest houses at the cemeteries upgraded from goddamn latrines to American country-club standards? That was me, Hammond. That's how seriously I take this job. Congress has given us quite a task transporting these women and seeing to their safety! They can't be lost like someone's old sock."

"I didn't exactly lose Mrs. Russell, sir—"

"She is in your party," Perkins reminded him.

Hammond referred to the papers on his clipboard as if he'd never seen them before.

"Party A, correct."

"So what has been done to find her?"

Hammond straightened up. "I interviewed the girls on the registration desk and they swear Mrs. Wilhelmina Russell never signed in at the hotel."

"And that's supposed to be good news?"

"I believe the duty officer is in error in stating that she arrived at Grand Central."

"Or," suggested Perkins, "she arrived at Grand Central and slipped away from the duty officer."

"He's a good man, very responsible. I can vouch for him."

"I see. And now you're a judge of character?"

"With respect, sir, it seems more likely that there

was a mix-up in the transport section, and that in fact Mrs. Russell took a different train—"

"Button it, would you? Your father would not accept lame excuses, so why should I?"

Hammond's cheeks turned pink. He was never not under scrutiny or being compared to his father. But he stood tall and didn't blink while Perkins let him broil.

"God help you if she's wandered off somewhere," the general said.

At the same time, Mrs. Selma Russell was moments away, on the train from Boston and about to arrive at Grand Central Terminal with Cora Blake and Katie McConnell. After a lovely supper in the dining car of roast duck breast in cherry sauce and wild rice, they had indulged in a glass of sherry, which put them out for fifty miles. Regaining consciousness, they dove into their itineraries, checking off the optional excursions —the Empire State Building and the Central Park Zoo—that they planned to go on together. Bolstered by the unity that had blossomed almost immediately, they were alert, eager, and ready to take on New York when the conductor announced Grand Central station.

The first-arriving members of Party A were met in style by a brisk employee of the railroad, whose entire job was to see to the needs of Gold Star Mothers. He wore a three-piece suit and a red carnation, organized the luggage and the porters, took them upstairs by special elevator and onto the street. By then it was dark and they were overwhelmed by the grandeur of the city at night. There was so much noise and commotion. The spotlit marquees. The white summer furs. Policemen above the crowds on beautifully groomed horses. Bakery windows filled with trays and trays of éclairs. Everything in New York was larger than life, Cora marveled, and so much more *important* than anywhere else.

The Hotel Commodore overlooked a plaza where taxis buzzed at reckless speeds. As the railroad man forged ahead into the traffic, Cora was seized by an automatic reaction to reach for Sammy's hand . . . followed by a wave of emptiness so powerful she wanted to lie down on the sidewalk and go to sleep, if sleep would end it. But her feet kept up their dutiful march, following the neat shoulders of the railroad man, numbed by the wound-up chatter of her companions, as they stepped off the curb and across the mad circle of traffic.

The hotel loomed before them, an enormous edifice of yellow sandstone, two wings and a courtyard, twenty stories high. Every window had a canopy and every window was lit. Cora, Katie, and Selma looked up, eyes rising slowly, incredulously, as if they were scaling the building itself, all the way to the roof, where an American flag was in full display on a stiff breeze, floodlit against the sky—the same gritty breeze that was gusting down Forty-second Street, lifting their skirts, smelling of old iron pipes and corn roasting on a nearby peddler's cart, a tin stove on wheels with a crooked chimney. The noise of horns and revving motors was like a deafening waterfall. A doorman came forward to guide them past a lush round fountain and up the red-carpeted steps.

While they entered the hotel, Lieutenant Hammond happened to be looking down at the glittering plaza from the floor-to-ceiling windows of the ballroom on the second floor, hardly realizing that the answer to the problem was right beneath his nose. The records he had requisitioned were in brown folders piled on a trolley, and for the past several hours he'd been poring over barely readable, tissue-thin carbon copies of the rosters detailing every pilgrim who was leaving on the S.S. *Harding*. The names were not alphabetical but listed by county and state, which meant he'd had to go through every one. Under *Maine* he'd located Mrs. Wilhelmina Russell of Prouts Neck, mother of Private Bradley Russell. In *Massachusetts*, he'd found Mrs. Selma Russell, mother of Private Elmore Russell, and saw that she was scheduled to arrive from Boston that night. In fact, she should be here now. If so, where was she?

He'd found the source of the problem but was

no closer to finding the missing women. There were two Mrs. Russells on this pilgrimage, both with sons in the New England Yankee Division. Still, the discrepancy didn't make sense, between the duty officer's report—that he had personally escorted "Mrs. Russell" yesterday—and this document that said she was about to arrive. He stretched his back, rose up on his toes, and knuckled his head all over to try to wake up. Who had arrived? Who was lost? It was like a math problem that didn't add up. He'd thought he was through with that kind of worry at West Point, but in fact, memorizing Latin and learning German and military science had been a lot easier than solving a logistical problem in real life. How to find a lost woman in the midst of millions? How to avoid being reamed by Perkins the following day?

"Lieutenant?"

He spun around quickly. It was Lucille—or Linda?—whom he'd just interviewed at the registration desk, standing in the shadowed doorway of the silent ballroom. Like him, she was on a twelve-hour shift. This morning she'd been perky enough, bending over in a revealing sweater. Now she looked like her face had melted.

"Mrs. Russell's here," she announced. "You said to tell you right away."

"Really?! You're an angel! You have my heartfelt and eternal thanks!"

119

She didn't respond. Not even a smile? The girl didn't care; she just wanted to go home. Not used to rebuff, he followed her to the lobby, where two women were talking. One was tall and dressed in black and spoke with an Irish accent. The other had dark blond hair beneath a red beret and wore a gray dress. She was younger-looking and prettier than most of the war mothers he'd seen. Whatever trouble she might have caused, he was cheered to have her on board.

"Mrs. Russell!" he said gaily. "Lieutenant Thomas Hammond. Delighted to meet you. I'll be leading your party."

"Happy to meet you, too," said the woman. "But I'm not Mrs. Russell. I'm Mrs. Blake. Cora Blake. And this is Mrs. Katie McConnell—"

"Yes, of course! You're both on my list! Welcome. Please forgive the mistake, we're a bit scattered tonight. We're expecting another pilgrim, Mrs. Russell."

"You lookin' for Mrs. Russell?" asked a southern voice. "She right here."

Hammond turned toward a large, grandmotherly woman he hadn't noticed before, sitting in a big chair near a palm tree. Something short-circuited in his brain and he was paralyzed.

"Mrs. Who?"

"Mrs. Selma Russell," the woman repeated slowly.

"We all came down from Boston together," Katie said.

Cora was momentarily puzzled into silence. She thought the lady in her party was named Wilhelmina. Maybe Selma was a nickname.

The longer the young man stood there staring, the more Selma's expression hardened into the cynical dark brown mask she'd worn outside the waiting room in South Station. It was her habit to distrust, and she was usually right.

Hammond managed to extend his hand, along with a winning smile.

"So *you're* our Mrs. Russell! Welcome to New York City," he said heartily, knowing he was doomed.

Things couldn't be more thoroughly loused up, and they weren't even on the boat.

7

Mrs. Minnie Seibert appeared to be staring at the young woman on the bus but actually she was in deep contemplation of the woman's hat, a navy pillbox that had a veil dotted with pearls. The pearls were nice, but it was the feathers that interested Minnie. She was certain they were hackle feathers from white stag roosters, of the same breed that she and her husband, Abraham, raised on their poultry farm outside Bangor—a high-priced feather that took well to dyeing. You could see these were of superior quality because of the true colors in the turquoise and teal that were fanned out on the navy blue hat like the tail of a miniature peacock.

Minnie was certain that she knew the wholesaler who sold the feathers to the milliner who made the hat. His name was Max Bodenheimer, the biggest feather man on the Lower East Side, who paid sixteen dollars a pound for the leavings Minnie's girls collected and packed, which Abraham drove down to the city twice a year. Max Bodenheimer. It had to be. And since Minnie had gotten on the bus at the corner of Broome Street, in the heart of the eastern European Jewish ghetto, and this young lady had boarded there as well, she had to be a *landsman* also—another Jew.

"*Iz dos Park Gas?*" Minnie said in Yiddish. *Is this Park Avenue?*

The woman replied in English: "Not yet, but soon. How far are you going?"

"Street number forty-two. Hotel Commodore."

"I get off at Fifty-seventh. I'll tell you at your stop."

"*A dank,*" Minnie replied automatically, but the woman did not acknowledge her thanks.

That hat must have cost her a pretty penny, Minnie thought, running her eyes over the blue suit with white trim and the open-toed pumps. She couldn't have been older than twenty-five, but already she was some kind of professional who knew her way around. She carried a case for a musical instrument, maybe a clarinet, and a smart leather portfolio. She wore her copper hair in waves and on her lips a thick layer of confident red. Minnie hadn't worn lipstick in ages. It would never have occurred to her. She was past lipstick and everything it suggested.

This person, however, took it upon herself to make her own rules. She understood Yiddish, but refused to speak it. What was wrong with the new generation who thought they were Americans *only?* Minnie had lived in this country thirty-eight years, she was an American, too, and she liked nice things, just like this lady with the clarinet. They'd had a house full of treasures in Russia—silver candlesticks and gold jewelry—and her father had been a physics teacher, before their homes and shops were burned down during the pogroms. As a child Minnie had been spat on, and her eight-year-old brother was kidnapped for three days by drunken peasants who tied him down until he agreed to be baptized as a Christian, but he never gave in and was rescued near starvation by their father and uncles. Minnie had seen what it cost to be a Jew in Russia at the turn of the century, which made it all the more precious in this day and age. There was a lot not to like about chicken farming in Maine, but within their tiny group of ten families they could live a Jewish life. Why didn't this free American citizen respect history enough to at least answer in her own language?

The bus sped uptown a mile a minute, even faster than the crazy traffic. Bessie Reiss, the cousin Minnie had been staying with on Houston Street, was the head bookkeeper in a glove factory, a *baleboosteh* who didn't take orders from anyone. It would have been nice to have her sitting beside her now. But Bessie had to go to work, so she'd put Minnie on the bus with instructions that once they turned onto Park Avenue it was *nishtikeit—nothing.* "Just keep your eye on the street signs and get off at number forty-two and ask anyone." But without Bessie or the teeming comfort of the old-country neighborhood, where you could talk to anyone in four languages, Minnie quickly lost all sense of where she was, and entered instead a familiar world of worry. She worried she'd get lost. She worried that she'd miss the breakfast at the hotel, the first big event of the pilgrimage. And the itinerary clearly stated, *"It is important for you to attend, as this will be an opportunity to meet the other members of your party."*

It was barely eight in the morning and already like a steambath. Even the hot air coming through the half-open windows of the bus was a relief. Minnie wore her best bright-pink-and-green-flowered cotton frock, which came down to the ankles, with a scoop neck and puffy sleeves. She carried a borrowed needlepoint handbag and a cardboard suitcase, and wore a white brimmed hat that brought out her naturally arched brows and deep-set slate-gray eyes. She had always been told she was the prettiest of her sisters, which led her to carry herself with no small amount of vanity, and had made it a long fall to the poverty of the chicken farm, unproductive land they had bought cheaply, where Isaac had been born in a ramshackle house held together with tarpaper.

By then the girls were married and moved to Bangor, in order to get away from their father's rants against capitalism, nationalism, Orthodox religion, and the illusion of romantic love, and because deep in their souls they knew the egg business, at least the way their inexperienced cooperative went at it, with trial-and-error methods and naïve utopian ideas, was hopeless. In a houschold that believed you could live a Jewish life of virtue without accepting Yahweh, late baby Isaac was still a gift from God for his mother. The two were deeply entwined in ways she'd never felt with anyone, not even her beloved parents. With the raising of an eyebrow, they would both go into spasms of hysterical laughter, unable to explain. When she was hurting, she didn't have to say a word—Isaac was there to lift the burden or to surprise her with a "science experiment," usually involving worms. She believed he was "a genius," like her father had been, and embraced Isaac's dream of becoming a pharmacist with such fervor that she took in tailoring and saved for years in order to buy him a chemistry set. He was the love of her life.

When Isaac joined the army, Minnie was distraught mainly because he'd won a scholarship to the Philadelphia College of Pharmacy and Science and she fretted that while he was gone the money would somehow evaporate. It was easier to worry about the scholarship than about the war, but she was somewhat mollified because he volunteered to be an ambulance driver, which meant he'd serve behind the lines. Abraham forbade Isaac going. "Patriotism is idiotic!" he yelled. "Your loyalty is right here. To your family." Isaac replied, "I'm an American. I'm going." His father took the sugar dish and threw it down so that it shattered on the floor. It was just a piece of china but the whole house seemed to shake. Minnie felt the impact through the soles of her feet and in her body, where it stayed.

Block by block the familiar neighborhood was slipping away and Minnie's apprehension grew. Storefronts covered in Hebrew lettering that had pickle barrels outside, tiny pocket-sized *shuls*, alleys packed with pushcarts, Orthodox men with their minds immersed in Torah, patrolling the streets in big beards and black hats, gave way in the wink of an eye to an endless barren street stretching far into the morning light—with a church on every corner. Although piano makers and newspaper publishers and even department stores had moved into the fancy cast-iron buildings on lower Park Avenue, to Minnie Seibert, New York City was a looming skyline of crosses. She'd grown up in Russia with a deep-seated fear of crosses because they meant death to Jews, and just last winter Gottlieb, their neighbor in Maine, had found a burning cross outside his house, left by the Ku Klux Klan.

Desperately in need of some sort of refuge, Minnie leaned toward the woman on the bus and tried once more in Yiddish.

"Gefelt mir dayn kapeleyush." I like your hat.

The woman didn't look up. "Thank you," she said briskly in English.

Minnie decided she had nothing more to say to this girl. She had what her grandmother would call "a fresh mouth." Even sitting down she was too busy to be polite. Or maybe she was embarrassed talking to an out-of-towner. She appeared to be involved in the pages she had taken from the portfolio. Minnie was amazed to see that they were music. The woman was reading music on the bus.

For some reason everything had stopped at Thirty-fourth Street. The bus didn't move, like it was trapped in cement. Something was going on. There was the unsettling howl of sirens and passengers had gotten up and crowded the windows. Outside, a well-dressed businessman was sprawled motionless on the sidewalk, and a policeman was waving cars away to make room for an ambulance. Minnie couldn't look. If the screaming sirens didn't stop, she'd jump right out of her skin. Isaac promised her that he'd be safe. He wrote from France to say he loved what he was doing and there was no cause for worry. His job was exciting and important. He'd pick up the wounded from a dressing station that was way behind the lines and drive at terrific speeds over country roads to the hospital in Verdun. The dressing station itself was supposed to be a safety zone. It had a big red cross on the roof, the international sign for hospital. Instead, the Germans used it as a target and bombed it from the air, just as Isaac and another driver were loading a casualty.

The bus was lurching forward but her heart was beating fast and her underarms were slippery with perspiration. She was going to be late for the breakfast. And she'd forgotten all about the Gold Star Mothers badge! She found the velvet box in her needlepoint handbag and opened the top. She'd pasted Isaac's military portrait on the inside cover so she could see him whenever she opened it. His hair was so short and plastered down and *parted neatly,* for the first time in his life. His smooth young face was half turned away so the eyes were looking back at her, gently sharing the sadness of their separation.

A loud buzzer sounded inside the bus and

Minnie flinched. The young woman had pulled the cord.

"Your stop is next," she told Minnie.

Minnie stood and hastily gathered her things, unaware that her fellow rider had glimpsed the soldier as he went back inside his box, and watched her pin the red, white, and blue badge on her dress. Minnie had all she could do to hang on to a strap as well as the cardboard suitcase and purse. When the bus jerked to a halt and the doors swung open, the young musician turned her face up to Minnie, who was swaying over her, and whispered shyly, "I'm sorry about your son. *Megn Got treystn du tsvishn der aveylim.*"

Minnie's eyes were smarting. The Yiddish words—*May God console you among the mourners*—wcrc from the old, old Hebrew, said to mourners in order to reassure them that God will take responsibility for their consolation. The rabbi who came from Bangor when Isaac died told them that when you grieve, you are not alone. You are with God and everybody else who grieves throughout time. Minnie had stopped believing in that god, but she knew a miracle when she saw one.

And here was another: people were lined up behind her, politely waiting for the Gold Star Mother to be the first one off the bus. The young musician looked embarrassed, as if she were the reason for this alarming pause in the pulse of New

York. She seemed unsure of what she'd said—if she had said it right, or if maybe it would have been better not to have said anything at all. Minnie let go of the strap and got her balance. She reached down with one hand and rested it tenderly on the woman's head—on the hat, actually—as if she had been one of her children; as if she were giving her child a blessing.

"Here she is!" Cora Blake cried as Mrs. Minnie Seibert joined the table. She took Minnie's hands in both of hers as if they were old friends. Their letters certainly had been intimate enough. As the first one to respond to her note of welcome, Minnie had a special place in Cora's personal pecking order.

"How are you?" she asked. "How was the trip?"

"Tiring," Minnie said.

"And your husband?"

"We're still married," Minnie said wryly.

"Did he understand?"

"All I can say is—I'm here."

Cora smiled and touched her arm. "You'll be glad. You'll see."

Minnie looked around. They were in the Dutch Room, a dining hall set aside by the Hotel Commodore for the pilgrims, a hodgepodge of ugly green chairs set around dozens of tables filled with several hundred chattering females making a din louder than the traffic in the street.

130

She noticed there were Christian angels painted on the ceiling . . . but what else was new?

Still standing, Cora tapped a water glass to get the table's attention away from the alluring American breakfast of grapefruit sections, sausage, bacon, waffles, eggs-as-you-like-them, smoked fish, toast, Ralston cereal, stewed prunes, pastries, coffee, and tea, which General Perkins himself had approved.

"This is Mrs. Minnie Seibert!" she announced triumphantly, as if Minnie had just won a race.

Smiling faces looked up in welcome and Minnie was introduced to Mrs. Selma Russell, an elderly Negro she immediately felt sympathy for because she seemed so burdened, even though she was sitting down, which reminded her of the family of black furniture movers who had driven their belongings from Bangor out to the farm. Nobody else would take the job because they'd be going back with an empty truck. Then there was Mrs. Katie McConnell, with short flaming red hair and bad teeth—Boston Irish, Minnie thought. When Cora whispered that Katie had lost *two* sons, Minnie's heart went out to the poor woman.

"But she doesn't talk about it," Cora added, and Minnie nodded in confidence.

Then Cora explained that the lady next to her in the olive drab army uniform was Lieutenant Lily Barnett, R.N., and that their liaison officer, Lieutenant Thomas Hammond, would be joining

131

them shortly. There was one more in their party, Mrs. Genevieve Olsen, who would arrive the day of departure and join them on the ship. Nurse Lily stood and invited Minnie to an empty chair. She was very solicitous. "Sit next to me," she said. "How are you feeling, Mrs. Seibert?"

"I'm fine," Minnie said, adding suspiciously, "Why do you ask?"

A waitress in a Dutch apron took her order and the pastry basket was passed her way. Minnie was ravenous. She wanted to eat everything on the table.

"I'll be accompanying you on the pilgrimage," Lily said.

"But I'm not sick."

Lily laughed. "Every party has a nurse. We want to take good care of you and be sure you have everything you need. It can be a strain," she added. She was an attractive girl with gorgeous cheekbones, a fair complexion, and a serious air. Her hair was pinned up under her military cap. She had a self-assured way of speaking that put Minnie at ease, relieved to be off that bus and in the arms of the U.S. Army. When breakfast arrived, it was a huge plate filled with scrambled eggs, whitefish, and a waffle with a square of melting butter. No matter what else Abraham thought of the government, they gave big portions.

"Who is coming to the Empire State Building?" Nurse Lily asked cheerfully.

Cora, Katie, and Selma raised their hands.

"We already said as much on the train," Katie said.

"Nobody's afraid of heights, I hope."

Mrs. Russell said, "Wouldn't know. Never been higher than a ladder."

You'd expect a grandmother who'd worked all her life to take things seriously, even bitterly, but those cloudy old eyes had a sly angle on life. She'd come out with dry little comments that caught you by surprise. Cora didn't notice that Selma was the only dark face in the room except for some of the help. Right now she was laughing to herself over eating ordinary fried eggs off fine china on a white tablecloth.

"We're awfully lucky," Nurse Lily was going on. "You know, the Empire State Building was just recently opened to the public."

Mrs. Seibert asked, "Are you sure it's safe?"

"Might be best to wait," Mrs. Russell suggested. "Case it decide to tip over."

Nurse Lily took a ladylike bite of toast. "It has to be safe, or the army wouldn't let us go."

"All right, count me in." Minnie shrugged. "What the heck."

She was feeling strangely giddy. All of this was different—not just the angels looking down, or the thin gold crosses Nurse Lily and Mrs. McConnell wore prominently around their necks, or the lake of syrup she'd recklessly poured over the waffle, but an altogether new feeling of acceptance. Every woman at the table—everyone in this enormous room—fat ones, skinny ones, ugly, whatever— wore a Gold Star badge. Abraham of course had refused, but Minnie had dutifully worn the torn black ribbon of the mourner for seven days after they got the news that Isaac had been killed—but thirteen years later you didn't go around wearing a badge. Here, you did. Because, like the rabbi from Bangor had said, the consolation for a mourner is that she shares with others not only this loss but all the misfortunes that come of living a full human life. Here, among those others, Minnie knew she belonged.

"Is that all you're eating?" she asked Katie McConnell, spying the remains of one boiled egg on her plate.

"Had my fill of oatmeal, thanks."

"How was it?"

Katie leaned close and whispered, "Mine is better."

Minnie scrunched up her nose. "Thin?"

Katie nodded.

"Nothing worse."

"Lumpy's worse. And there's no earthly reason. All it takes is a drop of patience."

"That I would agree with," Minnie said.

A man's voice interrupted: "Good morning, ladies."

Lieutenant Thomas Hammond had appeared at

the table. The presence of strong male youth, especially in uniform, caused eyes to brighten and posture to improve. He introduced himself and made the rounds, shaking hands and pausing to chat with each of the pilgrims, bringing in biographical anecdotes about them and their sons that he had memorized from the files. Training sessions had been held for this purpose. Last night at the final staff dinner, General Perkins had taken him and Lily Barnett aside with instructions on how to handle the Mrs. Russell mess according to the quartermaster general's orders—"with the least interruption to the normal lives of the pilgrims"—and Hammond was doing his best to be diplomatic.

"Nurse? Are we all ready?"

"Yes, Lieutenant."

Lily stood, ready to follow the plan. She was raised Catholic in an Irish enclave of Granite Falls, Minnesota, one of seven children, the next turn of the page in the story of the Mrs. Katie McConnells, who'd been part of the migration that left because of the great hunger resulting from the potato crop failures. There was nothing for girls in Ireland—no work, and only sons could inherit land. But second-generation Lily was able to graduate from the Presbyterian School of Nursing in Chicago. She worked as a visiting nurse in the Sleepy Valley section of the city, named for a population of drug addicts, which had given her the maturity that made Minnie feel she was in good hands, even though Lily was Hammond's age, barely twenty-three.

Her olive-drab uniform was a feminine version of his, with a skirt and a fitted jacket. They both held the rank of second lieutenant, although hers was a "relative rank" given to female contract workers, meaning they did not have an officer's privileges or pay. The two were similar in build, and attractive in the same young unencumbered American way—clear-eyed and undefended.

"Nurse? Is everybody going to the Empire State Building?"

"Yes, they are."

"Shall we?"

Lily grabbed her medical satchel with the Red Cross insignia and stewarded the group into the lobby, where hundreds of pilgrims going to different destinations were milling around the plaza looking for the right bus. Just before reaching the door, Lieutenant Hammond gently took Mrs. Selma Russell's arm.

"Madam, may I ask a favor? Would you mind coming with me?"

"Where're we going?"

"General Perkins would like a word," Hammond said.

"With me?"

"Yes, ma'am."

"What'd I do?"

"Nothing!" he said quickly. "No reason to be concerned."

She seemed confused. "Is it about my boy, Elmore?"

"Not at all. The general's office is upstairs. He just wants to speak to you, personally."

She instinctually resisted. "Ain't we suppose to get on a bus?"

Cora said, "I'll go with you, Selma."

Hammond was firm. "There's really no need."

Cora looked directly at Mrs. Russell. "I don't give two cents for the Empire State Building—"

Nurse Lily intervened: "This way, Mrs. Blake."

"She doesn't understand what's going on—"

"The general will explain."

Cora planted her feet. "Explain to *us*."

"There's been a mix-up," Hammond said. "Mrs. Russell has been placed in the wrong party. We apologize, but it's better to fix the problem now—"

Minnie and Katie both stopped in their tracks. This sudden break-up of their party disturbed the bonds that had just begun to crystallize. It was an uncertain beginning that threw everyone off.

"But she's part of our group," Katie said.

"Are the rest of us still in?" Minnie wondered.

"Yes, everything is the same," Hammond assured her, adding, "I'm glad to see you've all become friends. It's unfortunate."

Cora made a stand. "I'm staying with Mrs. Russell."

"It's all right, Cora," Selma said. "You go on along."

"Where are you taking her?" Cora demanded.

Lily and Hammond exchanged a glance.

"Mrs. Russell is changing parties," he said.

"Why is that?"

"There's been a clerical mistake. There's another pilgrim who is registered to be in your party. She's waiting to join you later."

"How can that be true?" Cora asked. "I'm the member coordinator. This other person wasn't on my list."

"Her name is Mrs. Russell, too. Mrs. Wilhelmina Russell."

Cora realized that was true. Selma. Wilhelmina. She'd been so distracted looking for Katie in the women's lounge, and so relieved to have found someone in her party, she hadn't paid attention, and out of politeness they had not exchanged first names.

"I know it's silly, but these things happen. The important thing is to give her a warm welcome when she arrives," Hammond said.

Katie and Minnie had already accepted the change. They hadn't been the ones to discover Mrs. Russell standing in the doorway, afraid to enter the women's waiting room. They hadn't sat with her and gotten to know her and provided an ear for her troubles.

"Fine," said Cora. "I'll change parties, too.

She's older and needs companionship. I don't mind. We're friends."

"We ain't friends," Selma said.

"What?"

Cora watched Selma's face close down, losing its sparkle.

"You a nice lady," Selma Russell told Cora Blake. "But we ain't friends and never could be."

"Come along now and say goodbye," Lily interrupted with authority, "so we can all sit together on the bus."

Cora was stunned. Nurse Lily drew her along with Katie and Minnie as Hammond took Mrs. Russell in the opposite direction to the service elevator. They got off at the mezzanine above the grand ballroom. She held on to the handrail as they walked slowly along the balcony above the war room.

"This is our HQ, you might say."

Hammond pointed down to the secretaries, the telegram and radio stations, waiters in white coats pushing coffee carts. Selma ignored him, staring straight ahead. They went through a fire door and down a service corridor that led to a maze of offices in the belly of the building, one giving onto the other with no windows.

Hammond offered Selma a steel-backed chair near a filing cabinet and an empty desk.

"The army took over the payroll department. The hotel wasn't too happy with us. Kind of a bare-bones operation up here. No secretaries, unfortunately. We use the typing pool downstairs. Can I get you some water?"

Selma paid no attention. She took a blue-and-yellow afghan from her bag and resumed crocheting.

"Isn't that pretty?" said Hammond. "You must have a lot of patience."

Selma took her time in answering.

"Patience . . . ain't always a virtue."

Hammond stood awkwardly in the bare room until a door opened crisply and General Perkins stepped out. Hammond saluted. The general shook Selma's hand and introduced himself.

"Well, we've solved the mystery," Perkins said. "There are two Mrs. Russells on this tour. What are the chances of that? The woman who belongs in Party A is Mrs. *Wilhelmina* Russell, not Mrs. Selma Russell." He smiled. "Which is you."

"Just tell me where to catch the bus."

"Madam, please, don't give it a thought. We'll take care of everything. A typist downstairs made a mistake and I deeply apologize. I'm sure you can understand that in an operation of this size, it's impossible to keep track of every detail."

"What exactly are you tryin' to tell me?"

"Somehow you—Mrs. Selma Russell—have been separated from your party and this *other*—Mrs. *Wilhelmina* Russell—is waiting uptown, in the YWCA in Harlem. You follow me?"

Selma nodded. "Very well."

"Good. The nurse will help pack your things and then she and the lieutenant will escort you."

"Harlem," she mused. "Well, that's the first good thing you said! They got a lot of wealthy folks up in Harlem. Nightclubs, too. Always wanted to see Harlem. I think I got peoples lives there."

"Probably not enough time for a visit." Perkins smiled.

"Wasn't planning on it."

"Again, our apologies. It's standard procedure for the colored mothers to go on separate tours and separate ships."

"Call it by it proper name," Selma said. "Segregation. I heard about that happening, but I thought, well, maybe it just ain't true. You know they tell all kinds of lies. Some of the black women like me, they refuse to go on the pilgrimage because of segregation, but I said, Nothin' gonna stop me from seein' my boy."

Hammond fought to remain perfectly still. Perkins was smiling and relaxed.

"As I said, a clerical mistake."

"Maybe I'm just old and slow. Didn't our boys all fight together? Ain't they all buried in the same place?"

"Yes, of course the black soldiers are buried with the white. The bodies were buried as they arrived—no distinction was made. In fact, we've got the American Buffalo Soldiers and the Bloody Bucket from Pennsylvania—both Negro divisions—right in Meuse-Argonne. Please understand, these traveling arrangements are for your own comfort."

"My own comfort would be to have my boy with me today."

Selma gathered her work and stood. As she left the room, Perkins spoke quietly to Hammond.

"Is the other one ready for transfer?" he asked.

"That's my understanding."

"No more mistakes."

"Understood, sir."

Having wrangled Cora onto the bus, Nurse Lily had come back upstairs and was waiting for them outside Perkins's office. As the three circled back around the balcony overlooking the ballroom to the service elevator, Hammond had a wild thought that Mrs. Russell might throw herself over, but it was he who was embarrassed and distraught.

"How do we get uptown?" Hammond asked through gritted teeth.

"Taxi," Lily told him. "I've got the petty cash."

Although the Empire State Building was just a dozen blocks from the hotel, the bus ride was tedious stop-and-go, with nothing to look at but glaring store windows and hordes of grim-looking people racing each other to the next traffic light.

The bus was packed with war mothers and wives, chattering, making friends, apprehensive, alert. Cora sat with a woman from another party. They didn't speak. She watched the city pass: pawn-shops and newsstands, tucked-away playhouses and movie theaters where people who had no homes could sleep for thirty cents a night, sightseers, slummers, sailors, sidewalks filled with sandwich boards, Turkish restaurants. She didn't know where Harlem was, and wondered what her former friend was seeing on the way there. Selma's words still stung.

Three private buses pulled to the curb on Thirty-fourth Street and pilgrims wearing badges took over the sidewalks in a dense parade, but Cora felt alone. She'd lost track of Minnie and Katie and was being pushed along anonymously in a tight group, crammed inside the bronze art deco lobby of the world's tallest building, waiting in a long line, and then stuffed into a tiny elevator—like the hot sardines she packed in cans—indecently close. The lift went up, and Cora closed her eyes while her ears screamed. Finally she stepped out onto the observation deck.

The wind was fierce and it was twenty degrees colder than down on the street. The curved iron railings did not look high enough. Cora hung back near the wall. Cinders flew into her eyes. She wanted to flee, but where do you go when you are standing on top of the world? What had she done to so offend Mrs. Russell? Why had she made a point of saying that they weren't friends and never could be? Why be so hurtful, when all that Cora meant was—

Katie was clutching her arm.

"Come! Minnie put a nickel in!"

She pushed Cora toward a telescope. Minnie's coin had activated the machine, causing it to start ticking like a clock. They made Cora step up on a metal box and look through two eyepieces. She saw bridges and wide-open bays with all sorts of boats and hundreds and hundreds of brown- and red-brick buildings, all in shocking detail. She saw window shades and water towers and seagulls. Then the ticking stopped and the view went black.

Cora stepped back while the other two raced like schoolgirls around the deck to look at the Hudson River on the other side. You can only see something for the first time once. Cora's world had expanded rapidly, but not from the vista. She remembered what Selma told her in the women's waiting room in Boston. *You got a lot to learn.*

Cora stepped up to the edge and put her fingers on the rail and let her hands absorb the coldness of the rusted iron. The city writhed and blew out smoke. It didn't compromise. It didn't promise fields of honor and forgetting. It separated black from white. Selma's parting words were sounding different now. *"We ain't friends,"* she had said, but she'd meant it as a friend would say it—to instruct you in your own illusions—intended in the kindest way.

8

The taxi climbed steadily uptown, outpacing the trolley cars and scattering slum children playing chalk games in the gutter, past shoppers jammed under the umbrellas of peddlers selling everything from shoes to frankfurters and lemonade—an uncountable number of Negro people from all over the country crammed into the northern grid of Manhattan. Blocks of row houses served double duty, as tenement apartments upstairs and storefronts down on the street, where you could buy auto parts, snuff, cheese and bread, get your gun repaired or your hair cut. Awnings reflected the scalding light of noon into banks of tenement windows, where residents had no qualms about stringing the family laundry. Airspace was living space in the crowded city.

Farther up they passed empty lots with nothing but rubble and the unemployed sitting around on wooden boxes, telling lies and killing time. Mrs. Russell stared intently out the window and commented only once, when they passed two wagons piled with cooking equipment and hitched to a horse; a traveling tin shop slowly working its way up Lenox Avenue.

"Will you look at that?" she said. "More pots and pans than the state of Georgia."

Lily asked when was the last time she was home.

"Nineteen oh-one, the year my daddy died. I went down for the funeral."

"You were living up North?"

Mrs. Selma Russell nodded and told the story of how her grandmama, who was known to have visions, looked at her palm and saw "needle and thread."

She laughed hoarsely and coughed. "I says, Sure, I sees them every day!"

Elmore was two years old and Selma was working on her daddy's farm in Sumter County, Georgia. The *very next day* after Grandmama saw the sign, a letter arrived from a girl Selma knew who had gone up North and found needlework, sewing at a manufacturer of men's and ladies' furnishings in downtown Boston. She wrote to say that the company was relocating to a brand-new building on Essex Street and they were hiring.

"So I left Elmore with my mama and came up," Selma said. "I didn't see my baby for seven years because I was livin' in a boardinghouse in a room not big enough for a mouse, just a bed with nails in the wall for clothes, one candle on the table.

Ever hear of Gordon Underwear? That was my first job and they still in business."

Lily smiled encouragingly. "And when did Elmore join you?"

He was already nine years old, Mrs. Russell said, when she was settled enough to raise him. By then she had two baby daughters and a steady man with a job in the railyards.

"What was your son like?" Lily asked.

Hammond admired the way Lily was able to distract their passenger from the disaster of the morning. If she could just keep her talking for another fifteen blocks, they'd be able to get Mrs. *Selma* Russell squared away, retrieve Mrs. *Wilhelmina* Russell, and put the whole mortifying situation behind them. When Hammond was a child, his family had lived in the Wardman Park Hotel, built to house the transient military and diplomatic community in D.C. It was an elegant brick building crowned by stone pediments, with more than a thousand rooms and residential suites—a busy, soldierly world unto itself. Hammond was part of a boys-only gang of army brats that built a hideout in the labyrinthine basement of the hotel, where they made friends with the children of the Negro help, sharing cigarettes and rumors of sex, stolen treats and escape routes hidden from adult eyes that led to freedom in Rock Creek Park and the zoo. On Armistice Day, November 11, 1918, they roamed together through the frenzied crowds that carried coffins and gruesome effigies of the Kaiser, searing into Hammond's imagination the belief that this was all due to his hero dad. A younger, black boy named Oscar had attached himself to Hammond, and whispered excitedly that he had a secret. While the rest of the world was drunk on victory, Hammond was led to a dark basement room with concrete walls lined with hundreds of ominous-looking gas meters, and then to a musty, spider-webbed corner where he and Oscar squatted down to watch a gray-striped alley cat giving birth.

Segregation had been a fact of childhood in Washington, D.C., and Hammond knew of course that troops were separated in the army, but he saw for the first time, in the case of Mrs. Russell, how distressing it was that real equality seemed achievable only by children, underground.

"Elmore?" Mrs. Russell smiled and clicked her tongue. "The world weren't ready for Elmore."

"What do you mean?" Hammond prompted, doing his share.

"He a special child. The way he was born, his mouth weren't right, so he got teased a lot, but he fight back. He was a good fighter. I tell him he the same as everybody else. You got a beautiful heart and Jesus love you. And your mama, she love you best of all."

"How did he get in the army?" Hammond wondered.

"We don't pay much attention to the war at first, it so far away. But when the president say everyone in the country has to get involved one hundred percent, Elmore was ready to answer the call of duty. I say, Honey, it ain't our fight, but a man come to the church and say all these good things about the army, how they can fix Elmore mouth for him. And that's exactly what they do."

"They did the surgery?" Lily guessed it was a simple operation of the type that should have been done when he was a baby.

Mrs. Russell told them how different Elmore looked afterward. Like he'd been waiting all his life to inhabit that uniform and that smile.

"They send him to France right away, and put him to work in a special unit call Service of Supply. He not too happy, say he rather be holding a rifle instead of the dead bodies they have him carry, but I say someone gots to."

Hammond shifted uncomfortably in the over-heated cab. He knew the SOS was an all-Negro unit where the soldiers were used as laborers, but wouldn't dare say anything to dim Mrs. Russell's pride.

"Anyways," Mrs. Russell was saying, "he take to the army like a fish to water and decide that when he come home, he's going into officer training school for colored folks. That the last I hear, even though it was a whole year later when I got the letter."

They rode in silence. Mrs. Russell's lithe brown fingers with red nails were calmly folded over the clasp of her purse. Her gaze was distant.

"I talk to Elmore every day. He tell me, Don't worry, Mama, I'm all right. I'm here with Jesus. I say, I know it, son. The Lord made you whole so you'd be ready to take Jesus's hand."

She opened the purse and dabbed her eyes with a handkerchief.

Lily breathed, "Amen," mostly to herself, but Hammond found his throat was strangled. He was over his head when it came to female emotion, useless, miscast in a maudlin drama where he didn't know the lines. He'd never even seen his mother cry. She did, of course, but not in front of the children. He recalled the one time she had really broken down, when they had to leave her childhood home in North Carolina to move to Washington, D.C., for his father's new posting. Hammond remembered being kept apart from his mother's helpless sobbing by a clean white door.

The taxi let them out at 135th Street in front of a newly built red-brick building eleven stories high. The tower was the tallest in the immediate skyline. It was a less grand version of the Hotel Commodore but with the same design of two wings capped by American flags. The main entrance was a humble doorway, but inside the floor was freshly waxed and there was a mural of African dancers in spokes of sunlight coming through jungle vines. The attendant who greeted them was a clean-cut young man in a short-sleeved shirt and bow tie who looked like he might have just come from church.

"I'll take you to your room, missus, and you can put up your feet."

Hammond felt it was his duty to sign off on behalf of the army.

"I hope all goes well for you, Mrs. Russell."

"Be a good boy," she said.

"Yes, ma'am."

She was tired; you could see the fight blown out of her. The attendant was encouraging. *"You're almost there. Just a little farther now."* Lily saw that Hammond was bewildered, hands limp at his sides. In his world, efficiency won the day—in sports and on the battlefield. If you studied the rules and learned to seize the advantage, things would unfold pretty much according to expectation. But it seemed the clock had stopped, leaving him suspended between the action, unaccustomed to the dead quiet of a strange halftime in which certain powers that could not be accounted for were somehow deciding the game. Watching Mrs. Selma Russell shuffle slowly toward the elevator, leaning hard on the attendant's arm, Hammond realized he had lost track of the goal.

Lily was simply practical. "Let's find Wilhelmina," she said, and asked a passing resident where the dining hall might be.

· · ·

They were shown into a plain room of square tables and ladder-back chairs. It was just before lunch, and cooks were setting up steam trays. There were slices of ham and grits and glazed sweet potatoes. No waiters in white jackets. No menu with many choices or lofty windows overlooking a plaza. The black pilgrims were to bus their own dishes and pile them on trays. It was easy to spot Mrs. Wilhelmina Russell. She was sitting alone, the only white face they had seen since they'd passed 125th Street.

"Don't worry, everything's taken care of," Hammond said.

Wilhelmina's eyes wavered back and forth across the empty room. "But I'm about to have lunch with my friends."

She was a lanky person—at one time a competitive tennis player—whose face had grown loose and horsey. Her tawny hair was faded by the sun; she had pale irises and eyebrows. She wore a pink rayon blouse with mismatched buttons that was not closed properly.

"Let me fix that," offered Lily, but the lady slapped her hand away.

"Who are you?" she asked again.

"We're from the army," Hammond said for the second time, becoming worried that he wasn't getting through. "And we're taking you to your hotel."

From her wide-eyed reaction, Hammond wondered if he'd phrased that in the best possible way. Maybe she thought anyone in uniform was the Reichswehr.

"There's a taxi waiting, just outside," he assured her.

"This is my hotel."

"No, you see, there's been a mistake."

Someone had carefully hung Wilhelmina's white sweater on the back of the chair as if to protect the heavy beaded appliqué of a pink carnation. Lily picked it up and discovered there was a handwritten note safety-pinned to the collar.

"Oh, that's for you," Wilhelmina said off-handedly.

Lily undid the note and read out loud: *"To Whom It May Concern: My wife, Mrs. Wilhelmina Russell, is not in a normal state of mind. She has just been released from the Maine Insane Asylum. Please see that she gets medical care. Please wire me at W. J. Russell & Crampton, Boston, if she causes any damage. Sincerely, Warren J. Russell. P.S. A bromide will help her headaches."*

"It's a sweet letter?" Wilhelmina said. "Isn't it?"

"Very sweet," Lily assured her, although her mind was racing with this new information.

"He's screwing a girl half his age," Wilhelmina added calmly.

"Your sweater is beautiful," Lily managed, not knowing what to say.

Wilhelmina seemed relaxed and unaffected by the revelation of her husband's infidelity.

"Do you like the appliqué?" she asked. "I made it in the hospital. This is what I'm doing now," she said, and pulled two needles and a piece of curling yellow knitting from a canvas bag.

Hammond said, "Very impressive," but his smile barely hid his impatience. He'd had enough of knitting and crocheting. He allowed Wilhelmina to walk ahead and grabbed Lily's arm. "What are we going to do?"

"Is General Perkins aware of her condition?"

"He never said anything to me. But that would explain the mix-up in the records. She wouldn't have gotten our communications if she was in an insane asylum. And the husband doesn't seem like much help."

"No wonder she never replied to Mrs. Blake's letters."

"Have you ever handled a mental case?"

"Lots of times," Lily said. "I did a rotation on a psychiatric ward."

"Good, because I think it best if we don't make a point of this with Perkins."

"Thomas, it'll be on her medical record," she said, surprised. "I'm sure he already knows."

"He's upset about the mix-up. No use stirring the pot."

His handsome brows were knit, his expression tight.

"You don't want him breathing down your neck, is that it?" Lily asked.

He nodded.

"In that case, let's do our best to get her back with the group quietly and without incident."

Outside the hotel the cab was waiting with the meter still whirling.

"Leave it to me to take care of Mrs. Russell," Lily said decisively. "Come on, before we run out of money to pay the taxi."

Wilhelmina slid into the backseat with Lily and took out her yarn. Hammond sat up front for the ride back to the Hotel Commodore.

"Don't worry, dear, we'll send for your bags," Lily told her.

"Everything fine?" Hammond asked, turning around.

"Yes," Lily answered brightly. "Mrs. Russell is about to show me her knitting."

"Very good," Hammond said, and exhaled with relief. He admired the way Lily had taken over and was confident now that she would hold up her end. He also couldn't help noticing how pretty she looked in the back of the cab, with her face turned toward the window as the city passed, wisps of strawberry-blond escaping from beneath the nurse's cap. He forced himself to turn around and stare at Fifth Avenue.

Having completed the murky and confusing journey from the dining room to the sidewalk to the taxi, Wilhelmina had settled herself in, engrossed now by the yellow bonnet she was making for the latest grandchild. Every time her husband, Warren J. Russell, the famous architect of grand shingle-style homes along the coast of Maine, had her committed—the latest had been the seventh—she would start another project. The bonnet was part of a winter ensemble for the newborn daughter of their younger daughter, Wilhelmina watched her fingers automatically work the strands. What a memory they had.

9

On the morning of departure, each of several dozen parties lined up on the pier behind their liaison officer. On this special day all the pilgrims were dressed alike for the photographers, in army-issued white dresses with white hip-length capes and frog clips to hold them closed, as if it were graduation day at a convent school. The costumes had been delivered to their hotel rooms, and this morning on the bus they'd been handed fresh corsages. The display of unity was a magnificent distraction from the purpose of the trip, both for the pilgrims and for the hometown victims of the economic collapse that had gripped the country, who might not have been able to pay their rent, might even be dozing on a bench with a newspaper for a blanket, but who would read in that paper how well President Hoover was taking care of the war mothers and widows, and could go back to sleep with the assurance that he really did know the right course of action for the country.

The pilgrims were leaving from the same pier where, thirteen years before, thousands of American soldiers—maybe their own sons—had debarked to fight the war in Europe. Now it was seething with more than four hundred women, plus military personnel, porters, regular passengers, well-wishers, police officers, and the crew. High above it all loomed the steamship S.S. *Harding*, bigger than any boat Cora could have imagined, with a black hull as high as a New York apartment building—even the lifeboats looked bigger than any craft that ever docked at Stonington Harbor.

Just days ago, she had been standing on her porch, vitalized by clean ocean air, Linwood and his truck waiting below as if they were off to the farmers' market in Blue Hill. Since then, she'd taken an all-day train trip, made and lost a friend from Georgia, met her first Jewish person and befriended an Irishwoman, and rushed from one dizzying site to another—the Empire State Building, Broadway, Grant's Tomb, the public library, Fifth Avenue, the Central Park Zoo— driven hard by Lieutenant Hammond and Nurse Lily according to an inflexible schedule that had to be checked off by the hour.

Everything moved too fast and New York City was dirty and full of itself, but Cora's eyes had been opened by being in the heart of it, the movement and roar, the tallness of the amazing edifices, the sun at such an unfamiliar high remove, flat sidewalks that stretched to infinity, mysterious steam shooting up from the middle of the street, diamonds in shop windows, flags of affluence flying from department stores and banks, doormen dressed like English gentry, flowering trees and marble mansions.

How could she describe it all to Linwood? She'd read the postcard he'd sent to the hotel with a sinking feeling that already they were a world apart:

Dearest Cora,

I hope this finds you well. I am currently working with a crew of two trucks and three men to calculate the measurements for a base map of our sector. I have several boils from walking through some grass that will have to be lanced. We found Caribou loam in granitic glacial till, but not enough to plant potatoes, so we have spared some farmers a lot of headache.

I hope you are having pleasant thoughts about me as I am about you. I look forward to your reply.

Yours faithfully,

Lin

She imagined him thrashing through the weeds in the straw fedora with binoculars around his neck and felt a rush of affection, as well as a tug toward home. Maybe for another island girl the past few days in the greatest city in the world would have been enough to last a lifetime, but Cora, inhabiting her mother's adventurous spirit, could almost taste the sultry air of those Caribbean voyages aboard the *Lara Leigh*. The exhilaration her mother must have felt under sail from their little harbor was probably not unlike the thrill of leaving home for college. Cora vividly remembered the unsteadiness of searching for her room in the freshman dormitory and the pure joy of finally dumping her things on an anonymous mattress that would be hers. New York was just the beginning: they were about to take on the Atlantic Ocean and beyond.

The throng on the dock had grown with the arrival of more newsmen and photographers, pressing the white-coated pilgrims closer together, until all Cora could see was tops of heads and sky. She wondered how Sammy had put up with the army—you couldn't get the boy to wear shoes, let alone march in a line. Last night she'd dreamed that she was assigned to Sammy's company as a cook. He was showing her the ropes—but when she looked at the huge pots and lines of hungry men, Cora had that sorrowful feeling again, spiraling down. She told him she couldn't do the job, and awoke to discover she was in tears. It had been so lovely to be with Sammy in the dream. Why hadn't she taken on the work and stayed?

A deep vibrating blast from the liner's foghorn seemed to fill her entire body. It was the cue for all the West Point liaison officers to draw their dress swords, hold them high above their heads, and lead their parties to the ship.

"Right this way! Pardon us! Stay close!" shouted Lieutenant Hammond, cutting through the multitude with Party A huddled behind him and Nurse Lily bringing up the rear. In the midst of this, Mrs. Seibert realized that she was missing her gloves.

"My gloves!" she cried. "I left them at the hotel!"

"Too hot for gloves," said Katie.

"What if we have an occasion? What if we meet the president of France?"

"You can wear my gloves," Wilhelmina offered.

Wilhelmina had been returned from Harlem, installed in the Hotel Commodore, and then almost immediately escorted to the farewell banquet that night, which had given Katie, Cora, and Minnie no chance to get to know her, but to Hammond's and Lily's relief, she had been quite friendly, and the others welcomed her without a hitch. Unused to spontaneous generosity, Minnie was wary of the offer.

"Thank you, but you'll need them," she said.

"It's all right," Wilhelmina replied.

She peeled off her white cotton gloves to reveal another pair exactly like them underneath.

"Take these," she insisted.

"That's very nice of you," Minnie said, not really understanding why her friend had two pairs. She had no intention of sticking her hands into someone else's finger holes, but not to be rude, she stuffed them in her bag.

Just before entering the red-carpeted gangway they hit a bottleneck. Reporters crammed in closer, calling out for the attention of their hometown pilgrims. *"Mrs. Pizzorelli from Chicago?* Chicago Sun*! Over here!"* Photographers rudely stuck their tripods wherever they wished, forcing everyone to walk around them. Each group was stopped for a snapshot: from factory workers to Indians wearing blankets and smoking cigars, they were ordinary American women equalized by their loss, a range of shyness, sadness, confusion, pride, and astonishment on their faces as a band played and an honor guard saluted.

"Sorry," Hammond told them. "Seems that we're stuck in traffic." He pivoted, checking his flock. "Everybody here?"

"All accounted for except Mrs. Olsen," Lily reassured him.

"Where is she?"

"Already on board."

"How do you know?" Hammond shouted over a particularly brash blast from the band.

Lily waited for the echo to dissolve from her ears. "She boarded at the VIP entry."

"God help us," Hammond said. "We can't lose another one."

"It's all right—the steward promised me the boat won't sail without her."

"He was just being nice to you."

"No, really," Lily said earnestly. "He told me she's a rich society woman."

"How rich?"

"I don't know, but she drove down from Boston in a limousine. Imagine the cost of the gas!"

Minnie, who had been standing close enough to overhear, immediately ducked back and told the group. "There's news."

Cora and Katie leaned close.

"We're going to get a *very rich woman.*"

Katie said, "You mean the lady from Boston?"

"Cambridge. Her name is Genevieve Olsen," Cora answered. "Her family owns a railroad."

Minnie's eyes opened wide. "Well, that explains it."

"A blue blood amongst the savages," Katie observed.

Cora jumped to Mrs. Olsen's defense. "That's not fair."

"Why would someone like that bother with us?" Minnie wondered.

"Because she lost her son, just like we all did, and she believes in the Gold Star Mothers," Cora replied stiffly. "She's a patriot! We wouldn't be standing here if she didn't go down to Washington and shake a few trees."

Katie looked thoughtful. "All the more reason to suspect."

Wilhelmina had leaned in to the circle. "Suspect what?"

"That she's bossy and wants her ways. I can tell ye, I've been employed in great houses on Beacon Hill where they have two or three servant girls, but even then you're up at six with one afternoon off a week, no time to yourself a'tall while you're in the house, and you have to fight tooth and nail just to be allowed to go to an evening's mass—"

Wilhelmina interrupted: "Where will she sleep?"

The others exchanged uneasy glances. They were beginning to realize that Wilhelmina wasn't shy about speaking whatever came into her head—which was often the same as what they had been thinking but were afraid to say. Sleeping arrangements were always one of the thornier issues to confront on the pilgrimages, and therefore skirted on both sides. On the train from Boston—with no assurance that the army would agree—Cora and Katie had planned to room together, hoping Minnie would double up with Mrs. Russell, but when she was removed from Party A, that left Katie and Cora together with Minnie on the outs, which made Cora feel bad, since Minnie had been so candid in her letters, so they'd invited her to share a triple, and Minnie had been moved to tears by the gesture. But now there was Wilhelmina. And Mrs. Olsen. Would they make a pair? At the same time, because Hammond had been warned to expect discord and requests for transfer, he'd held off as long as possible distributing their assignments. But Cora Blake was tapping on his shoulder like a very determined woodpecker. The time had come.

"Lieutenant Hammond! Where does everybody sleep?"

"I've put Mrs. Seibert together with Mrs. McConnell—"

Minnie and Katie stared at each other with shock and mistrust. Historic disregard of the Jews for the Irish—and vice versa—rose between them like columns of steam from the manholes of New York. Katie thought it would have been easy to get along with Cora Blake moderating from the middle. But now—an Irish maid and a Jewish chicken farmer? Who could say?

"And Mrs. Blake, I think you'll be comfortable with Mrs. Russell."

This was a surprise as well, but Cora saw no reason not to like Wilhelmina, so she smiled at her new roommate, who absently smiled back.

"And if anybody's worrying about Mrs. Olsen," Lily added, "don't. She's taken a private suite."

Any further conversation was drowned out by another warning blast from the foghorn. The crowd jolted and hurried forward. Then they saw the source of the problem: General Perkins was at the foot of the gangway making a speech into a microphone held by a radio man:

"As these fine ladies board the ship, we are reminded of the sacredness of their pilgrimage. For every cross in the American cemeteries of France . . . a boy. And for every . . . boy . . . a mother."

"Hold on to your hat!" said Wilhelmina, pressing hers to her head.

"Stay together!" Hammond ordered.

Flashbulbs exploded. Black bubbles floated across their vision, and then Party A was pushed onto the ship and up against a railing, where they were told to stay and watch the departure. The steward marched along, hitting a gong and shouting, "All ashore that's going ashore!" and some very drunk young people scrambled down the steps from the top, laughing and waving bottles of Champagne. Streamers were thrown from the decks. The foghorn sounded three more times and imperceptibly they began to move.

Katie, Cora, Wilhelmina, and Minnie stood side by side as they rolled in stately measure past the Statue of Liberty. Her face seemed to loom very large and close, as if she were following them with her huge eyes.

"She's very beautiful," Cora said.

"Like a madonna," Katie agreed.

"I remember when I came here," Minnie said. "My father sent for us from Russia. It was the first time we saw Papa in three years. We stayed with his brother on Houston Street. My uncle gave us bananas and we thought they were the worst thing we ever tasted."

"We were on Canal Street," Katie remembered. "You and I were neighbors and we didn't know it."

"The Irish and the Jews weren't such great neighbors," Minnie murmured.

Wilhelmina announced, "I was always here," which sent them into gales of silly laughter. Then, reverently, the four members of Party A watched the skyline slip into the mist, followed by a dilapidated boat called the *Lightship Ambrose*, which marked the last point in the New York Harbor channel.

That night at dinner in the formal dining room, well after everyone was seated and noisily attending to the honeydew melon appetizer, Mrs. Genevieve Olsen made a grand entrance. It was a white-tablecloth-and-armchair room, with gilded paneling in a chevron pattern, a small stage in the middle. She created quite an impression walking down the Persian-carpeted stairway on the arm of Lieutenant Hammond. Despite the difference in their ages, Hammond and Mrs. Olsen seemed a matched pair, each of them having come from old families whose roots in the military elite and the railroad industry mingled in the enriched soil of East Coast society. He wore a tuxedo and she a dramatic floor-length metallic gold lace evening gown with a plunging back, complemented by a spectacular diamond necklace and matching drop earrings.

"Ooh la la," Katie said behind her hand. "Here comes Mrs. Somebody."

As Mrs. Olsen approached the table, the others were simply struck dumb. Her gray hair was curled in perfect waves. She had a pleasant face with a too-wide nose, and a habit of tilting her head with the gamine smile of a boarding school queen. Her skin was snowy white and her eyes lively blue. She was not a beauty but had excellent carriage, and at age sixty-five a strong and confident bearing.

"Which of you is Cora Blake?"

"That would be me," Cora said.

"Get up so I can give you a proper greeting," Mrs. Olsen said with throaty vigor. "So wonderful to meet you at last. You're as lovely as your letters."

Katie watched from her seat at the table as the two stood there embracing like long-lost sisters. Decades of preparing meals and cleaning bathrooms for lesser women than Mrs. Olsen caused her hackles to rise like a mongrel dog looking for a fight. She was the one with the muscle when it came to running a household. But obedience was expected of Katie, by her employers as well as the church, and so she settled into a familiar resentment, as worn as the shiny spots on the Oriental rugs she vacuumed over and over.

On the other hand, Cora was feeling perfectly at home. Aside from having been deputized by Mrs. Olsen as member coordinator, and privy to her private correspondence all these months, Cora was quite familiar with summer people from Boston who had homes in Maine. As a teenager she'd sold them chanterelles picked in the forest and caramel cakes her mother made, and had babysat their children. She knew their stuffiness and their generosity. Some of those old-line Yankee women could be powerhouses on their own. Mrs. Olsen seemed the type who not only moored a forty-foot yacht in a private deepwater cove, but sailed it solo.

All of which gave way, for the two women in the middle of the grand dining room, to the kind of informality between folks of different social class on the island; as if they'd run into each other in Boyce's Grocery on Main Street, where everyone was an equal opportunity gossip.

"You make a handsome couple," Cora observed of Mrs. Olsen and Hammond.

"The lieutenant is the handsome half," she replied graciously. "Now, who is this charming young lady?"

168

Hammond introduced Nurse Lily, who rose and shook hands.

"It's an honor to meet you, Mrs. Olsen," Lily said. "Please join us."

Dressed for dinner in a teal-green day dress with a rhinestone belt that emphasized her tiny waist, rose-blond hair loosely caught up in a ribbon, Lily looked the role of every soldier's sweetheart, but steadfastly maintained the decorum of her rank. She was on duty, after all, ready to attend to the slightest indigestion, which she could see coming right up on an approaching waiter's tray. The second course was deviled eggs with Cheddar cheese and bacon, to be followed by French onion soup.

Minnie declined the eggs.

"But they're scrumptioulicious!" Wilhelmina insisted, stuffing one in her mouth, whole.

"She don't eat bacon," Katie explained.

Minnie shrugged. "I wrote to General Pershing when I got the letter asking me to come because my son was killed, and I told him, it's nice of you to invite me to France but I don't eat pork. We're not religious, but still. So I'm looking on the menu and what do I see? Pork roast, pork sausage—"

"She can't eat sausage?" Wilhelmina wondered. "What about luncheon meat? I couldn't live without my bologna on white."

"Nothing better than kosher salami," Minnie said.

"Give me Irish country bacon," Katie said.

Lily chimed in: "Has anyone here ever had real Chicago Polish sausage?"

"I don't know about that," Cora said, "but there's a woman on the island named Elizabeth Pascoe who makes pork sausage with maple syrup. I walk two miles just to get some before they're gone."

Katie elbowed Minnie. "That'll make a believer outta ya."

"Not likely," Minnie replied, fretting over what she would eat. She picked up the menu card and her eyes fell on Swedish Timbales with Chicken and Mushrooms, which sounded like a foreign orchestra, but she would try it.

On the other side of the table, Mrs. Olsen, veteran of countless dinner conversations with strangers, was asking Hammond where he was born.

"San Rafael, California. It was a romantic beginning. My parents met during the earthquake. My father was stationed at Fort Scott, helping to evacuate families by ferry to Oakland, and my mother was the daughter of a naval officer."

"The earth shook?"

Hammond smiled. "Yes, but I also have two younger sisters born in the Philippines, where we were posted before we moved back to North Carolina and then Washington, where we lived in the Wardman Park Hotel."

"Oh, the Wardman!" Mrs. Olsen exclaimed with a bright smile. "Do you know Colonel and Mrs. Harriman Bay?"

"They're good friends of my parents'!"

"I thought they might be—they've lived there for years and have a son just your age."

"Charlie. He played second base on my baseball team in high school. He's on Wall Street now."

"And Mr. and Mrs. George Swenson? She's a dear friend from Radcliffe."

Hammond slapped the table. "Absolutely. We've been out on their boat. But they moved, didn't they?"

"Yes, to the Hayes-Adams Hotel."

"Same architect who built the Waldman, am I right?"

Mrs. Olsen nodded, finishing a spoonful of the French onion soup while expertly avoiding strings of cheese.

"Poor Henry Waldman. He was my mother's cousin, and such a prolific man. You know he lost everything in the crash?"

"Thirty million, according to my mother, and she knows everything. She's in the Green Book," Hammond added, referring to the social list of Washington with a cynical roll of the eyes.

Mrs. Olsen nodded. "Well then, you must have done cotillion."

"Of course," Hammond said. "Club etiquette, coming-out balls, the whole bit."

"I'll bet you were a popular date."

He shrugged. "I've accompanied a few debutantes. They'd rather dance with me than their fathers."

"You're being modest," Mrs. Olsen said, slyly pointing with a manicured finger. "I'm sure you've left broken hearts all over Washington."

Hammond laughed, enjoying the flattery. "Yes, there's a plaque for the Hammond men at the Hayes-Adams Hotel."

"I love the Hayes-Adams," Mrs. Olsen declared. "We had the engagement party there for my son, Henry, and his fiancée."

"When was this?"

"Right before Henry went overseas. He was engaged to marry a very nice girl from Smith. She was going to devote her life to poetry. Henry was a surgeon, you know; he specialized in bones, and so he was very needed in France. Well," she said, sitting back as the waiter cleared their bowls, "he didn't return and it was all very sad. She went on to marry someone else. When you lived in Washington, did you take advantage of the museums?" she asked, changing the subject.

"Not as much as I should."

"I was just at the opening for an exhibit of new Chinese flower paintings at the Boston Museum of Fine Arts. The imagery was breathtaking. They're using much brighter colors and stronger lines than, say, the Qing Dynasty," she said. "I went back twice to try my hand at chrysanthemums, but it requires such discipline and control of the brush. I'll stick to my little sketches."

"I didn't know you were an artist, Mrs. Olsen," Cora said from across the table.

"Botanist, really. Just an amateur hobby," she replied. "Please call me Bobbie. I know, it has nothing to do with 'Genevieve,' but it's always been Bobbie. My father wanted a boy."

"We're grateful that you didn't oblige him," Hammond said.

Lily suppressed a giggle. Mrs. Olsen smiled, amused by his gallantry.

"I'm looking forward to studying the wildflowers of France," she said.

"Poppies?" he suggested.

"Of course," she answered, lowering her eyes. "The flower of remembering. But they also have a lot of what we have—campion and bluebells and so forth."

"Have you seen the lupine fields in Maine?" Cora asked.

Bobbie looked over with interest. "Yes, dear, didn't I tell you we have a house down east?"

"Where?"

"Oh, a little island."

"Which one?"

"Owl Island, outside Blue Hill Bay."

"I know the house! There's only one house on Owl Island, the Gilley House."

"That's right."

"I think I was there a long time ago, with my father. We went to scavenge a shipwreck. There was a shipwreck, right?"

"Yes, but oh my, it must have been in the eighteen hundreds, because we bought the island in 1908 . . ."

After that, Cora and Bobbie talked nonstop through the Welsh rarebit, Swedish timbales, broiled quail, cauliflower au gratin, and chicory salad. But just before the parade of petits fours, almond macaroons, and Nesselrode pie, the older woman complained that she wasn't well and would like to return to her cabin. Lily, instantly alert, jumped up from her chair and said she would accompany Mrs. Olsen.

"Are you feeling seasick?" Cora asked.

"I don't get seasick."

"Because I know a cure."

"What is that?" Bobbie asked, a hand to her forehead.

"Clam water."

Bobbie seemed to sway with dizziness at the suggestion. "I'll just say good night," she said swiftly, and Lily took her arm as they left.

Before the entertainment started, the waiters made sure each table was supplied with a choice of ten cheeses, three breads, raisins, crystalized ginger, and demitasse. The band played an introduction and a bald, big-eared master of ceremonies appeared on the tiny stage, announcing there would now be a talent show, starting with Mrs. Sadie Belmont of Baltimore, who would recite a poem. A skinny lady wearing glasses and a sparkly black dress was helped onstage. She stepped up to the microphone and read in a high-pitched voice:

"I wear a poppy on my breast
Where once a boyish head found rest.
And often when the day is done
I see again my soldier son.

He comes to me in such a way
That I can almost hear him say,
'Do not worry, Mother dear,
I am coming home some day.'

And when the tears unbidden start
I place a hand above my heart
To there caress a tousled head
But only find a poppy red."

During the applause Wilhelmina said disapprovingly, "We had better talent shows at the hospital. We put on the entire works of William Shakespeare."

"Is that so?" Hammond said, clapping loudly so the others wouldn't hear her. Party A had yet to be informed of Mrs. Wilhelmina Russell's history, as had anybody else in authority. He and Lily had been keeping close tabs on their charge, which he hoped would be enough. So far she hadn't displayed any symptoms of hysteria.

"Yes," Wilhelmina recollected with satisfaction. "It was a regular Shakespearean festival. Mr. Grimilski played all the parts himself. When he was between electric-shock treatments. It was quite enjoyable."

Hearing this, Hammond cast a panicked look at Lily, but she was chatting with Minnie about the effectiveness of castor oil for digestive problems. He hoped that Cora Blake could live with Mrs. Russell's idiosyncrasies. It was too late for him and Lily to admit they'd known all along she was a mental case. His military history professor had been fond of quoting Julius Caesar before he crossed the Rubicon: "*Iacta alea est*"—The die is cast.

The first thing you saw when you entered Cora and Wilhelmina's first-class cabin were the sunflowers. They smiled at you from a silver vase on a round table covered by a linen cloth, which was set beside an armchair. Two beds on either side of the room were made up in baby-blue blankets topped by throws of white rabbit fur. On one wall between them was a sink with glass shelving, on the other a dressing table with a mirror and space for hanging dresses. There was a water closet and shower behind a hidden door. The walls and headboards were covered with continuous gray felt, which rendered the room soundless. It was cleverly lit by recessed lamps that sent pools of light just where you'd want them. The only way you knew you were on a ship and not in a luxury hotel were the chrome rails around everything and two imposing steel portholes with no-nonsense bolts, but even they could be eliminated by a pull on a pair of maroon drapes.

They divvied up the shelves and drawers and made small talk as they prepared for bed, undressing by turn in the narrow WC. Wilhelmina tied a scarf around her fading blond hair and massaged her face with cream. Cora used soap and toweled off quickly.

"It's too bad that you never got my letters," Cora said.

"It's not your fault. In the hospital you don't always get your mail."

"Oh, were you sick?"

"On and off," Wilhelmina said. She spooned some powder from a jar into a glass of water and it fizzed. "Nervous headache," she explained.

"Would it be better if we turned out the lights?"

"Yes, thank you."

The smooth, fresh sheets felt wonderful after the long march down the pier to the ship and the excitement of boarding. They each touched a switch near their bed and found themselves floating in heavy darkness.

After a moment Cora said, "What do you do down in Prouts Neck?"

"Work on my tennis game. We live at the country club."

"I didn't know people could live there."

"My husband designed and built it, so they gave him a cottage. He's an architect, you see. He owns a firm in Boston. We met on the tennis courts at the club. He's not a player, but I was there one day with my dad, who was the caretaker, and they'd just finished building brand-new clay courts. We couldn't resist. I was hitting with my brother when Warren—who I had no idea would be my future husband—came storming out and ordered us to get off. Then he saw I was a pretty good player and sat down to watch. I was sixteen, he was twenty-four. We were both prodigies in our fields."

Her voice in the dark was strangely muffled in the soundproofed room.

"I always had athletic talent. I could have played any sport, but my father decided on tennis. He trained me from the time I was eight. He'd put a quarter down on the court and I had to keep practicing until I hit it three times in a row. I won everything. I was state champion."

"Really?"

"Nineteen sixteen. Then they canceled all the tournaments because of the war."

"What about after the war?"

Hesitant silence.

"I didn't go back."

Cora said, "When Sammy died I couldn't do anything for months. I didn't even have the strength to read—and I'm a librarian."

"I still play sometimes," Wilhelmina reflected. "My father said the trouble with my game was that I was too strong. He said I played like a man and should rely more on strategy and finesse. I only had one way, and that was power."

"Why did you stop playing?"

"I was having spells. The doctor said that tennis made it worse."

"Isn't that too bad?"

"I still play," Wilhelmina repeated, her voice growing tired. "When I'm well enough."

Cora waited but there seemed no more to say. "Good night."

"Good night."

Except there were the sunflowers. The flowers in the vase seemed to glow in the dark. That's because they always grow in sun, Wilhelmina thought, like the hot sun on the tennis court. They had big yellow faces on tall thin stalks. Taller than Bradley. Bradley, her middle child, was strong and took to the sport. She dressed him in miniature whites with the yellow and green stripes of the club. He'd climb up on the referee stand and watch her hit. He'd go into the sunflowers and retrieve the balls.

The last time she saw him was in the hospital when he'd come to say goodbye before shipping out. He had been wearing his fresh olive uniform with the stand-up collar and epaulets. Wilhelmina admired the brass buttons, fingering them until he pulled away. He knew the place well. He knew the sunroom with its row of wicker rocking chairs and barred windows, everything painted harsh industrial white. By the time he was a teenager, Bradley had seen his mother in and out of the asylum several times. It was a wrenching and unfathomable experience, because she could also be the most nurturing, attentive mother in the world, and then go out on the tennis court and be brilliant. He expected that she wouldn't understand where he was going, about the war, but Wilhelmina was in one of her cogent states and knew from reading the newspaper what the Allies faced on the Western Front. Still, she was optimistic and promised she'd be out by the time he came home.

"When your father is bored with his hussy," she'd said.

She hadn't meant to, and regretted it immediately. She'd known for years that Warren was taking advantage of her hospital stays in order to chase women. She imagined he'd seduce them with tales of loneliness and the hint of marriage to an up-and-coming architect if his wife, sadly, had to be committed for life. Somehow Wilhelmina had managed each time to climb out of the episodes of depression that flattened her, just in time to send her husband's latest paramour scurrying back under her rock, but the back-and-forth bouts of illness, infidelity, and recovery made her relationship with Warren a wretched parody of the game she excelled at on the court.

It was a competition she couldn't win. Repeated hospitalizations hammered at her vitality: there was the fever cure, where they exposed her to mosquitoes carrying malaria to induce infection that would purge the body; sleep therapy, which allowed the nervous system to recover by keeping the patient drugged for a week; hypothermia, whereby the body temperature was lowered almost to death by wrapping her in refrigerated blankets, with minimum nutrition supplied through a stomach tube. She could have endured everything but the look on her boy's face just then. He hadn't known about the affairs.

"What do you mean?" Bradley's cheeks were flaming. "Is Father cheating on you?"

"Never mind," she'd said, fumbling stupidly. "No. Not at all. It's the medicine. It makes me say things I don't mean. Your father would never—"

"Tell me," he demanded. "I'm going overseas, so tell me now."

"I hid it from you," Wilhelmina confessed. "You, as well as the girls. I didn't want my children to lose respect for their father."

"You think we didn't know something was wrong around here?"

"It's because I was sick."

"Sometimes you did have to go away, but then you came back and you were our mother. You still loved us but he always cared about his rich customers and his big firm in Boston. And his chippies, obviously."

"I'm not going to say don't be too hard on him, because he's been a cad."

"At least you're honest about it now."

"Don't tell the girls."

"Oh, Mother—they're not babies."

"Wait. Just wait until I'm out of here and they don't have to worry—"

"Do you want to go home?" Bradley asked, tight-jawed. "Because I'll get you out right now—"

"No, it's better for me here," she'd said desperately.

"But why? You're—you're perfectly normal. He's the one who's got a sick mind. How could he have you committed? I don't understand."

"Your father was worried because I wasn't doing the housework."

"So what? That's why we have maids."

"Yes, well, not fulfilling my wifely duties. It's not fair to him."

"How can he get away with that?" her son said, anguished.

"He's allowed to. It's the law."

Bradley went down on his knees in front of her and took both her hands.

"I love you. It's not fair what he's done."

"Oh, my sweetheart." She caressed his hair. "You go on and live your life."

"When I get back I'll get you out of here. You're not really sick and you never have been, have you?" He saw her unwillingness to answer, even now. "Mother, I'm going to war. Tell me the truth."

The word *war* made her sick to her stomach. Now she was afraid not to tell him.

"Your father wasn't wrong, Bradley. When you were born I had a nervous spell so bad I burned my tennis racquets. I was too ill even to take care of you. I've regretted it my whole life, that I wasn't able to hold you . . . that it was left to Grandma to take care of you and the . . . girls . . ."

His mother's pale eyes were glistening with tears.

"You're not crazy," he said, inspecting them. "You're just very, very sad."

"Yes. I'm sad about this, and I'm sad that you're going away."

"I promise," Bradley said, squeezing her hands. "I'll take care of you."

Then came the awful news that he had been

killed in France by a high-explosive shell. Wilhelmina had a complete nervous breakdown. After a lengthy hospital stay, she was able to return home under the care of a full-time nurse.

By 1931, Warren J. Russell was designing libraries and municipal buildings, spending most of his time in Boston. They were still married but leading separate lives. Wilhelmina had good days and bad. A good day was hitting a tennis ball with an old friend at the country club. A bad day was disappearing with the car and getting arrested for shoplifting in another state.

Where once there had been tenderness, despite her husband's other interests, there had been none since Bradley died—not until the very last moment before she boarded the train in Portland for New York City to join the Gold Star Mothers pilgrimage. Wilhelmina was clear-minded when she had said that she wanted to go to France to see Bradley's grave, and Warren had been so shocked by the return of her decisiveness that he'd said yes. But when they were finally at the train station, he was less sanguine. He kissed her cheek and fussed over the instructions to the army medical staff, pinning them at the last minute to her sweater—realizing that once she was gone, he would be alone with it. The loss. Suddenly it was dangerous to let her go, into a void that was not of their making but that they had intimately shared all these years. Tears rose in his eyes as the train pulled out. Even in her illness, she had always been here, within reach, and he was befuddled and somewhat frightened that now she was not.

Wilhelmina, on the other hand, was accustomed to the hurt that came along wherever she went, like the white cardigan with the beaded pink carnation she had painstakingly appliquéd in the hospital, one tiny bead at a time.

Their first full day at sea began with fog and high seas as a result of the rough weather they'd encountered the night before. Nobody slept well, and Hammond, who'd been up half the night, now had to document it all in the daily "Liaison Report for Party A," a detailed record required by the quartermaster general. By 11:00 a.m. the skies had cleared and most of the pilgrims were out on deck taking the sun. The Tropicale Day Room was fairly empty and seemed a good refuge from female voices. It featured bamboo chairs upholstered with palm trees and a white piano in front of a mural of dark-skinned women selling melons. Hammond lit a cigarette, opened the file, and began to write.

> 8:45 P.M. Mrs. Olsen left the dining room complaining of feeling ill. Mrs. Russell complained of a nervous headache and was given a triple bromide. Mrs. McConnell

complained of constipation and was told by Mrs. Seibert to eat prunes.

12:30 A.M. Unsettled weather caused the ship to roll dramatically. I was summoned from my room by a steward at the request of Nurse Barnett. Upon meeting her in the corridor she reported that Mrs. McConnell and Mrs. Seibert were having an argument about whether the portholes should be open in their stateroom. I went to Cabin 219 and found, in addition to the ladies above-mentioned, the night watchman. I found the portholes open and the room quite cold. Mrs. Seibert was in bed with a topcoat over her blanket as a covering, somewhat angrily saying that she was "freezing to death" and would not live with "an Eskimo." Mrs. McConnell complained that she was "burning up." When I closed the portholes she burst out crying and sobbing. The steward was called, and also the ship's carpenter. After consultation with everyone present, a wooden partition was erected to divide the room in half so each lady could have her private porthole. All were pleased with this arrangement.

He was interrupted when the very people he had hoped to avoid—Mrs. Seibert and Mrs.

McConnell—entered the Tropicale Day Room, accompanied by Mrs. Blake, who was looking unusually haggard. He snuffed the cigarette and closed the file.

"Hello, ladies. Tired of the sun?"

"Will ya play?" Katie asked. "We're looking for a fourth."

"What is it?"

"Gin."

Before he could reply, they'd swamped his table and produced a deck of cards.

"How is everyone?" he asked, resigned. "Sleep well?"

"Finally," said Katie, shuffling like a professional.

"She snores," Minnie said.

"So does she," Katie shot back.

"Mrs. Blake? How was your night?"

"Fine," Cora said. "Slept like a log."

She didn't want to say what had happened to Wilhelmina. That was private, and should not be mentioned over a card game. But in the middle of the night, her roommate had woken up screaming in the claustrophobic dark. It was a sound like nothing Cora had ever heard. Something between the crying of a wolf and the screech of a seabird—a new genus of creature imprisoned in Wilhelmina's body and clawing to get out. She was sitting up, eyes wide open, murmuring incoherently. Cora tried to get her to lie down, but she was as rigid as a corpse. Then, like the turn of a switch, it stopped. She relaxed and lay back, breathing softly. Cora was so shaken, she sat in the armchair, knees up, hugging her bare feet, while Wilhelmina slept peacefully until dawn.

Cora looked up from her cards, sensing someone coming toward them in the Tropicale Day Room. It was Nurse Lily, looking fresh as ever, unfazed by having had just a few hours' sleep owing to the porthole affair.

"There you are, Mrs. Blake! I've been looking for you. Sorry, but I need a favor. Mrs. Olsen is in her cabin, still not feeling well at all. I've given her bicarbonate of soda, but it hasn't done any good. She wanted to try your clam-water cure. Would you mind?"

"Of course not," Cora said, rising.

"Now what?" Katie mourned. "We need another hand."

"Join us, Lieutenant," Hammond said with a significant smile imploring, *Help me!* Lily was uncertain where her duties lay: in the cabin with Mrs. Olsen or shoring up the others? Cora made the decision for her.

"You stay," she said. "I'll take care of Bobbie."

"Okay," said Lily, taking her seat. "But watch out, everyone. Gin rummy is my game."

Mrs. Olsen's cabin turned out to be what the cruise line called a "deluxe apartment," consisting of a dining room, salon, multiple bedrooms, private decks, and a baby grand piano. Cora was guided by Mrs. Olsen's personal maid—French, in uniform—through chambers with molded ceilings and wallpapers in exotic patterns, rich carpeting upon which dainty furniture rested delicate birdlike claws, chaise longues every few feet in case you needed to lie down before you got to the bedroom. The suite was done in mauve, sensual and silky as in a Greta Garbo movie, and there were pots of orchids all around. Bobbie Olsen was lying on a dark hardwood bed made up with the pink crêpe de chine lace-trimmed sheets with which she always traveled. She wore a Japanese silk dressing gown and a turban because her hair was undone. Half-finished sketches of the orchids had been torn from her notebook and abandoned on the coverlet.

The room had been personalized with silver-framed photographs of her son, Henry Olsen, M.D., from a naked baby on a bear rug to a young man in a white coat, holding a black bag. There must have been a dozen pictures with nobody else in them, just Henry. He was a serious, good-looking chap with a calm, aristocratic bearing and a thin mustache. The maid resumed her task of inserting stretchers in her lady's shoes and placing them in rows.

"I'm sorry to make you come all the way up

here, but I'm really feeling like a dog," Bobbie said. "I can't even draw. The room is spinning and my stomach is having fits. You said clam water—and you know, I really believe in those island remedies. There are some very dear people who are caretakers at Gilley House, and they've come up with cures that have saved our lives more than once. So tell me, Cora, how do we get some clam water?"

"First you have to have clams—"

Bobbie interrupted her: "Instruct Ingrid, and she'll tell the cook. Be precise, because judging from the food last night, he doesn't know his ass from a fry pan."

"He's going to take a dozen clams," Cora told the maid. "Scrub them and rinse several times. Then he puts them in a pot with *two tablespoons* of water. No more—we don't want soup."

The maid nodded. "No soup."

"You cook them until the shells open, take out the meat, add the liquor to the water already in the pan, and strain it through cheesecloth twice."

"Thank you!" Bobbie sighed when the maid had left, repositioning a hot water bottle on her abdomen. "Surely, if you were home, you wouldn't throw out all that good clam meat?"

"No, ma'am," said Cora. "There's a hundred ways to use it."

"What's your favorite?"

"Chowder."

"Are times very hard in your town? Sit down," she said, indicating a tufted chair.

"All in all it hasn't been that bad. I wouldn't want to go over the same route again, but I'm not going to kick. I'm thankful we had a little bit to get along with. The kids never went hungry. They never had holes in their clothes. You know what they say—we're not poor, we just never had money."

"What about your husband?"

Bobbie was reclining on the soft pink sheets. Her eggshell-white skin was exposed in all its wrinkled glory, and her bright blue eyes were alert. She hid nothing, she pretended nothing. She was a cultured, very wealthy person and that was that.

Cora wished she could be as honest. She was tempted to confess it all to this benevolent dowager—what it was like to raise a child alone in an isolated New England town—but got cold feet and retreated to the safety of the story that she'd always told.

"My husband died," she said quickly. "What about yours?"

"The same. I pretty much raised Henry myself. Do you have other children?"

"No, just Sammy. My boy, who I lost. My sister, Avis, died from cholera and I'm raising her girls."

"Are they good girls? Do they help?"

"I try to bring them up to take care of them-selves. They're learning. Slowly. When I'm working at the library it's their job to have the garden stuff pulled. They're supposed to at least have the vegetables ready, but it doesn't always happen. It's not like when I was young. If we didn't toe the line, we'd know the consequences. Honestly, the problem is, their mother—my sister—passed away too young."

"Do you wish you had more of your own?"

"I wish I had my own little girl."

"I lost a little girl when she was two. She passed in my arms. But my son was lost a million miles from nowhere; I never saw his face or hugged him again."

Cora nodded. "All they sent were Sammy's clothes."

"There's not a day that goes by I don't feel guilt."

"You shouldn't," Cora said, although she, too, lived with remorse every day. If she hadn't been so hardheaded to think she could raise a boy alone . . . if Sammy'd had a father . . . maybe he wouldn't have left home and everything would be different.

"Well," said Bobbie, "when we get there, I expect to feel a great relief."

"I hardly know what to expect," Cora said. There was a knock on the door and a waiter entered, carrying a tray on his shoulder that held a steaming tureen. When it was uncovered, the scent of salt and seaweed filled the room. He ladled it out with a ridiculous flourish and withdrew. It's only broth, Cora thought.

Bobbie took a spoonful. "This is surprisingly good. Would you like some? You look a bit peaked."

"We had a rough night," Cora confessed, and then she told Bobbie about Wilhelmina's bad dream, and how she couldn't wake her from it.

"Did you tell the nurse?"

"I didn't think it was my place," Cora said.

"If it happens again, you should. For Wilhelmina's benefit *and* for yours. There's no reason to put up with that; you need your strength. Look, why don't you stay with me? It would be no trouble. I have more bedrooms here than God."

Cora didn't figure she could fall asleep in such a grand palace. She preferred her cozy bunk.

"That's all right. We'll be fine."

Bobbie let it drop, realizing the invitation had been inappropriate. "Thank you for the soup."

"Are you feeling better?"

"Yes, you know? I am!"

"Maybe you should take a nap."

"I never nap," said Bobbie briskly. "It only makes me tired. If you'll wait a minute, I'll get changed."

Bright sun hit their eyes as Cora and Bobbie walked along the main deck, where rows of

193

lounge chairs were taken by women in every manner of dress, reading books or chatting with their neighbors, others strolling by in groups of two and three. A cloudless, sapphire sky made a sparkling backdrop for the tableau, so placid compared to the chaos of boarding the ship; everything sorted, everyone content in this artificially female world, where there was no competition for attention by children or men, and many mothers, wives, caretakers, and workers could attend to themselves for the first time in their lives, happily unburdened and alone.

But Cora's view was darkened by the scene last night. She wondered if these tranquil pilgrims were beset with demons as frightening as Wilhelmina's had been; if they were crouching down inside everyone, including Cora. She hadn't seen her roommate since this morning, as she didn't come to breakfast, and considered whether it might be best to go down to the cabin and check. Her questions were answered when they came around the bow.

There, amid the lifeboats, a group of people were playing golf. It was just a tee-off, really, from a square of carpet on the deck. Six passengers or so were standing around, relaxed, fiddling with their drivers, a few men dressed in ties and caps, two women in ankle-length skirts, one of them Wilhelmina. It was her turn to hit the ball. She placed it, eyed it, became very still, disregarded the wavy hair streaming across her face, then executed a graceful swing, releasing enormous power with perfect timing as she struck the ball cleanly, sailing it into the air and over the side in a beautiful arc. Everyone applauded the shot. When she saw that Cora and Bobbie had been watching, she smiled and gave a cheerful wave. It was, after all, a bright and sunny day.

PARIS

10

One by one the women of Party A squeezed into the *thomp-thomp* of the revolving door of the Ambassador Hotel, clutching their handbags as if it would eat them alive. Spit out right into the middle of busy Boulevard Haussmann on their first day in Paris, they quickly became panic-stricken. Massive buildings eight stories high, with strange Egyptian motifs and Greek pillars, stretched on for miles, while traffic barreled in both directions; no one spoke English and everyone else sounded as if they were gargling mouthwash. They huddled together on the sidewalk like puppies who were hoping somebody would round them up and put them back in the basket.

If their gauche assortment of ready-made dresses, unfortunate hats, and lace-up shoes didn't mark them as American, the white satin sashes across their chests that read GOLD STAR MOTHER surely would. Out of nowhere, a middle-aged, well-tailored Frenchwoman sprung forward, gripping Katie's hand in both of hers and murmuring incomprehensibly before shaking her head in some kind of distress and hurrying on.

"What did she say?"

Bobbie translated: "She's thanking us for our service to France."

Katie blinked back tears. "Jesus Mary."

After that, the little entourage marshaled its pluck and began to walk together, four across, no longer worried about their small-town airs in this headstrong city. The exception was Bobbie Olsen, on her own, erect and commanding, wearing that day an oatmeal-colored linen suit and carrying a bag made of alligator skins, as smart as anything on two high heels tearing up the dirt to get to the stores at Galeries Lafayette. She knew how to *faire une balade*—saunter along, taking everything in: the café smells of cigarettes and coffee and beginnings of a chicken stew, or a peculiar three-sided clock high up on a pole so it could officiate over all sides of an intersection. You got the impression that Bobbie Olsen presided over every boulevard on which she strolled.

"Everyone says he was a genius," Hammond was confiding to Lily, "but personally, I can't stand these big avenues by Haussmann."

"Why? They're just streets."

She paused to adjust her army beret in a shopwindow. It was part of the nurses' travel outfit, which included a white poplin dress covered by a long navy cape. Hammond wore olive drabs, and although the ladies were dressed in ordinary clothes, the sashes across their chests

200

made the group unmistakable, especially since the tours had been widely covered by the French press. In their excitement and awe, the pilgrims scarcely noticed that people were stepping aside to allow them to pass.

Hammond watched Lily in the window, noticing what a striking figure she made in the white uniform and cape, the epitome of American pride, and that together they were a natural pair, even though she was entirely different from the girls he'd dated in Washington—either high-strung debutantes with whom you had to tread as carefully as steps in a French quadrille, or hard club women as competitive as men. He'd experienced true love only once during his teenage years, and that was with Carlota Rio Branco, petite, with Gypsy-dark hair, the eldest daughter of the Brazilian ambassador, who was stationed at the embassy office in the Wardman hotel.

Carlota was exotic. She claimed to have noble Spanish blood and could act as spoiled as the rest, but the freshness of the country girl was still in her, and she loved to break the rules. They conspired to get both families to spend a weekend at the Greenbrier resort in West Virginia, where they snuck away one night and lost their virginity together on the golf course under a crescent moon. He gave her a paper cigar ring. They were just seventeen when they were cruelly pulled apart by suspecting parents, and Carlota was sent back with her mother to Brazil. She was devastated when Hammond refused to fight it. At seventeen, people married in her country. But he followed his ambitions, withstood the deluge from all sides, and applied to West Point. In retrospect, he'd let Carlota go too easily. He'd never met anyone as solid and soft at the same time—until Second Lieutenant Lily Barnett. Like Carlota, she was a girl who knew what she wanted, and was as temptingly off-limits as the ambassador's daughter.

"Haussmann's plan is ruler-straight," he said, as they walked on. "Much too egotistical and grand."

"I think it fits the city to a T. Of course, I've only been in Paris twenty-four hours."

"But you do agree it's grand?"

"Compared to Chicago? Chicago is down and dirty with lots of people in reduced circumstances. In Paris, they don't care."

"They care a great deal," Hammond objected. "Certainly about their history and culture. Look at how they revere the military giants—Vauban, Lafayette, Napoleon Bonaparte, Joffre, who beat the Germans at the First Battle of the Marne—"

"I mean they don't care about the little people," she said impatiently.

"How do you know?"

"Just look—everything's a monument!"

"It's foolish to even talk about Paris and Chicago

in the same breath," Hammond said. "Chicago's a cow town."

"It's where I'm from, mister."

"Well, mooo to you."

She lifted her nose in mock distress. "You think I'm uneducated because I only went to nursing school."

"And you think I'm a snob," Hammond guessed with a smile.

"Why? Because you can name all the French generals?"

He laughed. "I apologize for that. I'm really a very down-to-earth type of fellow."

Lily looked away, buying time, knowing he was flirting with her and trying to figure out how to slow it down.

"No, Thomas, you're not a snob. You come off like someone bent on his career," she said with finality.

"Well, if all else fails, I can always be a tour guide," Hammond replied amiably. "Let's get away from all this noise." He raised his handkerchief high enough for the group to see and shouted, "Follow me, ladies!"

They turned off the avenue into the old quarter and smack into a neighborhood street market. The women stopped to examine every dead fish and pig's head on ice while Hammond and Lily waited awkwardly.

"Got a fag?" she said at last.

Hammond responded with two cigarettes.

"When did you start smoking?" he asked.

"Sixth grade," she said. "Even though I went to Catholic school, I was still a rebel."

"So you *are* the rebellious type," he said hopefully.

"You bet. They thought I was defying God by becoming a nurse."

"Not really."

"It's true. See, that's what people don't understand. I care as much about my career as anyone, and it was really hard to come by. Where I grew up, nursing wasn't considered a 'real profession,'" she said in a disdainful voice. "It was for women of low morals. The only reason I even applied to nursing school was our local vet, Dr. Malloy. I love animals and he used to let me tag along and help; then he figured I might be good at taking care of people. The school was free but my folks had to save up just for the fare to Chicago." She exhaled smoke. "I lived in a slum with two other students—the kind of place where gangsters were having shoot-outs, and people left newborn babies in a shoe box at our door. It was eye-opening, I'll tell you that, but we had a lot of fun."

"Sounds like fun," Hammond echoed, perplexed. He had somehow lost control of this conversation.

"Where did you go to school?" she asked.

"Mostly public schools. I'm just an army brat,"

he assured her. "My father was with the War Department, so we lived in Washington."

"I always wanted to see the capital of our nation. Maybe someday—"

"You should visit—" Hammond agreed, and almost stumbled into Mrs. Blake and Mrs. Olsen, who were just ahead of them, staring into a barrel seething with scaly silver fish.

"What do they call those?" Cora asked.

Bobbie questioned the vendor in French. "He says mullet. Not too pretty, are they?"

Cora was scrutinizing the greenish water.

"What's the matter, dear?"

"I'm trying to figure if the keg of salt mackerel I left down home is fairly ripe yet. Might be."

Bobbie blinked several times, attempting to understand. "Well," she said finally, "that's good news."

She took Cora's elbow as they waited on a busy corner for a line of taxicabs and bicycles to speed by. The day was overcast, but you could feel a pleasant heat behind the clouds. The trees were rank with summer. The group stayed in the coolness under the canopies of the tightly packed shops until Bobbie stopped, pointing at a display of flowers in tall pails across the street.

"Oh!" she exclaimed delightedly. "French market bouquets! I must make a sketch. Lieutenant, can we spare just a minute?"

"Of course," he said, and before anyone could

stop her, Bobbie was off the sidewalk and on her way to the florist's stall, pulling a tiny pad and small case of colored pencils from her alligator bag.

"Oh my!" Lily exclaimed, watching her run through traffic.

"I didn't see that," Hammond decided.

Cora couldn't tell what the big deal was. The arrangements were nice, but basically just round bunches of pink and white hydrangeas and green grasses tied up with herbs from the garden. She could do the same thing at home, and not give everyone a heart attack.

Finally Hammond went over, slipped his arm in Bobbie's, waited for the traffic light, and escorted her back across the street. Bobbie was bubbling with excitement.

"Thank you all very much for waiting," she said, slipping her materials inside the purse. "That was once in a lifetime!"

"I'm glad you're happy," Hammond remarked dryly.

"Very," she replied, patting his hand.

They kept going until they had reached the open crossroads of the Boulevard des Italiens. At night the marquee that poked the intersection like the prow of a steamer would be alive with moving lights advertising the shows, but now it was a dull corner filled with streetcars and midday shoppers.

"My feet are killing me. How much further we got to walk?" Minnie asked plaintively.

The morning seemed to stretch into infinity. *We have a hell of a way to go,* Hammond wanted to say. He checked his watch. With all this stopping and looking and sketching, they were almost an hour behind schedule. And Mrs. Russell was missing.

"Now we're in trouble," Hammond muttered to Lily.

"Don't worry, she's always late," said Minnie, who had sharp ears when it came to hearsay.

"There is *late* and there is *lost,*" Bobbie observed.

Praise the Lord; they were in front of a chocolate shop.

"Do you mind waiting inside?" Hammond asked.

They did not.

"Nurse Lily, would you please make sure nobody else goes wandering?"

"I'll guard the door," she promised, acknowledging the worried look in his eyes.

Hammond doubled back through the market streets, asking if anyone had seen *"une américaine folle."* Finally he spotted her—tall and bony, wearing the same pink blouse she had refused to change since they'd gotten on the ship, a white polka-dot skirt, and a broad velvet hat on a bird's nest of straw-colored hair, standing at the gate of a small house overgrown with ivy. She was attempting to bargain in English with a boy in knickers who was ringing the bell, selling something from a basket. Hammond only hoped that whatever it was, it was not alive.

"Oh, Lieutenant Hammond!" Wilhelmina smiled. "Please tell this young man I want fourteen."

Shoelaces. The basket was full of men's shoelaces. She wanted fourteen pairs in black. He paid for them without question, tipped the boy, stuffed them into his pockets, and took her back to the chocolate shop, where the ladies were comparing small white paper bags containing miniature chocolate baguettes and adorable chocolate hens. Fretfully, he checked his watch again.

"Everything all right?" Lily asked.

"If we don't hit every stop on the quartermaster's schedule, I'll be duck soup."

He hailed two cabs and marshaled the mothers inside, making sure to place himself in the one with Mrs. Russell, and put Lily in charge of the other. When they got to the Place Vendôme, he roared through the prepared speech in his instruction packet.

"The Place Vendôme is one of the finest squares in the world. It was designed in the pure classical style—"

"What about lunch?" Wilhelmina wanted to know.

"—the Vendôme Column is cast of the iron of twelve hundred enemy cannons. Napoleon stands on top, wearing the costume of a Roman emperor."

"Why?" Minnie asked.

"Because, from the beginning of time," Wilhelmina said solemnly, "man has had the urge to stand upon the highest summit, dressed in bedsheets."

Everybody cracked up laughing. The sun had gone again and a gentle haze was turning to rain. Red flowers spilled from the iron balconies, and the gold medallions on the doors of the Ministère de la Justice gleamed in the fickle light. As the rain filled the square with a soft gray volume of mist, they took refuge under the archway of an arcade of fine shops. An aristocratic-looking Spanish woman—straight-backed and dressed in black—was accompanied by her dark-eyed, artistic-looking son. Their arms were linked as they bent closer to the windows to discuss the jewels on display. Bobbie, gripping the alligator bag as if she would never let it go, watched the mother and son in the reflection of the glass, her expression openly longing.

Lunch was at Jacques's, where twice the price buys half the meal. It was a tiny cavelike joint with creaking floors and cane-backed chairs, probably a hundred years old, with ancient wood-planked walls—pretty much like being inside one of those fish barrels on the street. There was a small bar in back, and a steep staircase that looked as if it led directly to the underworld. Jacques, proprietor and solo waiter, was folding napkins into stiff white crowns because there was nothing else to do. The front room was empty as usual. When Party A entered, he stood up and opened his arms to embrace one and all, speaking in quaintly accented English. "Welcome, mothers of America! Ladies of distinction! We are honored." He made a show of moving tables and helping each individual to a seat.

"What kind of a place is this?" Minnie wondered.

Jacques cocked his head coquettishly. "It is an experience you will never forget."

Hammond gulped the sherry that had been wisely put before him. Moments later their man reappeared with a tray of squid, crayfish, and eel—all suckers and antennae, some still waving in the breeze, in order to show them that only the freshest seafood went into the soup.

"Lord help us," Cora said. "That's the stuff we throw away."

Katie drew herself up. "It's a different matter when you're hungry," she said indignantly.

"Maybe so, but they shouldn't charge money for the leavings."

"Mrs. Blake is right," Bobbie declared. "This is not acceptable."

Katie felt cornered. In Bobbie's tone she heard an airy dismissal of poor people everywhere, especially her relatives in Ireland, who would have been glad of eel's meat during the famine, or pig's guts, or anything.

"It's not something I'd expect you to understand, Mrs. Olsen. But that's all right, you'll never in your lifetime have the need."

She stood abruptly and shoved the chair back with such force that everything on the table shook, then turned on her heel and left in search of the ladies' room.

Bobbie called after her, "Mrs. McConnell, I only meant—"

"Let her go." Cora understood that they came from different ends of the earth, and could only hope things would be patched up later.

Bobbie let her hands fall in exasperation and gave up the ghost. She'd tried being decent with Katie, and all she'd gotten were smart quips and haughty looks, which would never be tolerated at home. Of course, they were not at home, and Mrs. McConnell was not in her employ, but as she'd learned long ago, there was little benefit in speaking below your station.

"We need to be patient with our Mrs. McConnell," Cora said quietly. "She doesn't like to mention it, but she lost two boys in the war."

Bobbie said nothing.

The others reacted with tut-tuts of sympathy.

Minnie nodded along, her eyes telling Cora she had never let on about Katie's secret, and Cora acknowledged the trust.

"Not ac-*cept*-able?" Jacques was crying. "*C'est la bouillabaisse!*"

"Le fish stew," Hammond echoed. The sherry was dry, and old as the walls. "The famous dish of France."

"Why don't we kite it out of here?" Wilhelmina suggested.

"It's on the schedule," Hammond answered grimly, meaning some army bureaucrat was on the take and they'd have to somehow get through this lunch.

Jacques looked hurt. Actually, the tray of tentacles was a shock tactic calculated to make them grateful for anything else that might follow. He and Hammond exchanged words and a flurry of hand motions until Jacques shrugged sadly and went away.

"All's well," Hammond said brightly. "He's bringing us the blackboard special."

Nobody would touch a drop of wine, so it was up to Hammond to take care of the bottle of table red that Jacques had brought. Katie returned looking harried, strays of red hair sticking out on end.

"What's the matter with you?" Minnie asked.

Katie had suffered a shock going to the ladies' room. She'd had to first practically feel her way along a dark passage with damp stone walls that smelled as if it had been tunneled out of a sewer, until finding an unmarked door barely lit by a sickly yellow lamp. She was afraid to go in there alone, which paradoxically made the urge more urgent. The door opened to a tiny chamber with sticky floors and grimy walls and a rusted-out toilet that seemed to have no way of flushing. She went anyway and afterward spent several unnerving minutes searching for a hanging chain or a handle on the back until finally spotting a pedal on the floor. The minuscule sink was just as filthy, gouged with blue-green stains, the faucets incomprehensibly marked *C* and *F.* The *C* faucet brought steaming hot water instead of cold, which sent her fleeing out the door without even fixing her hat, right into the arms of a leering Frenchman.

"I never seen nothin' like it!" she exclaimed. "The moment I get out of that revolting ladies' room there's a disgusting man standin' in the hall who puts his hand right up my skirt!"

Hammond demanded, "Where?"

"D'ya need a road map?" Katie snapped.

"I mean who—where is he—?"

"Behind that curtain there's another room," Katie said, pointing. "A man comes out and he don't have no teeth—I swear I shoulda knocked the daylights outta him."

"Sounds like someone already has," Wilhelmina remarked.

The blackboard special turned out to be—not surprisingly—mullet, three slices of fleshy fish that tasted like the mud in which they were spawned, set on a pond of yellow mustard sauce. The rice came in an upside-down cake. There were a few shreds of carrot, but you had to admit the plate was generously sprinkled with parsley. As they were finishing their custards, a strong smell of cigar smoke and the unmistakable *scrape-boom* of a snare drum were heard coming from the back.

"I'll bet it's a strip joint!" Bobbie exclaimed. "I've never been in one. Should we go see?"

"Not on yer life," Katie said, folding her arms.

"I want to!" Cora volunteered, thinking of the fishermen's shacks where ladies weren't allowed. She'd always been curious about those shadowy places men go that would give you the willies just to step inside, like the smoking parlors near the Bangor railroad station and the cheap palm gardens behind locked doors on Harlow Street. But with Bobbie along, she felt brave and was the first one out of her seat.

"That's my girl," Bobbie said, joining her.

Cora made a point of including Katie. "Come on, you know where it is."

Katie begrudgingly got up.

"Where are you all going?" Minnie asked.

"The library," Wilhelmina replied confidentially.

"That's what my husband always says. *Don't wait up, dear. I'm going to the library.*"

"Hold it one darn second!" Hammond called.

But they were already following Katie along the dank hall to an ominous black curtain, where they paused, giggling and poking each other, until Cora boldly pulled it back and was startled to be faced with the proprietor.

Bowing, Jacques said, "Please, come in! Don't be shy."

The ladies of Party A followed him into a small dark room with a tiny stage. Three or four scruffy male customers sat at tables, smoking and eyeing them lasciviously.

Minnie repeated, "What kind of a place *is* this?"

The lights went out. In total darkness, several things happened at once. A two-man orchestra rapped out an introduction. Hot white spotlights hit the stage and a woman with severely cut short black hair and big red lips appeared, covering herself with fans.

"Mothers of America!" she announced. "The French say, *How do you do?*"

She flung the fans away. She was not young and not wearing anything but underwear. Regular, bad white underwear, as if Jacques had asked the cook to do him a favor.

On the other side of the curtain, back in the restaurant, Hammond had taken the opportunity to move around the table in order to sit next to Lily.

"We should rescue our lost little sheep," she said, to fill an uncomfortable silence.

He stared into her face and she returned a questioning look. Alone in the deserted dining room at Jacques's, at a table still covered with dessert things and a forgotten plate of half-eaten mullet, he kissed her. Lily stood up so quickly the chair fell over.

She made big surprised eyes and gasped. "What was *that?*"

They heard applause and boos from the other side, and the women's voices growing louder as they returned down the hall.

"Oh, no!" cried Lily. "They're coming!"

They were both taken by a fit of giggles like kids about to be caught. Lily righted the chair and smoothed her uniform.

"Quick! Look like you're doing something!"

Hammond was laughing so hard his eyes teared up.

"What should I be doing?" he snorted helplessly, and searched in desperation for his wallet or a pen but discovered only that his pockets were full of shoelaces.

11

The following morning, the American journalist Griffin Reed was at his usual table in the barroom of the Ambassador Hotel, reading *Le Figaro*. Three archways gave way from the lobby to a local saloon that was a refuge from the tourists. The stained-glass ceiling let in colored light whose delicate hues cast a tone of respectability over the dark-suited men conducting business over croissants and cigars. The waiter brought Reed's usual café espresso along with a Cognac. They exchanged indifferent greetings, like workers clocking in for the day. The hotel's location on Boulevard Haussmann, near the office of American Express, had made it a convenient expat hangout where "the most brilliant authors who are writing in English today," as the press put it, could collect their rejection slips from the New York publishers and then stop by for a restorative drink.

Reed figured that's what had befallen Clancy Hayes, who had come through the arches looking ill. Hayes, employed as a foreign correspondent for AP, had moved to Paris from Illinois to write a novel. He was a shave-a-day fellow who always wore a suit and bow tie, the privileged son of a banking family, of the type Reed had no patience for, who was always telling you what it was "worth." *"It's worth reading,"* Hayes would say significantly, as if everything in life had a price and you should be grateful for his personal appraisal. He was also already halfway drunk.

Now he huddled over a banged-up manuscript wrapped in creased brown paper with an expression on his face as if his own book had jumped up and bitten him between the legs— which, Reed knew from having once tried to write a novel himself, was very possible.

"What's the word from New York?" Reed asked with an illicit shiver of glee.

"Lousy," Hayes mumbled.

Reed raised his espresso and a sympathetic eyebrow, but Hayes ignored him, heading quickly to the men's room. Reed didn't mind; he was aware that his most benevolent intentions could be misunderstood. Buttoned up in a tweed vest, jacket, and scarf, with his plastered hair, mustache, and round glasses, he gave the impression of a bourgeois bore.

It was galling that a hack like Clancy Hayes got work while Reed, who knew himself to be a real in-the-blood newsman, was pretty much out of the game. He'd been employed for several years on the proofreaders' bench at the Paris *Tribune*, fixing other people's copy in the basement alongside thunderous linotype machines. But when the American troops withdrew, English-language newspapers got into trouble, and the *Tribune* folded. Reed did book reviews and the odd travel piece for throwaways. It wasn't only because of changing times. The days of breaking news were over for Griffin Reed and the reason was his face, or, rather, the partial mask he wore to cover the unspeakable wounds to his face he had sustained in the trenches.

His new face was not displeasing, and certainly nobody in the barroom would trouble Reed because of it. The regulars knew him as the journalist who'd been tragically wounded while covering the American Expeditionary Forces. There were quite a few "tin noses" around after the war, the result of advanced machine guns that could fire up to six hundred rounds per minute, and of monster artillery capable of sustaining an extended battery of shells stuffed with bullets that exploded with deadly shrapnel. The upper-left quadrant of Reed's face, bone shattered by a rapid-fire machine gun, had been replaced by a partial covering made of a new lightweight amalgam of metals, thin as a calling card.

The mask replaced his nose, left cheek, and temple, and was cleverly secured by a pair of eyeglasses that hooked over his ears. It had been expertly painted to match his skin by an American sculptress, Florence Dean Powell, who had molded the device from photographs of Reed before the injury. Working in her Paris studio with an innovative plastic surgeon from Britain named Dr. James Blackmore, she had fixed Reed's prosthesis with a perpetually friendly look, as if surprised to discover the world was such a pleasant place. This was helped by the round glasses and jaunty mustache. With straight dark hair neatly parted and a scarf to cover the scars at his neck, Reed seemed from a distance to be another expat attempting to be Parisian, although he could never hide his California roots. Otherwise able-bodied, with broad shoulders and sturdy hands, he seemed from the neck down to be his old self: a Stanford University graduate from rancher stock whose people raised cattle in the Central Valley; a young man on the rise who'd never had to worry about his looks, or much else.

After Stanford, he took odd jobs picking fruit and working construction until he was hired to sell classifieds for the *Sacramento Bee*, and found he got along with the cynical, hard-drinking reporters a lot better than with the stiffs running the advertising department. His first byline, which he cut out and mailed to his mother, was a paragraph about a crash involving an ambulance and a police car, both racing to the same fire. He'd scooped it by following the sirens on his bicycle. Reed liked running with the cops—cruising the night, first on the murder scene. He discovered that people—especially heartbroken women—liked to tell him their stories. He was patient and heard things through. His square-built, all-American dimpled chin and inquisitive blue eyes helped. Corruption, psychotic killers, mudslides, bad crops, the boxing circuit, rodeos, kidnappings, county fairs, mummified remains in a bathtub, the house of a hundred cats—juicy small-town stories took him from Sacramento to local papers in Wyoming, Texas, Florida, New York, and finally Virginia, where his sensational exposé of an officer who had shot his wife sixteen times and buried her under their noses at Naval Station Norfolk was picked up by the wires, and he landed a job with the Associated Press.

He had been twenty-nine years old and impatient to get to the big time. It was spring of 1917, and the United States had just declared war on imperial Germany. Reed pressed for an overseas assignment, but was told he had to wait in line. In July the following year, he got his dream job, traveling with the first wave of troops to Belgium. He was there when the Americans joined the Allies at the third battle at Ypres, during the wettest autumn on record. Fighter planes were grounded. Without air support, the artillery couldn't hit the enemy's guns. Troops inching forward were trapped in sludge that turned to quicksand—open targets on both sides. The Germans launched a poison gas attack that caused asphyxiation and blindness, but its real purpose, because chlorine gas is heavier than air, was to force the Allied soldiers to climb out of the trenches into a bombardment of machine gun fire. Crawling over the top and gagging for oxygen, Reed was cut down with the rest.

As a journalist he'd always scored the inside line, that telling piece of color, because subjects had no reason not to trust such an earnest, easygoing fellow. Who would trust their story to him now, to this strange, unreadable countenance? Take the Gold Star Mothers pilgrimages, which came through the Ambassador Hotel on a regular basis. Over the past weeks he'd watched them arrive by the boatload from small-town America, cheerful and ignorant, seduced by first-class treatment by the U.S. government and lavish attention from the press, to accept, along with the badges and bouquets, the burden of the nation's violence and guilt. Reed spent many promising summer mornings deep in the shadows of the barroom, fascinated by the spirit of the female sex, her capacity for resilience. He knew that they, like him, had suffered greatly in the war, but he could not bridge the gap between his painful experience and those of the factory workers, midwestern housewives, farming women, and club ladies swarming Paris in giddy groups. The journalist in him knew there was more to the story.

The first time Reed saw Cora Blake was through the archway from his solitary table. He realized he was looking at something he had never seen

222

before. She had just come out the brass doors of the elevator and was standing between the palm trees on either side, looking like she had woken up on Mars. He knew she was one of them even though she was thankfully not wearing one of those inane banners. She did have on somebody else's dress, it seemed, cheap burgundy silk that hung loose on her frame, and a hat like a metallic flying saucer, fortuitously tilted to show the fine curve of her cheek. A woman with those kinds of looks deserved better tailoring, he thought. She seemed lost and eager at the same time. He liked her very much.

Clancy Hayes, now established in a banquette, along with a second glass of Pernod, had been joined in his misery of rejection by an American photographer named Jim Denver who on principle refused to comb his hair and favored pretentious Gypsy vests—peering ratlike at him out of small black-framed glasses. Denver's artwork showed up regularly in the *bouquinistes'* stalls along the Seine, but you had to ask for it, and then you would be handed a smudged box of postcards showing inventive things that could be done with two naked women, a parrot, and a chair. Denver was a useful guide to reefer dens but also a shameless gossip. He dealt in gossip, and in shame, and therefore made a good living in Paris.

Hayes and Denver had spotted Cora Blake, alone, at dead center of a huge Oriental carpet, an intricate motif of gold flowers and obscure shapes like an opium dream. She was turning in a circle, banging a scuffed black leather handbag against her calf, as if looking for someone she had yet to meet.

"There's our canary," Hayes said. "Stay close."

Denver hoisted up the big Speed Graphic camera and Hayes slid out of the banquette. Reed noticed that the newspaperman was now empty-handed.

"Tough break about your manuscript," Reed said.

"What would you know about it?"

"You'll send it out again, won't you?" he said with a curl of the lip.

"Already did," Hayes replied. "In the trash."

"But that's crazy, all that work—"

Hayes patted Reed condescendingly on the shoulder, as if he were the one needing sympathy.

"Don't let it upset you, buddy."

He pushed his photographer into the lobby, and the two of them headed for Cora.

"Excuse me," Hayes said softly, coming up from behind. "I may be wrong—but—do you happen to be a Gold Star Mother?"

"Yes, I am."

He mugged a surprised smile.

"But you look so young!"

"I was young."

She noticed that his skin was baby-soft from the

morning's barbering and his mustache ruler-straight, unlike Linwood Moody, who only shaved on Sundays. The image came to her of piles of rotting lobster shells near the pier.

"We're from the Associated Press," Hayes said. "Do you mind talking to us?"

Cora glanced at Jim Denver, lounging nearby with a disinterested look, brogues crossed and his weight on one foot, as if he were going to stand there like a flamingo forever, the Speed Graphic hanging casually at his side. The giveaway was his operatic black hair standing every which way. It said there was a madman rattling the bars inside.

"I don't think I mind," she said cautiously.

"What is your name and where are you from?"

"Mrs. Cora Blake from Deer Islc, Maine."

Hayes nodded as if this meant anything to him, and reached inside his jacket for a pencil.

"Will this be in the local paper?" Cora asked.

"Good chance of it, lady. We're syndicated across the country. The pilgrimages are a big story back home."

She nodded. "There were so many newspapermen asking so many questions when we left New York."

"Pack of animals," Hayes agreed.

Watching from the barroom, Reed noticed that the newsman was unsteady on his feet and slipped a little trying to place the pencil squarely on the pad. Reed could feel it coming at him from the back of the skull: the first pinpoint of rage.

"What is the name of your beloved?"

"Samuel Blake. My son, Sammy."

"Sympathies for your loss, Mrs. Blake."

"Thank you."

"You've traveled a long way to see the grave of your beloved dead hero son."

Cora looked flustered. "What do you mean?"

"It must be a terrible time for you," Hayes pushed on. "Tell us about the grief and anguish. The trepidation about seeing your dead son's grave."

"His grave?"

"What's it like to make the supreme sacrifice of motherhood?"

Cora's face was turning red. "What's it like?"

"When do you miss him the most? Mornings? Evenings? On his birthday?"

"What are you talking about? What about Sammy's birthday?"

She had taken a step backward, between the palm trees, but Hayes pressed forward, growling between his teeth to Denver to get the shot.

"Tell us, how old was Sammy when he died? Don't you miss your little boy?"

"Of course I do!" cried Cora tearfully, a hand to her throat.

Denver raised the camera, but Griffin Reed was there.

"Take a walk," he said, stepping in front of the lens.

Denver tried to move around him. "Get out of the way."

"The lady doesn't want to talk to you."

"Sure she does," said Hayes. "She said so herself."

Reed turned to Cora. "Is this man bothering you, miss?"

Cora glanced hesitantly at the stranger who had intervened. In her emotional state, all she saw was an odd expression and an old-fashioned mustache.

"I don't want to make any trouble," she said.

The brass doors opened, revealing that the elevator car was jam-packed with pilgrims, many still wearing white sashes across their bosoms, pushing forward like a stampede of aging dance hall contestants. The reporter and photographer were pushed away, swamped by an unstoppable surge of women.

"Stay out of my business," Denver warned Reed. He looked ready to fight.

"Not worth it," Hayes advised. "The man can't defend himself."

"Try me," said Reed.

"Take it easy, pal," said Hayes. "Just trying to make a living."

"Get lost," said Reed as the members of Party A swarmed around Cora. Denver and his henchman knew it was over for them and took a hike.

"I've been waiting forever!" Cora cried. "Where have you all been?"

"We had a mix-up," Bobbie began breathlessly, as the women looked from one to the other. "We agreed to meet in Mrs. Russell's room—"

"We said the lobby!" insisted Minnie.

"*Some* of us thought it prudent to look in on Mrs. Russell," Lily sighed.

"But she had gone to Mrs. Seibert's room—"

Lieutenant Hammond was coming across the lobby, at first smiling and then making uncertain eye contact with Lily. They hadn't spoken since yesterday, when they'd escorted the women back to the hotel after the clumsy embrace at Jacques's.

"Good morning," he said crisply.

"How are you, Lieutenant?" she replied.

"As well as can be expected."

She saw his discomfort and indicated that they should step away from the mothers.

They began to say "I'm sorry," both at the same time, and laughed self-consciously.

"You go," he said.

"I've got someone at home," Lily told him. "It's pretty serious. I know I should have told you, but—"

"Not at all," he said, interrupting. "I didn't mean to offend—"

She wanted to tell Hammond that she had thought about him all night, in spite of the truth of what she'd said—that she was practically engaged to David Sawyers, M.D., a promising young pediatrician at Presbyterian Hospital in Chicago. They'd been seeing each other for a year and were in many ways a good match. He was dedicated to medicine but loved the outdoors as much as she, promising that when they were married they would have a cabin to escape the city, with as many pigs, chickens, dogs and cats, horses, and goats as she desired. She loved David but also loved nursing, and knew she couldn't have both. Hospital rules prevented married women from working; she would have to choose. She'd volunteered for the pilgrimages in order to think it out. David promised he would wait.

"I'm not at all offended," she said, there in the lobby of the Ambassador Hotel. "Don't worry, we're still friends. Best to just get on with it."

"Thank you," he said, grateful she hadn't made a fool of him. He bucked up and waved the handkerchief over his head to get the attention of the group.

"Everybody ready to see Notre-Dame?" Hammond called. "Gloves, billfolds, room keys, umbrellas?"

"Dyin' to go," said Katie. "But it seems we've lost Mrs. Russell."

"Over there." Minnie pointed to the coffee table, where Mrs. Russell was stuffing her pockets with cookies.

Cora searched the lobby to thank her rescuer, but the strange man had disappeared.

The beggar with the crutch was one of the outcasts, along with hunchbacks and nuns with harelips, who gathered daily outside Notre-Dame Cathedral, kneeling with their cups in a silent multitude of suffering. Every time the army brought groups to the cathedral, the liaison officers would report on the same beggars harassing their parties from the same spots, heads bowed, striking postures of supplication, appealing to the sympathy—or horror—of the tourists streaming by. There were French veterans missing arms and legs, as well as street performers from all over the world, while from the heights of the magnificent façade the famous gargoyles kept watch over this human wreckage.

Holding his U.S. Army credentials high, Hammond led Party A past a juggler tossing crystal balls and boys in gaucho suits twirling bolos, threading between the visitors and silent panhandlers. Minnie was afraid of the looming church but not of the desperate people outside, and dropped some coins in the cup of the beggar who was half kneeling, leaning on his crutch. Katie, so excited about going inside she was practically shaking, wanted a photograph of herself in one of the magnificent doorways of the west front beside a carved saint. She posed behind the crippled beggar as Wilhelmina looked down into a box camera, moving it this way and that. Without any warning, the man was up on both feet—miraculously cured—trying to pull the camera away, but the former tennis player was stronger than he and hung on like a terrier. They wrestled back and forth until he finally let go, picked up his crutch, and aimed it like a rifle, calling everybody, in English, *"Shit!"*

"Leave him," said Hammond. "He's crazy."

"Fake!" called Wilhelmina. "You should be ashamed of yourself!"

The beggar shot her, machine-gun-like, with the crutch.

"Stop that now," ordered Hammond.

The *rat-tat-tat* continued. A crowd had formed a circle as if they were part of the entertainment.

Hammond scanned the plaza. "You'd think the French would have a cop on duty. All of you, move away from that man. I'll be right back," he said, and trotted off to look for a police kiosk.

"Come over here, ladies."

Lily steered them away from the incendiary scene—but an indignant well-dressed English couple had stepped up on behalf of the beggar.

"I saw what happened," said the husband. "The poor wretch didn't want you to take his picture."

"Nobody took a picture," said Lily.

"Clearly, he thought you did," sniffed the wife.

Cora said, "So what if he thought that?"

"Well, he was humiliated."

"Why?"

"You stole his humanity," pronounced the Englishman.

Cora was inflamed, both hands on her hips. *"Stole?"*

During this, the beggar had folded up his leg and sunk back into silence, head bowed, the crutch laid beside him, waiting for the next offering.

"Funny," said Cora. "He looks just fine now."

"You think that's a fine way to live?" said the man.

"I never said that—"

Bobbie was not about to have anyone criticize anyone in her group.

"This is not your business," she said dismissively. "The man was paid."

"Naturally," said the husband. "That's what you Yanks always say—"

"Go home, ya English bastards," Katie said from low in the throat. "Thirty years of killin' Catholics, what're you doing here, defacin' our church—"

Now they were shouting all at once:

"Fix everything with money," the Englishman barked. "The American way."

"You know there's a depression going on?" Minnie demanded.

"One would think our so-called English friends would be grateful," Bobbie declared. "After bailing you out of the war."

The man pointed a shaking finger.

"Have some respect. We lost our boy in the war."

"So did I," said Bobbie, breathing hard. "So did all of us. We're American war mothers and you can go to hell."

She opened her alligator bag and threw a handful of bills toward the beggar's cup, causing a feeding frenzy among the nearby scroungers.

The Englishman was stammering something and his wife, outraged by Bobbie's casual disposal of money—as though anyone could imagine there could ever be compensation for their anger and loss—lurched at the older woman as if to put hands around her neck. Cora sprang forward to pull her away from Bobbie, and the husband, trying to protect his wife, begin to swing a heavy camera on a leather strap over his head. Bobbie ducked and fell to the ground. Then Hammond came running with gendarmes, who helped her up and drew the English couple away.

"Those people don't deserve the time of day," Cora said breathlessly, an arm around Bobbie, who was leaning on her heavily as they stumbled away.

Lily shepherded the rest to the nearest bench while the sea of tourists closed behind them. Minnie was still barking at the English people, calling them "stupid idiots," until Lily convinced her to stop and come over with the rest.

"Mrs. Olsen doesn't look good," Wilhelmina told her flatly. The nurse pushed everyone aside to find Bobbie sitting listlessly on the bench beside Cora.

"Mrs. Olsen? Can you hear me?"

"Of course I can hear!" Bobbie retorted.

Lily took her pulse and appraised her pale skin.

"When was the last time you saw a doctor?" she asked.

"I had a complete physical right before we left. He said I'm fine to travel. I'm perfectly okay. No need," Bobbie reiterated, trying to stand up.

Lily gently pushed her down. "I want you to just sit here for a moment."

"It was those awful people," Bobbie said.

"I know. I saw it. An unprovoked attack."

The others hovered over her.

"Would you like a glass of water?" Minnie asked.

"That's an old wives' tale," Katie said.

Minnie folded her arms. "What would you suggest?"

"A shot of brandy, that'll bring her back."

"There's a place across the street," Cora offered, looking at a café.

Hammond joined them, having settled with the police. Claiming injuries, the English couple was being taken to a hospital.

"How is Mrs. Olsen?" Hammond asked Lily.

"She's had a shock and needs to rest. There's

some bruising on her knee. You go on with the others. I'll get a taxi and take her back to the hotel. Is that all right with you, Mrs. Olsen?"

Bobbie nodded weakly. "Notre-Dame will still be there. Of that we can be sure."

Hammond took out a small notebook and scribbled a reminder to write in the Liaison Report: *"14:30 Incident at Notre-Dame. Group assaulted by English tourists. Mrs. Olsen feels faint. Nurse takes her back to the hotel. French police resolve dispute."* It would turn out to be a crucial notation.

Clancy Hayes sat down at a table outside Les Deux Magots.

"Listen, Reed. I'm awfully sorry about this morning."

It was late that night. Hayes wasn't drunk anymore.

"You should get yourself a new monkey," said Reed, who was pretty well smashed. There came a point every day when the throb of his joints and the soreness from the mask had to be addressed. Alcohol, in quantity, helped.

"Denver's a hophead." Clancy lit a cigarette. "But he's good. He's over at Bricktop's taking snaps of Ellington."

"Bully for him."

"You know what it's like. I had to get the story. Food on the table." He shrugged.

Reed looked at Hayes in disbelief. His father owned a damn bank. His big baby eyes were pleading innocence. All he needed was a pacifier.

"You bullied that woman to get a story. *'Grieving mother mourns hero son'*—trashy entertainment for the desperate hordes waiting on bread lines."

"All's fair . . ."

"All's not fair."

"You would have done it. In your better days, my friend. Admit it."

"My better days are ahead, don't you know?" Reed finished the drink and signaled for another.

Hayes was looking frankly at the mask. "What's it like?"

"To have your face ripped off by a machine gun?"

"To only look one way. Nobody can tell what you're thinking."

Reed leaned close. He wanted Hayes's full attention.

"It's a hell of an advantage," Reed told him.

By the time they left, the streets had been glazed with a night shower, dark-stained and beautiful. They walked together. Hayes had the manuscript under his arm. You could hear the drip from the wet trees hitting the soiled brown paper.

"I thought you trashed it."

"Changed my mind. Decided to take your

advice and send it out again. They said they liked the writing," Hayes said hopefully.

They went to the entrance of the *métro*. In the well at the bottom of the staircase a student musician was playing folk melodies on a violin. The music echoed sweetly off the tiles. At this late hour there were no other passengers and few coins on his plate. At the top of the steps Reed turned to Hayes and hit him hard on the mouth. He sprawled halfway down. Reed picked him up and threw him the rest of the way. When he stopped at the bottom Reed was already there. He stood him up against the wall and let him have it with both fists. Then he took the manuscript and tore off the string. Hayes staggered toward him like a zombie. One eye was swollen shut.

"My book," he sobbed, gurgling blood.

"What's it *worth,* do you think?"

Reed was about to rip up the pages and toss them to the foul wind coming from below like fumes from a cesspool, but changed his mind and gave it back. He left Clancy Hayes clutching his manuscript and climbed the stairs to the wet boulevard.

The violinist kept on with his song.

12

Reed crossed the river and drifted north along the major avenues, turning corners at random until he found himself in a warren of narrow passageways off boulevard de Clichy. Wet cobblestones gleamed in the glowing signs of illicit hotels. It was three in the morning and the second-story shutters were closed. Occasionally a woman would materialize in the shadows of a doorway, unsmiling. He passed a familiar vestibule of pebbled glass at a bordello where he'd occasionally gone to visit two obedient Russian girls—JoJo and FanFan—who looked exactly alike, small-breasted and slimly built, barely twenty. Not tonight. He was at his best when he was free to walk the streets unnoticed. Paris at night required nothing of him and made no judgments.

He turned back down rue Amsterdam, jammed with horse-drawn engines that were sucking the muck out of sewers with huge snaking hoses. The stink made him gag. His stomach was cramping from too much whiskey, or maybe he'd pulled a muscle while pounding Hayes. At Madeleine he ignored a squad of ragpickers, and the pairs of bicycle police that were zipping around the Tuileries like bats with their black capes and high-pitched whistles. Through the gold-tipped bars of the gate he glimpsed a pair of lovers on a bench. Nothing changes, he observed. He recrossed the Seine and headed toward the Fifth, where bakeries and markets were coming to life; an old geezer was asleep on top of a cart of vegetables he'd just brought in from the countryside.

There's nothing worse than a writer without a story, Reed reflected morosely. Clancy Hayes *thought* he had a story, *hoped* he'd be one of the big boys someday, but Hayes had no real talent; he was nothing but an impersonation of a writer, using a false identity to accumulate a pile of bylines, which made anyone who was the real deal want to punch him in the face. What Hayes was grinding out was banal in every way, but *he had stories* and *kept on being hired,* and that's what burned Reed.

The craving to be back at the paper was like a physical need. Not being there was misery. Someone waiting for your words—even a half-assed editor—that's what mattered, because then you had a reason to be, to bear witness, which is what a real writer did. And after you'd lived with it and made it yours and wrestled it onto the page and locked it down, there was the victory lap. Defeating the naysayers. Rubbing their noses in it. Prudes, politicians, bankers, liars, mothers, fathers, and thieves. The day Wall Street crashed they'd had an orgy in the newsroom, set fires in wastebaskets and sent cherry bombs down the mail chutes, sex on top of the desks, everyone crazed with all-out perverse self-destructive joy. We can burn it down if we want to! Now, all that power gone and mourned. At best he'd been allowed to be the guy in the basement, shoveling other people's copy into the furnace in the belly of the beast. He needed a story like grass needs rain.

It was dawn when he reached the high white wall surrounding the three-story white brick house in the Latin Quarter. He unlocked the gate and was greeted by the happy burble of the fountain made by Florence Dean Powell, in which a pair of bronze boy-angels urinated at cross-purposes. He wondered if he would find the usual half dozen passed-out young homosexual males sprawled on the tangerine sofas in the living room. Florence's boys adored her. She was flamboyant, sarcastic, generous with money and alcohol, and, like them, had defied convention—in her case, by leaving Beacon Hill society and refusing to marry in order to devote herself to making art. Unlike those pompous cubists nobody could understand, Florence Dean Powell was a naturalist anyone who liked garden ornaments could admire.

Tonight the house was quiet and empty except for the tortoiseshell cat who was waiting for Reed on the stair. He picked her up and carried her to the second floor, past Florence's bedroom and on to his own, but had to let the cat go when an abdominal seizure made him duck into the hallway bathroom. Every joint in his body ached by the time he staggered to bed. The mattress gave in luxuriously under his weight. The cat was back, nosing under the blanket. If there was any part of him that wasn't broken, he didn't know about it.

Two and a half hours later, he was woken by Florence's accusing voice.

"You should have gotten me up."

It was a full-on summer morning and the room was saturated with sunlight. Reed knew because a red sea was flooding his inner eyelids. He hoped to keep them closed as long as possible.

"Why?" he managed.

He could hear the creak of a window opening on its crank and the clack of glassware and bottles being collected from around the room, feel warm air on the naked caverns of his face and where sensitive bare gums had receded above the teeth. Florence, who had fashioned his mask, was the only person allowed to see him in this condition.

"You were sick."

He smelled soap. She had picked up the device where he'd left it on the night table and was scrubbing it in a basin.

"I'm not sick."

"I heard you. Here." She tapped him with it. "What happened to your hand?"

His eyes opened. His hand had been resting on

his chest. He saw that his second and third fingers were black-and-blue. Come to think of it, they were throbbing like hell. She was standing over him with a tray against her hip on which she had matter-of-factly piled the detritus of his masculine den, including old newspapers and full ashtrays, used napkins, pill bottles, and a hypodermic syringe rolling around on a china saucer.

"Where were you last night?"

"Les Deux Magots."

"What happened?"

"Don't worry," Reed said, fitting the mask in place and the eyepieces around his ears. "Your reputation for keeping a half-crazed war casualty is intact."

Florence put the tray aside and sat down on the bed. She wore a sleeveless lilac dress that fell toga-style from the shoulders and gathered into a narrow belt, showing her taut figure and long, well-developed arms. She had strong brows and expressive hooded eyes, which she'd imbued with a dreamy air in an early self-portrait that now hung in her alma mater, the Massachusetts Normal Art School in Boston—a full-figure study in which she imagined herself as a repressed Victorian young lady with raven hair parted in the middle beneath an elaborate hat with a knotted veil, an old-fashioned dress with a bustle, and, in classic manner, holding a muff. In it her long face was tilted with a wistful look, as if asking a question or waiting for a reply, but then Florence had abandoned the romanticism and been honest in showing an unflattering jawline and the trembling lips of a needy sexual being.

Her attitude toward Reed was not unkind as she gently examined his injured hand.

"Let me get some oil of wintergreen."

"It's nothing," he said.

"In that case, can you please get dressed? Harold Gravois is expecting us."

Her habit of repeating both names was galling. Not just *Harold*. Not *Gravois*. But *Harold Gravois,* as if to keep hammering home that she, *Florence Dean Powell,* was acquainted with a famous painter. Of course, she might have never been invited to the great man's studio if Monsieur Gravois had not been seated next to Griffin Reed at a dinner party in the home of a bohemian painter in the Marais, and become intensely interested in his war injuries from an artistic point of view.

"I told you, Flo. I have no interest."

"This is a major artist."

"Who gives a damn?"

"You inspire him. That's important."

"To you."

Didn't he owe her? After thirteen surgeries and a year of convalescence in England, Reed had come into her sculptor's hands gravely disoriented, with the noseless, gaping, inhuman profile of an ape. She had made him back into a man and fallen in love with her creation, taken him into her life, and supported his addictions to alcohol and painkillers, as well as his despondent moods. If she wanted to loan him to a fellow artist, what was the problem?

"Yes, it's important to me for you to sit for Harold Gravois," she admitted, "but not for the reason that you think."

Reed sat up and swung his legs off the bed. "I think," he said, "it's so you can brag to your fairy friends. It would raise your status in *café society,*" he said disdainfully.

She followed him across the room. "It's not for me. It's for art."

"Can we skip the platitudes?"

"I mean it, Grif. It would be making art for the cause of peace."

"Peace? Isn't that a little grand?"

"The reason Harold Gravois wants to paint your likeness is to make a statement about the pointlessness of war. As a protest. *Un cri du coeur.* Wait—let me finish—it's not a realistic portrait that he wants, it isn't you, yourself—"

"Well, that's a relief."

"He's a *surrealist.* He paints in *abstractions.* He only wants to use the shapes and forms of the destruction of the human face. Nobody will recognize you."

"I won't do it."

Florence became infuriated. "Grif! I promised him you'd come."

"Your mistake, sweetheart."

"Don't embarrass me! I am sick of your self-pity," Florence raged. "You forget—I was there. I was there when they brought you into the studio looking like something not of this world. I was there during the darkest days, before anybody knew what to do with you—as well as a hundred thirty-two other terribly wounded soldiers just like yourself! I gave up my own work making art plus three years of my life to devote my God-given talents to Dr. Blackmore's clinic, so someone else might have a chance at normal life—"

Once the floodgates opened—and it often took just a nudge—there was no stopping her wounded indignation. Reed tried to escape, trotting quickly down the stairs, past rows of white plaster casts of the faces of former patients Florence and the surgeons had treated. She still insisted on keeping the eerie molds on the wall like trophies. His silent, frozen brethren. Many had been able to return to their families with self-respect and confidence. Many had not lived long and had been buried in their masks. They had been sustained for a while by the artist, ruthlessly honest in her way. If she was dissatisfied, she would smash a piece of sculpture as fearlessly as she had shaped it. Her top-floor studio was lined with buckets of clay shards, a reminder, as if he needed it after all these years, that Florence the creator was also Florence the destroyer.

"—but love means nothing to you, Grif," she was going on. "You're incapable of caring about anybody else—"

As they got to the bottom of the steps they heard someone knocking on the front door and saw the maid hurrying to answer it.

"Who is that?" Reed asked.

"Dr. Szabo. It's a Sunday. I could only get a Jew."

"Why can't you leave anything alone?"

"You were sick and you've *been* sick—"

The maid was announcing the doctor, a balding, middle-aged Hungarian in an immaculate three-piece brown suit and striped blue tie, wearing wire-rimmed glasses and a wan smile. They went into the living room, where the draperies had been swept open for better light, flooding the windows with lush views of the garden. The maid came back with tea.

"Beautiful home," said the doctor, opening his bag.

"Don't let him tell you that he's fine," Florence interjected. "He's had indigestion for over a week—"

"Thank you, Florence," Reed said shortly.

"Thank you, madame," the doctor echoed firmly. "Please wait outside."

When she was gone he efficiently got down to business, listening to Reed's chest and examining his ears.

"How often do you have stomach problems?"

"On and off."

"Too much wine?" asked the doctor with a friendly raise of an eyebrow.

"Could be."

"Smoke?"

"Not much."

"Is there still pain from the surgery? What do you take?"

"Laudanum by mouth. Morphine by injection."

He peered closely at the mask. "Would you mind taking that off?"

"Yes, I would."

The doctor accepted his refusal without protest. "May I look inside your mouth?"

Reed obliged and got poked with a wooden tongue depressor until he gagged.

"Sorry. How are your feet?"

"My feet?"

"Any numbness or pain?"

"Not that I notice," Reed lied. His feet were always tingling.

The doctor's eyes went back to the mask as if he couldn't look away. Reed bore the scrutiny as long as he could.

"Is there a problem, Doc?"

"What's that device made of?"

"Some kind of metal. A combination of metals, I think."

"My concern is that you may have plumbism," Dr. Szabo said crisply. "Lead poisoning. The symptoms can include gastrointestinal upset and peripheral neuropathy—numbness in the feet. But the main component of a positive diagnosis is based on proximity to a source of lead. We see it in children who have eaten paint that contains lead. It's possible that you've been exposed through the skin. I take it you've been wearing the device several hours a day, possibly for years? I'd like to take a blood sample; then we'll know. Please roll up your sleeve."

The stinging smell of the alcohol swab brought back terrible memories of gurneys, hallways, intractable pain that even morphine couldn't touch. Reed's heart kicked up as the doctor removed a tourniquet and a syringe from the bag.

"Why don't you lie down?" he suggested.

Reed didn't argue, stretching out on the tangerine sofa. He felt the rubber hose tighten above his elbow and the doctor's finger tapping a vein.

"If I do have lead poisoning, then what?"

"Who was your surgeon?"

"Dr. James Blackmore at London General Hospital."

He felt the needle go in and stay there as the glass tube slowly filled with his blood.

"Go back and see Dr. Blackmore. Facial surgery has changed a lot since the war. At the very least, you should have a new prosthetic made."

"It took months to get this one right."

"Mr. Reed, if the test comes back positive, you won't have a choice."

"Why is that?"

"This one is going to kill you."

13

It was the last day in Paris for Party A. The schedule had given them a free morning. In the afternoon they would join an assembly of French war mothers to lay a wreath at the Tomb of the Unknown Soldier at the Arc de Triomphe and then proceed to Restaurant Laurent for tea with dignitaries. First thing tomorrow, Party A, along with other groups in the same rotation, would board private buses for Verdun, which would be their base for several days of visiting the Meuse-Argonne American Cemetery and Memorial.

They were almost at their final destination, which is maybe why Cora had the dream. She saw Sammy in an empty room with wood floors and plain walls, like the farmhouse at Tide's End. The light in the room is what disturbed her the most. It was solemn and unchanging, and seemed to imply the conclusion of something. Sammy was just standing there, looking strangely patient and shockingly real, exactly as he had when he was sixteen. Outside there was nothing but clattering, nonstop rain.

When she woke up she felt so drained that she scarcely had the will to get dressed. Soon there was knocking and an insistent voice.

"Cora? It's Bobbie!"

The moment she opened the door, Bobbie saw Cora's distress and said, "What's wrong, dear?"

Cora turned away. She didn't know how to voice these things.

"I had a bad sleep."

Bobbie followed into the room. "Are you ill?"

"Just tired."

Cora became aware of her own selfishness. How could she forget what happened the day before?

"Are *you* all right, Bobbie?"

"Why shouldn't I be?"

"That terrible man at Notre-Dame."

"I'm perfectly fine," the older woman replied emphatically. "Full of piss and vinegar," she added, to emphasize the point.

Cora smiled. "You look nice."

Bobbie was already dressed for the afternoon's event at the Arc de Triomphe in a brown-and-white checkered jacket that nipped the waist, white scarf and pearls, a tiny green hat like an inverted teacup.

"It's lovely to have a morning off, isn't it?" she

said. "If I have to listen to those harpies in our group screeching at each other one more minute, I'll slit my throat. Let's get out of here. It's our last day in Paris and I promised an old friend I'd stop by before we go. She's invited us to lunch. Come on, now or never!"

Bobbie's tireless energy snapped things back to normal. The disheveled pillows no longer seemed a nest of sorrow. Cora fluffed them up and pulled at the heavy gold damask bedspread.

"I just have to make the bed."

"The hotel will do that for you."

"My mother used to say, 'A person who doesn't make their bed in the morning doesn't respect herself.'"

"And *my* mother used to say, 'Let the maid do it!'"

A black limousine was waiting at the side entrance of the hotel. A uniformed driver opened the door for Madame Olsen, then came around the other side and opened the door for Madame Blake. The backseat was made of soft leather and big enough for each of them to lie down and take a nap. Each had her own oval window with a little pleated curtain, through which to view the fancy shops slipping by.

Cora was taken by a spasm of giggles.

"What's the joke?"

"The last time I was on a car ride, we were going to the train station in Bangor. My fiancé took me

251

in his truck along with a pig. The pig was in back."

"And was there hay?" Bobbie wondered archly.

"No hay," said Cora, mimicking her superior tone. "But plenty of blood, that's for sure. It was really *half* a pig, on the way to market."

"Well," said Bobbie, "I'm sorry not to offer you such fascinating company, but if you feel homesick, we can stop by a butcher shop."

Cora laughed until she had to blow her nose.

"You never mentioned a fiancé. What's his name, and how long have you known him?"

"Linwood Moody. He's not really a fiancé, as we're not really engaged, although he's asked me."

"What does he do?"

"He's a soil scientist."

"Then he's certainly got his feet on the ground." Bobbie smiled at her own wit.

"That's true about Linwood," Cora acknowledged. "Sometimes I think if I'd married a proper husband, and not tried to raise a boy myself, Sammy would still be here."

"Why do you say that?" Bobbie wondered.

"If he'd had a father to stop him, he wouldn't have gone. He would have stayed another year under our roof and by that time the war would have been over."

"First of all, a *man* wouldn't have stopped him, a *man* would have *urged* his son to go and fight.

My husband would have thought it was a splendid idea for Henry to join the army, even though we had to rush the engagement. He had a large ego—he built apartment buildings and the like—and I think Henry inherited that sense of immunity from life's blows. I suppose as a surgeon you need to feel a godlike power," she mused. "Henry was always a confident young man, sometimes to the point of arrogance. He was quite certain he alone could change the world."

"He did," Cora said. "For the men he saved."

Bobbie briskly steered away from sentiment. "Now, what about this Linwood?" she said. "Is he the one?"

Cora thought about it. She'd sent him a postcard—as promised, the Eiffel Tower. But she hadn't said anything more encouraging than *"Everything is going well."*

"I think I'm ready," Cora said.

Bobbie shook her head. " 'I think I'm ready' entirely sidesteps the question."

"He's a good man."

"But?"

They glided over a bridge to the Left Bank, down wide avenues with crowded café terraces, twisting along elegant residential streets of elm trees and private courtyards.

Cora said regretfully, "Linwood would hate it here. New York and Paris would be much too fast for him, while all I can think about is, What's next? What's that building? What do they eat for breakfast? And look at their beautiful parks—"

"You're an explorer and he's a homebody," Bobbie said. "And home is a million miles away."

"You're right. We're different that way. I wonder if we'll ever see eye to eye?" she asked tremulously.

Bobbie patted her hand. "Don't worry dear. You'll be back soon and then you'll see."

Cora nodded and forced herself to smile. She could no longer tell one sadness from another.

They stopped at a tall white wall topped by a perfectly clipped hedge. The limousine driver accompanied them as far as the gateway and said he would wait. From there they entered a green oasis, quiet except for the sound of bubbling water and the mossy scent of wet stone, as they passed a fountain of two brass cupids apparently having a peeing contest.

"They have a funny sense of humor over here," Cora said.

"My friend, the one you are about to meet, did that sculpture," Bobbie said. "She's American and her name is Florence Dean Powell. I'm very close with her mother. We were sorority sisters at Radcliffe and serve together on the board of the Boston Museum of Fine Arts. Her mother is Abigail Powell, daughter of Eugene Randolf, the former senator from Massachusetts. I've known Florence all her life, and she's never changed from the little girl who wouldn't let you tie her shoe—she had to do everything herself. I suppose you can say she's succeeded! She's quite publicly refused to get married in order to devote herself to sculpting. Her mother was devastated when Florence moved to Paris after the war. She heard the call—Paris is the place to be! You have to admire her guts, but she seems to have fit right in with the Parisian way of life."

As they crossed the courtyard, a dark-haired man wearing a lustrous smoking jacket and slippers emerged from a back doorway. He had a pipe between his teeth and carried a pile of books under one arm, a bowl of coffee in the other hand, and there was a tortoiseshell cat riding on his shoulder. Without acknowledging the visitors, he disappeared into an opening in a hedge beyond which there appeared to be a small cottage.

"Are you sure she's not married?" Cora asked.

"Yes, I'm sure."

"Is *that* the way of life you're talking about?" Cora said with amusement. She understood what it was like for your relationship with a male to be the object of moral speculation.

"I wouldn't know," Bobbie said disapprovingly. "And I certainly won't ask her mother."

The maid answered the door. They entered to the scent of onions simmering in red wine.

"Bless her heart, she's making beef stew the real French way. Although of course she has a cook,"

Bobbie added tartly, still upset by the unknown male. "Thanks to her parents, who cater to her every whim—"

Florence Dean Powell was coming down from her studio upstairs.

"Hello, Bobbie!" she called. "Welcome! I'm so happy to see you!"

She wore a white blouse tied at the neck in a big soft bow, with a painter's smock over it. The maid carefully helped her off with the smock, which was covered with fine white dust. Underneath was a slim skirt to the knee and black pumps. Evidently Florence sculpted in high heels. Her black hair was up in a bun, which accentuated a long face with large limpid eyes.

"I'd embrace you, but all this dust—"

"No matter," Bobbie replied, as they delicately kissed on both cheeks. "Your mother sends her deepest love."

"Thank you. I miss her so!"

Bobbie introduced Cora and the two women shook hands.

"Are you on the pilgrimage also?"

Cora nodded. "My son, Sammy, was killed in 1918, the same year as Bobbie's son. They both served in the same division. But they didn't know each other," she felt compelled to add.

"It's just god-awful, isn't it? I knew Henry growing up. He was the handsome older cousin— not really a cousin, but we thought of him that way—all the girls had crushes on. He was very patient and remembered the names of my dolls. He was serious, almost Victorian in the way he liked to explain things, right, Bobbie?"

"Well, he never talked down. Not to servants *or* a child."

"I remember Henry taking me to the Public Garden to feed the geese. Maybe that's where I got my love of animals!"

"Florence is well known for her animal statues," Bobbie said. "She's got two wonderful rhinoceroses guarding the entrance of—what is it? A famous zoo."

"Lots of zoos," Florence said modestly. "And museums. Now I'm doing table sculptures, mostly tigers. People are scaling down these days."

"Ever do raccoons?"

"No, somehow I've missed raccoons."

"Sammy and his friends used to hunt raccoons because they were taking over the garbage dumps," Cora said with pride. "They'd get twenty-five cents apiece from the county."

Florence smiled and raised her eyebrows. "What a waste of a good coat!"

Cora caught more than a whiff of condescension. Her stomach tightened in defense of her son, the island, the entire state of Maine.

Florence was oblivious to the offense. "Why didn't you stay with me," she was asking, with a strong arm around Bobbie, "instead of a strange hotel?"

"There's so little time and they've been shuttling us all over. We have to be at the Arc de Triomphe at three."

"Oh, my, then we'd better sit down."

Florence led them down a hall. The scent of beef stew grew mouthwateringly intense. Although the house was well appointed, there were odd things around, mirrors everywhere, and rows of strange white plaster faces of men mounted on the wall.

"What are those?" Cora asked.

"Those are my brave boys," Florence said. "British and American soldiers who were wounded in the war. We gave them new life here."

"Florence helped men who suffered facial wounds," Bobbie said.

Cora swallowed hard, seeing the faces now as dead.

"This house used to be a clinic. I came over to study sculpture but I met an English doctor, James Blackmore, who was doing very advanced, very important work in the area of reconstructive surgery, and joined his staff as an artist. We lived and worked upstairs, and there used to be a surgery ward. Those are the molds we made of each wounded man. Then I'd use a photograph of the soldier from before the injury and make a mask that exactly covered the missing parts. I'd paint it to match his skin, and there you go."

"And afterward, how do they get along in society?" Bobbie asked.

"The best cases were able to regain their confidence and go back to their families. But some were too ashamed or afraid, or beyond our help, and they've wound up in homes for disfigured soldiers. I'd rather remember our successes. Some of them, you wouldn't know it at first. You'll see when you meet Griffin. He's out in the garden, with the cat."

Through the glass French doors of the dining room the garden looked like a painting itself—filled with wisteria and beds of tulips, and daffodils blooming in the shade. They could see the back of the man in the smoking jacket, seated at a small round table, half hidden by a pink chestnut tree.

"Are you sure?" Bobbie asked. "When we first came in he seemed to avoid us. I would hate to cause the poor fellow more discomfort—"

"No, no, he's a writer, so he's naturally antisocial. The mask allows him to have a normal life. You know, drink, go to prostitutes—all the normal things that writers do!" she added charmingly.

"Does he still get treatment?" Bobbie asked, wanting to reassure herself that he was only a visitor, albeit dressed as if he'd just gotten out of bed.

"No, he lives here."

There was a moment of confusion.

"He lives with *me*," Florence said quite clearly. Her eyes were merry. She seemed to enjoy shocking people. Cora sensed Bobbie flinching and felt protective of her new friend. She was trying to think of a civil way to put their hostess in her place when Florence opened the glass doors and called, "Grif? Come and say hello."

The cat jumped off his lap and the man in the smoking jacket walked toward them through the dappled shade. It was true. From a dozen paces, he didn't look scarred at all. He was of strong build and wore a friendly expression, along with a cheerfully un-American scarf knotted at his throat.

"Meet the journalist Griffin Reed."

"I know you!" Cora exclaimed without thinking.

"I know you, too," he replied in a kindhearted way.

Cora looked directly into his keen blue eyes and he gazed back with frank recognition. A shock went through her and she was embarrassed down to her toes, as if it were as obvious to everyone as it was to them that despite the appliance, the war, Florence, Linwood, and everything else, there was an unmistakable connection between these two strangers.

Reed's hand lingered in hers. His fingertips were soft in contrast to the fixed look on his face, which made the touch all the more illicit.

"We've already met," Cora managed.

"Have you really?" Florence asked. "How is that possible?"

"At the Hotel Ambassador."

"Ah, Griffin likes to go there and macerate with other gloomy writers. He doesn't write anymore, that's the problem. That's why you're depressed, darling."

"Who said I'm depressed? And if I was," Reed said genially, "how could you tell?"

Bobbie looked perplexed; Cora wasn't sure if it was okay to laugh.

Florence rolled her eyes. "That's one of his jokes."

"I was at American Express," said Reed. "Next door to the hotel. Then I had a little breakfast."

"All right," said Florence. "I forgive you."

Why should he be forgiven? Forgiven for what? Cora wanted to know.

"Griffin saved me from some terrible reporters," she said a bit too defiantly. "And I never got to thank him."

"She was cornered by that idiot Clancy Hayes," Reed explained. "And his junked-up photographer pal."

"Why on earth?"

"The Gold Star Mothers tours are big news in America."

Florence turned toward Cora. "What's wrong with that? Why not cooperate?"

"I would have, but—"

"He was provoking her to get a picture," Reed said impatiently. "That's all."

Florence caught his tone and dropped it. "Well then, good for you. I'm sure he'll never bother Cora again. Let's sit down."

"I'm going to beg off," Reed said.

"Are you all right?"

"Yes. Don't fuss. I've got some reading to do."

Florence patted his metal cheek. "Sorry, darling. There'll be soup for you."

They said their goodbyes and Reed went back into the garden.

"Oh my," said Bobbie, concerned. "Can he only eat soup?"

"It's just a bout of indigestion. He's had some tests, but the doctor thinks it's nervous stomach," Florence said, because that's what Reed had told her after Dr. Szabo left. He didn't want to turn over the rock about anything more serious if there wasn't a need.

Cora trailed behind and even glanced back through the glass one time to see if he was looking, but he was absorbed in his books. They sat at a table covered by a beautiful white cloth with crystal and silver, in a floral-wallpapered dining room with fresh flowers in big vases. They were served individual ramekins of lobster custard and then the maid brought rice, peas, and beef stew on platters and held them out for each guest to serve herself, which made Cora twitchy.

"How are you doing, Bobbie? Mother's worried that this might not be the best thing for you.

She's afraid the pilgrimage might bring everything back . . ."

"It never goes away, Florence," Bobbie said sternly.

"But you've carried on."

"Not really. The days just come and go. I used to be so active—entertaining and traveling and my charity work—but even though I had a wonderful marriage, without Henry I've lost the focus in life. He was everything to me. I always fretted about him, even when I knew he was safe. He was a sturdy little boy, but from the moment they're born, the worry doesn't stop. I always take pictures of him along with me, wherever I go, and I talk to him. I don't think you can understand if you've never had children."

Florence's jaw tightened but she assured Bobbie that she understood. They spoke of nieces and nephews while the dishes were cleared for the cheese course, and then chocolate mousse and a plate of truffles were served.

"If only I could have Henry back, for just a few minutes," Bobbie mused. "Don't you think so, Cora?"

"I dream a lot about Sammy."

"That's like having him back, isn't it?" Florence said.

Cora didn't answer. It's not how she saw it. She wished she didn't have those dreams. She wished she hadn't seen the plaster faces in the hallway.

"Florence, dear, as you know, we're leaving Paris tomorrow," Bobbie said. "It occurs to me, since you knew Henry and are such a close friend of the family, that you might like to come with me to visit his grave. It would mean a lot to me, and to your mother, I'm sure."

"How far is it?"

"How far is Verdun?" Bobbie asked.

"It's a two-hour drive if you don't stop."

"Would you?"

Florence answered, too quickly, "I'd love to, but I can't; I have a show coming up. I have to prepare."

Bobbie's opinion of her sank like a stone, but mostly she felt sorry for Florence's mother. Maybe it was best that her daughter lived in Paris so she didn't have to witness on a daily basis what a selfish woman her promising little girl had become.

"Well, one day, if you get around to it," Bobbie replied acidly. "Since you are right here. I haven't traveled much recently, but this is one trip I was determined to make."

There was a shift in the atmosphere and Bobbie stood up.

"We should go," she told Cora.

Florence saw them out with kisses on both cheeks and promises to write. The moment she closed the door, Bobbie and Cora knew exactly what the other was thinking.

"Sorry, but I'm not too good at hiding my likes and dislikes," Cora said.

Bobbie said, "I agree with you. She's changed. I've never seen anything like it, the way she keeps that poor man. Her mother would be appalled."

"He doesn't seem put off," Cora said. Then, to change the subject: "It's a nice house."

Bobbie shrugged and lifted her nose. "Maybe it's bohemian."

As they crossed the garden, Cora confessed that she really didn't want to go to the ceremony at the Arc de Triomphe.

"Don't you feel well?" Bobbie asked. "You seemed a little out of sorts this morning."

"No, I'm fine. It's just that I've had enough speechifying."

"The driver will take you to the hotel."

"I'd really just like to walk. It's my last day in Paris."

"But you don't know the way."

"Yes, I do," said Cora, and recited block by block where to turn left and how to get on Boulevard Saint Michel and across the river to Boulevard Haussmann.

"That's astonishing," Bobbie said. "How did you remember?"

Cora said, "I just know."

"All right then," Bobbie said. "I'll see you at dinner." Then she was in the limousine and Cora was free.

• • •

It was a relief to be on her own, away from schedules and lectures. She took her time, marveling at the assortment of new things on every block: Gypsy tearooms, interesting-looking food shops, strange old churches with domes. She was on the corner of rue Soufflot waiting for the traffic light to change when a man standing beside her said, "*Admettez-la, que vous êtes perdue.*"

"I'm sorry," Cora said. "I don't speak French."

"Then I'll say it in English," said the man. "*Admit it, you are lost.*"

It was Griffin Reed.

"I'm not lost."

"Which way are you going?"

"That way, toward the river."

"I'll go with you."

"Did you follow me here?"

"I felt like getting out. Would you like to get a drink?"

Cora was startled by the suggestion. "I don't think so—"

"Hot chocolate, then?"

"In the middle of June?"

"You have to try it the French way. I promise you, it's not like home."

They walked half a block to a *crêperie*, where they were served two tiny cups through a window. A cookie like a miniature waffle, light as air, nestled in the saucer.

"What do you call this?" Cora asked.

"*Chocolat chaud.* What do you think?"

"Not too bitter, not too sweet. I like it!"

"Thought you might. You're that kind of girl."

"What kind?"

"Not too bitter, not too sweet."

She just stared at him, amazed at his presumption. She wondered if the mask paradoxically made it easier for him to speak freely. She was beginning to read the subtleties of Reed's communication. The restless shoulders. Playful eyes. The lips you could glimpse in a fleeting smile. Graceful, unimprisoned hands, and a frank masculinity that inhabited his body. Away from Florence's house he seemed very different. She was surprised that she felt no pity but, rather, that she was in the presence of a human being as in touch with life as anyone she'd known. Being with him was more powerful than being with others, as if a nameless, transcendent force was reaching out to her from behind a prison wall.

"Have you been to the Luxembourg Gardens?" Reed asked.

Cora shook her head. He slipped his arm in hers and they walked down the street, legs synchronized in stride. He could feel her tension at finding herself with a strange man in a strange city, and tried to be reassuring.

"I'm not making a pass at you, just teaching you

how to be Parisian," he said, pulling her across a mad plaza full of traffic.

"Grif-*fin!*" she squealed, but held on as they ran to the entrance of the park.

"We have to get there before they take the sailboats in," Reed huffed, as they hurried down a path lined with perfectly spaced trees, all alike, until they came to a wide circular area.

"Here!" he said triumphantly. "This is all you need to know about Paris."

There were sculptures everywhere. Heroic figures and ordinary humans mingled like renderings of each other. Children in school uniforms chased deft little boats in a sailing pond in a luxurious garden ringed by apple-green trees pruned to look like lollipops. Reed pulled two metal chairs across the gravel with a loud scraping noise.

"You hear that sound? That's the sound of civilization."

It was impossible not to feel noble, arranged in chairs with the delicate play of water before them, surrounded by relaxed conversation in many languages. Late afternoon and she wasn't working! Not cleaning or cooking or trudging over the baking hot, pine-dusted trail from the cannery, sticky and stinking of gutted sardines. Near a marble wall in the garden two lovers were arguing, making large gestures at each other, until finally the young dark man with black hair and a sweeping raincoat walked off.

"Une affaire vite résolue!"

"What'd he say?"

"It's open and shut!"

Reed drew a small notebook from his breast pocket.

"You're writing that down?" she asked incredulously.

He nodded, slipping into that agreeable state of mind both drowsy and awake that would lead him through the wings and back onstage to an ongoing and brightly lit piece of his own private drama—a short story that he was secretly mulling over.

He closed the book. Cora pulled the skirt of her dress beneath her knees and sat up primly on the chair. They watched for a while without talking. Girls were playing a clapping game and church bells struck.

"I think I'm homesick for Maine," she said.

"I read somewhere that Maine is the place you're homesick for, even when you're there."

She looked at the French colors flying from the top of a white palace. The clouds opened up to a silver sky and the breeze was fresh and sinuous, everything in flux.

"How can I be homesick when this is all so beautiful?"

"You can have both," Reed said.

They sat quietly. "You miss your son," he said matter-of-factly.

She nodded. "Maybe that's Sammy, up there."

A lone seagull was crossing the sky.

"What about Sammy's father?" he asked. "What does he think of your coming here?"

"Sammy doesn't have a father," Cora said briefly. "I was never married."

Her fingers rose to cover her mouth as if to suppress the words, but she found she'd rather let them go.

"But you're a 'Mrs.,' aren't you? Or is that a false identity and you're really a German spy?"

He'd meant it as a lark and was surprised to discover it was partly true. She found herself continuing: "I got pregnant by a teacher my second year in Colby College. I was living in the dormitory. We were supposed to get married. He had a cottage almost an hour away, and I kept saying, Why do you want to be so far from Waterville, because that's where the school was, and then, when push came to shove, I finally found out that he was already married, with a wife and three children living in another town."

Reed moved closer, encouraging her to go on.

"He offered me the privilege of being his mistress and said he would pay for the child. I hated him. It destroyed my life. I left school, never finished, came home, and moved in with Mother on the family farm. It's called Tide's End, and it's on an island. My dad was a sea captain, he came and went, but when he retired he was very close to my son, Sammy. I made up a story that my

270

husband died of cholera. His real name was Curtis Westcott and he taught chemistry. I made up the name Mrs. Curtis Blake. Want to know how I came up with that? Six months pregnant, on the train back home from Waterville, I saw an advertisement in a magazine for Mrs. Blake's All-Purpose Tonic."

"Brilliant!"

"But it's a lie and I've lived it all my life."

"What else could you do? Give the baby away?"

"Oh, that would have been fine with Sammy's father. He didn't care about the baby. He just wanted me to keep quiet so it wouldn't cause a scandal at the college."

"There's nothing to be ashamed of, Cora. You believed this guy. You were young. How could you know?"

"But I'm not who I say I am, and thank God nobody in town found out the truth. They all believed that Curtis died of cholera. In a way, I killed him. I never told Sammy—that's what I feel the worst about. If Sammy had lived longer, he might have gotten to meet his father and decide things for himself—I don't know—but you see, it's my fault that he never had the choice."

"From what you say," Reed answered, "there was nothing to be gained from Sammy's knowing that his father was a louse."

Cora looked at him curiously. She had just

entrusted her deepest secret, without hesitation, to a perfect stranger. Well, he had already come to her rescue once. She thought about what Reed had jokingly said about a false identity. If "Mrs. Blake" was a disguise, what had been underneath all this time? It struck her deeply that if she wanted to, she could discard that mask, unlike her heartrending companion. They rested peacefully for a moment.

"Look at those flowers!" she exclaimed, pointing to the banks of yellow and orange zinnias, light and dark purple morning glories, black-eyed Susans, and geraniums that encircled a fountain.

"Which do you like best?"

"All, except for the geraniums," she answered finally.

"Why pick on poor geraniums?"

"The day before I had to take the train to New York City, I was walking to the neighbor's, my friend Elizabeth Pascoe, just outside the village, to buy some sausage. It was a fair day and I was thinking, *I should be happy*."

"You *should* be happy?"

"I was going to see my boy."

He said nothing.

"There's a patch of red geraniums by the side of the road, growing wild. Have you ever noticed that geraniums smell like they're dying?"

"No."

"They smell like turpentine."

Reed did not point out that the sense of smell was something he'd lost a lifetime ago.

"They smell like heat and dying. I always take the road past the graveyard. Why do I do that, when I could just as well go the other way? You know, the pastor said if I really loved my boy, I would be glad that he was dead. I should give his clothes to the poor, and be thankful that God had taken Sammy into Himself." She waited. "It's shameful, but I think that's a lot of bunk."

"I bet a lot of people feel that way but nobody has the guts to say it."

"Still, it's right for the country."

"That you're here?"

She nodded and stood up, stiff from sitting in the low-slung chair and the cooling down of the day.

"I should get back to the hotel."

He offered to accompany her and they started back on the long gravel path.

"What do you write for the newspaper?"

"I don't write anymore. I used to fix other people's stories, but the paper closed."

"You could still write."

He tapped his metal cheek. "Subjects don't like to talk to me."

She laughed. "I guess I'm the big exception, shooting my mouth off."

He didn't answer, but she could feel the strength

of understanding that seemed to come off his body.

"I've never told anybody the truth about Curtis. Not even my sweetheart at home."

"Ah," he said. "You have a sweetheart."

"You're surprised?"

"Not at all. I would be surprised if you didn't."

"His name is Linwood Moody."

"Rest assured, I won't tell Linwood. What does he do?"

"He teaches geology. He does soil surveys for the government."

Reed stopped in the middle of the path and took both her hands.

"I'm very happy for you, Cora." His touch was warm and sincere. "Maybe there is some happiness in the world."

"There is." She swallowed hard. "There can be."

They squeezed hands and then let go.

"You know what I'm thinking?" he asked as they walked on.

She dabbed the corner of her eye. She wished that he could have some happiness. "No. What?"

Reed pretended not to notice. "I'm thinking there's a good story here. Yours and Sammy's. You coming to France."

"Oh, come on, there's nothing special about it. There were four hundred ladies on that ship." She sniffed and gave a sideways glance. "Why? You think there is?"

"I'm not going to hustle you like that jerk in the hotel."

"I never thanked you properly for that."

"Not necessary."

"If you were going to write something," she ventured, ". . . what would it be?"

"Well, I'd have to know more about you and Sämmy. That's the story. A mother. A son. A war. Universal."

"Go on," she said impulsively. "Get out that little book."

Now he seemed to reverse direction, almost apologetic. "I might not get anyone to print the thing—"

"I don't care."

"Why?" he asked meaningfully. "You might not like a word I write."

"It doesn't matter," she said. "I want to tell you. I don't know why."

They walked through the park and continued along Boulevard Saint Michel, the words freely bubbling out, about how Sammy had joined the army after his grandfather died, the prayer she repeated several times a day while he was overseas, neighbors who helped with the farm work, the shameful wish that somewhere along the line she'd had another baby. The writer listened, the notebook filled up, and Cora could feel something lift, as if she'd tossed that thorny secret over her shoulder, left it to the pond and the flower beds and the bittersweet afternoon light.

When they reached the hotel, she and Griffin Reed said goodbye, shook hands, and wished each other well, both of them satisfied that an exchange had been made that was of lasting consequence. Later she would mark that moment, when they passed through the gold-kissed gates of the Luxembourg Gardens and she trusted him enough to tell her story, as the one that changed her life.

VERDUN

14

The road out of Paris followed the river, close to the tree-lined quays where early morning strollers were walking dogs not much bigger than their purses. The Seine was the color of cold green marble, as sluggish as the barges that moved so slowly they barely broke the surface. Hammond watched with mounting anxiety until they reached their first landmark, the Vélodrome de Vincennes, where the cycling track for the 1924 Summer Olympics had been built. He checked his watch.

"Right on time," he told Lily, who was beside him, up front near the driver. Party A took up two more rows, and beyond that it was a full house, with every seat taken by other pilgrims wearing their summer dresses and hats, chattering away beneath an invisible cloud of face powder.

"At this rate, including a rest stop at Montmirail and lunch, we should get to Verdun exactly on time. We'd better, or General Perkins will bust my buns. He always meets the buses himself." He sighed. "This is like transporting a division."

"Good practice," Lily murmured. She was deeply into her paperwork, filling out the health forms from yesterday.

"Right, if you had to move an army to India."

After the incident at Notre-Dame, formality

between them had given way to comradely accord, and they rested their feet together on Hammond's banjo case, which lay on the floor of the bus, writing in the leather folders open on their laps, like two industrious college students.

"What are you putting down about the departure this morning?" he asked, peering at her notes.

Lily read out loud: " *'The pilgrims were cooperative and alert. Mrs. Seibert requested an anti-nausea tablet for the bus. Then Mrs. Russell wanted one also.'* "

"Did you give it to them?"

"No, I said once we were on the bus, we'd see how they felt."

"Be sure to put that in the report."

"Why?"

"So nobody thinks you weren't on the ball."

Lily looked down at the page, still puzzled. "Why would they think that?"

"In case Mrs. S and Mrs. R heave all over Mrs. Q and you get blamed for not giving them the pills."

"Oh, Thomas—" Lily began in protest.

"You have to protect your ass, excuse my French. It's the name of the game in the army. Anyway, nobody's going to get sick. The road is straight as an arrow."

He stared out the window. The bus rolled under bridges and through an industrial sector until the houses thinned away and they were miles from

Paris, traveling due east. They passed through acres of combed green flatland, then another stone church identical to the last, presiding over the same-looking clusters of red-roofed houses.

"Hard to believe it," he mused. "What my father went through. What this must have looked like after the Battle of Verdun. I mean, literally, it was a bloodbath, hundreds of thousands of French casualties. God knows what he saw, whatever was left after the trench rats had their fill, it must have been an open graveyard—like Halloween for real—do you know, after a while the French just piled all the bones together and buried them in a huge ossuary? That would be something to see. Luckily the Americans didn't have to do anything like that, we had the luxury so to speak of individual burials, well, because we scarcely lost as many as our allies—"

"Thomas." Lily had to repeat his name to stop the excited flow of words. "Why did you ever go to West Point?"

"Following my father. Why not? He graduated with MacArthur in 1905, became a colonel, won the Distinguished Service Award from the army, and now he's just been appointed a commissioner of New York City. You can go anywhere from the academy. It gives you an enormous boost. I remember my dad showing me his gas mask and it was so exciting and strange, I thought the army must have sent him to outer space."

"I don't see why anyone would *want* to fight a war."

"Because our generation can do it better," Hammond answered without hesitation. "And the signs are that it will happen again. There are four million unemployed in Germany right now, and by all accounts the republic is heading into a bank failure—meanwhile, the Nazi Party keeps creeping up in the vote. Europe is ripe for fascism; no matter what the isolationists say, the U.S. Army has to be ready. You understand—you're just like me. Strong moral fiber—"

"Gosh, what a compliment!"

"Come on, I bet you wouldn't ask anyone to do what you wouldn't do, right?"

"Like what?"

Hammond considered the question. "What's the worst thing you ever had to do as a nurse?"

"I'd say walking into a tenement where a family of seven was living in one room, all with active tuberculosis, two corpses in the middle of piles of trash, one of them a six-month-old baby."

"But you stayed and treated them."

"I stayed and treated them. But that wasn't the worst—"

In his enthusiasm Hammond cut her off: "You see, that's why if you believe in democracy, you have to fight for it. More than that, my father always said, it's the responsibility of the more educated to be leaders of men. I mean this"—he gestured around the bus bumping along with its cargo of pilgrims—"this is a sacred honor. But it's also an opportunity to prove that I can get it done—whatever's needed. Ask me, I'll do it. That's the stuff that makes an officer, you get it? We leave on time, we arrive on time. We make every stop on the schedule. I will see to the comfort and safety of these ladies with the same commitment"—his fingers curled into a fist—"as you would leading troops on a march. That's what I mean by covering your ass."

Hammond was almost breathless when he finished and the color was high in his cheeks. His hair was all glossy black tufts from the number of times he'd exasperatedly run his fingers through it, struggling to explain.

"And I suppose I can't help thinking, given the way the world is going, it could turn out that one day some bright young lieutenant right out of West Point might be accompanying my own mother." His voice shook slightly. "On this same pilgrimage."

Lily's smile was filled with light and pity. How much she wanted to protect him then. "Okay, Thomas, you've convinced me," she said. "I'll put it in that I didn't give them the pills, *sheesh!*"

"You're welcome," Hammond said, and they went back to their reports, unaware that in the rows behind them, morale was fracturing among the troops.

Bobbie was reading *Le Figaro*, Cora beside her in the window seat with the tartan travel bag on her lap like a comforting pet. She'd put the Willa Cather novel away in order to study the farmland. It was different from Maine's. Hugely open, not bounded by wood lots. They made hay into round jelly rolls here, not square bales. They had bone-white cows. You didn't see a soul, maybe a lone bicyclist, and Cora imagined that unlike Big Ole Uncle Percy clawing between clotheslines of perpetually damp laundry for a drunken pee off the rocks, French country life was as spick-and-span as the brick-lined streets of their perfect little towns.

Across the aisle, Minnie and Katie were arguing over how to cook a chicken.

"First you fry the bacon—" Katie was saying.

"For boiled chicken, are you crazy? A little water, a carrot maybe for color," Minnie said. "Unless you don't have such a good bird," she sniffed.

"Don't make no difference," Katie replied tartly. "Any chicken will improve itself when it's stewed with bacon and a good cup of Guinness."

"I always cook my chicken naked," Minnie declared.

Wilhelmina, sitting alone, turned in her seat, alarmed. "Don't you wear an apron?"

Nobody reacted. They were used to Wilhelmina's eccentric view of things. Bobbie put her newspaper down and joined in.

"My son, Henry, loved my orange tea cake. When he was in medical school, I sent it to him every week."

Bobbie's intrusion brought the argument to a halt. Immediately the debaters dropped their positions and realigned—Katie and Minnie, with occasionally Wilhelmina dragged along, against Bobbie and Cora—a split in loyalties that had been widening since those two had gone off on their own in Paris.

"Whose cake was it again?" Katie asked.

"My aunt's recipe. Who knows where it came from?"

"Probably the help," Katie said, and Minnie nodded.

Cora gave up her view through the window and leaned toward the discussion. "What's the difference where the recipe came from as long as the darn cake got to France?"

"If Mrs. McConnell is going to make Mrs. Olsen's orange tea cake," Wilhelmina explained patiently, "she will need the recipe."

"Mrs. Olsen didn't make the cake," Katie corrected her. "I guarantee. Her kitchen maid made the cake. That's the heart of the matter."

"Not everybody has to be a baker," Cora said.

Bobbie laid a hand on hers. "Let it go, dear."

"Sure, if it doesn't please ya, drop it," Katie said.

"You've got that right, Mrs. McConnell,"

Bobbie said, switching to the vernacular with an edge. "I did not *whip up* that cake. But Henry loved it anyway. Does that clear the air?"

"Not entirely, if you want to know the truth."

"What are you up to, Katie?" Cora asked. "I thought we all were friends."

"Until you two go gallivanting off."

"When was this?"

"Yesterday. While the rest of us were at the Arc of Triumph, along with the French mothers. They put on a very pretty ceremony, but you took it upon yourselves to skip it."

At the memory of her walk in the Luxembourg Gardens with Griffin Reed, Cora's face reddened. At the time she'd forgotten all about the ceremony, an explanation that hardly mattered now.

"I . . . was just too tired," she said lamely.

"And then her ladyship arrives late, like the queen of England."

"We were embarrassed on behalf of America," Minnie quietly agreed.

"They're nutso," Wilhelmina told Cora. "Don't listen to them."

Bobbie pinched the inside of her wrists in order to distract herself from making a rude remark, a skill she'd been taught in boarding school.

"Mrs. McConnell, you're going way too far. I know you lost two boys, and I'm very sorry if it makes things harder for you—"

"That has nothing to do with it! We're here to bring honor to each and every soldier," Katie went on. "Not to go traipsing about on our own whenever we like. The rest of us ordinary types were there."

Cora took a breath. All the way to the back of the bus, the forty or so other pilgrims were chatting contentedly, and up front, Hammond was unpacking his banjo. They were due for a rest stop any minute. She sensed that one quick move could snap Party A back into place like a dislocated shoulder. It would require the same manipulation she used when her three nieces started to argue and fuss: put the enemies together.

She stood up and stepped over Bobbie.

"Let's switch seats," she said to Minnie, standing over her in the aisle. "You go next to Mrs. Olsen and I'll sit with Mrs. McConnell and then nobody will feel left out."

"What about me?" Wilhelmina asked.

"Shhh!" hissed Bobbie, at her wit's end. "Listen to the song!"

Lieutenant Hammond was strolling down the aisle, playing show tunes to appreciative smiles. In the flurry of confusion, Cora was able to get Minnie to switch seats, which set the thing at rest for the moment. The pilgrims from other parties were already singing along with the lighthearted lyrics: *"Sweetheart, sweetheart, will you love me forever? Will you remember the day? When we were happy in May?"* as if to erase the language that had rent their hearts: *"Killed in battle." "On detail and later found dead."* But the dark days were done. It was all sorted. What the army had destroyed it had now put in order, in neat rows in a field of honor. Soon they would be with their sons. Until then they could rest at ease in each other's company and the headlong forward motion of the bus.

As they drove through the village of Meaux, the sun came out, warming a layer of rippled clouds. They passed the little town of La Ferté-sous-Jouarre, where every window had a lace curtain, and made the Montmirail rest stop at exactly 10:00 a.m., arriving at the city of Chalons-sur-Marne at 1:00 p.m. for a luncheon of *consommé à la royale*, olives, salted almonds and celery, potatoes Brabant, Brussels sprouts, supreme of chicken, mushrooms à la Sabine, Canton sherbet, Parisian sweets, crackers, cheese, and café noir, in the dining room of a large white hotel with cheerful striped canopies over the windows.

Not surprisingly, most of the pilgrims dozed through the rest of the trip, but Cora was alert, as if a tiny motor had been triggered inside, wound up with a key like a mantelpiece clock. It was thinking about Griffin Reed. He'd started something and now it was going all by itself. She noticed that the landscape was changing again. Red poppies were showing up in the weeds. The fields were wheat-colored and flat, the way Cora imagined California to be—a blank landscape with an ocean out there somewhere. The way Reed had talked about his hometown, it was sunny all the time and everyone had an orange tree and lived in the desert, where they were scalded into madness by their own greed, which made California sound like a Bible tale with a moral no one could explain. His father had passed on, but his mother still lived on the ranch where he'd grown up, in what they called the Central Valley, possibly another scriptural reference. Reed hadn't been back since before the war. The last his mother knew, he was working for an American newspaper living the expat life in the lively cafés of Paris—happy, and doing exactly what he loved.

It was almost uncanny how well they'd gotten along. They talked—well, she talked and he took notes—all the way back to the hotel. When he spoke it was like a gentleman, in a measured voice, in long effortless streams of thought that she found mesmerizingly close to the manner of her professors at college, who had made her feel eager and bright, worthy of their interest. How did Griffin see her? Was she more than an ordinary person trying to raise three girls and make ends meet? Was she actually, in some way, up to his standard? Equal to Florence Dean Powell?

He did leave Florence's house to follow her. There must have been a reason. Was it only to get her story and get his career back on track? He liked Cora's plainspokenness, she could tell. Didn't he say that she could "cut to the bone"? Maybe he was tired of Florence's demands. Anyone would be. She was by far the vainest woman Cora had ever met, looking into every mirror she passed—and there were several big heavy mirrors in that house, which Griffin avoided. You could see they made him squirm, so why not take them down? Because she'd saved his life—and wanted him never to forget. Cora had the terrifying idea of pushing Florence down the stairs!

To calm herself, she thought of Linwood. Good, reliable Linwood. Linwood didn't bother with things he couldn't touch or see. He was content. He enjoyed the regularity of his working days, filling in the colored areas on his maps. He was the kind of person you'd ask to join a card game—easy to talk to at a church supper or social affair. Big and reliable. Not thin and driven, like Griffin Reed, with that strange magnetism, a languorous mix of sadness and desire. That was it about Reed, she thought, summoning up what she remembered from a long-ago class in English poetry—he was a romantic. Linwood was a pragmatist. He'd spent an entire summer building a wooden tower in the middle of the forest, just for the doing of it, so he could haul himself up there once in a blue moon and look over the tops of the trees. What a waste of wood! But that's what some men do, she thought: they spend a lot of time and effort in the hope of getting above themselves.

"Ladies!" Hammond announced with a flourish of banjo chords. "We will arrive at our destination in exactly fifteen minutes!"

The peasants walking beside the road sensed the bus behind them. Maybe it was the female chorus of "Over There" coming through the open windows that alerted them, because from the way they stumbled indecisively in their late afternoon march back from the vineyards, they seemed to have heard the English words before and knew their meaning. *The Yanks are coming, / The drums rum-tumming everywhere . . ."* The men stopped and removed their caps. The boys pulled handfuls of Queen Anne's lace from the weeds, tossing them at the bus flashing by, cheering as they hit. The adults stood at attention. *"We're coming over, / And we won't come back till it's over over there!"* The flowers blew back in a wash of rubber-scented air. The animated faces of the American women and those of the solemn, weather-beaten men met, eclipsed, and passed.

Inside the bus, the banjo music carried them with a feeling of triumph to St. Paul's Gate, a massive stone archway topped with battlements that looked like a piece broken off a castle. It marked the official entrance to the city of Verdun.

But the anticipation of arriving at a charming river town lasted only as long as it took to sweep beneath the arch. Instantly they were inside a war zone, hardly changed since the battle of 1916. The raw, unreconstructed ruins of the city were a shock that broke off the young lieutenant's song and made the busload of women gasp audibly.

Monumental walls of salmon-colored limestone blocks were all that remained on a street of bombarded buildings, standing in a row like gargantuan books of stone with the pages ripped from their spines, the knowledge they once held in wasted rubble at their feet. There were some cheap newer structures in the German style, half-timbered with brown tile roofs that stood out in the damage like bandages on a wound. The buses made their way down to a residential section near the river that had largely been spared, except for perilous cracks in some of the steeply pitched roofs. The medium-sized Hôtel Nouvel, where they were staying, had survived intact on a brick-laid street of three-story row houses with frayed shutters. Destruction was so widespread that the undamaged buildings looked out of place, as if they were really stone façades behind which the rooms would be exposed to the sky, skeletal and abandoned.

The front door to the hotel opened and General Perkins stepped out, startlingly alive against this dreary backdrop. He wore a peaked hat, riding breeches, and an olive tunic with bars on the chest and gold on the shoulders. His boots and belt were as polished as the tack on a champion dressage horse, and he held himself tall, collected, and alert. All in all, a stallion.

Hammond hurried up the steps and saluted.

"Lieutenant Hammond, sir. Liaison officer of Party A."

"Fine job, Lieutenant. Right on time."

"Thank you, sir."

"Everything all right?" he asked. "Nobody sick on the bus?"

"No sir. Everybody's fine thanks to Nurse Barnett," he said generously.

Perkins peered down at Lily, who was waiting at the bottom of the stairs to lead their party into the hotel, looking like an innocent out of a modern fairy tale, strawberry-blond curls falling on the shoulders of the navy cape, a pure white dress.

"That nurse must be you," he said.

"Second Lieutenant Barnett," she said. "An honor to meet you, sir."

Since she was not commissioned, she was not required to salute.

"Keep up the good work."

"Yes, sir, I'll do my best."

The tired crow's-feet around the eyes and windswept creases in his cheeks attested to the gravity of his duties. He was a soldier through and through, not a figurehead for show; you knew he'd been in the crux of war, the real bloody, awful thing. It was awe-inspiring and a little bit scary just to be standing close.

"Let's move this along," Perkins said.

Hammond stepped to. "Right away, sir."

As the pilgrims filed into the hotel he stood erect and shook the hand of each and every one, looking into her eyes and asking where she was from and where her son had served. Each loss was his loss. And he meant it.

The hotel owners, a family originally from Germany, had tried to pump some life into the enterprise by transforming it into a pretentious Normandy castle. They'd put in a false beams-and-stucco ceiling with a heavy iron candelabra. Flickering electric torches cast yellowish figures on the fake stone walls. There was a huge walk-in fireplace with long-handled copper pans hanging off the mantel. Ornate wood-carved chests, heavy as frigates, were tucked into every corner.

"Isn't this attractive!" Bobbie exclaimed, to head off any accusations of snobbism.

"I'm pleased just to be off that bus," Katie remarked.

"So am I," Bobbie agreed, sinking into the closest armchair.

"Are you all right?" Cora asked.

"Just catching my breath."

"Should I get the nurse?"

"No need. I'm ready for a whiskey," she said, patting her chest.

The lobby was filling quickly with American women and their luggage as pilgrims streamed off the buses parked in special spots outside. The owner of the hotel was a scowling older man with some kind of a disfiguring disease that had crippled his fingers. He sat in a wheelchair behind the desk, giving orders to his middle-aged son, who wore a beard and a breezy attitude, ignoring his father's constant harangue. The owner's wife cowered near the cash drawer, afraid of him, but you could tell she was mean to the penny. Hammond was arguing with the older man in French.

"What's he saying?" Lily asked.

"He claims to have only four rooms available, although the reservation for Party A clearly states seven," said Hammond, glancing fearfully at the door. "Perkins will have my nuts."

"Don't worry," Lily replied calmly. "The general is still outside, meeting and greeting."

"He's trying to gouge us. You watch, Perkins will come in and miraculously he'll have seven. 'But it'll cost, monsieur—'"

"Pooh on that," Lily said. "Here's what we'll do. We'll take the four rooms and double up the mothers. I'll bunk with Mrs. Russell."

"You don't mind?"

"I can handle her," Lily said.

Hammond felt a rush of gratitude that Lily could be so practical and would have told her so, except at that moment Perkins did enter the foyer, causing a stir of interest among the women waiting for their rooms.

"Meet you here," Hammond said in an urgent whisper. "In the lobby. After they're asleep."

"Later, alligator," Lily promised.

Hammond's eyes rose over her head. "Oh good Lord," he murmured, as Wilhelmina Russell walked up to him with a wide, vacuous smile, a scarlet parrot perched on her wrist. She looked quite rumpled, as she'd refused to wear anything but the pink blouse she'd had on since New York.

"Isn't he magnificent?" Wilhelmina said. "He was sitting there in the parlor, all alone."

"Isn't it nice you've made a friend?"

"Oh, I knew him the moment I saw him. I said, Bradley?"

Hammond peered at the black eye-disks of the parrot, roving around as if looking for the answers to many questions.

"Your son, Bradley?"

"Yes," Mrs. Russell said. "I'm certain it's him. But don't tell anyone, they'll never believe it."

"Of course they will," Hammond assured her kindly.

Finally a maid came to take Cora and Bobbie to their room. The maid offered to help Bobbie out of the chair, but she waved her off.

"Don't get old," she advised.

"You're not old," Cora said as they left the lobby. "Walter Conary is old. He's ninety-two and lives in North Deer Isle. He cuts trees off his wood lot and just dug his own well. Imagine that. Digs a well at ninety-two."

"That's what you call optimism," Bobbie said, with a throaty laugh.

The maid guiding them was a stick-thin twig of a girl in a uniform that would have fit a nine-year-old. All three made it into an elevator built for two. Cora wondered if she was part of the wretched family that owned the place, because she kept slavishly tidying up along the way, making sure the linen closet was locked, collecting stray newspapers under her arm, all the time chatting it up with Bobbie in French, as they made their way down an endless corridor to the last room, which had a big metal key in the middle of the door.

It was airless and smelled like someone had left cheese rinds under the beds. The maid checked the towels and tugged at the window. It wouldn't open. She fussed with it, gave up, and left. There were two single white iron beds covered with cotton lace spreads, a desk and a chair, and a skinny white dressing table with a mirror. The wallpaper had narrow stripes and the carpeting a geometric pattern that repeated itself tediously, not unlike some of their companions, Bobbie thought. When they sat on the beds, the mattresses caved in under them.

"We could transfer to a better hotel," Bobbie said. "But I wouldn't want to start a class war. I hope I don't offend you, too."

"I don't get offended. I get mad, but being offended? Not worth the trouble. You've been very nice to me from the start, when you first wrote those letters. You were the first person who really understood what I went through. As far as the others—you just have to brush it off."

"Thank you for saying that, Cora. I've always believed in being who I am. When I work with the poor, I make it a point to wear my jewels. *They* are who *they* are; why should I pretend? It only makes everyone uncomfortable." She lay down on top of the coverlet and the springs squeaked. "I'm too tired to take off my shoes."

Cora yawned. "When is dinner?"

"Seven-thirty. But you and I are going down for that drink as soon as humanly possible. Did you see that terrible man at the desk?"

"What happened to him?" Cora asked, lying back on a lumpy pillow that smelled of hair oil. "Was it a stroke?"

"They say that man and his wife were collaborators during the war."

"What do you mean?"

"You realize that we are very close to Germany? Just twenty miles to the border, which is why the

Germans and the French have historically fought over this place. Really it was for the coal deposits. They each claimed the land was theirs, all the way back to ancient times. There are a lot of native Germans here; a large German influence. This couple who own the hotel, the Bachmanns, they lived in Verdun and they had a shop. He was a watchmaker."

"With those hands?"

"Well, that's *exactly* the story. Verdun was a crucial objective for the Germans. If the Germans took Verdun, it would have had a very dispiriting effect on the French—and England might have just given up the war and gone home. The rumor is the Bachmanns were sending secret information to the German high command."

"How?"

"They hid a telegraph machine in the back room. It was inside a case that looked like a clock."

"How do you know?"

"That little maid told me. She doesn't like her employers, that much is obvious. When the watchmaker was discovered, he was tortured by the French army. To make sure he never did it again, they broke his hands."

"Is it true?"

"Why not?"

"It makes you sick," Cora said. "The whole thing. Makes you feel sick to your stomach."

Bobbie hadn't moved. She was still wearing her plum-colored travel suit and pearls.

"We'll be home soon," she sighed.

Cora's spirit of adventure had faded to a low point. The tense bus ride and now this dreary room had briefly extinguished the joy of anticipation, which is the traveler's spark.

"I wish I were home right now."

"And what would you be doing, Cora dear?"

"Cooking supper. Turning ice cream. The girls love ice cream on a summer night. Except I forgot—we're out of sugar."

Both were quiet, looking up at a silent ceiling fan. It was still very bright outside. Evening would come late.

"They were such a great distance from home," Cora said at last.

"But, you know, at the time, nothing seemed more natural. It was a noble thing to go over there and help our friends fight the Germans . . . And I naïvely believed that because Henry was a doctor, he would be safe. I believed a lot of things that weren't right—like sending him away to boarding school. It was 'what one did.' Henry was so bright, I was pompous enough to think there wasn't a school in Boston that was good enough. But you know what? He would have become a doctor anyway. Looking back, what was the point of missing all those years with him?"

Cora thought of all the missing years with

Sammy and hoped Bobbie didn't see the tears coursing down her cheeks. She flattened them with the palm of a hand.

"I've never seen such a depressing town," her companion said at last. "You'd think they'd have fixed it up by now. Or at least, for God's sake, please drive the buses around in some other direction. Seeing the results of a bomb barrage does not make a very good first impression. I'm going to talk to the general about it. He seems to be an intelligent man." She swung her legs off the bed and straightened her pearls. "Promise that you'll come and stay with me at the Gilley House," she said briskly. "We're not going to allow this wonderful friendship to slip off into oblivion when we get back home, like so many things. Agreed?"

After distributing the medication on her last round of the night, Lily came down to the lobby to wait for Hammond. She'd brushed her hair into soft waves and changed into a raspberry-colored polka-dot dress with a narrow belt. It was a little after 9:30 and she could hear music coming from the street through the open door of the hotel. She drifted into the doorway. She was in the mood for fun, and by night Verdun looked much more inviting. Where there were no lights, there was inky blackness that erased the ruins; and where there were lights, there was excitement.

She took a few steps in the direction of the music. They weren't officially given time off, so they'd just have to steal it. She was looking forward to getting a little tipsy in a waterside café. She'd go there with Thomas Hammond. They'd smoke and drink but nothing would happen because she was in love with David Sawyers, M.D., who at this moment was probably on afternoon rounds in the acute cases nursery of Chicago's Presbyterian Hospital. Her nursing friends always teased her about how lucky she'd be to marry a pediatrician because he'd know how to make babies, and that they'd better save up, because any kid that came from a doctor and a nurse would be doomed to go into medicine. But she would have to quit nursing if she married David, and the picture of caring for a yowling newborn while he was gone working long hours was unsettling. Alone in the lamp-lit street, balancing in heels between the cracks of the bricks, she felt the spookiness of Verdun sink into her skin, and she had the strong feeling that deep down she did not know where she belonged. Serving the down-and-out neighborhoods of Chicago, where she was useful and free? Engaged to a doctor so that she felt protected? Halfway around the world, pretending to know what to say to these dear old ladies who were stuck in the past? God, she needed David right now. She could always talk to him. He was just two years older, but taking care of desperately ill children had given him a shrewd outlook on things.

"Nurse Lily? Could that be you?"

Underneath the lighted canopy of a neighborhood market, in between wooden cartons of produce and flowers, a couple of small tables were set out where local couples could take coffee and pastries. There was General Perkins, alone with a cigar and a bottle of wine for company.

"Lieutenant Barnett!" He waved her over. He still wore the riding boots he'd had on at dinner but the tunic was unbuttoned at the neck. "Lovely dress." His eyes moved over her. "A damn sight better than a service uniform."

"Thank you, sir."

He got to his feet. "You know we are in the region of Champagne? Will you join me? I mean, not here. We'll find someplace suitable. And oysters, if they have them."

"I'm meeting Lieutenant Hammond."

Perkins looked across the street at the hotel. "Then where the hell is he?"

"I'm early," she lied.

"Let's take a walk." He placed her arm in his. "Don't worry, I'll have you back. Just to see the Meuse River. Have you seen the Meuse River?"

She realized he was slightly drunk.

"Let's just sit." She pulled back toward the table. "That way when Thomas comes, we won't miss him—"

"Who? Oh, Colonel Hammond's son. Well, in that case we'll be discreet," he said, with a nudge. "Come along, you need the fresh air."

Intimidated, she allowed him to lead her down to the water. He told her stories about growing up on a tobacco farm and his first days as an officer in the Philippines. Five minutes, she decided, and looked at her watch to be sure. There was no clear way to the river. Where the road quit and the streetlights faded was an impassable field of debris left over from the shelling. Gnarled pieces of iron, piles of splintered wood, whole planks and window frames, railings and hunks of concrete. Beyond it was a black ribbon of water, and on the other shore, the looming outlines of dozens of bombed-out homes, their faces ripped off to expose empty floors, guts kicked out and spilling down the embankment. Fragments of signs could be seen in the shadows—*"Maison des Plumes" ". . . des Gants"*—more terrifying than the rubble they had seen by daylight because the brokenness had become part of the night and the vastness.

"I hope the mothers don't see this."

"They should know what their sons died for. You'd better get used to it if you want to be an army nurse."

"I have no intention of becoming an army nurse," Lily told him. She'd started to shiver. Five minutes were up. "I need to go. Tomorrow at the

304

cemetery is going to be trying. I hardly know what to say to them."

"Not up to the challenge?" He flicked the remains of the cigar into the dark.

"I don't see how what I say can change anything. Or, for that matter, how it will help them to travel all this way just to look at a marker in the middle of nowhere."

"Have you ever lost someone?"

"Just my dog."

"You're right. You're way too young for this. But so were their boys." He'd dropped her hand. He was sober now. "Look, if we hadn't been in this war, Europe would have fallen. If it weren't for the bravery of the American soldier, this is what the whole piss-soaked continent would have looked like. Those mothers know it, and they're proud as hell that their boys knew how to fight. You don't have to say a damn thing."

"I'm sorry—" Lily felt small and close to tears. "I just don't know where I fit in all of it, and if—"

"It doesn't mean a goddamned thing," Perkins interrupted. "Right at this moment, all you need to know is you're alive. We're here and we're alive. If there's one thing I learned on the battlefield, it's that we must never waste a moment of life, because it will be gone. Like that."

He pulled her strongly to him and covered her mouth with his and kissed her deeply. No hesitation, no retreat. The first taste was inviting and her body wanted more, but almost instantaneously she thought, *This can't happen,* and froze, trapped by the ironlike tendons in his arms, holding her so close she couldn't move. She pushed against him until he released his grip, and swayed backward from the shock of having been so electrifyingly overwhelmed.

"Stop it," she gasped.

He took her face in both his hands and gazed at her in the poor reflected light.

"You're very pretty, you know."

She looked into his eyes, afraid. "I have to go."

"Lieutenant!" he said gently. "Don't be shy, it's okay. Are you a virgin?"

"None of your business," she shot back despite the tremble in her voice. "Are you married?"

"Of course. I have four daughters. Which is why you're right and you should go back to your Lieutenant Hammond," he said, releasing her.

"I'm only meeting him for a drink," Lily replied, adding defensively, "Lieutenant Hammond is a fellow officer. I'm engaged to a doctor back home."

"Best of luck," Perkins said dryly.

They walked up the street, side by side, his hands in his pockets. His mood shifted, and she hoped she was safely out of the woods.

"You're not like these women, Lieutenant. Don't let them depress you. They're through, and you're just starting out. You're a ball of fire and men like pretty girls. You should use what you've got."

"Use it, how?" She wondered if by some trick of fate this commander, with all his worldly experience, might know the answer to the questions she'd been asking about her future.

He laughed. "It's how you live your life. The trick is being on the spot. When the need arises, the real warrior does what needs to be done. He acts cleanly, and never quits. He always moves forward, never just holds his position. He's ruthless, and he's a son of a bitch, but in the end, his actions benefit the kingdom."

"I have no idea what you're talking about."

"Who gives a shit? I have to leave for Paris tomorrow. But you'll be back there in a few days, and all of this will be behind you. Your first tour of duty. Mission accomplished, won't that be great?"

He was so changeable, she thought it best to agree.

"Yes, it will."

They were almost at the hotel. Perkins left her with a nod and walked into a pool of darkness, leaving her stranded. Thomas Hammond would be waiting. They'd gossip about Party A. Who had a headache and who was catty about whom? What was the schedule for tomorrow? They'd talk about where to go for a drink. Hammond wouldn't have any money, so they'd end up at one of the tables at the neighborhood vegetable market, drinking cheap wine and straining to hear the music coming from the farther banks of the river at a café neither of them could afford, and all of that would be a relief.

"Where were you?" Hammond asked when Lily came into the lobby. Two women from another party were eyeing her suspiciously, as if she were a trollop off the street.

She had no intention of telling him what had just happened. "Just taking a walk."

"I was about to give up."

"Sorry. I needed the air."

"You look nice."

"Thanks."

"I'll be done in a jiff."

She saw his reports laid out on a coffee table. Hammond was perfect for the army. He would always do the right thing.

"I'm just making a note that Mrs. Seibert had another argument with Mrs. McConnell, and that Mrs. Russell believes her son came back as a parrot," Hammond was saying. "I love them enormously, but honestly, sometimes it's hard to keep a straight face."

Lily barely heard him, suddenly exhausted.

"Should I put the parrot in the report?" he asked.

"Let it rest," she said distractedly.

"You're right. Next she'll say he came back as that armchair."

"Thomas," she said. "Tomorrow's going to be a big day."

"Feeling pooped?"

She nodded.

"Shame to waste that dress."

"It's not going anywhere. Will you give me a rain check?"

Thomas really was a sweet kid. Almost like a brother, like the boys she knew in high school.

"Of course," he said. "Another time."

She gave him a tired smile and left. A few minutes later, when the general came into the lobby smoking a fresh cigar, Hammond was still writing in his diary.

"Burning the midnight oil, Lieutenant?"

"All this paperwork." He shrugged.

"I'm going back to Paris in the morning. But I'll be reading your reports."

"I'll try to keep them interesting. Good night, sir. Have a good drive back."

"Good night."

Perkins retrieved his room key from the night clerk. Shoulders squared, he chugged up the stairs alone.

15

Griffin Reed stayed home, barefoot and in his pajamas. When he was writing he never needed to pass beyond the white walls of the garden. He barely saw anything around him; his mind chased a progression of ideas that kept evaporating whenever he got close. Occasionally a phrase would emerge like a neon sign out of the mist and he'd grab for it with pen and paper, miss it completely, then toss the note aside and veer away. Soon there was a trail of notes blowing across the property, each one urgent and forgotten. He snapped at the maid not to pick anything up. He'd find himself on the floor, on the bed, staring out the window, walking down the steps to make a cup of tea, clipping leaves in the potting shed, dropping the clippers, back in the kitchen, looking at the mail. He lived in a muffled corner of his mind that was not illuminated by any kind of logic or salvation. It was like drinking laudanum without the swoon. His stomach was still upset and his appetite was down. Sometimes he'd pop a chocolate in his mouth or peel an orange.

He had been a newsman who could deliver copy as fast as the Teletype could spit it out, but since the *Tribune* had shut down, living this pampered life with Florence had clogged the works of his writing machine. He felt like a middle-aged old codger compared to the hard body he had inhabited when he first came overseas for the Associated Press. *A strong spine,* his father used to say. *You need a strong spine in life.* He knew he had something in Cora Blake's story. He needed to put into words the power that had taken hold of him.

The problem was that Cora's story was not unique. Nor was it really a story. There was no corruption to expose, no crime to make the reader cringe. There was no dramatic crisis, except for the death of Private Sammy Blake at Meuse-Argonne, and that was very old news. As he worked it in his mind, he first saw the angle as a close-up look at a victim of politics—a decent, hardworking woman who had no choice in her country going to war and claiming her only child. An ordinary tragedy.

Too ordinary. Too often told. For a newspaper-man, there was never doubt. The hook was there in capital letters: THIEF STEALS LINCOLN'S HEAD. DEAD BABY FOUND ALIVE. But this was something new. He had to look inside *himself* to discover the core. What had drawn him to Cora Blake out of the crowd in the lobby of the Ambassador Hotel? Why was he so burned when Clancy Hayes tried to bully her that he punched the guy out?

Was it because the moment he saw Cora he had

wanted her—in the way he would have before the injury—watching her body move inside the too-big dress, and a virtuous profile you could carve on a cameo? Under other circumstances he would have been happy just to pursue her, to be close to her by any means. Was it because when they were together he felt like his former self; but the only way he could possess her now was in words?

His bones ached. He unhooked the mask from his ears and gently pulled where the metal stuck to his skin. He wiped it down with antiseptic, noticing more chips on the metallic lining. They hadn't gotten the results of the test for lead poisoning back yet, but in any case the English facial surgeon, Dr. Blackmore, had agreed with Dr. Szabo that it was urgent to replace the mask. Reed was to travel to London in ten days to prepare for a fitting that would require some preliminary surgery. *"Given your excellent health, even if the results on the test are positive for lead, you probably have several weeks before it begins to damage the organs, but science isn't always accurate,"* Dr. Blackmore had written. *"Best to err on the side of caution, so please make an appointment at London General Hospital as soon as possible."* The mask would be of a new material, even more lifelike, Florence said. She of course would accompany him to England and supervise the fitting. Maybe he'd choose a different expression this time, he thought. Maybe it would be the face of a snarling Chinese tiger. Reed swabbed the healed-over craters in his face, not thinking about Florence or the pounding in his head, back in the drift of his story.

It had to be Cora and her son and the things she'd told him when they walked back from the Luxembourg Gardens, freely and openly, out of kindness, or reparation to a wounded man, it didn't matter. She'd talked to Reed because nobody else would, and now he'd do what was necessary to make people give a damn. A woman's point of view was not the kind of thing newspapers generally reported. Maybe, he thought wryly, because newspapers were run by men. They assigned reporters to cover the pilgrimages, but the editors only wanted the pro forma stuff: names, hometowns, the sights they saw and how much it cost. But they never went to the core. If you went to the core, it would make readers weep.

He fitted the mask back over his ragged cheekbones and pawed through the mess on his desk until he found a small address book made of worn leather with gilt-edged pages. It listed the whereabouts of every American expat mover and shaker in Paris, from politicians to madams, and represented a decade of collecting information and knowing what to trade and with whom. He wondered what Clancy Hayes would say his little book was "worth."

His old paper was out of business, so he looked at the entry for the *International Herald Tribune*. There were three names crossed out before the current news editor's, Walter Marley. They hadn't met before, but Reed knew he was also a veteran of the Associated Press, with a quick mind and no patience. To snag Marley's interest, he'd have to get the story of the Gold Star Mothers down to one sentence. One phrase. Then he had it, in one word: *bravery.*

Over the phone, Marley said he'd like to have a look. He agreed the story had to run while the pilgrims were still in France, which meant in the next few days. Reed had stayed up until four in the morning writing, and by ten o'clock was on the *métro* on the way to the Champs-Élysées, where the *Herald* was headquartered. On the train he took the typewritten pages out of his portfolio but could not restrain his pencil from continuing to work them over. The story of a mother and son, separated by duty but united by courage, was rich. Maybe, if he told it well, and if Walter pushed it hard, this would turn out to be a classic in war reporting, like Kirke L. Simpson's articles on the burying of the Unknown Soldier at Arlington after the war, for which he'd won the Pulitzer Prize. Reed knew the famous quote by heart. Remembering it now, he found that the rhythm of the words seemed to match the rocking of the train:

"Under the wide and starry skies of his own homeland, America's unknown dead from France sleeps tonight, a soldier home from the wars."

He came out of the *métro* station and walked toward rue de Berri, where the paper had recently moved into a modern nine-story building. Walter Marley emerged from a wooden door in a glass-partitioned office. He was about forty, wearing a blue three-piece suit, with an old-fashioned watch fob at the vest. He had wire-rimmed glasses and was not balding gracefully. Living in Paris seemed to have had no effect on his American vulgarity. He shook Reed's hand, and then asked him to leave.

Reed held out his work.

"You're not even going to read it?"

"Nope."

"You said you wanted to see it."

"That was yesterday."

"Okay, things change—"

"Some things don't."

"This is a story readers want to hear."

"Maybe, but I ain't buying. Nice to meet you."

"Just hold on."

"We've got nothin' to talk about."

Reed studied Marley's wary eyes. He knew the type. Marley was a small man who belonged in a small town, where he could act like a big man. He was like the guy who owned the only auto repair shop for miles. If your car broke down, he'd have you by the nuts. Marley was the kind of newsman who went for headline stories, easy and quick. He had the bullishness of the news business, but not the heart. Not the feeling for its subjects.

"What's the deal?" asked Reed, not budging. "You have someone else on the story?"

"Well, I did until you cold-cocked him."

"Clancy Hayes?"

"Who do you think?"

"Since when does Hayes work for the *Herald*?"

"Since he got fired from AP."

"For what? Drunk and disorderly? When was this?"

"Couple days ago."

"He's let go from AP and you hire him? That's slick, Walter."

"I can't discuss company policy. Be a good kid and take a walk."

Reed had a finger pointing close to Marley's chest.

"Get this straight. Hayes manhandled a grief-stricken woman in order to get her to cry for a cheap photo. He was drunk and way out of line. That's the guy you hired."

"Step back, fella."

Reed did not step back. "What's your beef?"

Marley raised his chin and looked at Reed through the bottoms of his glasses. "You can't go around clocking my reporters."

"That's crap," said Reed. "You don't give a

damn about Clancy Hayes. You don't even know him. You don't know my work and you don't know me. Or is it that you just don't like my face?"

"Christ," said Marley, truly shaken, which was Reed's intent. "Look, we all feel for what you went through—And what . . . how hard . . . I'd like to help, but—"

"Come on, Walter. Spit it out."

Reed peered at him directly through the mask with luminous eyes that had seen hell, and Marley crumpled.

"Okay, I'll level with you. I was interested in what you had to say, which is why I called you in. Then I got the word to kill it—directly from New York."

Reed was confused. The *Herald Tribune* was owned by the *New York Times*, but why would they bother with a small overseas matter like hiring a local hack?

"I had to clear your story, and the New York office wasn't buying. It's not from editorial," Marley added quickly. "They know you're good."

"Yeah, yeah, I'm the best thing since sliced bread," said Reed impatiently. "So?"

"It came from the board of directors."

"I don't get it."

"It's the kid's father, okay? Gerald Hayes. Clancy's father. He's one of those East Coast movers and shakers, politically connected, on the board of the *Times*. Hell, he owns the paper's fucking bank. Clancy doesn't like you, so he poisoned the well. What can I say?"

Reed just laughed. "Not a thing, Walter. Not a thing."

"You don't deserve this—"

"Tell it to the judge," Reed said, not looking back.

As he walked out the door, Marley called after him, "Skip the wire services, too."

An hour later Reed was in the offices of the French daily *Le Matin*. They bought "An American War Mother's Story" for five francs but wouldn't pay for a translator, so he had to sit there and translate his own words himself.

At a wooden table piled with old bundled newsprint, dictating to an overeager secretary with curly black hair and body odor, he consoled himself that at least *Le Matin* was a major newspaper with national distribution in France. Tomorrow morning, office workers in Lyon would be moved to tears over their café au lait. And you had to appreciate the irony. He'd survived a hail of German bullets to be blacklisted in the English-speaking press by some little pisser who had to run to his daddy. The secretary was waiting for his golden sentences, fingertips on the keys. He had to get on with it. The piece had to run somewhere, and soon—even if it ran in French. The story possessed a certain shelf life and beyond that, it would spoil like curdled milk.

16

The morning of the visit to the cemetery, Lily was still in foggy twilight when she came down to the breakfast room, wearing her white uniform and feeling like hell. She hadn't slept all night, wrestling first with guilt about David back home and then with indignation about where things might have led with the general; whirling thoughts she couldn't contain, like moths flying out of a cupboard. She was going to die today in a thousand ways. She'd been warned by her supervisor in New York that this would be the most trying time of the tour and that the ladies were going to need all the comfort she could provide. She wished she could find some comfort herself.

To her annoyance, Hammond was as enthusiastic as ever. He had wrangled an omelette and bacon from the skinny little maid, and was loading his plate with everything on the sideboard.

"How'd you sleep?" he asked.

"Lousy."

"You turned in early."

"Didn't help."

She reached across him for a cup. The hotel's weak coffee would have to do.

"Why are you in such a good mood?" she muttered.

"I know it will be difficult for them, but frankly, between you, me, and the lamppost, I'll be tremendously relieved when we deliver the mothers to their destination. This trip has been a bear."

Lily thought about what Perkins had told her as they'd walked to the river—how he'd been put to work at the age of five stacking tobacco leaves on the family farm, won a scholarship to the University of the South, served as first lieutenant in a war she'd never heard of, thirty years ago in the Philippines. In a soft voice he described burying his first dead comrade there on the beach, and giving his first order to execute the man who'd shot him, a Filipino rebel, by a strangulation machine called a *garrote*.

"It's what they mean by *putting the screws to you.*" He'd squeezed her neck, which made her cringe with a strange thrill. "The prisoner is put in a metal collar and a screw is driven through the collar until it snaps the spine in two."

Perkins had said it as matter-of-factly as how to install a window or fix a lamp. It was simply what needed to be done. He was as unemotional about murder as David was passionate about saving lives—even embracing Lily's dream of having a farm where they'd take in unwanted animals. She was lucky to have such a wonderful man at home, and relieved that the general had left for Paris that morning. She should say five

Hail Marys in gratitude for never having to see him again.

And she should add a few for having a comrade like Thomas, reliable and true, wearing dress blues today, his clean-shaven face looking young and painfully sincere.

"What I'm really excited about," he was saying as they carried their breakfast things, "is seeing the actual places where my father fought."

The dining room was in flux as other parties came downstairs for breakfast or to board their buses. Most of their group was still at the table, except for Minnie, who had been pacing outside for over an hour, on the lookout for a bus that still wasn't due for another fifteen minutes. Katie seemed particularly pale in the washed-out way of redheads, her features melded to an exhausted flatness against the gloomy beading on the collar of her black dress.

"Did you get any rest, Mrs. McConnell?" Lily asked.

Katie shook her head. "None a'tall."

After yesterday's long bus ride from Paris, the spartan hotel room had provided no consolation for Katie and her roommate, Minnie, on the night before their climactic visit to the cemetery.

"The bed's too hard," Minnie had complained, tugging at the thin sheets.

"Better than the kitchen floor, where I used to

sleep," Katie had replied. Her bed, too, felt like a pancake on a plank of wood.

Minnie was clearing her throat. She had a night cough just like Katie's husband, Ian. A grating *ah–huh-huh-huh.*

"Take some water," Katie told her, as she always told him.

Minnie obligingly drank a glass, part of a nightly routine that was exasperating but somehow soothing for both of them. In the same way, their bedtime conversations were often about things they'd endured as new immigrants. Although the stories they told were about hard times, it was calming to drift between wakefulness and sleep in a common past.

"The relatives would come over from Russia," Minnie said when she'd caught her breath, "and stay in my uncle's apartment on Houston Street. There were so many of us, we had to take turns sleeping under the sink."

"I'm not speaking of first arriving here," Katie said. "I was already a grown-up woman, a maid-of-all-work almost three years, and the kitchen floor's where they put me to sleep. They treated us terrible, but one thing I made sure of: I never let them call me by my first name. It was always Mrs. McConnell, and I made sure that it stuck."

Memories had been coming to Katie at night and lingering during the day, as if being on the verge of seeing her boys had triggered a desire to sum up the past—the lonely years as an inexperienced sixteen-year-old who only knew how to boil potatoes, plunked down in service to a family of five in an isolated outpost of Boston called Jamaica Plain. No church in walking distance. Her first mistress called her a "stupid Hibernian" because she'd never heard of a fancy vegetable with the puzzling name of "iceberg lettuce." She didn't have those problems now. Currently she worked for a banker's family in a well-kept brownstone in the Back Bay. The wife was the nervous type who was glad for Katie to run the house; they were decent enough, but every time she went out to hang the laundry she would break out in giggles—and couldn't help laughing now.

"What's so funny, Mrs. McConnell?"

"I was thinkin' of the time my husband took the boys to visit the police division on Boylston Street. Ian's brother, Jack, was a sergeant there, and he showed them the Stanley Steamer. You heard about it?"

"Sure I have," said Minnie in her know-it-all way. "It's to iron clothes."

"It's a *car*," Katie said, rolling her eyes. "Why would they be ironing in a police station?"

"To have nice uniforms."

"Oh, go on. It's a motorcar they used to have way back when Tim and Dolan were kids. There's a regular man who drives it, and then a specially high seat for the patrol officer to see over the backyard fences. It's the first warm day of spring," Katie went on, "and my husband and their uncle take the boys for a ride in the Stanley Steamer. They come back and Timmy—he's the older one, the smarty-pants—he says, 'Papa has the best job! He drives around and around looking for ladies with no clothes!' "

Minnie inhaled with exaggerated shock. She felt privileged to be hearing about Katie's boys and wanted it to continue. "Where on earth did they take them?"

"That's what I wanted to know," Katie agreed. "Ian says, 'I swear, we only went to Back Bay,' and I accuse him of being a liar, thinking him and his brother, they probably took the boys to see the seamy side of life—so he finally admits that when Tim and Dolan were up there with him on the seat, they look over the fence and see a lady in her backyard hanging laundry in the altogether! Why not? It was a warm day . . ." she managed, whooping.

"Then what happened?" Minnie urged her on. "Did she get arrested?"

"No, what happened was Tim decided to become a policeman on the spot and Dolan says he'd drive him! And every time I go out in the missus's backyard I have to laugh. Oh, me," she said, calming down and become reflective. "The army says two men from one family don't have to go, but they both enlisted. They refused to be apart."

"It must be terrible to lose two."

"They're together, like they always were," Katie said with forced stoicism. She wanted that to be the end of it. She shut off the lamp, but sensed there was something unfinished in the air.

"What is it now, Mrs. Seibert?"

"Your little boy with polio—" Minnie finally managed from the dimness. "Will he ever walk again?"

"He's walkin' just fine—" she began sharply, but put a brake on it, remembering that meekness overcomes anger, and she could use some of that. Mrs. Seibert meant the best, even if she was always, excuse the expression, putting her foot in it. "I'm sorry, Minnie, I know what you're askin'," she said. "He'll likely always need his crutches, but that won't stop him none. He comes from a fightin' family."

"That's good," Minnie murmured sleepily. "I'm glad for you."

Every night at ten o'clock Katie's family in Ballinlough, Ireland, would gather on their knees on the dirt floor of the cottage and say their beads. Katie waited until Minnie was snoring, and at the hour of ten, kneeling on a poor rug over the rough planks of the Hôtel Nouvel, she did the same, praying for the eternal souls of her sons. Then she fingered the beads all over again, in penance for having just told her friend Mrs. Seibert an out-and-out lie about the reason Tim and Dolan had been laid together in France; asking for forgiveness because she was too mortal and weak to admit the truth.

Minnie kept up her watch for the bus outside, while the others were still in the hotel breakfast room. Bobbie was complaining of heartburn, which required bicarbonate of soda, and Cora had an upset stomach, for which she was given spirit of chloroform—all of which would be duly noted by Hammond and Lily in their daily reports—and Katie, for the first time anyone on the pilgrimage could remember, began to cry, for which there seemed to be no cure except the understanding arm of the young nurse around her shoulders. When Minnie appeared at the doorway in a frenzy, announcing that their bus had arrived, there was a good deal of primping and last-minute running upstairs to change sweaters and hats, because it was important to look good for their sons.

The army had leased a tiny regional bus, like a blue breadbox on wheels. At this time of day it would normally have been transporting house-wives between the outlying villages and the shops in Verdun, which had given the driver, Émile, the hard-earned patience of a wagon mule. He took each lady's hand, bowed, and helped her on board. His crinkled smile, huge brush mustache, and sad brown eyes beneath a workman's cap were reassuring.

Although Lily had worried that the extent of devastation when they drove through the city would be a shock, there was no way to avoid it. Ahead of them was a two-wheeled cart transporting a wine barrel and there was no place to pass. They were forced to go at a snail's pace along a street that had been totally flattened, nothing left but chimney stacks in mounds of ash. Turning the corner, they passed a block where the buildings had been sliced in half. Between the walls of cascading plaster, they could look straight into the rooms. Even the structures that had remained whole were pitted by shells, and the narrow shutters blasted into piles of slats. Someone had once opened those windows, glad to see the day.

"Look at that poor house," said Bobbie. "On its last legs."

"Just like us," Minnie sighed.

"Speak for yourself," Katie said indignantly.

Bobbie and Cora, again sitting together, raised eyebrows and smiled.

"Why not laugh?" Bobbie said.

"Why not?" Cora agreed.

But there was still a knot in Cora's stomach from this morning, when she'd unwrapped the tissue from the dress she'd sewn to wear this day—the one of light heather-gray wool with a white collar. She'd worried that wool might be too hot for France in June, but knew that later it would still be a practical piece of clothing for autumn in Maine. As it turned out, the day was sunny but cool and the dress was just right. The red beret and black pumps she'd bought for this moment topped it off perfectly.

Everything else was quickly becoming unreal. Just outside the window of the bus the remains of Verdun seemed distant, like looking at a newsreel of a far-off war. Strange how all destroyed cities look the same. Although the proof was right before her eyes, it was impossible to believe that people really did these things to each other. She was grateful to have raised Sammy in the safest place on earth. Because it had been just the two of them, Sammy was all she had when the situation demanded the strength of blood ties, and he'd stood up to it like a man.

He had been just shy of sixteen, too old to hold his mother's hand, but he staunchly did so, as they walked unsteadily down the narrow drafty mortuary room to view her father home from the sea for the last time. Sammy's grip was stronger. His tears waited for hers. Cora's mother was sitting in a chair weeping into her palms, surrounded by neighbors and friends. Her father, wearing his best jacket and tie, looked small in his coffin. His eyes were unnaturally shut as if being forced to look down in deference to some-thing, which was very unlike him, as Captain

Frederick Harding had been outspoken in his views, and never backed off from his broad-minded opinions in that conservative town. She touched his forehead, hard and cold as ice, and tried to comprehend that he would never move, never speak. She wondered how it was possible to live for the first time in a world without her father's presence, while Sammy stood beside her, casually and exquisitely alive.

The road broke from the ruined city and ran across a vista of spacious fields, bringing with it sweet summer smells of fresh manure and flowering weeds. The farmland would have felt like home to Sammy, but when he was here, she knew, it didn't look like this, quiet in the distance, scattered with red poppies. The open plain would have been crawling with weapons and men and a slew of animals drafted into service—mules and horses to pull the guns, pigeons and dogs to carry messages. There would be pockets of fire and exploding shells. Squadrons felled by poison gas.

Lieutenant Hammond got up in the front of the bus and began to describe the Battle of Verdun with the enthusiasm of a radio announcer, and that's when the foreignness of everything hit. Cora felt detached from reality, as if the little blue bus were time-traveling in the bubble of war, viewing the world as if the flamethrowers and artillery were still grappling to no end—as if nothing had changed, or would ever change, but only they, the mothers, could see it.

"Those are the three hills defending Verdun," Hammond said. "If the Germans had taken the last hill, Verdun would have fallen. It wasn't a crucial military target, but it would have gutted the French spirit. That's why a lot of monuments around here show soldiers defiantly planting their swords in the earth down to the hilt. The French motto was, This far and no farther. '*Ils ne passeront pas*!'—They shall not pass."

Wilhelmina raised her hand. "Is this where they died?"

"Well, yes, you see the Germans lost over four hundred thousand, and the Allies—"

Bobbie spoke up. "She means our sons."

"Is that what you're asking?"

Wilhelmina nodded.

"No, ma'am," Hammond said awkwardly, trying to meet the flat yellow eyes that were staring at him like a cat. "That would be farther along the Meuse River. We'll visit that battleground tomorrow. In fact"—his voice picked up—"you'll get to walk where they walked."

"Okay," said Wilhelmina and resumed twisting the button on her blouse.

The bus bumped along in silence. Hammond glanced at Lily, who nodded at him to go on.

"The Germans mounted a mammoth offensive, and the Allies fought back with everything they had. This whole area was an epic battle of artillery, using every scrap of wood available to give cover to the guns. The French had the big stuff—six-inchers—which they lent to the Americans. We had railway guns that were sixteen inches across, taken off navy ships, but they could only fire every fifteen minutes. Not a big effect on the battle. If you miss, you get a big hole and a few dead cows."

At the crossroads at Madeleine Farm, they took a rest stop and then switched from the little blue breadbox to a *charabanc*, an open bus with a roof made of canvas, which could navigate the rough roads better, and would carry them the rest of the way.

From there it was a bumpy ride in the open-air coach. No longer separated from the countryside even by window glass, they were at once immersed in warm air, green smells, and birdsong, as if every sense had been sharpened. Now that they had come so close, the careful layers of security laid down by the army were losing their protective magic—the chaperoned travel, prepared meals, all the amenities, and medical attention night and day. Like true pilgrims, they'd reached the point where they had to leave behind everything they had known. As if stripped of possessions, barefoot, and dressed in sackcloth, they were defenseless, except for a flimsy canvas roof, which left them vulnerable to heat, and insect-laden updrafts expelled by the forest, subtle waves of pollen, and gut-churning anticipation.

The road had been rutted by spring rains. As they lurched along, it was easy to understand why it had taken an army to move the army, when Hammond described La Voie Sacrée, the Sacred Way, a stretch of road to the south that moved 3,500 trucks a day between a town called Bar-le-Duc and Verdun, the lifeline of supply to the French who were defending the city.

"A truck would pass every fourteen seconds," he shouted over the grinding of their own tires. "Hard to believe, isn't it? Even more amazing, they first had to *quarry* the stone to *build* the road, and then a dozen battalions were needed to work night and day just to maintain it!"

They nodded absently, staring at the peaceful fields where locals were collecting armfuls of blue cornflowers.

"Isn't it a lovely habit of the French?" Bobbie said. "Letting wildflowers grow? I can't wait until they let us loose so we can get a closer look."

They finally turned onto a paved road. The ride became smooth and the clatter of rocks hitting the underside of the coach quit the moment they entered the gates of the Meuse-Argonne American Cemetery. They passed between two white stone towers topped with spread-winged eagles, and followed the driveway to a large oval pond, where they parked. All that time the silence in the bus had been twisting tighter. In fact, Cora had been holding her breath. As she stepped down from the coach, there was an overwhelming sense of disorientation. They were here. But where? Someone guided her into the shade, where she stood numbly with the others. She felt weak and wanted to sit down. The sun was steamy; her heels sank into the soft grass.

A tall thin man in a dark suit was coming toward them, followed by two ladies, also wearing suits. He was the superintendent of the cemetery; they were the hostesses. The superintendent shook hands with Lieutenant Hammond, and the hostesses maneuvered the hesitant visitors around the pond. The same ominous feeling she'd had leaving the island now welled up in Cora. At this time in June, the Lily Pond back home would be carpeted with waxy white blooms, surrounded by daisies and lupine, and children knee-deep in mud trying to catch frogs. Here there were naked stalks and scummy green water in a concrete pool. The main reception building on the hill looked like any other suburban American house, vaguely Colonial with a red roof. The lawn had not been planted yet; it was just brown dirt. Her legs resisted going up the flagstone path but she forced herself to follow the others around the pool and up the steps.

It was cooler inside. Lemonade and sandwiches were waiting on silver trays in the foyer. The floor and windows were spotlessly clean and sunshiny bright. A white staircase led upstairs to the super-intendent's residence, and there were rooms to either side on the ground floor. The navy blue decor, the flags and certificates, and the friendliness of the hostesses shouted U.S.A., but the pilgrims behaved as if this place didn't really belong to them, speaking in soft tones, as they would in someone else's fancy home. It reminded Cora of cake and punch in the office of the dean of English at Colby College. Everyone afraid to break a glass.

The staff presented maps indicating the location of each of their son's graves. Chairs were available for resting throughout the grounds, they were told, and they were encouraged to spend as much time as they wished. Tea would be served from three to five.

Bobbie Olsen was first out of the door, armed with directions, head up, marching into the light. She walked past the circular pool and down the steps to the mall, which was divided into rectangular grassy areas filled with parallel rows of white headstones. She headed to a colonnade of trees to the left, noting that they were square-cut lindens, and found Henry's grave a few steps in, which was convenient, because by then she was alarmingly short of breath, almost as much as at Notre-Dame. Luckily there was a folding chair nearby, which she moved into the shade several yards from the stone.

She sat there gazing at it until her body settled down. Henry seemed away, but at a comfortable distance, as he had been, many times, at the other end of a long table filled with happy guests. They'd pepper him with incessant questions about their health but he would answer genially. She'd admire his aristocratic profile, the dark gloss of his hair, and round glasses flashing in the glow of multiple candelabras—proud of his youthful authority in the midst of such accomplished people.

A fresh breeze swept the Meuse-Argonne cemetery. Shadows moving through the grass reminded Bobbie of the telephone call she'd received from General Skip Reilly, Retired, a dear friend who served with her on the board of the Boston Museum of Fine Arts and was also involved in building the National Gallery in Washington, D.C., who'd been asked by a mutual friend in the War Department to personally deliver the devastating news that Dr. Olsen had been killed in a bombing raid. She'd thanked Skip, hung up the phone, gone to the vestibule for her hat and coat, ignored the concern of the maid, and walked through the gate of her Cambridge mansion and down a short leafy street that led to the river.

She had to keep walking. She followed the route she always did, north along the banks of the Charles toward Harvard Bridge, through dancing autumn leaves, past students in pairs and bicyclists, barely aware of the cars along Memorial Drive. She had a favorite bench with a view of the three arches of the bridge, and the gentle circular reflections in the water were always soothing. She passed an older woman seated there, contentedly reading a book. That used to be Bobbie, but no longer.

No matter how fast she walked on that cold fall afternoon, she could not escape the sharp-edged shadows of the bare sycamores that grated against the stone apartment buildings fronting the water. The shadows haunted her with their precise renderings of the real live trees. She felt them wrap around the corners of the buildings like a hand around her neck, ephemeral and nonexistent, but with terrible power. A trick of light had fleetingly transformed the placid façades into something that seemed alive, but was not. Like her son. How can you touch a shadow?

You cannot, and it's been a fact for thirteen years, thought Bobbie, straightening up in the uncomfortable chair. She pulled the black veil down from her hat so that it shaded her eyes, and folded her gloved hands in her lap. But touching him was hardly relevant, was it, since she was staring at his grave? There was nothing to be done, she told herself firmly. She was here, that's the only thing that mattered now. She'd done it. She had made the trip. She took a deep draft of the pollen-scented air of rural France and closed her eyes and thought of Henry. And with that, Bobbie Olsen was at peace.

As they passed, Hammond and Katie saw Bobbie seated primly on the folding chair, and discreetly left her to her thoughts. Katie'd had difficulty leaving the protection of the administration house and Hammond asked if she'd like company. She said yes and he offered his arm. She steadied herself and began to talk, searching for a subject that would save her from acknowledging the heartache out loud. Almost any deep emotion came tagged with transgression, personal things that should be addressed in the confessional, between herself and a servant of God. Here in the raw sunlight with this boy would have been unseemly.

"You know, my mother never wanted me to leave Ireland," she began, as if telling an amusing anecdote. "She even hid my ticket. But my sister told me where, and I found it, and I went down and booked the passage. There was nothin' anyone could do about it then! My husband is Irish but American-born, and that was a big catch for a country girl. I surely wrote home and let 'em know."

They were just outside the door of the main house, facing a row of red, white, and blue flags, bright and solemn on their golden staffs topped with eagles, and beyond that lay America's sons.

"But now I'm an American, too," Katie McConnell said.

Hammond waited patiently, and when the moment was right, walked her with military grace down the steps to find the graves of the brothers, side by side. They were way past Henry Olsen, M.D., nearer to the Memorial Chapel and halfway across the long unbroken row. Katie walked right up and kissed the stones, one and then the other, and touched them lovingly. Hammond set a chair down for her and withdrew. Lily was accompanying Wilhelmina, he knew, and Minnie, clutching a tiny black Hebrew prayer book, assured him this was something she must tend to alone. She seemed dignified by her faith, and her steps were slow but poised as she went in the direction of a Star of David headstone, prominent in a sea of Latin crosses.

Cora had lingered behind, slowed by dread in the pit of her stomach. Having come this far, she was surprised by how difficult these last steps were proving to be. When she finally walked out the door of the main house, she was met by the overwhelming sight of the entire layout of the cemetery. It must have been more than a hundred acres. There was still much open construction. The trees were in. The rows of 14,247 pristine stones were stark against the green. The view from up here on the hill stunned the heart. There were so many markers that they blurred together. Or was it her tears?

Sammy's stone was located in Plot C, Row 44, Grave 16. Drifting along in a dream, she passed mothers from other groups, black and white, floating in a similar state of disbelief and awe. The stones were larger than life, waist-high and of pure white marble. She came to his name, as featureless as the rest. It was supposed to be Sammy but it was only letters.

SAMUEL BLAKE PVT
3321475
Yankee Division
Maine
October 22, 1918

She stared and stared. "Sammy?" she said out loud. "It's Mama. I'm here."

There was no answer. The cross was puzzling. It was so big. It held no religious significance for her. It seemed like a stump with arms and no face—mute and frozen in time—an army of young men transformed into anonymous symbols. She knelt on the grass that rolled on seamlessly between the rows, and blindly felt the ground with her hands. Was he there? The cross said nothing. She took the shells they'd collected on Great Spruce Island from the pocket in the dress she'd sewn in for that purpose, and laid them tenderly at the foot of the marble, holding in her mind the sound of wavelets lapping the rocks of their cove, as if she could transport that image through the airwaves to Sammy. It was important for Sammy to know the cove was there like always, quiet and untouched, and that she passed it almost every day. She missed him so. A great and nameless force, more powerful than sadness, overcame her. She wept and said out loud, *"Don't leave!"*—the words she'd uttered when she received the letter brought to the door of the farmhouse by postmaster Eli Grimble, accompanied by the doctor and the minister. It had been written in pencil by hand and was scarcely readable, probably dashed off because the officer had so many to write:

11/7-18
Mrs. Cora Blake
   Deeply regret to inform you that Private Sammy Blake infantry is officially reported as killed in action October 22.
   Harris—Adjunct General

She'd gripped the letter saying, *"Don't leave!"* And years later, to Linwood in the middle of the night, "He shouldn't be there. He doesn't deserve to be there. Alone, in the cold ground." Linwood held her and stroked her shuddering shoulders and said, "That's not where he is." Where was he? Would he come back with her to Maine on those mystic airwaves—or did he live here now among the white stones? She knew that he had loved her with all the strength of his being, with a son's undeniable and abiding love. But she wept because he was on the other side of the curtain, at the same time knowing that her tears were useless because they, like everything, would pass. Every time she thought it was done and wanted to flee, she couldn't. Like waves in the ocean, it took a breath, pulled back, and knocked her down again.

Her reddened eyes squinted against the brightness of the sky. Silence entered her ears and pressed against her brain. Did anybody laugh here? Did anyone rejoice at happy memories? Or did that not serve our country? She stood up, running her fingers along the stone, noting the smooth edgework. She knew something that she hadn't known before. She'd always imagined Sammy falling alone in suspended space like a stage backdrop, but now she saw a marble forest of young men who were dead, and knew that Sammy was, had been, and always would be in their company. A spasm of grief almost doubled her up—for her boy, for all the boys, and for the lives they never had. And then, a moment ago unbearable, it left her like the breeze.

17

It was a new day at the Hôtel Nouvel. When the pilgrims came down to breakfast, they found roses on the tables. The stingy cornflakes were gone and the sideboard had been loaded with platters of sausage, along with toasted baguettes and scrambled eggs. The owner's wife stood at a portable stove wearing a clean apron and making crêpes filled with sautéed apples. Even the coffee smelled richer.

As they stood in line, Lily whispered, "What's going on?"

"I don't know," said Hammond. "We never asked for all this."

"Maybe they finally realized they should be grateful to the U.S. Army for putting us up in their hotel."

"As long as they don't put it on the bill," Hammond said, smothering his crêpes with a thick layer of Chantilly cream.

Bobbie was waving everyone over to an empty table, and one by one the others joined, including Lily and Hammond. Since Cora and Bobbie were roommates and Minnie and Katie, despite their bickering, were still a pair—and Wilhelmina went wherever the wind blew—it was unusual for all of them to eat together. But after the visit to the graves, everyone seemed to want the security of the group. Just as they'd settled, two glass-paneled doors opened, and the owner of the hotel was wheeled into the breakfast room by his son.

Both were clean-shaven and wearing fresh shirts. The old man was beaming and waving a claw as if to an admiring crowd.

"*Mon père est bien conscient,*" explained the son, "*que les mères américaines nous ont rendus célèbres.*"

"He says that today the hotel is famous," Bobbie said, "because of the American mothers."

"Why because of us?" Minnie asked.

The son had given Hammond a copy of *Le Matin*.

"*C'est à la page trois,*" he said. "*Il parle de notre hôtel.*"

Bobbie translated: "He says it's in the French newspaper that the pilgrimage is staying here." She leaned over Hammond to read a few lines, skeptically arching an eyebrow. "Obviously, they never asked *our* opinion of the place."

Hammond was quickly scanning the text. "Mrs. Blake! This article is all about you."

"Me?"

" '*The story of an American mother named Cora Blake who traveled 3,300 miles to visit her son's grave at Meuse-Argonne American Cemetery is just one of thousands of pilgrims who have made the journey, but it is a special story of enduring mother love . . .' "*

Bobbie's eyes widened. "Did our Grif write that?"

Hammond nodded. " 'By Griffin Reed.' Listen to this: *'Her brilliant blue eyes filling with tears, Mrs. Cora Blake explained that she had come to France in order to lay seashells on the grave of her son, Samuel, so that he'd never be far from the town in Maine where she raised him—'* "

Katie folded her hands over her purse with exaggerated gentility. "Isn't that nice."

"But who is Griffin Reed?" Minnie wanted to know.

"A friend of mine," Bobbie said casually.

Katie examined a spoon. "They call this polished? This would never pass muster in my mistress's house." She replaced it, exchanging a look with Minnie. "That explains it."

"Explains what?" Cora asked.

"How you got to be in the newspaper," Minnie piped up.

"Money talks," Wilhelmina agreed sagely.

Lily thought Wilhelmina looked more doped than usual. She wondered if the crafty old gal had gotten into the Red Cross satchel in their room.

"Excuse me," Bobbie said, in the gravelly superior voice she might use to dismiss a taxi driver. "Are you implying that because an article appears in a French newspaper, it's somehow a result of *my* influence?"

Minnie zipped a finger across her lips. "I never said a word."

"I must have a lot of pull! Can't you believe anything just *happens?*"

"*Somebody* was pulling strings. The article should have been about all of us—not just one."

"Write a letter to the editor," Wilhelmina suggested.

"You know, Minnie? That's just mean," Cora said in defense of Grif. "You make it sound like I intentionally tried to leave everyone else out—"

"She's not blaming you—" Katie said.

Cora turned on her. "Yes, she is—"

"It's up to the newspaper, what they say," Bobbie put in.

"Ladies!" Hammond said sharply. "Decorum, please!"

They lowered their eyes and ate in tense silence. Another reason the group didn't travel in tight formation was the friction that had been building between Minnie and Bobbie. Minnie boiled over Bobbie's optimism, and Bobbie was impatient with Minnie's prickly insistence that nothing would turn out right. While they'd been traveling, alliances had formed and re-formed, but now that they were in still waters, everything could fester—nerves, terror, exhaustion, prejudice—and everyone was low on reserves. Although they'd been given markers—plain and simple, in precisely plotted rows—the pilgrims were finding themselves in uncharted emotional territory.

Hammond snapped the newspaper shut. The crêpes were congealing like sludge in his stomach.

"All right, fine. Here's the schedule for today. First we go to Romagne to view the area where the Yankee Division fought in the Meuse-Argonne Offensive, and then we picnic in the woods by the Marne River."

"How does that sound?" Lily prompted cheerfully.

Katie said, "No."

"No?"

Katie had been pursued by bad dreams of headless trolls; the last place she wanted to go was into the woods. She stood up at the table. "It's a curse to go picnicking when we're here to pray."

Hammond began, "But of course we can pray—"

"I won't be part of it," Katie said. "I'll get me a taxi to the cemetery and the rest of you can party all ye like."

Hammond was on his feet as well. "Hold it, wait, calm down, Mrs. McConnell. We're all going to the cemetery together."

Katie put a hand on her hip. "And when is that? All I'm hearin' is larkin' about on picnics—"

"We're going in the afternoon," Lily said

smoothly. "We thought it would be cooler and more comfortable later in the day. Is that all right with you? Everyone?"

Heads were nodding.

"Well, you should've made that clear at the beginnin'!" Katie said, and sat down hard, clearly unsettled.

"If there's no more dissent, I'll go and see about the bus."

With a severe look at all of them, Hammond left the table, followed by Lily, who was on the way to her room to collect the Red Cross bag. From her point of view, a picnic meant bug bites and sunburn.

"Bully for you," she told Hammond as they crossed the lobby.

"They're like a bunch of children. Sometimes I want to thrash them."

"Almost home," Lily promised.

"Halfway, anyway."

Back at the table, the others noticed that Katie was silently pressing a hand to her mouth and her shoulders were trembling.

"Are you all right?" Cora asked.

"I'm just so happy we're going to the grave-yard," she said, although they could see she was crying.

"Of course you are," Bobbie said, eager to prove her magnanimous side.

"What I just said . . . that's a lie," Katie managed

finally. "I'm not happy a'tall." She sobbed into a napkin.

"Maybe it's just too hard . . ." Minnie whispered. "Losing both."

Katie shook her head. "It's because they're over here."

"But Tim and Dolan are together, like they always were," Minnie said, her arched eyebrows knit in concern. "Isn't that what you wanted?"

"We wanted them home."

"We all did, dear," Wilhelmina said sympathetically.

Katie wiped her eyes. "We wanted them close, in the parish cemetery. But we didn't have the money. We only had enough to bring one back. We couldn't do that, could we? Leave the other one alone? When we got the letter askin' where they were to be laid to rest, we had to say overseas, both together, side by side, the way they always were. But I have to tell ye—when I saw them yesterday—it broke me up all over again, knowin' they're here and I have to say goodbye. Forever, this time."

There was agonized silence.

Cora searched for some way to ease it, but there really wasn't any. Remembering her lonely decision to bury Sammy in France, she simply said, "It's a hard choice."

"We tried to put the best face on, we said it was the patriotic thing to do. But inside we were ashamed. We bore it in private, Ian and myself. And to be honest, everybody has troubles, nobody wants to hear yours."

Wilhelmina nodded. "They think you're crazy and put you in a hospital," she said, but no one was paying attention.

"What about your husband?" Cora asked.

"The boys in Ian's district put a plaque up at the station house for Tim and Dolan. My husband is a teetotaler, but he goes out to the pub and of course, they're Irish, so they're great talkers. Me, I'm all alone at the mistress's house. I can't say a word to anyone. It's like a tomb of silence around me and my sons. Thank goodness our church in Dorchester is just down the block. I go to the early mass every day, because I know He listens."

Bobbie put her fist down gently on the table and said firmly, "There's no shame in it. You're a brave person. Everyone can see that."

Katie raised her reddened eyes, about to challenge Bobbie, but in the older woman's steady blue stare she saw benevolence and under-standing, and she softened.

"Would you like to see a picture of my boys, Mrs. Olsen?"

"Very much."

Katie opened her purse and took out a dog-eared studio portrait of two sharp-featured young men with dark hair parted in the middle, posed before a curtain with their hands in the pockets of their vests. At once everyone got up from their chairs and spontaneously crowded around—to admire the photograph, to touch her in some way. Hands squeezed her hands. Hands patted her back.

Bobbie leaned over and said quietly to nobody in particular, "We all do what we have to do, and it may not always be noble. Myself included. I would lie, cheat, and steal if it had to do with my son. Wouldn't you?"

Before anyone could answer, the German family came marching back into the breakfast room carrying wicker hampers of food and leather holders with bottles of wine. The old man in his wheelchair was holding a pile of folded blankets in his lap.

"*Avec nos compliments*," said the son with a bow. "*Veuillez profiter.*"

"Ah!" Bobbie said with relief. "Here's our picnic!"

18

The day was glorious, filled to the brim with warmth and summer fragrance. High white clouds swelled across the sky as the breadbox bus, with Émile driving, took the road going north from Verdun along the river to Brieulles-sur-Marne. Hammond opened the official U.S. Army Expeditionary Forces map of northwestern

Europe. It was a khaki-colored sheet backed with linen that unfolded into rectangular segments, so that he could easily isolate the battle zones of the Argonne.

"We're almost there," he announced. "Just after this next town."

Émile honked and waved at a country woman carrying shopping bags. She waved back, puzzled because the blue bus wasn't stopping as usual. Instead, it made a laborious circle around a war monument and continued northwest toward the Argonne Forest. In less than an hour they'd passed several farming villages, each less populated the farther they got from Verdun. This was nothing but a single muddy street with no one in sight. The only sound was the echo of cows hallooing and frantic barking from a pink-bellied mutt in a doorway who was shivering with mange. Cora noticed swallows veering into an open barn. She glimpsed a farmer milking on a three-legged stool.

"You see that roof?" Hammond called as they passed the barn. "That's old galvanized iron they pulled from the trenches."

Cora strained to look out the window. "Where are the trenches?"

Hammond ran a finger along the color-coded markings. "They're a bit ahead, mostly up in the forest now. These fields have been pretty well scavenged."

When they were back out in rolling countryside, Hammond announced that they had reached the forward line of the American Expeditionary Forces during the Meuse-Argonne Offensive, the final chapter in the war. Although civilians might picture disciplined formations advancing neatly, he knew from his studies that the fighting was chaotic. Untrained troops reporting for duty were told to "go where the smoke is thickest"—in other words, were thrown into the bonfire like human wood chips. It was common for half of a company of 250 replacements to be dead within an hour. A commander of four companies of 1,000 men had to figure on losing 60 to 80 percent. The numbers had been drilled into Hammond at West Point as an example of an unwarranted strategy drawn up by egotistic generals with their heads in the military tactics of the last century.

The American plan had been to attack the German city of Metz, which the high command believed would have cut off the enemy's railroad lines, but British general Sir Douglas Haig had another idea, which was for *his* army to punch through the German-held Hindenberg Line, farther north at Le Cateau. Haig prevailed. The Americans took responsibility for the Argonne, figuring that if Haig had claimed the victory that ended the war, the Americans could at least hold up the Meuse-Argonne Offensive as the crucial mission that pushed the Brits over the top.

The problem was that the Brits didn't really need support to get through the Hindenberg Line, and meanwhile, the American forces had overly committed to the Argonne, with not enough time to prepare or staff to supervise. They eventually cleared the forest and pushed to the city of Sedan after an excruciatingly slow crawl in which Hammond's father, Colonel Thomas West Hammond, had commanded a regiment, over rough terrain in a complete downpour, resulting in the bloodiest single engagement in American history, and seen by officers even then as tragically unnecessary.

Émile slowed down and honked at two peacocks that were walking blithely down the center of the road, causing a burst of excitement as the women stood up to see, but Hammond's thoughts were grim. He believed in his country and his superiors, and that President Wilson had been correct when he said, "The world must be made safe for democracy—the right is more precious than peace," so when they'd settled down, he assumed his military posture in the front of the bus, and bravely met the expectations of the mothers in his care. His duty was to represent the army, not to rewrite history. But he could show it to them in a more gentle light.

With the expectant faces of the pilgrims before him, he gestured at the distant hills. "Here you have it. This is where the Allies made the final push to end the war. Mind you, there had already been four years of fighting, with the British and French holding the line at enormous cost—but now, in September of 1918, here come the Americans!"

Everyone on the little bus broke out in applause. Wilhelmina put two fingers in her mouth and whistled. Hammond smiled, more uncomfortable than ever to be a stand-in for their sons. He was supposed to justify how a boy from Boston or Prouts Neck ends up dead in France because of a war between decaying monarchies whose top brass cared more about the plumage on their helmets than the blood on the ground. He could see in their eager eyes that they wanted to trust what he was saying. They had to go home with something. It was up to him to deliver.

"The Germans were afraid. When they knew the Americans were coming, they launched the Spring Offensive—but when we actually arrived, and finally took our place beside the French, at Saint-Mihiel on September twelfth, frankly, it struck a killing blow to the enemy's morale. Our boys didn't have much experience, but they did have moxie, and more than anything, they were determined to defend freedom. The Germans quickly knew they were finished. The last great battles of the American Expeditionary Forces, which were fought right here on these fields, led directly led to the Armistice on November eleventh. Your sons made the ultimate sacrifice for peace. And we all know they couldn't have done it without the mothers who stood beside them, every step of the way. You should be very, very proud."

There was more applause. Hammond exhaled with relief, instructed Émile to pull over, and one by one they helped the mothers step down. For several moments the American women stood uncertainly at the side of the road, in their cloche hats and light summer coats, staring at a field of millet grass.

"What was it like?" Cora asked quietly.

"See the bumpiness of this ground? This is French and American artillery firing that way and German artillery firing back. See that hill? We were absolutely wanting that hill."

"What about those trees way back there?"

"I believe that's a stream. It's likely that the Germans were bunkered up behind it."

"Can we see it?"

"No, sorry," said Hammond. "It's possible that the field still contains unexploded shells."

Cora didn't really want to walk out there. The atmosphere that hung over the empty field was strangely hushed. She knew what the soil would be, blackened like the burned-out clumps that fell out of Sammy's scorched uniform when she unfolded it from the package from the War Department that she hadn't gotten herself to open for several days. It was as if the violence of those deaths had sunk in and corrupted the very earth.

But she persisted: "And our soldiers? Where were they?"

"Trying to push across. But it wasn't nice and pretty like this. Imagine dust and noise so thick you can't hear anybody talk. Crater holes and dead horses. The Germans would set up and cover themselves with grass so the Allies couldn't tell where the fire was coming from. And if anyone got too close to the hills, they had a nasty way of stringing barbed wire across the trees with gaps in the wire and machine guns aimed at the openings. We had to guess their position and shell where we thought the lines were. Sometimes we'd shell our own men." He stopped, afraid he'd gone too far. "There are always regrettable mistakes in war, but the point is, by the end we had two million troops over here—and that's the key to why the Allies won."

Cora had another question, but Wilhelmina broke into her thoughts.

"If they fought here and died here," she asked, "how did they get to the cemetery?"

"No need for you to worry about the details."

"How did they keep track? Of who was who? Some of our boys were blown to smithereens, you know."

Her remark, tossed off so matter-of-factly, had a numbing effect on the group. Cora bit her lip and

Minnie had a coughing fit. Katie held her pocketbook up to shield her eyes from the sun, the better to hide beneath it. Only Bobbie and Wilhelmina drilled demanding looks at the young lieutenant.

"That's what the army is in business for, Mrs. Russell. Keeping track."

"You owe us an explanation," Bobbie insisted. "How *did* they know, with all that smoke and noise you describe?"

"Fair enough."

Hammond squared his shoulders and explained that the army had a special burial unit. For every soldier, it was a priority and sacred duty to tend to the fallen, which meant to properly care for and identify the remains. His voice came from the gut, from the place that held the things he deeply believed. He was surprised by its authority.

"If a man fell, his comrades would pull him out. If they were under fire, the burial unit would follow. This was a great contribution of the Negro soldiers. Often they'd be assigned the duty of picking up the dead. A temporary wooden cross would be erected with the name, serial number, and division. Sometimes they'd hang his dog tags on the cross. After the war, the remains were moved by the burial unit from the battlefield to the American cemeteries. Believe me, the records were immaculate."

Wilhelmina's long furrowed face seemed to

have no expression at all. Under the shade of a straw hat, her eyes were lowered and unreadable. She kept fingering the top button buried in the frills of her blouse.

"Has he answered your question, dear?" Bobbie asked gently.

Wilhelmina didn't respond. Another local blue bus went by, kicking up pebbles. Its driver honked at Émile, who was squatting against a wheel, smoking a pipe. He gave the thumbs-up. *Tout va bien.*

Hammond looked at the others. "Who's ready for a picnic?"

It was high noon and they were burning in the sun. Cora spotted a bunch of wild strawberries by the side of the road and went to pick them, handing round the tiny fruit so that the women entered the bus with a taste like sweet candy teardrops on their tongues. Wilhelmina kept looking back at the trees in the distance.

"I had a letter," she said. "They told me that where Bradley died was in a field, with a farmhouse and a cannon. Is that near here?"

"Most likely it is," said Hammond, and guided her back on the bus.

The map showed a picnic spot a few kilometers away. On one side of the road was an uncharted farmer's field—on the other side, dense woods and a stream that looked promising. When the bus pulled into a turnout, they could hear the cooling sound of rushing water. Émile helped the ladies along a short trail that ended at a flat slab of rock overlooking a waterfall gently sluicing into a deep green pool, in which they could see the alluring shapes of well-fed trout. Sunlight warmed the rock and filtered through the canopy of beech trees.

"It's a Renoir!" Bobbie exclaimed when the wicker baskets had been unpacked and the food laid out on the blankets. The hotel, perhaps overestimating the effect Griffin Reed's article would have on their occupancy rate, had sent terrines of country pâté, hard-boiled eggs, cucumber salad, cheeses, baguettes both plain and filled with meats, and individual fruit tarts wrapped in cloth.

Minnie peeked at hers. "Who likes peach?"

Hammond offered to trade his blueberry.

"Peaches any day," he said robustly.

"Wild blueberries are the best for pies," Cora said. She took a careful bite of the famous French tart crust. "They put in a lot more sugar than we do. And they use real butter, not shortening. No wonder," she said admiringly. "Sammy used to love my wild-blueberry pie."

"And who picked the blueberries?" Bobbie teased.

"Who do you think? You'd never get Sammy to stay long enough to do a whole pail. He'd eat it all right, but spend every waking hour down at the cove. He loved his model boats."

"You let him become spoiled," Bobbie said.

"How can you not spoil them?" asked Katie.

"I'll tell you how," Bobbie said. "The Bible, soap, and spinach!"

They all laughed.

"Looking back," Bobbie continued, "at that long march through childhood—the illnesses and worries about school and if he's making the grade, and the types of friends he has—all of that—I wish I hadn't been such a martinet. I wish that Henry and I'd had more time together and just . . . more fun."

"We can all stand to have more fun," Hammond said, and began to undo the buckles on a large wicker basket lent by the hotel that looked as if it belonged on an African safari. He got the thing open. Inside were compartments for glasses and a bottle of Champagne.

"Thank you, but we couldn't," Wilhelmina responded sweepingly, as if they were at a formal dinner.

Bobbie laughed. "Of course we can!"

Minnie looked worried. "Not in the middle of the day. We'll get the collywobbles."

"This is the region where they make the best Champagne in the world," Hammond said. "Case closed!"

He popped the cork in an arc into the woods.

Lily drew the glasses out from their sleeves inside the basket.

"To all of us who have shared this pilgrimage. It's been a privilege," he said, and they all toasted. "To your brave sons."

Minnie's chin began to tremble.

"Oh, stop it, Minnie," Bobbie scolded. "I remember my boy in the sunlight, don't you? I thought you Jewish people have a word for it."

"*L'chaim*?" asked Minnie doubtfully.

Bobbie looked stumped. "Yes, that!" she said enthusiastically. "Down the hatch," she added and tossed back the Champagne.

Lily said she was going down to the water. Hammond watched as she leaned against a tree and discreetly lifted her skirt. Bending one leg while balancing on the other, she unrolled her stockings one by one, stuffed them in her shoes, and pressed her bare toes with pleasure against the smooth rock, running her fingers through her golden hair, shaking it out with abandon. She couldn't have looked more fetching or less like a second lieutenant army nurse. He was wondering idly if he could change her mind about the doctor at home when she shattered that thought by inviting everyone to come down to the water.

"It's lovely and cool down here," she called, waving.

Katie and Wilhelmina were on their way but Minnie's eyes were drooping.

"That cocktail went to my head," she said, dragging a blanket to a bed of leaves. She lay down, careful to tuck her dress discreetly around the marbled flesh of her calves, and was instantly asleep.

"Aha!" Katie pointed. "She snores! You tell her. She snores!"

Cora got up and brushed herself off. "I'm going to explore."

"Hold up, Mrs. Blake. Let's check the map," Hammond said, producing it from the haversack on his web belt, which also held a canteen. "Yes, it's okay if you go up there a bit," he said, indicating a trail leading to a rise. "It's been cleared of ordnance. Just stay on this side of the road."

"Do you want to come, Bobbie?" Cora asked.

Bobbie declined. She'd already gotten out her sketchbook and pencils.

"There are flowers here I've never seen. They may be a species of iris."

"Don't go too far," Hammond cautioned Cora. "We have to get back on the bus in ten minutes."

Cora gave him the "okay" sign. He counted heads. Wilhelmina and Katie were taking off their shoes. Standing in the middle of the stream, Lily looked dreamy and at peace. She was holding the skirt of her dress above her knees. The water made respectful ripples around her legs, and inside the white uniform, her body was outlined by the sun.

Hammond tore himself away from the view. "Mrs. Olsen?" he asked. "Need a hand?"

"I'll be along presently," she said, fussing with the sketching kit. "Trying to get myself organized."

Just as she was about to join them at the stream, Bobbie noticed a large stand of what looked like bellflowers across the road. They were much more vigorous than anything she'd seen at home—at least three feet tall, with large cone-shaped flowers in deep blue hanging along the stalks. They'd make a wonderful composition, she thought, a striking mass of violet against the yellow straw. She decided to skip the gathering at the stream and capture it on paper. She was accustomed to doing whatever she liked, and damn the torpedoes.

In short order Cora was out of sight of the picnic spot, relieved to be away from the forced companionship and the closeness of other female bodies. To be alone and in the woods was a luxury that she missed. For several minutes she followed a trail that went uphill and then leveled off into a thick oak forest. Strangely, she didn't hear any birds. The trees were weak and thin, not like the solid pines of Maine; these were saplings, she realized, that must have grown up since the war. That meant this area had been under fire. Slowly a chill crept through her. She could still hear the stream below but she was up high enough to look through the gaps in the trees and see the field on the other side of the road on which they had driven. A familiar shape rose in her mind—the shape of Sammy's last moments.

She only knew them as an outline gleaned from a couple of paragraphs. She'd been working in the cannery when the second letter came—the one from Sammy's sergeant. It was official, typed on letterhead, and arrived a month after the hand-scrawled notice of death. It was still early winter but there'd been a break in the frost, so she could stand outside comfortably just in her sweater and gut-soaked apron. The sergeant was writing to provide details in order for her to know the extent of Sammy's heroism.

Because of his skills with a rifle, Private Blake had been sent with six other men on a scouting mission to determine whether the Germans occupied a tiny village near a stream (the sergeant had written "a flood") called the Moussin. It was a risky mission because they had to cross open fields. They'd gone almost two hundred yards before being cut down by a machine gun nest, just as Hammond had described it, hidden by grass. Sammy was killed between the hill and the flood; nobody in the scouting party made it to the village and apparently the effort to secure it was abandoned.

Cora stood motionless in the fungal heat rising from the forest floor. It was still incomprehensible that she was standing under the French sun, on French soil, close—maybe just beyond these very woods—to where her boy's life was ended. She'd so often seen him being shot in dreams, hit and floating to the ground. She'd dreamed it all in silence and there was no pain on his childlike face. But there was so much pain as she stood there. She was like a lightning rod for pain. Her soft woman's body seemed to fill with the silent wasted loss of hundreds of thousands of young men whose nonbeing was as tangible as the missing generations of oak trees.

Her feet were moving on their own. One foot stepped forward, the other swung through to the next step. The ground was spongy and her attention turned to not tripping on the briars that crept along the ground. Her eyes fell on hard chalky-white shards that looked out of place in all that green. She picked them up and fingered the ridged surfaces. Could these be seashells? Instinctively she looked at the sky for gulls. That's how you found broken shells back home; the gulls would drop them on the rocks near the sea. But there were no gulls or rocks or ocean for hundreds of miles. A few paces on she spotted a lead ball the size of a marble that, when she picked it up, was unusually heavy in the palm of her hand. It must be from what they called a shrapnel shell, she realized—hundreds of bullets were packed inside to explode in all directions into peoples' flesh. She dropped it and focused on the forest canopy in order to calm her breath.

She recognized that she was on top of a berm, like a spine that followed the curves in the hills. On one side, where the hill fell away, she could make out that the ground had been dug into dips and folds, and was undulating in an unnatural way. The foliage that covered it seemed to grow in a zigzag pattern. She felt the familiar hum that always guided her through the Maine woods. She got her bearings. If she'd remembered correctly the way Lieutenant Hammond had described the Meuse-Argonne Offensive, this would have been the enemy's position. She was looking at German trenches.

Those were the trees where they would have strung barbed wire, with openings in the wire and machine guns aimed at the gaps, so that when the Allies advanced, they'd be herded into the bullets like animals to a slaughterhouse. She turned from the ridge and made a pact with her fear to walk five more minutes before turning back. Then she would have seen everything she had come to France to see. The hum had deserted her, replaced by a disorienting wail. She was stopped by an impenetrable stand of blackthorn, dense spiky branches like the vines that grew over Sleeping Beauty. She understood the story for the first time. Only imaginary fairy-tale magic could cut through such deeply rooted evil. There was evil all around.

Something had turned the birch trees lurid green. The bark was emerald when it should have been white, probably, she realized, from the copper in all the shells that must be in the ground. And just on her left was an enormous crater, a perfect circle scooped out of the earth at least fifteen feet deep and twenty feet across, halfway filled with seedlings and forest debris.

She turned around where the brambles blocked the way. If she'd gone a little farther she would have come to an intact German bunker the Americans had failed to blow up when they liberated the area, now infested with bees. She would have made out old wooden beds and realized that young men had slept there, and that if they'd taken off their helmets in the semi-dark, she would have seen hollow pairs of human eyes.

Cora came back to the picnic spot stunned by her discoveries. She wanted to grab Hammond and take him up there and show him everything so he could explain, in that excited voice she'd come to trust, what had happened and why. To tell Bobbie all about the crater and confess the strange thought she'd had, that little Sammy and his boyhood friends would have loved that big hole, would have slid down on their heels and dived headlong into the leaves.

The ladies had already returned from the stream. They were moving slowly, grumbling about mosquitoes, seeming to still be dazed from the heavy lunch and afternoon heat while Hammond and Lily folded up the blankets.

"Where were you?" he asked sharply.

"Just up there."

"I was about to go after you."

Cora told Hammond she'd found some trenches and a giant hole. "What was it?"

"Most likely from an American howitzer. The Germans were up here for four years," he said, as if she should have known. "They chopped down trees for barracks and brought in supplies on a small rail train, built communication lines. They were always one skip ahead."

"How could they do all that without anybody knowing?"

He shook out a blanket.

"They had collaborators," he said darkly. "Where's Mrs. Olsen? Didn't she go with you?"

Cora shook her head. "Isn't she with you? Look what I found." She opened her hand and showed him the white shards. "How do you think they got there?"

"Those are oyster shells," he said distractedly.

"I thought so!"

"The Germans used to eat oysters and drink schnapps. They said the oysters gave you the passion to fight. And the schnapps got you drunk so you could. Anybody seen Mrs. Olsen?" Hammond asked to no reply.

"She probably went somewhere to pee," Lily said. "Should I go look?"

Hammond picked up his web belt and took a drink from the canteen that was attached. He looked at his watch. "Damn it to hell," he remarked crossly. "We're supposed to be on the way."

Cora squinted into the sun. A dry wind was blowing her dress. She couldn't see anything but high grass in the neighboring farmer's field. It crossed her mind uneasily that maybe Bobbie had wandered off, like Elizabeth Pascoe's mother on her way to the cemetery. She went down to the road and stood still and listened to the whispering of the straw. She heard Bobbie's voice calling for help, far away and weak as a baby bird's.

"Thomas!" Cora waved frantically. "She's there!"

Hammond dropped the belt and sprinted past Cora, who ran behind him through sharp waist-high grass.

"Hold steady!" Hammond shouted. "We're coming."

Fifty yards in they found Bobbie lying near the clump of bellflowers on a matted mound of straw where she'd fallen, legs twisted beneath her, sketchbook tossed nearby.

"I'm afraid I've been clumsy," Bobbie said. "I was walking along looking at the flowers, and next thing I knew, I was on the ground!"

There was straw in her hair and her makeup had streaked. Cora remembered how determined Bobbie had been to sketch the florist's bouquets in Paris, not hesitating to rush across a busy street, but this time she'd been tripped up by a concealed danger.

Her foot had been caught in a tangle of rusty barbed wire, and blood was running from the punctures of the spikes. She was tethered to the spot.

"I've been trying to stand—"

"Don't do that," said Hammond, appraising the situation. "Try to relax."

"Something happened to my knee."

Cora could see the swelling starting to rise. She stood up in the grass and bellowed, *"Li-ly! Nurse Lily!* I'll go get her—"

Hammond grabbed Cora's arm and said, "No."

"Why?"

"It's a bit more complicated than that. Mrs. Olsen, try not to move."

"I'm not about to get on a train," Bobbie said. Even flat-out in the middle of a pasture her sense of irony had not abandoned her.

"Look at this."

Hammond pointed. Cora followed his finger as it moved along the tangle of wire, which was wrapped around what appeared to be a piece of an old farm implement—a fourteen-inch wooden handle with a metal head.

"What is it?"

"A German stick grenade."

"That's a grenade?"

"Yes, it's a grenade. They attached them to sticks and lobbed them into the trenches."

"Could it still explode?"

He didn't answer. "Go tell Émile. Get the women out of here. Get the police. Tell them we've got a dud-fired German Stielhandgranate 24 wrapped around a lady's leg."

"Should I—?"

"Go," he commanded.

Cora turned and ran.

Bobbie was looking placidly at Hammond. Her eyes were old and calm. "You too," she said.

"I'm not going to leave you," he replied.

19

The faster Cora pushed through the high grass, the harder it became to keep moving forward. The thick stems would not yield. She swept them aside but their sharp edges cut her hands and whipped across her eyes. She inhaled a noseful of chaff and was blinded by tears. Her foot hit a heavy metal object and she tripped and sprawled into the standing field, pierced all over by shafts of straw. When she got to her feet and whirled around to see what had caused her to fall, her legs began to shake like the shivering village dog's. She'd fallen over a cylindrical brass shell five inches in diameter that still had its high-explosive nose.

"Thomas!" she screamed, waving. *"Thomas!"*

His head and shoulders appeared out of the yellow stalks.

"Go—just go!"

"The field is full of bombs. Look! They're everywhere!"

She and Hammond stood stock-still, fifty yards apart, watching clouds and sun roll over the sighing grass. As their vision settled in the rippling light, they began to discern the remnants of a battle that had been overgrown and hidden. The rusted wheels of a field gun. A human jaw.

"Thomas! It's a battlefield!"

Hammond could see it now. The grotesque litter of war was all around them, emerging from the changing shadows like hidden pictures in a child's book. A charred gas mask. A glove with the skeletal hand still in it.

"Nobody is to come out here, those are my orders. Do you understand?"

"Yes."

"Go back! Find a telephone!" Hammond called.

"I can't move."

"Why? Are you caught?"

Cora stared at the shell. Faintly striped with red and green, it looked threatening, unstable, those lead balls inside poised to blow. She might have been on a ledge a hundred feet above a granite gorge for the paralyzing venom that filled her body, causing her to tremble so violently her teeth were clicking; so light-headed she might faint.

"I just can't."

The thing was alive. She knew it.

Hammond's voice surprised her with its confidence.

"Mrs. Blake, listen to me. Take one step at a time. Exactly the way you came. Steady your mind. Think of your son."

Cora pictured Sammy. She took a step.

"That's it! Make Samuel proud of you," Hammond said. "Keep going!"

The first wild thought that came to her was of the races on the Fourth of July, in the park after the parade. She was hopping along in a burlap sack, one hop at a time, laughing so hard she might wee, and there was Sammy at the finish line, urging, *"Mom! Mom!,"* his face summer-flushed and serious because this race was the most important thing in the world—his little man's arms covered with downy hair reaching out to tag her while his toes dug in behind the chalk—five or six years old and still obedient to the rules—and she held on with all her might to reach that earnest face, the most important thing in the world, as she picked her way through the living minefield.

Lily was running to meet her when Cora stumbled onto the road.

"What happened?"

"There are explosives left over from the war."

Lily gasped. Her eyes went over Cora's head. "Where's Mrs. Olsen?"

"She got her foot tangled up with a grenade."

"I've got to help—"

Cora grabbed Lily's arm. "You can't. It's dangerous."

"It's my duty—"

"You need to take care of the others. The lieutenant's orders are for everyone to keep away." Cora startled when she saw that the turnout was empty. "Where's the bus? Where's Émile?"

"He went to get gasoline—"

"That's the stupidest thing I ever heard!" Cora blurted, half crazed, tramping toward the group waiting in the shade.

Lily followed. "Émile said the gas pump was in the opposite direction from the cemetery, so when—"

Cora interrupted: "I don't care what he said!" She snapped out, "How far did he go?"

"Mrs. Blake, calm down. We thought there would be enough time—"

"There is no time! How far are we from the village? We need help. Can we walk?"

"I'll get the map."

The others drifted over curiously as Lily

fumbled with the haversack. Cora wiped the sweat from her forehead and peered down the empty road. They were out in the open and, if that thing went off, completely trapped. Lily found the U.S. Army chart and Cora knelt beside her in the dirt, quickly orienting it to north.

"Where are we?" Lily asked.

Cora pointed. Linwood had taught her how to read maps. "There. The nearest town is Cheppy."

Wilhelmina leaned over Cora's shoulder. "Are we lost?"

"Don't be silly," Katie answered mildly. "The bus will be back any minute."

Lily was on her feet. "It's too far. I'm going to help Thomas."

Cora stood and got in front of her. "I say you don't."

"I'm sorry, but you don't have a say—"

"If you disobey his orders, I'll report you myself."

Minnie looked between them. "What is going on?"

"Where *is* Bobbie?" Katie asked.

"She stepped on a bomb!" Cora said in exasperation.

"Sweet Jesus up in heaven," Katie breathed.

Minnie cried, "What should we do?"

Cora tried to think. "It isn't safe. We can't help them; it's best for us to go."

Minnie pressed a hand to her mouth. Katie gripped Cora's sleeve with an accusing stare.

"Just abandon them, like that?"

"They can't move," Cora told her desperately. "Bobbie's got that wire wrapped around her leg."

Wilhelmina suggested they get out of there. "Pronto."

"Look!" Minnie cried. "There's a car!"

They all ran to the side of the road. Only Lily remained. She kissed her crucifix.

"Please be with Thomas, please," she whispered.

Hammond took his jacket off. The heat of the afternoon was brutal. The bleeding had stopped and he'd had time to examine the grenade—"to know the enemy" as they said—and he could see that the situation was bad. The "spoon," the time fuse, had already come off, which meant the thing could detonate at any time.

"Where is everyone?" Bobbie murmured.

"I've asked them to stay away for the moment."

She nodded. "We don't want to put anyone else in danger."

"Just taking precautions," Hammond replied lightly.

"I wish you'd go."

"We're getting out of here together. This thing might not even be live. After all, it's been lying around for years—"

"Don't fib, Thomas," Bobbie said. Her tongue moved over her parched lips. "I raised a boy of my own, you know."

Her eyes were dull and her skin had taken on a greenish pallor. Hammond badly wished he had not dropped his belt with his canteen when he'd run into the field. He tried to weigh the greater danger: the damn thing blowing up or her becoming dehydrated and going into shock.

"Tell me what you're doing, son. I'd like to follow along."

"Textbook would be to dispose of the ordnance by blowing it up, but obviously we can't do that, so the next best thing is to separate *you* from *it,* so maybe if we can remove the shoe . . ."

He untied the laces carefully, but the slightest movement made Bobbie groan.

"My foot's all swollen up."

He sat back on his heels. He had no tools, no knife. He scanned the old battlefield for something sharp to cut the wires, but all he saw were a couple of half-empty sandbags oozing the earth they'd been stuffed with.

"You just rest," he said idiotically, and scrambled through the brush to drag the sandbags, one by one, around the woman. Sweating like a pig, he went back to the shoe.

He looked at his work and realized he had accomplished nothing.

"If we can just slip this off . . ."

But he couldn't manipulate the shoe without causing her to squirm in pain and disturb the pull cord to the grenade, which was wrapped around

377

the barbed wire. With the spoon gone, they were at grave risk. The slightest movement could set off a blast.

"Can we go now?" Bobbie said dreamily.

"Almost there," Hammond promised, feeling like a lousy, cheap, cockeyed liar.

Her eyes had closed. Then she was still for a long moment.

"Mrs. Olsen?"

Panicked, he groped for a pulse. Her wrist was so thin it disappeared inside his hand.

"Henry?" she said quite clearly. "Would you mind closing the door, dear?"

The driver of the car was dressed in a suit and hat and his female companion wore a corsage. They roared right by, ignoring the commotion by the side of the road and keeping their eyes straight ahead, as if they were late to be somewhere. Distraught, the women returned to the shade.

"Did you see that man? That man refused to stop!"

Wilhelmina stomped her foot with frustration. Her hat was crooked and her hair was lank. Random bits of straw clung to her clothes, which were covered with dust. She looked to Cora like a colt that had rolled in a pile of manure.

"Of course not," Minnie cried. "Waving your arms and jumping up and down like a crazy person. Who would stop for a crazy person?"

"Another crazy person?" Wilhelmina suggested.

Katie pointed. "Look!"

The blue bus was lumbering back. It stopped in a cloud of foul exhaust. Émile climbed out, eating an apple.

Minnie hit him with her purse. "Where were you?!"

"*Quel est votre problème, madame?*" he cried, jumping away.

"We have to go," said Cora. "Now. Find a telephone. Where's the nearest phone?"

Émile was confused. Didn't they want to go to the cemetery? He was supposed to keep to the schedule.

"*Mais il n'est pas temps de revenir à l'hôtel. Nous n'allons pas au cimetière?*" he asked, tossing the apple core.

"Oh hell," said Cora. "Nobody here speaks French. *Telephone!*" she fairly shouted. She pointed to the field and mimed a huge explosion. "A bomb. A German bomb!"

Émile understood.

Hammond had decided that the only course of action was to try to defuse the grenade himself. He took out a handkerchief and wiped the moisture from his face and hands. Then he wrapped the cloth around two twists of the barbed wire and pulled gently. Slowly he eased the wires far enough apart to be able to get his hands through.

He could just reach inside the knot of cords and wires to get his fingers around the head of the grenade.

Gingerly, he tried to unscrew the top. His plan was to disrupt the chain of explosives by removing the top and the pull cord in one piece.

They were rusted tight.

He applied more pressure.

Grimacing, he twisted harder. Bobbie moaned.

"Where is it?" shouted a man in French.

Startled, Hammond almost dropped the whole assembly. Émile was standing a few paces away, bravely offering a bucket of water.

"What the hell are you doing here?" Hammond demanded, also in French. "These things can blow on impact!"

"Those fucking Germans. This happens every day—"

"Get something to cut these wires. Hurry!"

Émile set the bucket down and ran back toward the road.

"And watch where you step! There's live shit all over the place."

Hammond turned back to the corroded top of the grenade. His fingers were slick with sweat. The orange rust came off in his hands. It was hopeless. He needed a demolitions expert. Or at least a wrench. He set everything down and waited for Émile. The sun was low in the grass. It was coming on evening and a veil of jumpy insects had appeared over the field. Or had they been drawn by the proximity of death? he wondered grimly. He jammed some sticks into the ground and hung his jacket over them, creating a bit of shade for Mrs. Olsen. Her breath was sounding shallow and her thin lips sucked like a baby's.

The driver returned with a pair of rusty garden shears that barely closed.

"Thank you," said Hammond in French. *"Now get lost! And get those women on the bus and far away."*

Émile's weathered face looked grave but he didn't argue. With a somber tip of his cloth cap, he was gone.

Hammond tried to keep his thoughts away from everything but the puzzle that lay before him. It was a purely mechanical problem. It could be solved. All he had to do was follow the knots, like untangling Christmas lights. He would do this slowly and deliberately, no matter how long it took—there were still hours of daylight left. He had to use both hands to manipulate the rusty shears. He made three careful snips in the barbed wire and pried it loose. All of it came away except one batch still hooked on the pull cord of the grenade. Snaking a hand through, Hammond attempted to free the last piece and slashed a finger on a barb, producing a spurt of blood and stinging pain. His hand jerked involuntarily. The pull cord yanked at the detonator, where the spoon had been. He held his breath.

They were safe.

Then the thing started smoking.

Wildly he cut through the rest of the wire, grabbed the wooden handle, pulled it loose, and hurled the grenade with all his strength, end over end into the sky, throwing his body across Bobbie's. Three seconds later, the earth erupted. There was a flash of fire and a booming explosion that was heard two miles away. The shock waves filled his body and clogged his ears. The pilgrims were already on the bus with the motor running when the blast went off. The whole thing shook. Two windows shattered. Glass flew as they screamed and crouched down in the aisle.

When it was quiet they lifted their heads, pulling themselves up stiffly, asking if everyone was all right. There were torn stockings and scraped knees. Émile had turned off the engine and stumbled outside, a hand to his scalp where he was bleeding from being knocked against a pole. One by one the others ventured out clutching their purses. Émile tried to help them down from the bus. Wilhelmina, tall and solid on her feet, took that job as Lily tended to Émile's wound from her Red Cross bag.

They looked across the road. There was no sound, no movement but the shushing of the grass. Cora felt the world shut down. Her whole body trembled as if it couldn't support the weight of everything anymore, and finally she gave in to tears.

Someone put an arm around her. It was Minnie.

"No more bangs, that's a good sign, yes? They'll be okay. Keep thinking, *God is good, they'll be okay.*"

Just then Hammond emerged from the meadow carrying Bobbie in his arms, both of them tattered, bloodied, filthy, and alive. No war heroes ever had a more emotional welcome, as the mothers surrounded them with tears of joy and cheers of relief, like a regular homecoming parade.

"Please put me down," Bobbie said. "I feel ridiculous."

Lily supported her as she gingerly found her feet. "Easy on the knee."

"I can walk."

They helped her to stand.

"Okay?" Hammond asked.

"Marvelous. Thank you. What a guy, right, girls?"

The women applauded with whistles and hoots.

"You should have seen it," Bobbie said. "He threw that nasty old thing away like Babe Ruth himself."

"Not at all." Hammond blushed beneath the ruddy sunburn, dirt, and sweat.

Lily gave him a punch on the arm. "Aces up. Brilliant job."

Minnie fanned her bosom with her pocketbook. "See? I told you."

Katie laughed and poked him in the chest. "You're going to get a medal, *right here!*"

"Mrs. Olsen was the brave one," Hammond said.

"Mrs. Olsen needs to rest," Lily said firmly.

Wiping her eyes, Cora came forward and took her friend's arm. "Come on, Bobbie. Let's go on the bus and sit down."

"Horsefeathers!" Bobbie declared. "What a story this will make at my bridge club! Now— where's the rest of that Champagne?"

At once both her legs gave out and she collapsed into a net of loving arms that eased her to the ground. Lily pulled smelling salts from the Red Cross bag and put them under Bobbie's nose but there was no response. She wasn't breathing. Lily tried chest compressions but nothing changed. The women grabbed for one another—hands, arms, skirts—whatever was closest—holding tight in a protective circle. Lily grabbed a stethoscope from the bag and probed for a heartbeat, but Bobbie's face had settled into stony silence. Lily looked up and her moist eyes were filled with terror.

Wilhelmina nodded. "I've seen this before. She's left us."

"No!" said Hammond wildly. "It can't be!"

Cora rocked Bobbie's shoulders. She rocked harder, but she knew.

They stared down at the motionless body.

Lily had an iron grip on Hammond's forearm. "Thomas—?"

He couldn't answer. He was sobbing.

Émile climbed in and started up the bus but nobody would leave Bobbie. Hammond composed himself and helped Lily cover her with a picnic blanket. The rest sat down against the trees in the dusk.

"We'll go to the cemetery tomorrow," Katie said numbly, and the rest simply nodded.

Émile drove back to the market where he'd gotten the gas. A phone call was placed to the police station in Cheppy, and an hour later a patrolman arrived in a dust-covered sedan, followed by an ambulance. Lily helped the dazed women back onto the bus. Mechanically they sorted out sweaters and hats and articles from purses that had been strewn about after the explosion. Staring into the dark they rode back to the hotel, while Hammond stayed and made his report.

20

General Perkins arrived in Verdun by motorcar from Paris before noon. He wore the same olive-drab riding jacket and high leather boots, but this time his sharp features were set with displeasure rather than welcome, and the insignias of power sewn into the uniform seemed far from merely decorative. Straight-backed, he trotted up the hotel steps followed by his aides-de-camp. Lieutenant Hammond and Lily were waiting at the door, exactly where he'd welcomed the pilgrims days before with warm words and a handshake. Hammond saluted but the general kept going.

"All activities are suspended," he said. "Nobody is to leave the hotel."

He strode past Lily without a nod. Inside, the German family hovered nervously, the son standing guard beside his father in the wheelchair. With a few terse words, the aides had arranged for a room to serve as the command post for the inquiry into the unexpected death of Mrs. Genevieve "Bobbie" Olsen. The French police would no doubt be involved, but for now the matter was in American hands. Hearing the word *enquête* made the wife behind the counter visibly cringe. Coffee was arranged.

"Lieutenant Hammond? Please come in," Perkins said, opening a door to a room off the lobby. "Nurse? I'll see you later."

"Yes, sir," Lily said, but Perkins ignored the reply, motioning the lieutenant to come inside.

They were using the parlor, a dank corner with fern-green wallpaper carpeted with purple flowers like an overgrown swamp. It was outfitted with broken-down wicker tables and chairs and a scarred upright piano. One wall was taken up by a heavy, ornate gold-framed mirror; the kind featured in horror movies, Hammond noted, where the hero peers into the glass and sees himself reflected as a ghoul.

"Sit down, Hammond," the general said, lighting a pipe. "This is unfortunate."

"Very sad, sir."

"Do you know who Mrs. Olsen was?"

"Yes, sir. She was a very nice woman."

"I'm talking about her background."

"She came from a wealthy family in Cambridge. She was interested in art, and—"

"It's a bit more than that, Hammond. Her grandfather built the New England railroad. She comes from one of the richest families in the country. You know what that means?"

Hammond searched for the answer and found his voice had shriveled to a chirp. "It will be in the papers?"

Perkins tossed the dead match into an ashtray. "Correct."

Hammond cleared his throat. "I take responsibility, sir."

"How is that?"

"Mrs. Olsen had been drinking, sir."

"Drinking?"

"Champagne. It was provided by the hotel . . . for a picnic."

"What are you saying? That she died from an overdose of Champagne?"

"I don't know, but she also—"

Perkins interrupted with a cold laugh. "In that case, Hammond, why fight the Germans? Why not invite them over for hors d'oeuvres?"

He got up and paced, smoke trailing behind him, so that the small room became filled with the sickly sweet smell of Revelation pipe tobacco.

"Don't be so quick to hang yourself, Hammond. You're a hero, don't you know? You risked your life to defuse a fucking German stick bomb and save a Gold Star Mother. The fact that she succumbed afterward, well, that was an unforeseen outcome, but goddamnit, you did your part. You're a poster boy for the American soldier. If anybody asks, it was a tragic incident that in no way reflects on the U.S. Army or the pilgrimages."

Hammond considered this. The patrol officer from Cheppy had been a tall, skinny youth his age, with a curved back, graceless face, and light brown mustache, who looked more like a delivery boy than a cop. "*Chance dure, ami*," he'd said nervously. He seemed to want assurance from the man in the U.S. Army uniform with the gold bar that things were under control, which is what Hammond had hoped in vain to get from his French counterpart. The two ambulance drivers who took care of the body were older, matter-of-fact, and shook Hammond's hand before driving off. None of them questioned the circumstances.

"The police were cooperative, sir," Hammond replied.

"Good. Our mission here in France is to show the U.S. Army in the best light. And certainly not to ruffle the waters with our allies." Perkins knocked the pipe against his palm, emptying the bowl into the ashtray. "The only remaining question will be cause of death."

Hammond's heartbeat spiked. It was the question that had kept him up last night, examining the scenario piece by piece to be certain there was nothing he had done that showed dereliction of duty. Still, he readied himself for a grilling. He would hold his ground.

"How did she get into that field?"

"Mrs. Olsen went there of her own volition, sir. I expressly warned them to stay on our side of the road because there was known to be unexploded ordnance in the area. She disobeyed my orders."

"I doubt a woman like Mrs. Olsen took orders from anyone."

"I'm afraid not, sir."

"What was she doing there?"

"She wanted to sketch a flower."

This drew a wry look from General Perkins. Mrs. Olsen's imperious behavior did not surprise him in the least.

"I believe I was quite clear. I have witnesses—"

"Take it easy, Hammond," Perkins interrupted. "No need to start turning over rocks. We go through the motions of an investigation, and then it's just a matter of paperwork. The faster we get Mrs. Olsen's body back to the family, the sooner this is over. Once the French medical examiner signs off, it's out of our hands. All we need are the medical records."

"Yes, sir. I'll get them right away."

Lily had been sitting in the lobby in a cracked leather armchair, rereading her notations on Mrs. Olsen while nervously waiting to be called. She was fairly sure the poor woman died of cardiac failure but there was nothing to back that up—no indication of previously existing heart disease. If there had been, her family doctor would not have allowed her to make the trip or, depending on the diagnosis, would have prescribed nitroglycerine or at least a sedative. But there wasn't anything like that on the medical form. It came down to the fact that Mrs. Olsen had been sixty-five, the oldest person on the pilgrimage. She died of natural causes due to nervousness and exertion; certainly the general could see that.

It was the other matter, their brief assignation by the river, that was much more troubling. She had confidence in her nursing care; it was Perkins she was worried about. That kiss made her vulnerable. She sat there berating herself for not reacting even faster than she had. She'd hesitated half a second—shocked, pulled in, flattered—until her brain woke up and she pushed him away. The iciness she'd felt when he arrived frightened her. Was it because she'd turned him down? Was he going to take it out on her now? It was little comfort to recall that he'd boasted about garroting a man in the Philippines without a blink.

She sprang up the moment Hammond came through the parlor door.

"How'd it go?" she asked.

"He wants to see Mrs. Olsen's medical records."

"I have them." But she withheld the papers.

Hammond gave her a hard stare. "Don't tell me there's a problem, Lily."

"There isn't a problem," Lily said. "That's what—"

"All right then, *give*." He snapped the folder out of her hands. "He wants them *now*," he said.

"Why?"

"He's looking for cause of death," Hammond answered.

The seriousness of the situation had truly sunk in. This was not like the war games they played at the academy, moving toy soldiers around on a table grid, drawing battle plans on a chalkboard. The relics in the field where Bobbie died jumped out at him. That grenade was real.

"But you know what really killed her?" Hammond said, reflecting briefly. "The waste of war." He headed to the parlor.

"Thomas?"

"What?"

She could see from his tense, drawn face that things were rough inside.

"Don't worry," she said gently. "Nobody will find anything unfavorable in my report." Meaning she'd made sure that he'd come off well.

"Thank you." Hammond lowered his eyes and the tips of his ears burned red. "I admit what happened afterward was not my proudest moment as an officer."

"But completely understandable."

"I guess I never really watched anyone die before."

"Even if you had, I can promise that you never get used to it. How do you think I feel? I'm the one who was supposed to save her."

"But there was nothing to be done." He meant it as a question.

"No," she assured him. "There was not."

"I hope the brass sees it that way."

She hesitated. "Thomas?" she asked tremulously. "Are we in trouble?"

"I'll let you know," he said, and closed the door behind him, feeling the pressure of looking out not only for his own welfare but also Lily's.

Cora watched from the window of her room as a stream of unusual characters entered the hotel. Normally all you'd see in the mornings were housewives dragging grocery bags and corralling young children, and elderly men shuffling through their worn routines. Once in a while a peddler of knives or cotton goods would pass, leading a horse-drawn wagon. Today there were more taxis than usual, as trains arrived at the station carrying newsmen and some important-looking officials from Paris. A cluster of villagers had gathered in front of the hotel to ogle the goings-on. Cora longed to get a closer look, to get outdoors and breathe the fresh, brackish air, but not only were the streets in ruins for blocks, they had been told not to leave the hotel, on orders of General Perkins. She saw a postman impatiently pushing through the crowd to the entrance. The sight of him nudged her back to the writing desk, where she'd left a half-finished letter to Linwood. She'd probably be home by the time it arrived, but she had such a craving for someone to talk to; someone who knew her well. She glanced toward Bobbie's sad, empty bed.

"*. . . I never thought I could be close to such a wealthy lady, but there's a kind of friendship that goes beyond money or the color of your skin. I'm glad Bobbie got to say goodbye to her boy, which was the most important thing to her and she would—*"

There was timid knock. Cora got up from the desk and opened the door to find the little maid holding an envelope.

"*Excusez-moi, madame,*" she said. "*Il y a un télégramme pour vous.*"

The maid looked emaciated in her washed out too-big black dress, and childlike black stockings and ballet slippers. There were circles under her eyes.

"Aren't they feeding you enough?" Cora asked.

"*Merci. J'espère que vous profitez bien du reste de votre séjour.*"

They nodded and smiled, neither understanding the other, and the girl gave her the letter and left. Cora assumed it was from the Adjunct General's Office—a travel reminder or a change in schedule. She opened the envelope. Inside was a cable from Paris.

ARRIVING TONIGHT. GRIF

When Lily was finally called into the parlor, she could see right away that the General Reginald Perkins she now faced was not the same as the man who had kissed her in the darkness near the river. This Perkins was all official business, the senior mechanic called in to fix the engine and make the airplane fly. That, and only that, was the mission. He had moved things around so he could station himself behind a card table placed in the center of the room—the flimsiest of barricades—but it served to make clear who was questioning whom.

"Please sit down," he said.

The only choice was a wicker rocking chair.

"How are you?" he asked in neutral tone that could be interpreted as intimate or completely disinterested.

Lily took the cue and replied as if nothing had happened between them.

"I'm fine, thank you, sir. I'm very sorry that we lost Mrs. Olsen. It was a shock to everyone."

He smiled a bit as if to put her at ease. "I'm sure that you did nothing wrong—"

"I would hope so, General Perkins."

"You understand the situation. Questions will be asked."

She straightened up as best she could in the rocking chair and kept her gaze steady.

"It's all in my report, but go ahead."

"I understand Mrs. Olsen went peacefully. Is that so?"

"Yes, sir. There wasn't any pain. She collapsed and stopped breathing. It was over very fast."

"Did you attempt to revive her? How?"

"Smelling salts."

"And when she did not wake up, you knew it wasn't just a fainting spell—"

"I immediately checked for a heartbeat. There wasn't any heartbeat."

"Then what did you do?" He waited. "I'm asking what the medical examiner will ask. No need to worry, it's all a formality. Papers need to be signed so the body can be released back to the family. Hopefully on the next boat."

"I performed several chest compressions and checked again for vital signs. There were none. We were out in the woods, there was no hope of getting to a hospital—"

"Meaning there was no chance she could be revived?"

Lily solemnly shook her head. "She was gone."

"And the cause? In your opinion?"

"Cardiac arrest. But I can't find any indication of heart disease in her record."

Perkins was tapping a pencil on the papers as if to call her attention to something she'd failed to see.

"It could be her doctor back home missed something. Doesn't mean she wasn't sick when she arrived. We have an elderly woman traveling overseas under terrific strain. Nobody's going to question what happened."

"Why should they?" Lily asked, trying to hide her alarm.

"They should not," Perkins agreed, closing the folder. He stood but did not offer his hand. "Thank you, Lieutenant."

"You're welcome, sir."

She was hoping for a final telling look—a confidential gaze to let her know that everything was all right—but he was studying his papers, eyes downcast. She withdrew smartly, determined not to show what the interview had taken out of her. She was sweating indecently and worn to the bone, as if she'd just passed orals at nursing school but without the thrill. It was more a feeling of cautious relief that they seemed to be on the same track. They'd both played their roles and gotten through their obligatory scene with the unspoken understanding—she hoped—that the whole business at the river was forgotten.

The women of Party A had been .told by Hammond not to talk to strangers about the matter of Mrs. Olsen and to be aware that the press might seek them out. They spent the afternoon mostly resting in their rooms, which was a necessity after yesterday's ordeal. Later that evening they met in the dining room and, feeling very conspiratorial, took a table in the back. After dinner, Lily organized a game of gin rummy, while Hammond, at loose ends, wandered in the hotel garden. Outside he smelled a waft of tobacco smoke. Following the red arc of a cigarette, he was shocked to discover it was Mrs. Blake who was smoking.

"Have a coffin nail," Cora said, handing him the pack she had bought at the desk.

"Bad joke, considering the circumstances, eh?" Hammond replied.

Cora folded her arms and inhaled. "Does it matter?"

They stood on a small brick path in awkward silence. The beds of waist-high lavender released a dense oily smell.

"I can't wait to get out of this place," Cora said.

"Ready to go home?"

She nodded. "I thought we'd see each other in Maine, and that Bobbie and I would be friends forever." She sighed. "What about you, Thomas? You never expected to have to face something like this, did you?"

"I'd like to say the army prepares you for anything—but—no, ma'am."

Cora smiled a little in the dark, feeling warm toward the boy—like Sammy, thrust out into the world so young, and taking on the world's heaviest burdens. That's what we do to our kids, she reflected. Give them our failures. Our wars and the results of wars. Abandoned farms and busted banks.

It was a mild summer night and the rear doors to the lobby were open, spilling light. Someone in the parlor was banging out "I Got Rhythm" on the piano, accompanied by a warbling soprano chorus of other Gold Star Mothers who were guests at the hotel.

"This can't be much fun. Chaperoning a bunch of chattering ninnies."

Hammond laughed. "I'll miss every one of you."

"You can't wait to get back to your buddies. But

you were very brave, and I'm proud of you. What you did. You saved Mrs. Olsen's life."

"Almost saved it," he said miserably.

"You have nothing to be ashamed of."

Hammond rubbed the side of his nose with the hand that held the cigarette in a pose of Continental angst. "Except for crying like a baby."

"It only goes to show that you're a human being with a heart."

The pianist switched to a ragtime version of "I Got Rhythm." Nobody could keep up with the words, and the whole thing collapsed into dissonance.

"Doesn't matter in the army. In the army you're supposed to follow orders and cover your ass."

"Maybe you're not suited for the army."

"Every male in my family has been an officer, going back to the Civil War."

"Bully for them. What about you?"

He smoked, pondered, cleared his throat.

"I still believe there's nothing more important than defending your country, and if I fail at that, there's not much else worth doing."

"There are other ways to serve your country."

"But not the Hammond way."

The music stopped and they heard weak applause.

"Let's go inside," he suggested. "I think there's punch."

Hammond stepped away so that she could go

first through the open doors into the lobby, where Griffin Reed and Florence Dean Powell had just arrived on the train from Paris. She was at the reception desk, briskly speaking in French to the hotel owner's cowering wife, impatiently tapping a black-gloved finger on the faux marble counter, a magnetizing figure in a sweeping raven-black mourning dress and a black hat trailing black feathers. Her lips were tightened in a disapproving frown. The sight of her caused a sour reaction in the back of Cora's throat.

Reed, also elegantly dressed in black, looked like a suitable partner to this determined lady, except when he turned his head and you saw that pleasant look of perpetually mild amusement that didn't go with the tension that was buzzing around Florence like a pack of wasps. While she argued with the wife, the owner of the hotel was sermonizing Reed in French, telling some elaborate tale, having maneuvered his wheelchair so he could offer a hand crippled by war in camaraderie with the wounded man behind the mask. Reed welcomed Cora with relief when she came over to introduce Lieutenant Hammond.

"I admired your story in *Le Matin*," Hammond said.

"Mrs. Blake was an inspiring subject," answered Reed.

"All I did was answer his questions," Cora said modestly.

"I know General Perkins appreciated the good things you said about the tours."

"I'm glad to hear it," said Reed. "Then he'll be inclined to help clear things up."

"Is there a problem?" Hammond asked.

"My friend, Miss Powell, was very close to Bobbie Olsen. She's concerned about what happened."

"The army sends its deepest condolences, believe me," Hammond replied.

"Miss Powell won't be satisfied until she's assured by General Perkins that everything was done correctly."

"I'll see what I can do," said Hammond, who couldn't take his eyes off the mask. Then he was unable to stop himself. "Shame about your injury," he blurted. "Where did it happen?"

"Ypres."

"Infantry?"

"I was covering the war for AP. There was a gas attack and I stood up in the trench. No air."

"Sorry to hear it."

"I knew the risks," Reed said offhandedly.

Hammond nodded and offered his hand. "We appreciate your service to the country."

Reed shook with the young man and Cora was pleased to see that Hammond had regained his self-control. She gave him an encouraging smile, which he ignored, excusing himself to settle whatever Florence had stirred up at the reception desk.

"Are you all right?" Cora asked.

"I could ask the same," said Reed.

Inside the prison of the mask she found his eyes were alive and warm, no different from the way he'd regarded her from the first; watchfully, even protectively, when they'd sat on the bench in the Luxembourg Gardens and she'd been thankful for his understanding company.

"I can't get over it," Cora said, shaking her head.

"Bobbie thought the world of you—"

"Finally!" Florence interrupted, sweeping between them. "The young man says he'll get his superior officer to tell me exactly what is going on. I'm so upset, I can't even cry."

"Cora was there when it happened," Reed reminded her.

"Terrible," Florence said, greeting Cora with a quick double kiss. "Just terrible."

"She was a remarkable lady." Cora found that her throat was still thick with emotion.

"Very strong," Florence agreed. "And she very much wanted to go on this trip."

"Yes," Cora said, "she told me."

"She *insisted,*" Florence went on. "Nobody could stop her."

"Why would anybody want to try?"

"Well, because of her heart."

"She wasn't sick."

"Oh, yes. Bobbie had a weak heart. Did have, for years."

"Are you sure?" Cora asked, looking back and forth between them, but Reed just shrugged.

"Of course I'm sure," said Florence with a shake of glossy black feathers. "I've known her a little bit longer than you."

"She never said a word."

"She wouldn't have. That was Bobbie. In charge to the end."

"So it was natural causes," Reed said. "That should be a relief to everyone."

Florence removed her gloves. "I suppose the medicine she was taking just wasn't strong enough."

"Bobbie never took any medicine."

"Maybe you just didn't—" Florence began.

Cora interrupted: "No, I would have seen. We shared a room, we were together twelve hours a day. She had no reason to hide it. I would have known."

"This doesn't make sense. Bobbie had congestive heart failure and knew she had to take her pills. She was always very good about it."

"Are you saying she skipped them?" Reed asked. "Why would she?"

"She didn't skip them," Cora said. "She never got them. Everyone else had their medicine. The nurse gave it out each morning—"

"And none for Bobbie?"

"None for Bobbie," Cora echoed, wondering why.

"Well," said Florence. "That decides it. There will be a full inquest. It was the army's responsibility, and they should have seen to it. I knew something was wrong."

"Wasn't it on her record?" Reed asked.

"Of course it was! Why wasn't she supervised? You see? We were right to come here. If it wasn't for me, they'd sweep this right under the rug. I'm going to insist that the American ambassador be involved! We owe it to Bobbie and her family," she said, answering Reed's skeptical look. "My poor mother will be devastated; she and Bobbie were sorority sisters at Radcliffe. I have to push this along, if for no reason other than Mother's peace of mind." She stopped to survey the castle decor of the Hôtel Nouvel. "Is this what the army considers first class? I don't know how Bobbie could take it."

"She didn't care," said Cora coldly. "She came here to see Henry."

"Florence, why don't you leave it alone?" said Reed.

"You look irked."

"I am irked," he replied. "It's over and done."

"Let's not argue," Florence said. "We're all too tired. To be continued," she promised Cora with a chummy smile.

They said their good nights. Reed and Florence were shown to an elevator in another part of the lobby and escorted to the room she'd reserved on the top floor. It was the best in the house—still not up to Parisian standards, but a far cry from the iron beds, contracted for the pilgrimages, that would have fit in with a hospital ward. From a frosted glass door they entered a passageway with mirrored closets that opened to a spacious suite with two twin beds, armchairs and a small couch, nicely carved oak bureaus. Clearly unoccupied for quite some time, the room was filled with dead air. The decor—headboards, bedspreads, bolsters, upholstery, heavy drapes—was done entirely in an orange japonaiserie fabric patterned with storks, which, along with the stifling scent of fresh lilies in a vase on the dressing table, created the claustrophobic effect of being inside a candy box offered by a bellicose aunt.

"Dear God, please call down for a drink," Florence said.

Reed picked up the phone and ordered a bottle of Gordon's gin, ice, and lime. Florence unpinned her black feathered hat and looked inside a drawer. "I don't even want to put my clothes in there. Poor Bobbie."

"Where's my medicine?" Reed asked.

"In the traveling case. I'll make you up a shot."

"I can do it. How long are we in Verdun?" he asked, rummaging until he found a brown glass bottle containing fine white powder.

"I didn't think more than a day, but now, with the inquest—"

"Really, Flo, what's the point of making a fuss?"

"I'm standing up for Bobbie. I'd like to think she'd stand up for me. Let's get the ball rolling, and then we can be out of this hellhole. No matter what, we can't stay later than Wednesday because we're booked for London."

"And when is that?" Reed was preoccupied by mixing the powder with distilled water from another vial.

"We leave Paris Thursday and arrive in London Thursday night. You check in to London General Hospital on Friday—"

She was interrupted by the ringing phone.

"Oh, hell. What now? *Gin, lime, and ice.* How can they get that wrong?" She picked up the receiver and said in her public voice, "Yes? This is Florence Dean Powell."

Reed liked it better when she did it because then he didn't have to fool around with the rubber hose with the needle between his teeth like a tawdry jazz musician in the back room of a cellar club, but these days he couldn't go very long without numbing the pounding ache that radiated from multiple points in his body, the problem being that the points kept changing and he had to keep chasing them like hounds after a cartoon rabbit, he was thinking, as the drug bloomed.

Flying with the Japanese storks that had lifted off the bed, he looked down from the ceiling to see that Florence was no longer on the phone

406

and her habitual expression of superiority had abandoned her.

"What's the matter, dear?" he asked.

"That was Dr. Szabo. Remember Dr. Szabo, who examined you at home?"

"Good old Dr. Szabo."

"He's gotten the results of the blood test back. Grif, they aren't good."

"Why not?"

"You've got a dangerously high level of lead in your blood. It's—everywhere in your system."

"All right," said Reed, drifting.

"I told him we were leaving for London," Florence went on rapidly, as if she'd been accused of something and had to defend herself, "and that you would get the mask replaced by Saturday."

"Then everything's fine."

She stared at him and suddenly began to knead her hands together.

"Take it off!" she screamed. "Take it off right now!"

The cry caused his nerves to explode. He fumbled at the mask with shaking fingers until he'd lifted it away and the pressure on his bones and ears was less.

"Much better," Florence was saying. "I can't stand to think of you soaking in that contamination."

"Better?" Reed laughed silently in slow motion until his eyes filled with tears.

Florence watched as he slowly nodded out, envying such total intoxication. Dr. Szabo's diagnosis had been more upsetting than she'd let on. "He has lead poisoning. People die from this," he'd said. "Don't wait a day longer." She decided to quickly settle Bobbie's affairs tomorrow and get them on the train to Paris, then straight on to the port of Calais. When she heard a knock she turned off the lamp at the side of the bed so that Reed's naked face would be covered by darkness, then greeted the waiter at the door and asked him to leave the tray in the entryway. When he left she poured a large drink, went back into the bedroom, and sat alone in the dark.

21

The police station was a short walk from the hotel, behind a medieval fortress on the Pont Chaussée that once stood as the entrance to the city. It was a summer day to lift the spirits. Weeping willows anchored along the riverbank had finally turned brilliant green, proclamations of new growth despite the rubble. The air was calm and insects had not yet risen off the water, that crisp time of morning before the sun strikes, when it is still cool enough to work out solutions to sticky problems, like the Olsen crisis. The downtown streets that had remained intact were filled with summer visitors to the monuments and battlegrounds. Locals met in breakfast rooms or strolled along with fresh baguettes under their arms, as if everyone except General Reginald Perkins was carrying on the business of life without a care in the world, beneath lampposts festooned with baskets of excruciatingly cheerful scarlet geraniums.

"You'd better clean up this mess," the American ambassador in Paris had barked over a bad connection at the hotel. "I just had a call from the Quartermaster General's Office in Washington, D.C. They're plenty sore about the demise of Madame Olsen, in case you haven't heard."

"I've already got an earful from Florence Dean Powell," Perkins replied.

"I know Florence Dean Powell," the ambassador said with some surprise. "She's the artist, right? A socialite from Boston. She moves here and becomes a bohemian—you know, the serious artist type who never misses a party? I've seen her around with that journalist with the tin nose, poor bastard. What's her interest in Mrs. Olsen?"

"They are all bosom buddies from Boston society, money coming out of their ears. Florence Powell grew up at the old lady's knee. She's demanding an inquest and claims to speak for the family. Don't worry, I'll take her to dinner and she'll calm right down."

"It's a squeeze play," said the man in Paris. "The

Olsen lawyers have already put army HQ on notice. The family wants a full explanation of where, when, and why Mrs. Olsen passed—on your watch," he added.

"She was elderly, Mr. Ambassador. It was an act of God."

"Then find out who is His servant on earth, because they want answers. The Olsens own a railroad, for Christ's sake, as well as a couple of Senate seats."

Perkins had held the receiver away from his ear. He already knew the drill. *Who can we pin this on?*

"Someone needs to be held accountable," the ambassador was saying with gratifying predictability. "We've shipped thousands of Gold Star Mothers overseas without a tragedy. Those are powerful people in the Beacon Hill crowd. The longer the family waits, the higher it goes up the ladder. If they're unhappy, you and I will be personally hearing from the president. As long as the country's in a depression, the pilgrimages are political gold and he doesn't want them tarnished by scandal."

"Then we can't be scratching our balls hanging around for an inquest. You know the French. They'll drag this out forever."

The ambassador was silent. "Do we have any reason to suspect foul play?"

The general chuckled. "You mean like someone

slipped arsenic in the old lady's tea? That would be a pisser. The simple truth is, she had a weak heart."

The ambassador sounded relieved. "So that's the story."

"Not entirely. Florence Dean Powell's got a notion that we fucked it up somehow, that Olsen never got her medicine—and she's up in arms about it."

"Christ, they'll say we murdered American motherhood."

"I'll take care of it."

"Just get the body the hell back to the United States before this hits the press."

"Right, but the body can't be released without papers signed by the French police service."

"You won a war, General," the ambassador had said, inflating the facts to match what he knew to be the size of Perkins's ego. "You can handle a local sheriff."

The weather was changing rapidly. The air had become humid with the scent of rain. As Perkins left the city center and neared the police station, the cheeriness of downtown gave way to desolation. Weeds grew between the bricks in the sidewalk and most of the houses were shuttered and silent. It was hard to say if they were still occupied. The general passed a decrepit dwelling badly pocked by shells, with a pair of basement doors melded shut by rust. The family must have hidden down there during the siege—seven months of bombardments that could go on ten hours at a stretch. *Savagery!* Perkins thought, taken by a wave of war fever so passionate that his groin grew hot and his teeth clenched. The cocksucking Huns, to have the audacity to think they could destroy Paris and the civilized world. The cowardly abomination of their weapons— gasoline flamethrowers, poison gas, bombs that fell on London from silent zeppelins floating too high for airplanes—what lousy perverted minds invented these killing machines? They threw out the rule book on the order of combat, where armies faced each other fairly on open fields, and almost won by sheer drunken barbarism. But they did not. Win. Because here he was, an American commander, walking free on French soil, and up on a hill there was a monument overlooking the city that proclaimed, *They shall not pass!* It was an epic battle of wills to the very end, and he wanted the turmoil and intense concentration of it all over again, the elation of brotherhood, the colossal importance of it all, to be in the burning center of history, his mind inventing revenge scenarios of mowing down Germans with their own machine guns, at the same time picturing himself in the center of a heroic cavalry charge, cracking skulls with the satisfying smack of a polo mallet that had suddenly appeared in his hand, and he carried on like this, in a dream state of murderous rapture, until the street ended at the river and he found himself beneath the steely blue lamps of the police station.

One thing Perkins could tell right away was that the Verdun chief of police was not a horseman. He was slightly built, with a sparse ring of brown hair, wearing a brown pin-striped suit with cuffed trousers. His round cheeks blended right in with his bald scalp, making his head look like a smooth granite egg. His office smelled of mold; it had bars on the windows, daguerreotypes of ancient police chiefs on the yellowing walls, and a cabinet that held a fake beard and a pair of infants' shoes—artifacts of local crime.

The chief sat behind his desk and folded his hands on an empty blotter. The knuckles were rash-red, as if he had weak circulation or had just come in from the cold. He stared at the American commander without a trace of humility. Had he been, as the ambassador suggested, a lawman of the Wild West, his smug expression would have been saying, *Just try it.* Pitiful, really, from a bureaucrat who, by the looks of him, had never fired a gun.

"Washington wants the remains on the next boat back to the United States," Perkins said, getting off the opening shot in rapid French.

"Without question," answered the chief. "Once we have determined this was not a homicide."

"It was not a homicide."

"What was the cause of death?"

"Heart failure."

There was a rumble of thunder and fat drops of rain began to slap against the dirty windows.

"You know this, how?"

"She had heart trouble."

"You don't mind if we do an autopsy?"

"No skin off my ass."

The chief opened a drawer and took out a piece of paper. Then he unscrewed a fountain pen, very slowly. The general was finding the splotchy, hairy red knuckles more repulsive by the minute.

"How long will this take?"

"We are a small city with only one coroner on loan, and he has to travel from Orléans. At this moment he is working on a domestic murder case in Auxerre that will take several days. Once the coroner performs the autopsy, he will send the results to the police laboratory in Lyon. By then we will have run into the summer holidays . . . So . . . assuming no undue complications . . . you can have the body back in four to six weeks."

The general flashed a dismissive smile.

"Let's save ourselves the trouble."

"Please?"

"The lady had a heart condition. Sign the papers and get on with it."

"You say there's a condition, but show me no proof. Do you have proof?"

General Perkins tapped his stars. "Proof."

The chief set his pen down. "I understand that

Madame Olsen had friends in high places. Even so, nothing can proceed without a proper investigation."

"Sure it can. You're in charge of this burg, you can do anything you damn well want."

"We are trying to do something here," the police chief said sternly. "We are rebuilding this city. I must authorize the closing of certain roads, review permits, meet with council members and the mayor ad nauseam. Now, as you can see, we are overrun with tourists, and the pickpockets that come with them. I have other things on my mind, General, besides your troubles."

Perkins stood, infuriated. "Do you think I personally visit the local police on every case that involves an American citizen? I hoped I didn't need to spell it out, but the United States government expects you to cooperate."

"We have laws when it comes to releasing bodies, especially to a foreign power. I am sure it's the same in your country."

"In my country, we go out of our way to help our allies."

"What can I do? I'm just a local policeman," the chief said mournfully. "I can't just skip the rules."

"We didn't skip over horse crap when it came to pulling you people out of the war."

The chief stood also. "With proper authorization we will send Madame Olsen on her sad journey home."

"What the hell is your problem?"

Heads shorter, the chief appraised the general with a superior stare. His little red fists were clenched.

"The Americans think they have the right to run the world. Well, not everyone agrees," he said, adding for emphasis, *"Salaud arrogant."*

The general laughed. "Let's see who's left standing next time around," he said, putting on his cap.

After the aides-de-camp had finished interviewing each of the pilgrims, the ban was lifted on staying at the hotel, but by then the summer cloudburst had turned to steady rain. The best plan Hammond could come up with to keep the mothers occupied was a hastily arranged visit to a local produce market that was housed in an indoor arcade a few blocks away. Crazy with cabin fever, Cora was eager to go anywhere, but nobody else was interested except Minnie. Katie said she'd seen enough vegetables to last a lifetime, and as they drew closer to departure, Wilhelmina had become more deluded. She now believed that every day was the last, and kept packing and unpacking her suitcase. The night before she had put on her clothes three times between the hours of 12:30 a.m. and 4:00 a.m., and today, thanks to a double bromide, she was sleeping it off, with Lily watching over her.

Equipped with big black umbrellas provided by the hotel, Minnie and Cora tramped through the downpour.

"Have you heard from home?" Cora asked, remembering the difficulties Minnie had faced over leaving despite her husband's objections.

Minnie shook her head. "I told them not to bother to write. I said I'm on vacation. Not such a vacation, but—"

"Good for you," Cora said heartily.

"I can't think what it will be like to be back."

"Very different," Cora said.

"I'm dreading it."

"Who wants to go back to work?"

"They won't understand."

"Nobody can unless you've done it. We've seen so many unusual things—"

"Like that lady in Paris?"

"The stripper?"

Minnie nodded and they began to giggle together. High-pitched silly laughter.

"That lady had a lot of nerve taking off her clothes!" Minnie said. "With everything hanging out . . ."

"You don't think Abraham would go for that?"

Minnie guffawed until her eyes ran with tears. "Her or me?"

"Oh my Lord," Cora said, catching her breath, "how can you begin to tell about Paris?"

Minnie was wearing a green cloth coat with a

tattered fox collar, the only coat she owned, which had to do for four seasons and was never right for any single one. The coat was too warm for the summer rain in France, but in her mind, "better than freezing." The needlepoint handbag, lent by a neighbor in the chicken farm cooperative, hung over one wrist and with the other hand she managed the man-sized dripping black umbrella. Dwarfed beneath it, she made a shambling figure, one that had traveled across continents and back, pursued, liberated, harnessed, terrorized, and freed again, bone-weary except for her large, lively operatic Russian eyes.

"When we were in Paris," she reflected, "I was thinking to myself, Minnie, this is the place you could have been happy."

They'd reached the big glass doors to the market, where a man in a black-and-white striped chef's uniform was maneuvering a cart loaded with crates of strawberries.

He held the door open with one foot, balancing the cart as they passed. Inside the arcade it was chilly and smelled of refrigerated meat. There were aisles devoted to whole fish on ice or just sides of beef. Tables were laden with summer offerings on checkered cloths scattered with flowers. The cauliflowers were enormous. There were baskets of peaches, plums, tomatoes, squash, and melons. One stall had nothing but sausages in white casings, with names scratched on tiny blackboards like a cast of characters: *Noix de Jambon, Saucisson au Choix, Merguez, Andouillette*. Minnie went on to the postcard stall while Cora entered the *pâtisserie*. They agreed to meet at a perfume store that looked enticing.

Ripe strawberries and the damp smell of sawdust brought Cora back to the Saturday market at the fairgrounds in the town of Blue Hill. In bad weather it would move inside the main building and the huge barn door would be open to curtains of rain, while all of them in heavy sweaters in the middle of summer—mother, sister Avis, and Cora—sold shortcakes. She remembered the way they worked, so easily, lovingly, almost without words, weaving in and out of one another's way as they ladled sweet macerated berries from large mason jars onto tender homemade biscuits. And the spoonfuls of whipped cream they swiped on the side! Those first days in Paris Cora had been drawn to every bakery window, but now, looking at the whorls, tarts, puffs, and cones lined up in perfect rows, analyzing their construction no longer held her interest; and Cora knew it was time to go home.

The *pâtisserie* had a few small tables taken up by middle-aged women with shopping bags at their feet. There was only one man, huddled in a corner with his back to the door. Unlike the slight Europeans with ethereal builds, he was a robust male wearing a silk smoking jacket and slippers, incongruous in the inclement weather, and his dark hair had been flattened by rain. He seemed to be bent over, almost embracing, a gold-leafed notebook on the round marble table before him, in which he was writing deliberately, as if each word counted.

As she passed he didn't look up. By now Cora was used to lively—or at least curious—glances from Frenchmen on the street, having discovered that the currency in Paris was not the franc but, as Bobbie put it, the *frisson*, and so she was feeling intentionally snubbed by this man, even a little put off, especially when she realized it was Griffin Reed.

"Hello, stranger," she said, standing right in front of him. "Did you think I wouldn't see you?"

He continued to write.

"I was hoping you wouldn't."

At the same time, Minnie Seibert appeared in the doorway of the *pâtisserie*, calling out, "Mrs. Blake! Aren't you coming to the perfume store?"

"In a sec," Cora replied.

But instead of leaving, Minnie advanced through the door like a miniature Mark I tank.

"Are you getting something? I'll keep you company," she offered.

Even though he had resolutely not looked up, Cora knew that Reed was smiling over his notebook. Neither moved nor gave any sign that they were acquainted, a mutual reaction to the invasion of this other; an unstated agreement that they'd rather be left alone together. Besides, the fastest way of getting rid of Minnie was to eliminate any hint of gossip she might run back and share with Katie and the rest.

"I just can't make up my mind," Cora said of the array of cakes. "You go. I'll meet you there."

Minnie directed a sigh at the napoleons. "I get fat just looking."

When Minnie had finally retreated, Reed gestured for Cora to join him. She pulled over a wire-back chair and sat with her elbows on the marble tabletop, gazing frankly at Reed. She now knew where to find him, beyond the glasses, in the deepest recess of his eyes, where there were no constraints.

"You were hoping I'd ignore you?" she asked.

"Then I wouldn't have to talk to you."

"I thought you liked talking to me."

"I do and I don't."

She gave him a playful frown. "Why are you all wet?"

"It's raining."

"Why didn't you take an umbrella?"

"Didn't occur to me."

"Why are you here?"

"Felt like a coffee."

"I mean it, Grif. Why'd you come to Verdun?"

"Florence asked me to. She was all broken up about Bobbie."

Cora had her doubts that Florence could be broken up about anyone. For a moment she wondered if he'd come to see her.

"What are you writing?" she asked. "Is it another article?"

He looked at the notebook. "This?" He shook his head. "No, it's just for me. It's almost impossible to get anyone to publish anything serious these days. The English-language rags keep folding. Not enough Americans left to read them. As for the *Herald*, they don't like me. Doesn't matter, everybody's getting out of Paris, it's the end of days."

"Don't be morbid."

"I was lucky to get *Le Matin* to take that story. Do you want a coffee?"

"No, thanks. They read it to us in English."

He finished the dregs in his cup. "Then you know what I said about you."

"Yes, and I'm happy you didn't tell about Sammy's father. You kept my secret."

"I told you that I would. What'd you think of the rest of the article?"

"Honest? I was kind of embarrassed."

"Really?"

"You made me sound like something I'm not."

"I didn't mean it that way."

"I'm a mother, Grif. I'm nothing special. I love my boy and I'm proud of his service to our country. Every war mother feels that way. It's the pain that hurts, but the pride that stays with you."

"Baloney. That's not what you said on our walk."

"Of course I did!"

"No, you didn't." He held up a hand to block her response. "I was listening! You said you had your doubts. It's in the piece, I reported what you said. You said all this pomp and circumstance is a bunch of bull—okay, you didn't put it that way— but it made you ask yourself what a war mother is really supposed to do. Wave the flag? Lie down under the wheels of a police car to prevent another war? It's a damn hard proposition. You told me that you drive yourself crazy, even now, asking over and over if you could have stopped Sammy from going—"

"I couldn't!" Cora cried.

"Of course you couldn't." Reed spoke soothingly and his eyes were soft. "There's no way you could have stopped him. He would have left home eventually, or if he didn't, resent it for the rest of his life. My mother didn't want me to leave California. She sure as hell isn't happy I'm in France."

"It must have been awful for her when you got hurt."

Reed said, "She doesn't know," and rubbed his temples where the eyeglasses pressed over his ears. He gulped the last in his water glass. He found that he was thirsty all the time.

"Are you all right?" Cora asked.

"Tight, that's all," Reed said. "Need to get this thing replaced. Go on."

"Your mom . . . she doesn't know? What did you tell her when you were in the hospital?"

"I got the nurses to write cheery letters saying I had superficial wounds. When I was well enough, I kept up the story. Living in Paris. Writing for the paper. Life's a bed of roses."

"Even now . . . she still doesn't know?"

He shook his head.

"But, Grif, you have to tell her sometime."

"I'd rather spare her the suffering."

"But when she sees you—?"

"She won't be seeing me. I have no plans to go back."

Cora was stunned. "You mean you're never going home? What if she gets sick—"

"Mom is a rancher. She's strong as a horse. When the time comes, my sister in San Francisco will take care of things."

"What does your sister think is going on?"

"She thinks the same thing. That I'm a war correspondent, a Parisian expat living with an artist."

"Oh, Grif," Cora said emotionally, "you won't see your mother? Ever again?"

"She's old now. What's the point?"

"But it's so much worse not to see your son. I'd give anything if Sammy were alive. I wouldn't care if he were missing an arm or a leg or anything just to see him—" She stopped. She was making him feel ashamed. "Well, anyway. I guess Minnie's waiting for me at the perfume store," she said.

"I'd go with you, but I wouldn't be much use in a perfume store without a nose. That's a joke."

Cora snorted with exasperation. "A stupid joke. I don't even see it anymore."

"I know you don't."

They were quiet. He reached across to take her hand.

"May I?"

"Yes."

His fingers tightened around hers. She closed her eyes and took everything in. The softness of his skin. The sureness of his grip. The warmth that was passing to her.

"Grif, if you and I were ever fated to meet, it was so that you'd write to your mother."

He laughed hard and enjoyed it. "You're one of a kind, you know that?"

"Please don't hurt her. Please."

"It would kill her to see me like this, Cora."

She tightened her grasp. "You're her child. Your life is the most important thing in the world to her. She'll never stop loving you. Go and see her. Think about it."

"All right."

She released his hand. They pushed their chairs

away and left the *pâtisserie* and entered the dank air of the arcade.

"What about your plans?" he asked. "When you get home?"

"Linwood's asked me to marry him. My family owns a farm on the island and he's thinking we could start it up again."

"Congratulations to the both of you."

But Cora lingered in the busy corridor. "I haven't said yes."

"What are you waiting for? Don't be a chump. You said this guy makes you happy, so grab it. I think that's where you want to go," Reed said, indicating a passage to the right.

Minnie was waiting outside the perfume store when Cora joined her.

"Did you go in yet?" she asked.

Minnie shook her head. "It doesn't interest me. Let's go back."

"We have to at least take a look."

"You go. I'll wait."

Cora poked her head in. The store was like a feminine bazaar in a city of the senses, jam-packed with manicure sets, hairbrushes and ribbons, mirrors, bracelets, washcloths, lotions and creams, stacks of perfume boxes displayed by color: red, white, purple, silver, black. The glass cases were bordered in gold. Red hearts on paper doilies adorned the walls; shimmery golden curtains hid the back rooms. Asleep on a pink cushion on the floor were two white toy poodles with pink collars.

"Come on, they're not going to bite you," Cora said, grabbing Minnie's purse strap and pulling her through the door.

Instead of a counter there was a large cream-colored sideboard that might have been lifted from a palace. It had a pair of glass doors with panes that radiated from crystal hubs like the rays of the sun. There were squiggly gold-leaf motifs all over, and it had curvy legs and those strange birdlike feet. The owner of the shop was wearing a white coat like a pharmacist. He introduced himself in English as "René from Belgium," as if not to be mistaken for German.

"Ah!" he said, admiring their badges. "Gold Star Mothers! I am honored." He kissed each of their hands. Cora giggled and Minnie melted. "May I have the honor of finding your fragrances?" he asked.

Minnie, who usually tied her hair in a kerchief and wore men's extra-small overalls, was dumbstruck.

"We don't know our fragrances."

He invited them to sit, indicating two stools with furry white cushions—last year's dogs, Cora thought, trying to untwist her lips from a smirk. René was in his early forties and dark-complexioned, the most meticulously groomed man she had ever seen. His skin was smooth and perfect, hair slicked back, a black swami mustache wriggling above soft womanly lips.

"Do you ladies have time to hear a little story about the most sought-after perfume in the world?" he asked.

Cora tried to picture René in an undershirt sitting down to supper in an overheated kitchen with an ordinary wife, but it only made her almost laugh out loud and want to pee.

"We really have to get back to the hotel," she said, but to her surprise Minnie, who had been too shy to enter and tried to escape, was now completely mesmerized.

"We have a minute," Minnie said, so Cora sat down on the poodle fur.

René's white teeth flashed as he told of a rare flower that bloomed in the Arabian Desert with an essence that drove men mad—so potent that this particular flower had been the object of wars and intrigue since the Middle Ages. He claimed there was a painting of it hanging in the Vatican.

"A famous sheik gave this precious tincture to me."

He took out a box made of ivory and removed from a velvet inlay a round glass flask no larger than a silver dollar, took out the stopper, and offered each of them a precious sniff. It was unusual, all right. More like cinnamon than roses, with a hint of thistle, Cora imagined.

"Somewhere in the world there exists a special fragrance for every woman," he murmured. "But if one is to discover this treasure, one needs a guide." He began to assemble bottles and spritzers on the curvy counter. "You wouldn't go into a dark, scary cave all alone, would you?"

Minnie shook her head, wide-eyed, and for the next quarter hour they got drunk smelling extracts of citrus, gardenia, oak, honeysuckle, lilac, moss, grass, vanilla. But when René from Belgium presented the perfect scent for Millie in a red-and-white candy-striped box, and one for Cora in a curved purple flask with a gold tassel at the neck, the prices were so outlandish that they jumped off the stools.

"For what's in that box I could buy a refrigerator," Minnie said.

René seemed poised for this response.

"I completely understand. How about a more petite souvenir?" he said, and slid a rack of lipsticks under their tired noses. "This is the number one lipstick in France. You cannot get it in the United States. I sell a lot of these. And for Gold Star Mothers there is a very special price."

Minnie was as enchanted as a child by the untouched tongues of color in their movie-star gold cases and kept screwing them up and down saying, "I haven't worn lipstick in years. My husband doesn't like me to. He says it's a bourgeois indulgence."

René's expression became stern. "Beauty is not an indulgence. Beauty is a force of life, but it must be cultivated. Forget your husband. You owe it to yourself."

With much coaching, Minnie finally decided on a bright shade of coral.

"And for you, madame? This one called Jolie would look beautiful with your eyes."

Cora told René no thanks. She'd spent her souvenir money on trinkets for her nieces and a cigarette lighter for Linwood.

"Next time," promised René, and they watched as he tenderly wrapped the lipstick in lavender tissue paper and slipped it into a dainty bag and handed it over.

"No, wait—put it on," Cora urged.

Minnie took the package. "I'm going to save it."

"What for?"

"A special occasion," she decided.

22

Just in time," Hammond said when they got back to the hotel.

Wilhelmina, Lily, and Katie were waiting in the lobby when Cora and Minnie arrived from the indoor market. They shook out their umbrellas and gathered curiously around Hammond, who was going through a pile of sturdy, oversize brown envelopes bearing the seal of the quartermaster general. He read from the instructions:

"These packets are for your final visit to the cemetery tomorrow. They contain mementos provided for your comfort and to create lasting memories."

He distributed them, quietly putting aside the one for Bobbie. Inside each envelope was an American flag and two dowels that screwed together to make a sturdy post, a Bible, an eggshell-blue box, and a leather-bound folder. Cora opened the blue box to discover a beautiful medal by Tiffany's jewelers on a luxurious red, white, and blue ribbon, meant to be worn around the neck. It was made of brass, heavy in the hand, and depicted a cruise ship breaking the surf between the Statue of Liberty and the Eiffel Tower. The words GOLD STAR MOTHERS TOURS TO EUROPE were inscribed below, and a golden star was embedded above the ship. She enfolded the medal in her fingers, grateful to the artist who had understood the weight and heft of their loss.

Minnie was the first to discover a small canvas pouch in her packet.

"What is this," she asked. "A tea bag?"

"It's for collecting earth," Hammond explained.

"Earth?" echoed Katie.

"What am I, a geologist?" Minnie quipped to nervous laughter.

Hammond cleared his throat. "For the grave," he

said. "In case you want to take some earth from the grave back home."

The expressions on the faces of Party A ranged from puzzlement to dismay. Cora remembered the requests she'd received before she left Maine from war mothers who couldn't travel to bring back dirt from their sons' graves. Forgotten until now, the names were still in her ribbon-bound packets back home in the library desk. The thought made her feel guilty and defeated. Even if she'd tried, there had been too many for her to fill.

Katie and Wilhelmina sat on either side of Lily on the settee. Vowing to fly right and finish with outstanding marks for the rest of the tour, Lily turned to Katie, who was stroking the two photographs mounted in her leather book.

"Your boys are so handsome," she said. "They look just like you."

"Tim is like my husband, Dolan is like me," Katie said. "Tim wanted to be a policeman. Dolan, he didn't know. He once said he wanted to be a baseball player," she said, half smiling, half sniffling.

Lily nodded sympathetically and handed her a tissue.

"What about you, Minnie?" she said. "May I finally meet Isaac?"

Minnie handed over a photograph of a proud-looking young man with dark hair and a determined set to his mouth and eyes. Even in uniform he seemed more like a scientist than a soldier.

"See that? You could tell Isaac was always thinking of something," Minnie remarked. "When he was ten he had an idea for a camera where you could see the pictures right away. I said, Why don't you make it so you could see the future?" She laughed. "Then he tells me, Ma! I have another big idea—how to fit beer into a can!"

Lily smiled. "Just like a boy," she said.

Cora was lost in the official army photograph of Sammy. At first there had been that jolt of recognition in seeing the face of her child, just as it had been when she'd seen him in life—even in the most mundane places—picking him out from his classmates on the rocks that formed the school playground, glimpsing him coming up from the pier—her child's face imprinted in the deepest part of her, for which she would have run through flames.

The jolts came again and again: the hooded eyes—her sea captain father's brown eyes—looking straight into the camera with the suspicion of a frontiersman staring down a city man; the rounded cheeks gently shaded by the gray tones of the photograph to make it appear as if he were too young to shave. Did he shave at sixteen? She couldn't remember. He wore no cap, just a brazen pompadour with a blond sheen.

The picture was cropped below the double

pockets of his khaki uniform, which had a stand-up collar and epaulets with small brass buttons. She caressed the photograph with her eyes, touching every inch of it until it came to life, until she could feel the texture of his woolen tunic and stiffened hair. Bringing it up close to her face, she could make out *U.S.* on one of the brass collar disks, and an eagle on the other. She counted every fair hair in his eyebrows to where they faded into an unfinished bridge over the nose. She admired the finely shaped ears and the slightly full cheeks with a hint of dimple at the chin. She was amazed at the serenity he showed in facing the camera; facing the war. His half-turned smile said he still had secrets from his mother.

Wilhelmina hadn't said a word. She held the leather book in her lap and ran a finger over the gold lettering, *Pvt. Bradley Russell.*

Lily turned to her. "Is that your Bradley? Can I have a look?"

"Sure you can."

Wilhelmina opened the portfolio, looked at the photograph, and collapsed on Lily's shoulder, fainted dead away.

Oh God, thought Lily, struggling to hold her up. *Not again!*

The rest of them froze, reflexively hugging the pictures of their sons. Hammond, along with other hotel guests who rushed to their aid, helped to ease Wilhelmina down on the couch. *"Get help,"* people said in several languages, *"Call a doctor,"* *"Get water,"* *"Get ice,"* *"Slap her face"*—while Lily scrambled for the Red Cross bag, always close at hand since Mrs. Olsen—but Wilhelmina was already awake, coughing and blinking rapidly.

Hammond retrieved her remembrance book, which had fallen open on the floor. He clapped it shut but it was too late; they had all seen. Instead of a photograph of a square-jawed blond young man of Scots-German ancestry who resembled his mother, this soldier came from somewhere far away from Maine tennis clubs and shingle-style mansions by the sea. He wore the same private's uniform as the rest, along with a private's beret, except that he was Negro, and his photo was inscribed *Elmore A. Russell Pvt—Yankee Division—Massachusetts.*

"Who is that? Who is Elmore Russell?" Minnie asked.

"That's Selma Russell's son!" Katie exclaimed.

"Good Lord," Cora said. "Do you really think—"

"He was in the Yankee Division—"

Wilhelmina was sitting up with the help of Lily's arm braced around her shoulders.

"Of course!" Hammond said heartily. "The papers got mixed up and she was accidentally put in our party. Nurse Lily and I took her up to Harlem so she could be with her people, and at the same time, we retrieved *our* Mrs. Russell." He turned to Wilhelmina. "Do you remember that? When we came to get you at your other hotel?"

Wilhelmina seemed numb. Her eyes were large and watery.

"She doesn't remember," Cora said.

Hammond bent over so he could speak directly into Wilhelmina's pallid face. "This is a bur-eau-cratic error. Do you understand? They've given you the wrong paperwork, that's all."

Wilhelmina said, "That's not him."

"We know, dear," Lily said soothingly. "But it's going to be fine. We'll get you the right folder. It'll all be straightened out."

Wilhelmina was fingering the top button on her blouse, a habit that by now was driving everyone mad. The poor garment was gray with wear. Cora could hear Bobbie saying, *Will somebody please put that thing out of its misery?*

Wilhelmina began to moan in an unsettling way. Like an old wooden cottage shifting its bones, thought Cora; like a gale building in the trees.

"What's the matter, Wilhelmina?" she asked quietly.

The glistening eyes rolled toward Cora. "Who is in my baby's grave?"

"Bradley!" Hammond fairly shouted with frustration. "Somebody put the wrong thing in this envelope. Your son is exactly where he should be!"

"Why should we believe anything you tell us?"

In an instant Katie's features had been transformed—stiffened with anger, but also by the same habit of self-respect that had insisted on her being called "Mrs. McConnell" at work.

Hammond was at a loss to deflect this bolt out of the blue. "Why not?" he faltered.

"How do we know?" she demanded. "I for one am sick of it. Sick of takin' orders, marchin' here and sittin' there and listenin' to a lot of babble when all we have is your say-so."

Cora, for whom the world had been so sadly reassuring when she held Sammy's face in her hands, now saw reality dizzily shift, like a camera moving to the right and then swinging way too quickly back to the left.

"Maybe it's not Bradley," Cora ventured. "Maybe it really is the Negro boy under Bradley's stone."

Lily and Hammond exchanged an uncertain look. "That's not possible," he said.

"My son went off to do his duty," Minnie began quietly.

A store of hurts and injustices and impotent rage had finally been loosed and the anguish poured out.

"That's all I know. They tell me that he died in action, he's driving an ambulance at the time. So, fine. They give me the approximate location of the incident and the number of his marker so I can find it in the cemetery when I go to France. But now, after everything we've been through, I'm sitting here kicking myself because I never questioned."

"Why should you question?" Katie said. "I don't care if it's the army or the pope—you're not allowed to question, not allowed to ask."

"Who asked?" Minnie said indignantly. "Nobody asked me."

"Thomas," said Cora. "You have to do something."

Hammond took in the room full of troubled faces. "We'll get to the bottom of this. I promise."

The parlor was stifling; he had to get out. Without pausing to think, he walked across the lobby to the main entrance and into the rain. It was wonderfully liberating to allow himself to get soaked. He felt the strength of his legs as he strode past the ruined city blocks down to the river. The farther he got from the mothers, the more clearly he was able to see himself. He was not a tour guide, or a West Point cadet: he was a commissioned officer, like two generations of Hammond men before him. Walking in the rain along a snaking footpath that followed the Meuse, he realized that he was, almost literally, following in his father's footsteps.

In wartime the job of an officer was straightforward. His father had pursued a twenty-nine-year career with no wrong turns. At West Point,

Colonel Hammond was a mathematics whiz and star football player. He served in the Philippines, graduated from the War College in 1923, and became an instructor there. During the war he was secretary of the general staff of the American Expeditionary Forces in France and commanded the Twenty-eighth Infantry of the First Division in a legendary march to Sedan, for which he was awarded the army's Distinguished Service Medal.

It was fair to say that the old man's first and only true love had been the army. Retired now, he'd told his son that when he was done as a commissioner of New York City, he would build a house close to his beloved West Point, and, Hammond thought, probably inscribe over the door the Horace Porter quote he often recited like a prayer.

Here the Academy sits enthroned in the fastness of the legendary Highlands; the cold, gray rugged rocks which form her battlements are symbolic of the rigor of the discipline exacted of her children; her towering hills seem to lift man near to his God; the mist-laden storm clouds may lower above her, but they break upon her crags and peaks as hostile lines of battle have so often broken up on the sword points of her heroic sons.

As the younger Hammond thrashed along, he would have liked to quash that inflated, hypocritical rhetoric the same way his boots were crushing the black grit in the puddles that filled the shell holes gouged in the path. At the Academy he, too, had been a believer, until he'd discovered in his short time as liaison officer on the pilgrimage that holding on to your principles was infinitely harder outside those cold, gray battlements. The way they taught things like strategy, using the means to the end, like a gigantic game of chess with human pawns, had nothing to do with what he'd seen in the faces of those mothers holding portraits of their sons and looking to him for answers. Were they being told the truth or not? They were questioning the authority of the army and, for the first time in his life, Hammond was questioning it, too.

The rain came down unmercifully in the open crags of the destroyed buildings along the riverfront, running down the last dregs of wallpaper in rooms never meant to be exposed to misty air. The few small boats tethered in the Meuse took a beating. He tramped along the footpath until he came to a bridge that led out of Verdun to the high muddy fields, and then he was truly in his father's world.

Hammond knew the facts as thoroughly as he knew his math tables and Latin verbs. His father's achievements were part of West Point lore. On the night of November 6, 1918, Colonel Hammond, then a captain, had commanded the Twenty-eighth Infantry on an agonizing trek to Sedan. Earlier that morning his regiment had attacked the French town of Mouzon in a battle that should have earned them a day's rest, but at 2:00 p.m. they received orders to assemble. The mules were dead and so two men were assigned to carry the 37mm Hotchkiss mountain guns, which weighed more than a hundred pounds. The shells alone were a pound each. After surviving the Battle of Mouzon, with no meals and no stopping, under heavy rain, his father's men began a torturous march over roads that had been torn to pieces by enormous shell holes. They had started out exhausted and now, without food or strength, they still had fourteen miles to go.

Young Lieutenant Hammond crested a hill and looked back at the mauled towers of Verdun. The rain slapped his face and he let it. He was breathless from the slog through heavy mud, but his heaving lungs were baby's slumber compared to the reserves his father must have had to call on as he walked beside the men in the dark, keeping them going with the promise of crossing the border of Germany in victory at the end. The long unbearable night was barely over at 7:00 a.m. when they finally broke through the woods south of the town of Chéhéry and climbed the last rise that overlooked Sedan, where they once again faced open warfare until the French arrived at 4:00 p.m. and the American Twenty-eighth retired from the line.

Colonel Hammond had led a thirty-three-mile march that took fifty hours, with no food, heavy fighting at both ends. As he promised, they marched into Germany as part of the Army of Occupation, and the regiment was decorated with the French Ordre de l'Étoile Noire.

That was what it took to be an officer.

Cora Blake was right. He was obligated to act on behalf of his charges—but how? All Lieutenant Hammond knew was that he was standing on a hill that had been contested by great armies where men had died whispering, *They shall not pass.* His feet were cold and his uniform water-logged, and he had no answer as to how to be his hero father's heroic son; the chances of that were about as likely as being hit by lightning.

The hotel had a new man at the desk. Hired for the tourist season, he was better-looking and more educated than the owner's hopeless offspring. After politely inquiring as to the acceptability of the stay, he told Mr. Reed that he'd had another letter.

"It came this morning," he said, crisply producing an envelope with a local stamp.

It was in French with a return address in Bar-le-Duc, a river town to the south. He handed it over with the rest of the mail. Just as Reed was leaving the front desk, Hammond came in from the rain.

"Who dragged you through the mud, soldier?" Reed asked.

"Any number of people," Hammond said, watching Reed flip through a dozen envelopes. "Aren't you a popular fellow?"

"It's a result of the story that ran in *Le Matin.*"

"Must have hit a nerve," commented Hammond.

"They're all from French war mothers," Reed said. "First the editor didn't want to buy the damn thing, but now they're clamoring for a follow-up."

"Congratulations."

"I wish I had something more to say, but frankly, I'm burned out on the subject of war mothers." Reed gave him a droll look. "I hate to sound like one of them, but you should get out of those wet clothes."

Hammond didn't move, apparently lost in thought.

"You're dripping," Reed reminded him.

"Sorry," said Hammond, snapping awake. "I'm in a bit of a muddle."

"Can I help?"

Hammond told Reed about the mix-up between the two Mrs. Russells and their packets, and the demands of Party A for proof of who was buried in Bradley Russell's grave. "It's gone beyond

Wilhelmina Russell," Hammond went on. "Now the rest are up in arms. They don't know what to believe, and I don't know what to tell them."

"How can you tell them what you don't know?" Reed responded. "Ask General Perkins."

"Ask him what?"

"Do what you're supposed to do—be their liaison. Tell him they want to be heard."

Hammond nodded slowly. "It would be the most direct way."

Reed watched him for a moment. "If you do it, I want to be there."

"The general might not like that."

"He'll like it fine, if he has nothing to hide."

Reed could almost see Hammond puzzle it out. Poor kid: *Whom should he trust? How much could he risk? What was Reed getting out of it?*

"Having you there would be a tremendous boost," Hammond finally decided.

"Are you sure?" prodded Reed, just to seal the deal. "It could be risky business for you."

"Let them hear it from the horse's mouth."

"Frankly, you'd be helping me out. It's a hell of a lead," Reed mused. "If it's true the army jumbled up the remains of a black soldier and a white soldier who both died serving our country— with their mothers looking on—that's the kind of thing that warms an editor's stone-cold heart."

Hammond said he'd let Reed know the arrangements, and the two shook hands.

• • •

Perkins agreed to meet with the women. He considered it the soft but necessary part of his job, like attending luncheons for army wives in Washington—a piece of cake. Hammond was glad to make good on his promise to Cora Blake, but later that afternoon, when he called at the general's suite to escort him downstairs, Perkins was in a touchy mood. He'd been summoned from his midday meal for another demanding phone call from the ambassador in Paris. Through a fellowship of "friends," meaning fellow homosexuals in the State Department, the ambassador had been able to stave off the news of the lady billionaire's unexplained death on a government-sponsored program abroad so that it didn't cross the threshold of the White House, but that situation was severely time-limited and about to expire.

Perkins snapped back that he was handling it, when in fact he had nothing at all. His aides had driven overnight to Paris and returned with sacks of documents on the members of Party A. They'd helped him lay everything out on three card tables pushed together in the living room of his suite. For hours the general had pored over fragile carbon copies on onionskin and inky cables fresh off the Teletype from New York, looking to pin this on someone or something. Mrs. Olsen's general health. Her behavior. Who she got along with, who she provoked. The food she ate, complaints lodged with the nurse, her nightly shot of whiskey. The medical form itself was simply a row of ailments to be checked off by the pilgrim. "Yes" to headaches, she had indicated in blue ink, frequent colds, arthritis, eye problems, and allergy to bee stings, but no red flags that would point to a heart condition.

Nevertheless, when he strode into the parlor where the women were assembled, he seemed confident as ever.

"You're looking optimistic, sir," Hammond remarked.

"I never walk into a room unless I know I'm going to win," Perkins said with a wink.

Tea and cakes had been laid out, but for the first time in memory, nobody touched the food. The women of Party A were already seated in wicker chairs. The only person missing was Griffin Reed.

"He said he'd be here," Hammond told Cora worriedly.

"I haven't seen him."

"He really wanted to write about it. Something's wrong."

While Perkins made the rounds, chatting with the pilgrims, Hammond went outside to the desk. They called Reed's room and when there was no answer, sent the bellman to check.

Hammond came back saying, "He's nowhere. What the hell?"

"Give him a minute."

"We can't wait, Mrs. Blake. The general's in a foul mood already."

"It isn't like him, especially if it has to do with the newspaper—"

"The important thing is, you've got Perkins's attention," Hammond said. "Use it and don't back down."

The general was calling for quiet.

"Good afternoon, ladies!"

He stood in front of the piano like a kindly professor. Hammond marveled at how his demeanor had changed the moment he'd crossed the threshold. He appeared to be nothing but conciliatory.

"How can I help you?"

There was silence as the women looked at each other. They hadn't planned their attack.

"I understand you have a question?" he prompted.

Minnie spoke up: "I marched for the right for women to vote. When we came to this country, my mother and I worked in the garment district, and I watched while two policemen beat her up for joining the union. So I'm not afraid of a fight."

The general raised his hands and backed away theatrically. "But I am!" he said, and got a laugh. He was beginning to win them over.

Not Minnie. She was glaring. "All right, if you think it's funny—" She picked up her purse to leave.

"Please, Mrs. Seibert," said the general, who had done his homework. "I meant no offense. I understand your son, Isaac, was an ambulance driver and he performed heroically, despite a cowardly attack by the Germans on his dressing station. My personal condolences for your loss. We're on the same side, and I am at your service."

Minnie's head jerked side to side and her lips trembled.

"It has to do with Mrs. Russell," she said, less certain. "Tell him, Wilhelmina."

Wilhelmina's eyes were wide and she scarcely blinked, almost catatonic, as she held the leather-bound folder against her chest.

"Show him," Katie urged.

When Wilhelmina didn't respond, Lily said, "May I?"

She gently pried the folder from Wilhelmina's arms and presented it to the general.

"Thank you, Nurse."

"You're welcome, General Perkins," she said, avoiding his eyes.

Perkins glanced at the photograph of the Negro boy, closed the folder, and gave it back.

"What happened here, Lieutenant?"

Hammond stepped forward.

"If you remember, sir, there is another Gold Star mother on the tour also named Mrs. Russell, one of the Negro pilgrims."

"I thought this was all sorted out in New York."

448

"It was, after each Mrs. Russell was sent to her proper hotel, but you see, because of the initial mix-up, it's natural for there to be a question, now . . . about this."

"About a picture?"

"About the burial procedures. I think they'd like reassurance that everything was carried out in the proper way."

"I see. Well, I'm in a position to know, as I redesigned the Graves Registration Service myself. But never mind about me, ask any soldier. His number one priority is taking care of his own. No man will ever be left behind. I promise you, our records are meticulous."

"What about Mrs. Selma Russell?" Cora asked from the back of the room. "What does she say?"

"She's apparently been spared the trouble of this."

"Why is that?" Cora said even more loudly. "Didn't she also get the wrong picture of her son? What did *she* think when she saw a white soldier?"

"I couldn't tell you," said the general, losing patience.

"They don't get pictures of their boys?"

"They don't get a goddamned high-class leather-bound book like this," he shot back.

"So a colored mother, for instance, wouldn't know," Cora said, "if something was wrong."

"My job is to get every American citizen on this

tour from A to B, safely and securely. Just like in war, the commander keeps his eye on the horizon. I don't approve every detail, Mrs. Blake, but it is customary to separate white from black. It's the way things are done. Ask them, and they will tell you they prefer to be with their own people. As for this—somebody slipped in the wrong picture, and that's the end of it."

Cora could hear Bobbie's voice in her head, and she spoke it.

"Don't you talk down to us," she said. "We've been told for a fact the bodies lay on the battlefield for months before they were moved. How can we be sure our sons are buried where you say they are?"

"The U.S. Battle Monuments Commission spent many years building the most beautiful cemeteries in the world—"

"That's not what she's saying—" Katie interrupted.

"We want proof!" Minnie cried.

"You have to take it on trust."

"We have no trust left in our hearts," she answered.

"With respect, the U.S. government has devoted a lot of time and millions of dollars to take care of you."

"We gave our sons for our country," Katie said.

"And we've given you a first-class ocean cruise."

"If I wanted a boat ride, I'd go to Staten Island," Minnie remarked to herself.

"From what I've seen, the war was futile, stupid, and avoidable," Cora added. There, she'd said it.

"That's damned unpatriotic."

"My family has a patriotic record going back to the Revolution. No one can say that I'm disloyal to my country when I say never again will we sacrifice our children for wars on foreign soil. Wrongs cannot be righted by blood. Happiness can never be the result of senseless deaths. We mothers know."

"I know all about mothers. My mother was a great woman," declared the general. "She taught me discipline from an early age—"

Lily could see, not without some satisfaction, that Perkins was losing his audience. They were frowning and restless; they didn't like being compared to another "great woman." *Don't tell about stacking tobacco leaves when you were five,* she thought—but the general did, and ended his speech even more poorly: "In the matter of burial records, the matter is closed. No more accusations. Let my soldiers rest in peace."

His soldiers? Lily thought. That's rather grand.

It inflamed them.

"We want answers!" Cora shouted, and the rest echoed her cry.

"I've been more than forthcoming. Good day," said the general and headed toward the door.

451

Cora looked imploringly at Hammond for help. The others turned expectantly in his direction, and his heart stirred with pride. Party A, which had fought over portholes and how to cook a chicken, had rallied into a hell of a fighting unit. He saw heartbreak and self-respect. He saw fear. He saw Lily, selflessly fussing to keep Wilhelmina's sweater over her shoulders, and knew that his most deep-seated loyalties had profoundly changed.

"There is a way to settle this, sir," Hammond called after his superior.

"It's settled as far as I'm concerned," Perkins said.

"You might want to give it a second thought."

"Why would I do that?"

"Because there are still remaining doubts."

"Not in my mind."

"If you're so sure about it, then you won't mind calling the burial officer in Paris."

The general halted. He glared at the lieutenant. "The hell I will," he snapped, his neck turning red. "Do you really believe the army would callously and cruelly dump bodies in a grave?"

"I believe anything can happen in a war, sir. And any citizen has the right to know, even women. Give them the proof they deserve, or I'll personally make sure this inquiry gets into the hands of the press."

"Watch what you're saying. I don't care whose

son you are, you're dangerously close to insubordination."

Hammond felt a wave of certainty roll through him. "Do you really believe everything the higher-ups tell you?" he said.

"It doesn't matter what I believe. I do my duty. Because I am a soldier, through and through. And you are not."

The hotel put on a private reception that night to honor the pilgrims at the end of their tour—five courses and a speech by the mayor of Verdun. Just before dessert, Cora excused herself and left. She was worried about Grif. She hadn't seen him all day and nobody was answering in his room. On her way upstairs she caught sight of Florence Dean Powell and General Perkins sharing a table in the main dining room. She noticed that Florence had abandoned her mourning clothes for a swank blue knit silk dress with knife-edge pleats, and that they were laughing over cocktails. Cora was glad: if Florence was here, Reed was most likely alone.

She went up to their suite. From the hallway she could hear music playing from a radio inside. She knocked but there was no response. She pounded harder.

The door opened, apparently by itself. Reed had let it swing wide while he turned and disappeared into the darkness of the room. He'd been expecting Florence.

"Forget your key?" he said irritably over his shoulder.

"It's Cora."

He kept his back to her with one hand pushed out, ordering her to wait. She couldn't help glimpse a sliver of his ruined profile while he fitted on the mask. The shades were drawn and the room was dark except for a single lamp with a scarf thrown over it, which cast the walls in smoky blue. The music on the radio was jazz. He motioned her inside.

"It's safe," he said when Cora still hesitated in the doorway. "The monster is back in his cage."

He climbed into bed and lay back on the pillows. His hair was still unkempt from the rain. He wore pajamas. In the shadows the mask took over. Its benevolent expression seemed grotesque—all the more so because for the first time she couldn't find the real man underneath.

"Grif, are you all right?"

He didn't answer. His silence frightened her, and the way his neck arched stiffly on the pillow as if he were in pain. The nightstand was crammed with liquor bottles, dirty glasses, ashtrays, and vials of powder. The room had a wet animal smell. A sob escaped him, a harrowing sound that seemed to come from a person different from the self-assured man she knew.

"What are you doing here?" he asked tiredly.

Her anger at his absence at the meeting was

dissipated by the haunting surroundings, and she found herself almost pleading.

"We waited for you as long as we could. Perkins was there. Why didn't you show up?"

He didn't seem to hear. "What did the general think of your request?"

"Ask Florence. She's down there talking to him now. Did you know that?"

"She said it's about Bobbie, that's all I know."

"Where have you been all day?" Cora asked.

"Right here, what do you think?"

"Drunk?"

"As much as possible."

"But when we sent the bellman up—"

"I paid him to go away. You should go, too. This is no place for a nice girl."

"Thomas said you would be there when we talked to General Perkins."

"War is hell. I was going to tell the world."

With effort, she held on to her patience. "And?"

"But you see," he said with a languorous wave of the hand, "I'm really not up to it."

"You can write about anything."

"Cora, I'm a morphine addict. I can't even get out of bed."

She stared at the debris on the side table. "No."

"Yes, I have fallen into the arms of Morpheus, and happily so. Joyously so."

She stood to remove the scarf from the lamp.

"Let's get some light into this room—"

"Stop that!" he called fiercely. "Stop that now!"

"I won't let you." She tried to pull him out of the bed. "Get *up!*"

He threw her off. "I can't. Besides, I don't want to."

She was breathless. "Where is Florence? Why doesn't she help you?"

"Florence is the one who gets me the dope."

Cora was horrified. "How can she?"

"She gets it from her doctor friends from the old clinic days. Pure, medical quality. Doesn't compare to the junk on the street. I literally can't live without her."

"She wants you to think that. She makes you sick and keeps you sick."

He sighed. "It isn't Florence. At least, not only Florence."

"She's the monster!" Cora cried. "I can't stand her keeping you under her spell—"

"I'm not under anybody's spell, and if you don't cut it out, I'll stick you with one of these," he said, lazily lifting a needle from the bedside table.

"I'm making things worse. I'll go."

"You are. But stay." He took a sip of something from a smudged wineglass. "Please."

With two fingers she delicately removed some female underthings from the seat of a diminutive chair, dropped them on the floor, and pulled it closer to the bed.

"You're really hurting, aren't you?"

"The doctor says I've too much lead in my system. It leached out from the mask. Too much lead," he said, laughing. "Sounds like a bad western."

"What are they going to do about it?"

"Going to London to get a new one of these. Easy aces. Leaving tomorrow." His words were slurring. "Gotta get it done, pronto."

"Then you should."

"Do you know that I came to Verdun only to see you?"

"No."

"Yes, because I had to see you one more time before you left for America."

"You didn't."

"You're right," he said. "I only wanted your story. I came to pick your bones."

She drew the scarf off the lamp where it had shaded the light. Reed grimaced and pulled away, squinting at the brightness. Cora playfully wove the scarf back and forth across her face like a dancer's veil, then tied it over her eyes.

"Now we're the same," she said.

"How is that?"

"You can take off the mask and I won't see."

"It's still there, isn't it? Say, do you have a cigarette?"

Still with the scarf blinding her, Cora went through exaggerated motions of finding the cigarettes in her skirt pocket and holding them out toward him. His warm assuring fingers closed around hers as they had at the *pâtisserie.* He took a cigarette. His hand was gone. She clutched the pack with the scarf still over her eyes and hand outstretched, poised. Untaken. She heard the swipe of the match, smelled sulfur in the air and then smoke, and then the crackle of burning tobacco shreds as he drew in deeply.

"It doesn't matter." He exhaled. "Because life is a hallucination. Everything's in pieces and we can't put it together. The only purpose of life is to create an exquisite corpse and I think I've done an excellent job, don't you?"

"Don't talk like that," Cora said.

She untied the scarf and arranged it back over the lamp, then stood and moved the chair back into place, leaving the underthings on the floor.

"I hope everything goes well in London."

"I have the best doctor in the world."

"Good. Well. Stay in touch."

"How?"

"Write to me at the library."

He gave her the "okay" sign. She quietly closed the door.

He sorted through the letters from the French war mothers. The one he'd just received from Bar-le-Duc interested him the most. It was from a Mademoiselle Champaux, who claimed to have known Sammy Blake, a private in the American army, during the war.

23

The last day felt like the first day, like quickening in the weather when the season turns. You could feel the change in the windy hallways as the rooms were aired, and see it in the eager faces of the extra staff that was hired for the midsummer crowds. Business would be picking up; despite the ominous signs in Germany, Europe was going on vacation. A regatta was scheduled to spend a week docked on the river and a classical music festival was opening in town. Taxis and tour buses were active and the temperature climbed. Party A of the American Gold Star Mothers Tour was soon to be a past entry in the ledger of the Hôtel Nouvel.

Perkins was needed back at the office for the next round of pilgrimages. He notified the burial service as Hammond had requested—insisted, the cheeky little snot—on the grounds that it was more expedient to delegate the matter of Party A to another senior officer.

The final visit to the cemetery was postponed until the afternoon due to the arrival of the chief American burial officer, Major Arlen Wistosky, a soft-bodied and mustachioed career man from a family of ironworkers in upstate New York, who arrived from Paris under stormy skies. His job was to oversee the administration of the U.S. war memorials in Europe. He'd brought two official cars to carry the pilgrims to the field where Private Bradley Russell was killed. He'd never been required to fill a request like this from a family member before, but having served in these same chaotic conditions, he understood why it might be asked, and having himself climbed out of the trench under fire to retrieve his best friend's body, he felt deep pride and a personal obligation to make sure the public knew that the burial records were clean.

Major Wistosky had the documents to prove that the remains of Bradley Russell had been accurately tagged. The problem was, the young soldier had suffered a direct hit and his body parts had been so widely scattered they had been impossible to retrieve. Wistosky, wearing a full dress uniform and standing with his aides by the lobby entrance as the women of Party A filed out of the breakfast room, identified himself and shook hands with each one, hoping, as he looked into their dignified faces, that he would not be called upon to explain these details, especially to the boy's mother, a tall blondish lady whose stare was vague and whose fingers, when he gently took her hand, were cold as ice.

The young liaison officer, Lieutenant Hammond, looked like he knew the score.

"What about your Mrs. Russell?" Wistosky

asked while the ladies were being ushered into the cars.

"She's stronger than she looks," Hammond told him.

"I hope she's up to this."

"We're usually accompanied by a nurse," Hammond said, glancing furtively at the closed parlor door. Lily had been summoned by the great man at breakfast and he hadn't seen her since. "I believe she's having an interview with General Perkins about another case."

"Well, not to worry. I always carry brandy for emergencies." Wistosky patted a hidden flask. "In case she becomes hysterical." He clapped Hammond on the back. "Buck up, son. You'll see worse."

Once they were out of town and on the country road, the headlights on the official cars could barely penetrate the mist that had settled over the fields. They stopped at a place along the front where the ground was still spongy and pock-marked by shells. They climbed out and stood by the side of the road, empty in both directions. The pilgrims stood close together, forming a subdued-looking group in the dark formal clothes they'd worn for the final visit to the cemetery later that day. The clouds were spreading. In the distance were a few charred trees like hasty slashes of charcoal against a paper-white sky.

"We'd better proceed," Hammond advised the major.

Wistosky unfolded a map.

"Private Bradley Russell's division was stationed all along this sector. We don't know exactly where your son fought, Mrs. Russell, but we do know where he died. Our burial files indicate it was Trench 8, Hill 295." He showed them where Hill 295 was identified on the map, and then pointed to a rise in the landscape. "That spot, right there."

Wilhelmina was blinking rapidly. "Yes?"

"Do you really want the details, madam?" To Hammond he said sotto voce, "Lieutenant, you may not be aware, but this was a bottle burial."

Minnie heard. "What does that mean?" she asked.

The wind had picked up and light mist was dampening their clothing.

Wilhelmina spoke: "It means they didn't have enough to bury, dear. All that was left of my son, Bradley, fit into a bottle."

The eyes kept blinking as if unaware that two large salt-colored tears had rolled down her ashen cheeks. Hammond, who had come prepared, took several folded handkerchiefs from his pocket and distributed them to Wilhelmina, Cora, Katie, and Minnie—who already had her hand out.

"Would you like Major Wistosky to go on, Mrs. Russell?" Hammond asked gently.

"I would."

Wistosky read from the file: "On September thirtieth, Private Bradley Russell was killed by a high-explosive shell. The skeleton was disarticulated, with fractures of the legs and pelvis. The head was shattered. The dog tag was nailed to a post above the remains. Final identification was made from dental records and a button from the uniform."

Wilhelmina was worrying at her blouse again.

Cora said, "Stop, Wilhelmina, you're going to rip that right off—"

And then she did. The thread broke and the top button of the pink blouse fell to the ground. Cora picked it up and held it in the palm of her hand. Small, compact, and made of brass. She recognized it as a button from the epaulet of a U.S. Army field jacket, just like the one Sammy wore in his photo.

"Is that the button—?"

"They sent it to me. It's all that was left."

Cora remembered receiving the shredded remains of Sammy's uniform. She knew now exactly what she'd done with them. She'd wrapped them up with rocks and buried them at sea. If she'd had only a button, she would have surely drowned herself in madness like Wilhelmina.

The wind picked up. Dirt was blowing from the open field, mixing with rain and the smell of earth.

Hammond asked if they were finished.

"You want the rest of the story?"

"Yes," they chorused, strongly and without hesitation.

Katie was fingering the beads of her rosary.

The burial officer read on: "The remains were disinterred from Grave 18, American Battle Area Cemetery Malancourt, and reburied April 26, 1919, in Meuse-Argonne American cemetery located at Romagne-sous-Montfaucon, Meuse, France, Grave 6, Row 12, Block E."

"May I see your memory book, Mrs. Russell?" Hammond opened the leather folio with the photo of the Negro soldier that had caused Wilhelmina to faint. He read off the coordinates listed as his gravesite, and they were the same as what the major had just said.

"It's true," he told Wilhelmina. "This is where Bradley fell, and here's the proof of where he's buried. You can rest easy now. They gave you the wrong picture, that's all. Bradley's whereabouts are accounted for. He is where they say he is."

Cora spoke up: "Wilhelmina got a letter from the sergeant saying Bradley died near a farmhouse and a cannon. Where are they?"

"Couldn't say for sure," said Major Wistosky. "That's not the types of things they put on the map."

"Let's sort this once and for all," Hammond decided.

He took his binoculars out of their case. Rain

blurred the lenses, but two hundred yards back, by an old tree break, he could see a stone farmhouse, recently rebuilt.

"There's the farmhouse."

As he moved the glass across furrows of wet mud, his heart skipped. He focused in on the nose of a half-sunk barrel. It looked like an 18-pounder field gun.

"Any way you put it, that's a cannon. Just as the sergeant said."

Wilhelmina was tugging on the sleeve of Wistosky's uniform.

"Is my Bradley in the cemetery? In his proper resting place?"

"I'm afraid so, ma'am," said the burial officer.

When Griffin Reed and Florence Dean Powell came downstairs to check out of the hotel, he surprised her by asking the desk man to order a taxi to Bar-le-Duc.

"That's a very nice town," the desk man told them. "It has many old buildings from the Middle Ages. Lots of history. You'll enjoy it."

"What is this about?" Florence asked.

"I'm going there."

"Now? We don't have time for sightseeing. We have to make the train to Paris."

"This is important."

"Darling, if we miss our connection from Paris to Calais, we'll miss the last boat to Dover and your appointment at the hospital. This is silly. We have to leave right now." She turned to the desk clerk. "We need a taxi to the train station."

"Bar-le-Duc," Reed insisted.

The desk clerk looked back and forth between them, mildly amused by the kind of domestic disagreement he saw a dozen times a day. "Um, well, they're in opposite directions, madame—"

"Get two taxis," Reed told him.

"Of course, monsieur." He was looking over their heads. "Good morning, General."

Behind them the parlor door had opened and General Perkins strode out with papers under his arm. A moment later, Lieutenant Lily Barnett followed and resolutely crossed the lobby with a determined look on her face, eyes fixed on the staircase straight ahead, which she mounted quickly.

Perkins and Florence greeted each other with double kisses, great friends after enjoying dinner together the night before.

"You'll be relieved to know the matter we discussed is taken care of," he told her.

"That's wonderful, Reggie. I'm very grateful, and I'm sure the family will express its appreciation to the army."

"Please, madam, it's my job. I wish I could say it was a pleasure, but at least it's over, and Mrs. Olsen can be laid to rest."

"Poor Bobbie. She didn't deserve this."

"Clear your mind of it. You've done all you could."

The bellboy came to load their bags.

"Grif?" said Florence. "Stop dreaming. We have to go."

Reed had been absorbed by the letter. He'd already read it multiple times.

"You go on ahead."

Florence let out a patronizing sigh. "All right. What's in Bar-le-Duc?"

"A lead on a story."

"Is it really important?"

"I don't know—that's why I have to talk to her. She's a Frenchwoman named Mademoiselle Champaux. She read the story on the American war mothers and recognized the name Mrs. Blake. She claims to have information about her son, Samuel."

"So what does she want? Money?"

"No, for God's sake, Florence—"

"It's very possible that she knew him," Perkins interjected. "Bar-le-Duc was a staging area for the Allies, the beginning of La Voie Sacrée, the Sacred Way. You've heard of that? It was the main supply route to Verdun. If this woman was there during the war, she would have seen the Americans marching right through town. Believe me, the French were happy to see us."

"But he's already done the article—" Florence began.

"The editor wants more," Reed said impatiently.

"Sounds damn interesting," Perkins agreed. "Everyone loves a wartime romance."

"I'm not so sure it's a romance. She could be a grandmother."

"But, Grif." Florence was close to pleading. "You have to see Dr. Blackmore in London—"

"We will, we will. Give me the tickets. You go ahead."

"No, you're in no condition. I'll go with you. I'll wait in the taxi."

"Absolutely not," said Reed, horrified by the notion of Florence getting near a source. "This is work. If I have to, I'll take a later train, but in any case, I'll meet you in Calais in time to make the Channel crossing." He waited while she fumbled through her purse.

She gave him his train tickets. "Hurry up then."

Reed made sure he had his pocket notebook, then headed for the door. When he was gone, a whirlwind seemed to settle down in the lobby.

"Well, he's excited," the general observed.

Florence made a wry face. "He's the most selfish man in the world. Get him on a *story* and he can't think of anything or anyone else."

She rolled her eyes and asked the deskman to call a second cab.

"Let me give you a lift," Perkins offered.

"Thanks, but the train station isn't far. I'd hate to put you out."

"The hell with that. I'm done here anyway, on my way back to Paris. Let's take a drive."

"Sounds like fun," Florence agreed with a smile in her eyes.

He offered his arm. "My car is outside."

It was an immaculate black cabriolet with two American flags flying from the windshield. The bellboy loaded their bags and opened the door. Florence gracefully stepped on the running board and eased in beside the general, who explained that he liked to do his own driving. They had a short wait while a policeman directed traffic that had stalled at the end of the street. Verdun was finally rebuilding itself. Dust, tar fumes, and exhaust from heavy trucks permeated the air over the open car. Ahead of them they could see men swinging pickaxes and blocking the road. Finally the policeman waved them forward and the glorious automobile sailed past the ruins on fat whitewalls.

From the window of her hotel room, where she was packing her bags, Lily Barnett watched it go.

She was waiting in the lobby when Major Wistosky brought the group back from the field and they dispersed to rest in their rooms. Hammond saw that Lily was in civilian clothes with a suitcase at her feet, and thought for a crazy moment she'd been given leave for a job well done.

"I didn't want to go without saying goodbye," she said.

"Why aren't you in uniform?"

"I was fired."

"What on earth happened?"

"That hypocrite is blaming me. He's sending me home."

"Perkins? Blaming you for what?"

"That Mrs. Olsen died."

She was composed but her eyes were red and swollen.

Hammond drew up an ottoman and they sat knee to knee. "What did he do to you?"

"He called me in and said he had proof that I didn't take care of her right. But I did."

"Of course you did. How'd he get that idea?"

"From the liaison reports."

"*My* liaison reports?"

"Oh, he had it all." She counted on her fingers. "*One,* I said it was okay for her to have clam water—"

"What the hell is clam water?"

"It's a remedy for seasickness; it came from Mrs. Blake on the ship."

"That seems a lifetime ago."

"Believe me, clam water can't hurt you. In fact, it's good for you. But never mind. Number *two,* going back to what happened at Notre-Dame when that horrible man attacked us and Mrs. Olsen felt faint. But she was fine—"

"Absolutely fine!" Hammond agreed.

"You said I gave her a bromide."

"Well, you did, and there wasn't any harm in that. Was there?"

"Not unless you think someone has a heart condition and should be sent straight to the hospital." Her voice shook with sarcasm. "*Three strikes, you're out*—she received *bicarbonate of soda* for heartburn! Instead of me performing surgery on the spot, I suppose."

"This is all bogus horseshit. I don't know what he's up to, shifting the blame onto you, but I never meant to imply you did anything wrong. Let me talk to him—"

"He's already left for Paris. He took that woman who came with the American journalist with the facial wounds."

"Florence Dean Powell?"

"I guess. Perkins says it was on Mrs. Olsen's medical record the whole time. That she had congenital heart failure and was supposed to take her pills. He's accusing me of negligence because according to him everything that seemed like indigestion was a heart attack about to happen. So you see, it's all my fault."

"That's grossly unfair."

"He gave me a choice—sign a statement that I take full responsibility and go home or face a disciplinary board."

"But—is it true? Was it on her record?"

"I said to him, it's not on her record. And there's no prescription for heart pills. I've been caring for this lady for weeks! He showed it to me. There was an X in the box for heart disease. But it wasn't there before, I swear it wasn't. I would not have missed something like that. I'm a good nurse!"

"Then he's a forger and an out-and-out liar, and you should take your chances with the board."

She wiped a strand of hair from her damp cheek. "He said it would be his word against mine."

"I'll back you up a hundred percent," Hammond said.

"It won't help."

"Why not?"

Their faces were close; close as brother and sister, urgently whispering about their murderous parents. Still, she could not confess the kiss. Perkins hadn't threatened her with it, but he hadn't needed to. The implication was clear that if she didn't take the blame, he would tell the board she'd seduced him. They'd see it as part of her unworthy character. What chance did she have against a military panel of Perkins's buddies? But that's not why she'd given up the fight. It was because she couldn't fight alone, and who would stand up for her? If she had to go before the nursing board, they'd be even more disapproving than the men. The only shelter in this unforgiving world was David. More than anything right now she craved his steady company and the security of being in his arms, valued and protected.

"It won't work. Don't get mud all over your shoes because of me, Thomas."

"He can't do this—"

"He can do anything he likes."

"He's a coward." Hammond spit the words. "He's not covering his ass, he's covering his fear."

"Whatever you want to call it," Lily sighed.

"What about the pilgrims? They need you."

"The official reason is that I had to go back for a family emergency—and please don't upset them with the truth. An army nurse will meet you in Paris for the trip home."

"Well, that's just swell—"

"I'm quitting the army," Lily said. "I don't want any part of it."

"I'm ashamed of the army," Hammond said. "I really am."

"I'm quitting nursing, too."

"You're just saying that because you're mad."

"I mean it. You can't have it both ways."

"Bull. You can do anything you want, too. You're a terrific nurse, Lily. Don't give it up."

"You're a nice kid, Thomas, but you're hopelessly naïve."

"Thanks a lot, pal—"

"Can't you see how it works? The hospital has a rule that married women can't work there. You can either be a nurse or a wife. Not both."

He didn't know. He'd never heard about such things. His own mother had always been a housewife and his father had gone to his job.

"That's tough," he said slowly. "What are you going to do?"

"What would you do?"

"Kill the bastard."

"Besides that."

Hammond was at a loss. She waited, seeing that he finally understood her position.

"I'm going back to Chicago to marry David. I'm going to be a doctor's wife and keep house and make sure he has everything he needs to do his work. It's too late for me, but you can still follow your ideals," she said earnestly. "Your principles in life, like we talked about."

"Remind me what they are again?" he asked ironically.

"Change the world for the better, remember?"

"Oh, yes. Fight for democracy."

"It's a good fight. You go on, Thomas. And when you look back, remember I said you could do it."

"Sure," he said, but it was as if a trapdoor had opened and his soul had fallen out. Is this what so-called honorable men did every day, let alone what they did under fire? His belief in "the right" seemed flimsy. Questionable. The whole undertaking was questionable. When Lily said she would quit nursing, his first thought was to quit the army, too. It was not his father's army. Not when you had petty minds like Reginald Perkins's running things—and if he stayed, that's the way it would be. His father was legend. Perkins was real.

Lily stood and picked up the suitcase. He took it from her and set it back on the ground and for a long time they clung to each other like abandoned children.

Griffin Reed read the address of the house out loud for the second or third time. It was frustrating beyond endurance that the shaven-headed taxi driver from Verdun with the neck of a bull and the brain of a pea had promised, *"Pas de problème"* when Reed questioned whether he knew the town of Bar-le-Duc, and of course, the moment they arrived they became lost. The result was a maddening tour of tangled streets, back and forth over several bridges and up and down hills, looking for 19½ rue du Port, the return address on the letter from Mademoiselle Champaux. There was no listing for a telephone under that name, but Reed had a strong hunch he could find her, because in some inexplicable way he believed she had been waiting for him all these years.

He'd adapted to the rhythm of pain in the gut and swings of relief provided by the shots, but the physical ailments that had been growing worse seemed pushed back by the force of the letter in his hand. His instincts said the French lady was sharing what she'd seen of Sammy Blake thirteen years ago because she felt for his American mother, plain and simple. He wasn't watching the street signs or haranguing the driver, he was drawing pieces of the picture together according to a shape in his mind. Writing questions to ask in his notebook. The editor had been hopeful they could get the two-part series syndicated in the English-speaking press. Reed also didn't mind that a major piece of reporting like that would be a spit in the eye for Clancy Hayes and his kind.

The taxi stopped at the dead end of rue Saint-François. Reed had been so engrossed in fantasies of triumph and revenge that he no idea how or why they'd gotten there. The driver was explaining that a passerby had told him to turn right. They were overlooking a stretch of still water that showed the reflection of two-story salmon-colored houses on the opposite bank with flat red roofs and sky-blue shutters. There was no one in sight except two young girls leading a goat. Reed told the driver to catch up and ask again for 19½ rue du Port. Politely. They stopped and obligingly pointed behind the houses and offered to show them how to get across, but there was no way for all of them to fit in the taxi, and so Reed had to endure an agonizingly slow procession of the girls, the goat, and the taxi inching along banks of weeds until they came to a footbridge.

He jumped out of the cab and ordered the driver

to wait. The footbridge led over the water into a hidden alley between the houses, and from there to a second bridge over a narrow canal. Bar-le-Duc had been spared from shelling during the war, and this maze of half-sunk buildings must have dated from the fifteenth century. Number 19½ was on a canal, one step up from the water, a weathered stone façade with a heavy wooden door half covered in peeling green paint. It was opened by an attractive woman in her early thirties, wearing an apron over a brown cotton peasant dress with a handmade lace collar. From the doorway Reed could see an elderly man at the kitchen table sorting through a bowl of red currants and beside him an aged woman using the traditional method of removing the seeds by piercing them with a goose quill. The white-washed walls had been aged by the soot of the fireplace to the sheen of an old meerschaum pipe.

"Good afternoon," said the young woman in French. The morning light crossed her face. She was fair-skinned and unflinching even when she saw the mask.

Reed continued in her language: "War wound. I hope I didn't frighten you. Are you Mademoiselle Champaux?"

The woman nodded. "Can I help you?"

"I'm an American. My name is Griffin Reed."

Her blue eyes widened. "Griffin Reed, the writer?"

"I received your letter about a soldier named Samuel Blake. Is it true that you knew him?"

"I knew him briefly."

"Can I have a moment of your time?"

She repeated the information to the elderly couple, who replied that Monsieur Reed should come in and be offered coffee and croissants with currant jelly, the specialty of the region. He sat with them and ate their croissant and swallowed their coffee, and when he had enough to write something, he got up from the table.

"Thank you for your kindness. I'm sorry but I have to go—"

Mademoiselle Champaux, who had been easy and cooperative, became insistent.

"Excuse me, but it said in the newspaper the American mothers are visiting this area—"

"Yes."

The young woman untied the apron.

"Take me to meet Madame Blake."

"I can't do that. My car is waiting and I have to make a train."

As he folded his notebook, a young man came through the front door; muddy clothes, trailing straw, hauling a basket of currants. He had dark hair and languorous limbs. Reed recognized him instantly and the heart inside the tin man broke.

"Is this your son?"

She nodded, the apron still in her hands.

Reed determined how long it would take to get to the cemetery and back to Verdun in order to make the afternoon train to Paris. He believed he could beat the clock. He said he would take her. The woman told the boy he'd better change his clothes.

They found Cora at Sammy's stone, planting the shaft of the American flag she had been given firmly in the grass. She was dry-eyed and, in a way, almost at home.

"Grif!" she said in surprise. "What on earth are you doing here? I thought you'd be gone."

"I'm on my way, but there's somebody you have to meet."

Cora straightened and found herself facing a woman she'd never seen before, wearing an oddly old-fashioned brown dress with a lace collar.

"This is Mademoiselle Lucienne Champaux."

She was good-looking, obviously French, and Cora assumed she had something to do with the cemetery.

"Pleased to meet you," Cora said.

The woman smiled and shook her hand.

"She doesn't speak English," Reed said.

"Oh!" said Cora awkwardly. "Sorry. I don't speak French."

"She read the article and wrote to the news-paper. I just found her. Just this morning. She's from the town of Bar-le-Duc. It isn't far, just down the Voie Sacrée. I had to bring you two together before you left for America."

"Why?"

"Because she knew Sammy."

Cora gasped and put both hands over her mouth.

"How—how did this happen?"

"The Americans passed through her village. It was a supply area for the Meuse-Argonne Offensive, we had truckloads going up to Verdun. The soldiers marched through the streets and all the girls fell in love with them. They threw flowers at the troops, and evidently, Mademoiselle Champaux gave Sammy a bar of soap."

The woman smiled and said, "*Savon*," her hands describing a bar of soap.

"You saw Sammy?" Cora cried, taking the woman's hands in hers. "You talked to him?"

As Mademoiselle Champaux spoke, Reed translated.

"She says he had a mischievous gleam in his eye. He was beautiful. He had blond hair and smoked a corncob pipe."

"He smoked a pipe!" Cora gave a wild laugh. "Why, that little stinker!"

"They all did, she says. They thought they were big men, you know. He was only there two days, but he told her all about you—his mother—and the village where you live."

"He did? Really?"

Mademoiselle Champaux nodded. Her eyes welled and so did Cora's.

"She remembers his words—'I know my mama is angry because I'm over here but one day she'll know why.' She asked what made him join the army and he said because it wasn't right that the Germans were killing people. He has in his mind the life of one child. That is why he fights. He said if one child can grow up in a free world, then it will be worth it."

Cora was overwhelmed. Her Sammy had been enough of a man to say such a thing? She was smiling, giddy and heartbroken at the same time.

"She says that child is here, and he wants to meet you."

"Well, that's very nice."

"Cora," Reed said, "he's your grandson."

The boy was sitting in the shade of the tombstone that belonged to the fellow next door, leaning up against the cross. He was young, almost the same age as Sammy when he left home. He wore a soft cotton shirt and washed-out blue shorts. His legs were drawn up and his head rested on his scabbed knees, a shock of hair over his forehead.

"That's your grandson, Cora," Reed said again, because she hadn't moved.

"*Dites bonjour*," Mademoiselle Champaux urged the boy.

The boy reluctantly got up and stepped forward. "Hello, *Grand-mère*," he said awkwardly.

His hair was dark but he had Sammy's hooded eyes and the shape of his face. He gave Cora a quick shy hug, barely touching, as if his arms were around a barrel. She went cold down to her feet.

Reed said, "His name is François."

François looked as if he'd rather be anywhere else, and Cora was speechless. She wondered how she'd ever learn to talk to him; she'd forgotten what to say to a young man. But as she basked in his childlike presence slowly something rekindled and began to shine. She had nothing to learn; she had it all inside.

"François," she said, as Reed translated, "do you like boats?"

"I like boats."

"Your father loved boats. Where I live, we have a beautiful harbor with lots of sailboats. Big ones. Would you like to come and visit?"

"In America? Yes."

"Would you like to see where your father grew up?"

The boy nodded. Cora squeezed her eyes shut. She looked again at François. He was still there and his mother was still there—the young woman with whom her son had fallen in love for two days during the war. The sun was shining in the boy's dark brown hair. She took him in her arms and held on tight until finally he embraced her, too, his arms firm and strong. She felt his body and the bones in his body and the life in the bones.

"Grif—" she wept, but he was gone.

In other parts of the cemetery, Katie McConnell draped her mother's black rosary beads over Tim's memorial and her grandmother's rosary over Dolan's. Minnie Seibert put three small rocks on the carved Star of David that marked Isaac's grave, the traditional Jewish sign that a mourner has been there; that the loved one is remembered even after the mourner is gone. Wilhelmina Russell sat in a chair under a tree from which she could keep watch over Bradley's grave, the button from his jacket still in her hand.

Reed left François and his mother at the Meuse-Argonne cemetery with Cora and climbed back into the taxi for the ride to the train station in Verdun. They made good time until they got to the entrance to the city at St. Paul's Gate and found it blocked by a column of slow-moving trucks piled with debris from excavated buildings. Reed urged the driver to find another way in, but he replied that it was the same everywhere. It's like that all the time now, he complained. The entire city is a construction zone and everything stops for roadwork. But it was better in the long run, he drawled on, because the restoration of Verdun and the development of nearby war monuments would draw more visitors each year. Things were finally looking up in this battered part of the world.

As a result of the delay, Reed missed the train to Paris by eight minutes. He was forced to wait another hour and a half for the next departure, during which he sat on an oak bench in a cindery draft between the tracks. His interest in the story had flown away like the pigeons taking off on the warm air currents. He was worn out from too many rounds of morphine and his mind wasn't working right. It was hard to concentrate on how the thoughts connected. He had a coffee but it didn't keep him from falling asleep immediately upon boarding the next train.

When he arrived in Paris for the transfer to Calais, the numbers on the destination board were spinning nightmarishly fast. For one sickening moment he felt completely disoriented. He was in the Gare du Nord, right? He stared up at the huge glass-and-iron vault. Right, yes of course, he knew it like the back of his hand. The last train to Calais, connecting to the ferry that would take him to Dover, England, was leaving in five minutes. He calculated the chances of hoofing it to the track and buying a ticket on the train or trying for one at the booth where half a dozen people were waiting. The man at the front of the line let him go first because he was a war vet. Reed got the last seat.

Down on Track 12, it looked like the beginning

of a mass exodus from Europe. The conductors were motioning everyone to move along. Reed clutched his ticket at the end of a long slow line of passengers. When he finally got on board he found himself in a third-class car filled with Jews and other émigrés from Austria and Poland, surrounded by bundles they had brought of all shapes and sizes—feather beds, teapots, musical instruments, and umbrellas, tied on with rope. Many wore their heavy winter coats although it was hot and close. Women wiped their children's tears with the corners of their shawls, while the men kept their heads in religious books. In the babble of languages, Reed could make out talk of a plague of consumption in Belgium. He was feeling weak himself from ducking through the crowd in the great hall of the station, and could not catch his breath until he made it to the second-class coach and finally threw himself into his window seat. A few minutes later a large French-woman with painted nails and a loud dress sat down beside him, a little white dog on her lap. He looked at his watch as the train pulled out. Two hours and fifteen minutes to Calais, where Florence would be waiting with a fresh supply of drugs, then across the Channel to London and the end of pain under the chill embrace of anesthesia, and then waking up to a new life.

More passengers kept cramming onto the train. Second class was filled with people standing in the aisle. Reed listened to the conversation of the couple across the aisle to keep his mind off the cramps in his legs. They were an English family who had rented a summer place in the south of France. Weary from caring for the children without a nanny, they were happy to be going home. They exchanged sections of the newspaper and talked about the possibility of another war.

"We'll have to fight it all over again," said the wife.

"Not at all. Nobody can afford a second war. The powers that be will never let it happen," pronounced the husband. He had a weak, whiny voice and seemed to work in finance. "Shall we find the dining car?"

"I don't think we should risk it. Someone might take our seats," said the nervous wife. She wouldn't let the boy and girl pet the Frenchwoman's dog.

Eventually the husband got up and came back with bags of chips for the children, complaining that there was nothing else. Reed couldn't think about food, although he realized that he hadn't eaten all day. His fingers were stiff and a strange bluish mottling had appeared on the backs of his hands. He swallowed the last dose of laudanum and listened to the wheels of the train and took comfort in their drumbeat, counting the minutes away. It was a long time since he'd smelled sea air.

Two hours later the train pulled into the station

on schedule at the port of Calais. All the passengers stood at once, grabbing for their luggage. The English couple woke their children. The loudly dressed lady's dog was making high-pitched yelps. Griffin Reed's lifeless body had slumped on its side against the window, the mask halfway fallen off. The aisles were already crowded with emigrants pushing forward, dragging unwieldy packages and heavy suit-cases, and everyone got all bollixed up as they slowed at the sight. Some picked up their solemn-eyed children and turned them away. Some knew what he was and lowered their gaze. Behind them still were boxcars of passengers anxious to make the last boat to England. Alarmists shouted, "Where is the conductor?" and there was shoving to get off.

The French lady had gotten up in shock. Clutching her dog, she quickly wedged her body into the human river. The English children scrambled out of their seats in her wake. One of them spotted a letter near Reed's outstretched shoe and reached across the forbidden territory of the filthy floor to snatch it.

"What have you got there?" asked the husband. The girl handed it up.

"What is it?" asked the wife.

"It's a letter addressed to Modesto, California, U.S.A. 'The Circle R Ranch.' "

"How American."

"That poor man must have dropped it. Did you see him?"

"Yes, and I was hoping the children didn't."

"We should give it to the porter."

"God knows where the porter *is*," said the wife, straining to look over heads.

"Well, we can't just leave it here."

The crowd was pushing forward. Afraid to be separated, they picked up the children and carried them.

"We can't go back, we'll miss the boat."

"Never mind, I'll post it myself," the husband said.

"You always say you'll do things, and then you never do," the wife remarked. They were almost to the platform between the cars. Outside it was cold and dark. His wife was always accusing him of falling short. It was true he hadn't served during the war and he'd always felt lesser for it. This letter, which had somehow come into his hands, would be his redemption. As if to seal the promise, he cast a quick look back at the man who'd done it; made the sacrifice. A kind person had covered his face. Helping the children off the high steps of the train, the Englishman distractedly slipped the letter Griffin Reed had written to his mother into his pocket, with every intention of mailing it from London.

488

HOME

24

The weather on the westward voyage was severe. A swarm of gales pursued the ship all the way across the Atlantic, one after the other with no calm in between, and as a result, everyone on board was constantly sick. The dining rooms were empty. Stewards delivered meals to cabins, where they were rarely touched. The infirm were told to stay in their rooms and not attempt to walk the shifting corridors.

The new nurse assigned to Hammond's party was Captain Jane Carlson, R.N., from North Carolina, in her forties, a thickset spinster with a friendly face and short dark springy curls she did up every night with pins, who was not a contract worker for the War Department like Lily Barnett, searching out and trying different ways, but career army; Captain Carlson was done and settled and knew what she was about. She liked to say that after twenty-two years in the military, nothing could surprise her, and by entering that restricted world at an early age, she'd made sure of it.

Captain Carlson was the perfect person—and something of a hero—to have been the one who rushed after Wilhelmina when Cora awoke from a groggy nap to find the bed across the cabin empty and her roommate gone. The gray felt soundproofing and the tempest's roar had prevented Cora from hearing Wilhelmina's departure. Staggering along the passageway, knocked from wall to wall, Cora called out to the nurse, who was finishing her rounds, and found herself forcefully about-faced, escorted back to the room with a viselike grip around the arm, and ordered to stay inside.

The ship's alarm sounded until Wilhelmina was spotted by some other Gold Star Mothers who had wrapped themselves in blankets and were lying inert on lounge chairs inside a glassed-in promenade, hoping a breath of sea air would help. Captain Carlson got there first, in time to see Wilhelmina, drenched by rain, looking like a tall thin pale naked ghost, in nothing but a clinging white nightgown, hanging on to the rail as sickly green waves broke over the side.

Thinking of nothing but duty, Carlson slid the door open and took on the storm.

Outside was wild chaos. Alarmed passengers were hit by fifty-mile-an-hour winds whipping sideways, blowing sharp bullets of rain, but Carlson put her head down and ground forward, grappling toward an orange buoy secured to the ship by a coil of rope. She wrestled it from the mounting but the water-soaked hemp was surprisingly heavy and threw her off balance as the ship listed to almost forty-five degrees. Tossed onto her back, Carlson tumbled end over end down the flooded deck until colliding with Wilhelmina and together they landed in a heap against the white iron rail, half drowning in salt water. The sea inhaled before the next surge of deadly power and by then two seamen harnessed by cables were sliding toward them through the blinding squall, and the stunned onlookers who had crowded the wind-soaked gallery witnessed a dramatic rescue at sea that would be the first thing from their lips when asked about the pilgrimage.

Hammond had been miserable since Lily's departure, and the rocky crossing kept him confined to his own despair. It was not just the loss of her lively companionship that made him want to punch the wall, but the way she'd been ripped out by the roots and tossed aside by General Perkins, and the depressing reality that the machinery of the bureaucracy would keep the commander safe from scrutiny. Stuck in a claustrophobic bunk and rolling with the storm, Hammond glared at the gray-painted ceiling twelve inches from his face, disillusioned, and at the same time trapped by the institution he had worshipped all his life.

The emergency alarm got him on his feet and out the door. He sprinted toward the shouts and commotion coming from the upper deck, tripping over floors that kept tipping like a funhouse. The ship's doctor was already supervising Wilhelmina's transport on a stretcher to the infirmary when

Hammond appeared, and they exchanged a few words while clearing gawkers from blocking the path. Wilhelmina looked dead but the doctor said she'd had a shot for the pain. Captain Carlson was lying prostrate on a lounge, attended to by the ship's nurses. There was blood all over her uniform. Word was spreading fast of the incident and Hammond thought it prudent to gather the troops.

"How is Wilhelmina?" Cora asked when he called at her cabin.

"The doctor thinks it's a broken shoulder."

"Oh, dear!"

"I know," Hammond said, supporting her as they made their way to Katie and Minnie's room. "What on earth was she doing out there?"

It was purely rhetorical. No one would ever know. Minnie opened the door looking as normal as ever. She was one of the few who hadn't become ill. Their cabin was exactly like Cora and Wilhelmina's, and the weighted vase of flowers and jars of cosmetics kept sliding around in their trays just as they did in hers, sloshing like coins in a pocket with the movement of the ship.

"It's a shame," Minnie said when Hammond explained Wilhelmina's venture.

"She's expected to recover," he said. "The nurse as well."

"Will she ever be able to play tennis?" Cora wondered.

"Why is it God takes away the thing you love best?" Minnie sighed. "Beethoven was deaf, you know."

Katie had been lying in bed, sick as a dog, one arm thrown across her eyes. "But Cora got a grandson. What do you make of that?"

Minnie thought about it. "There's always the exception," she decided.

"Will François visit you in Maine?" Hammond asked.

"I don't see how, it's so expensive."

"You'll find a way. Mrs. McConnell?" He tapped Katie's wrist. "Sorry to disturb you, but are you able to sit up?"

"I can try."

"Slowly," Hammond cautioned.

Katie made it to an upright position and seemed surprised.

"Not too bad. I'm must be gettin' my sea legs. Just in time to be off this mad boat."

"I'm counting the hours," Cora sighed.

"I have something for you," Hammond told Katie.

She took a sip of water and rubbed her eyes. "Really? And what would that be, Thomas?"

He drew two rosaries out of his pocket.

She gawked at the sight of them. "For Jesus's sake!"

"I believe these are yours. You left them at the cemetery."

"Of course I did! I meant to! What did you think?"

Hammond shrugged. "They were returned to me by the cemetery staff."

"Did you drop them?" Cora asked.

"Not a'tall!" Katie replied indignantly. "I would not lose sight of them—they belonged to my mother and her mother, who used to get down on their knees every night in the cottage in Ballinlough—"

"Sorry!" Cora said, hoping to head off another tale of dear Ireland.

"No, of course I didn't lose them; what I did was, I hung them up, one around Tim and one around Dolan. How'd they come to be back to me?"

"Maybe you're not allowed to decorate," Minnie suggested.

"I don't know," Hammond said, letting the beads fall into her open hand. "But here they are, for whatever reason."

"God bless the U.S. Army." Katie stared at the rosaries, dazed. "I suppose."

Twenty-eight hours later the S.S. *Harding* sailed back into New York Harbor. They'd left the storms behind and it was a fair summer's day with high clouds and blue sky when they passed the Statue of Liberty and made the mammoth approach to the pier. The hours passed slowly while they waited on board for the customs inspection, but finally they were released back down the gangway, tramping along with a crowd of other passengers eager to touch solid ground. Wilhelmina, with one arm and shoulder in a white plaster cast, came down in a wheelchair pushed by Captain Carlson, limping along despite a cast on one foot, like heroes from a different war, except there were no bands or newspapermen to make a fuss, just the usual wharf rats—a few police officers, souvenir hucksters, luckless orphans and prostitutes, sailors on leave.

Hammond led his group, now reduced to three, toward the line of buses waiting to take several hundred Gold Star Mothers back to the Hotel Commodore. While they waited in the hot sun, a middle-aged man wearing a seersucker suit and straw boater, and clutching a bouquet of roses, came trotting down the rows of women, asking for Mrs. Russell in Party A. He was directed to Hammond and hurried over, wiping the moisture from his ruddy cheeks with a big white handkerchief.

"Hello, son, I'm Warren J. Russell and I'm looking for my wife, Wilhelmina. I hope I'm not too late and she hasn't gone anywhere. Impossible to find anyone in this crowd. I've been told she's around here somewhere, possibly with you?"

His words alerted Cora, Minnie, and Katie. They turned around to get a good look at Warren

J. Russell, the architect of grand houses and the husband who had committed his wife to an insane asylum in order to run off with a secretary. He was not as superior-acting as they might have imagined; in fact he seemed disordered and all higgledy-piggledy, with his red bow tie askew, and sweating like a horse in the city heat. Eyebrows were raised among the women as all three had the same thought: *So it didn't work out so well with the floozy.*

"Pleased to meet you, sir," Hammond said, giving him the same once-over. "Your wife is right there. We weren't told she was to be picked up."

"It's a last-minute surprise. Thought we'd spend a few nights at the Waldorf and take a leisurely drive up north." He squinted at the crowd. "Where is she, you say?"

"Under that awning. You see the lady in the wheelchair with the nurse?"

William J. Russell did not recognize his wife, much thinner, wearing an unfamiliar lemon-yellow turban to cover the abrasions on her scalp and an ungainly cast that held one arm in the air. Incredibly, the nurse who attended her was wearing a cast, too.

"Good Lord, what happened?"

"We had an unusually stormy crossing. Mrs. Russell took a fall and fractured her shoulder. The doctor says—"

Warren J. Russell took off in a lopsided lope to where Wilhelmina sat, oblivious, and they watched as he embraced her, went down on his knees in front of her, and presented the bouquet of roses. She responded with the faintest of smiles.

Minnie zipped her lips. "I'm not going to say a word."

They said their goodbyes in the lobby of the Hotel Commodore. Cora drew Hammond aside.

"I need to tell you something, Thomas. I've been thinking about it, and I don't believe Bobbie's death was an accident."

It took him totally by surprise. "How can you say that? You were there—you saw what happened."

"I don't mean it was anybody's fault. Bobbie knew she was sick," Cora said. "Maybe she realized that her heart condition was getting worse. I honestly think she was afraid that if she told anyone they wouldn't let her go on the pilgrimage. All she wanted was to see Henry. She did say once that she'd lie, cheat, and steal if it had to do with the welfare of her children. She intentionally lied on her record."

"You're saying Mrs. Olsen left off any mention of heart disease?"

"That's right."

"Which is why there were no prescriptions for medication," Hammond said, starting to boil on

Lily's behalf. She'd been right about Perkins altering the record.

Cora nodded. "I'm telling you now because I don't want you to go off thinking you did anything wrong. It was Bobbie's will—and you know how strong that could be. You did a fine job, Thomas. We're all grateful. And you'll make the right decisions in the future, I know you will."

"I hope so," Hammond said grimly.

"What are your plans?"

"I've got another tour of duty on the pilgrimages," he said, but his mind was elsewhere.

"And then?"

"Prepare for the next war, I guess."

"I hope not, I really do."

"You're right," Hammond said, animated by a new idea. "I'm not."

"Not what?"

He looked at his watch. "Excuse me, I have to call my father. He's probably still at the club."

Cora smiled, bemused. "All right."

"I wonder what he'll think of the diplomatic corps."

"For you?"

"I think so, yes." Hammond's eyes were eager and bright. "Thank you for everything, Mrs. Blake," he said, vigorously shaking her hand. "Best of luck to you."

Cora knew she shouldn't kiss him goodbye, but

she did anyway, a gentle brush of her lips on the soft stubble of a manly young cheek.

Minnie planned to catch the downtown bus and go back to see her cousin Bessie, who worked at the glove factory, before going up to Bangor and her husband, daughters, and the chicken farm. When the hugs and kisses were over and pledges of lifelong friendships made; when Cora and Katie had gone up to their rooms for an overnight stay and Hammond had reported to the command center on the second floor, where he made a call to arrange dinner with his father that night, Minnie picked up the cardboard suitcase and walked across the lobby of the hotel and down a short hallway until she found the ladies' room. She was alone. She looked at herself in the mirror. She fixed her white brimmed hat. She placed the needlepoint purse on the marble counter and unzipped an inner compartment where she'd kept her treasure, the lipstick she'd bought in the perfume store in Verdun. She carefully unwrapped the lavender tissue. Leaning close to the mirror, she colored her lips coral red, and then stood back, marveling at the way it made her whole face come alive.

Cora and Katie took the train first-class back to Boston. This time they knew the ropes and ordered oysters Rockefeller. During that last, quiet leg of the journey, without the interference of others, they were free to speak plainly to each other with the commonality of New Englanders who, underneath it all, shared an acceptance of things. The winters did that, they agreed. You knew you were going to take a pounding and you just had to make the best of it. It was easy to talk that way with the bloom of summer going by outside the windows, but that was part of it too, the short season that brought garden tomatoes and squash at the end of it. Made you appreciate things while you had them.

When they emerged from the platform at South Station, the McConnell clan was there to meet them, and it warmed Cora's heart to see Sergeant Ian McConnell, with tears caught in his fair lashes, embrace his wife. The aunts and cousins crowded around but little Damian couldn't wait and scrabbled fast with crutches whirling until he was back in his mother's arms.

Katie held her child close. "I'll never forget you," she told Cora.

"Come to Maine. Please, I mean it. My nieces will love Damian."

"We will. For leaf season!" Katie called gaily, borne away by her family. "I'm so happy for you and your new grandson, Cora. Treasure him. It's a miracle."

On the train up to Bangor, Cora removed the Gold Star badge, glad to be an ordinary person again.

She settled the tartan travel bag comfortably in her lap as her mind buzzed with all the things she had to do. It was almost the Fourth of July. The weight of the work ahead came down on her. There would be bunting to dig out of the cellar and hang—she could count on the nieces not to have done it yet—strawberries to pick, pies to bake, potholders to sew for the tourists, the garden to put in order, then before you knew it, school. Would she sell her shortcakes? The girls would be a mess. They'd need haircuts and serious baths, like dogs with brambles. Who knew where Big Ole Uncle Percy would be— hopefully not in jail. And she hated to think of the condition of the library card catalog.

She was grateful for the time she'd had with Katie McConnell. It's funny how you can get to know a person in the most offhand way, like sharing a train ride together after an entire transatlantic adventure. Katie was salt of the earth. She understood what it meant to do without, so when she'd said François had been a miracle, she knew what she was talking about. A miracle is something unexpected; something to be grateful for, that changes your life. The miracle was meeting Griffin Reed.

When she thought back on how it happened, Cora sensed an invisible hand. The fact that Grif had found her grandson—that could not have happened by chance. It was Sammy, she decided. Sammy's spirit, guiding everything. She no longer remembered the faceless stone cross as anonymous and cold; now she believed that Sammy had been there all along. Her fingers absently climbed the window glass, as if to touch the faces that were gone from her. Sammy's and Griffin Reed's. But it made her smile and feel glad to know that Grif would be taken care of, safe in London with the best doctors in the world, and she dreamed of what he'd look like, whole.

When she awoke, they were crossing the bridge with Union Station in Bangor just ahead. The railway house no longer seemed like something in a fairy tale, as when she'd left. It seemed quite ordinary—but she was excited about seeing the harbor again, the way it opened up so modestly to the sea. It would be glorious, all gilded in sunset light—the place from which her mother had sailed away to see the world.

The Fourth of July! It came boomeranging back at her—she'd forgotten that she was chairman of the church fair! Oh no, another slew of tasks that would have be accomplished, fast. Then she remembered that she'd put Mrs. Celery Face, Essie Jordan, in charge of the crafts committee, so at least that would be a load off . . . And all at once, she realized how she could bring François to Maine. The Martha Washington Benevolent Society would be proud, she was sure, to raise the money to pay for the son of an island patriot to return. The train slowed as it pulled into the station. She could see Linwood's car. He would be waiting for her inside. The ride hadn't taken that long at all, she thought. The way home is always shorter.

Postscript

Although the characters and events in this book are fictional, the work was inspired by the diary of Colonel Thomas Hammond, son of Colonel Thomas West Hammond, whose first assignment as a graduate of West Point was to accompany a party of Gold Star Mothers as a liaison officer on the pilgrimage to France. As a result of his experience with the war mothers on that tour, Hammond decided not to follow his father's path in combat infantry and instead went into strategy and ultimately diplomacy, serving as a military attaché at the embassy in Paris. The author is deeply grateful to Nicholas Hammond and his family for access to the story of his father and grandfather, who are both buried with honors at Arlington National Cemetery.

The character of Florence Dean Powell is loosely based on an American sculptor named Anna Coleman Ladd, who brought her skill to the Studio for Portrait Masks in Paris, 1917, a clinic for wounded soldiers administered by the Red Cross. They followed the work of Sir Harold Gillies, a British pioneer in the field of facial reconstruction, which had become a desperate need resulting from the nature of trench warfare. During the Battle of the Somme, Gillies's team at

London General Hospital received 2,000 cases in one day.

The total mobilized forces of the United States during World War I came to 4,355,000. Casualties were 323,018, of which 116,516 were fatalities. Today the Meuse-Argonne American Cemetery is a memorial park commemorating more than 14,000 war dead, including 486 unknown soldiers.

To learn more about the Gold Star Mothers, go to www.aprilsmith.net.

Acknowledgments

From the first time Nicholas Hammond showed me the diary his father kept of the Gold Star Mothers pilgrimages to the publication of this novel has been a twenty-five-year journey. Despite my determination to tell this story, it would never have been realized without the dedication of two possibly more determined women: my dazzling agent, Molly Friedrich, and the famously revered editor at Alfred A. Knopf, Carole Baron. They both saw the potential, and the necessity, of giving voice to those forgotten by history, and they employed the full power of their talents to make it happen. I am honored to have joined the ranks of lucky authors whose work has been elevated beyond their wildest dreams by Carole Baron's unique combination of incisiveness, patience, strength, and spot-on instinct that is almost magical. Thank you, Carole, for standing in the trenches with me. And thanks to Ruthie Reisner—no more able assistant has ever existed—as well as to the marketing and publicity team at Knopf, under the sustaining leadership of publisher and editor in chief, Sonny Mehta.

Many sources contributed to the veracity of this book, chief among them the generous inhabitants of Deer Isle, Maine, who took a stranger with a notebook (always dangerous) into their homes: Michelle Kydd Lee, Claudette and Loring Kydd, Neva Beck, Mary Cousins, Anita Pickering, Connie Weiberg, and Tinker Crouch and Joyce Gray of the Deer Isle Historical Society. Thanks to Carrie Frazier and Joy Horowitz for help along the way. The Maine Folklife Center, at the University of Maine and the online Maine Memory Network have done a vital job of preserving our heritage and I'm grateful for their excellent work, as well as for the astonishing resources of the National Archives in Washington, D.C., which include original War Department documentation of the pilgrimages.

I am indebted to Jerry and Gail Savitz, who shared memories of Jewish chicken farming; Bruce Hoskins, for his knowledge of soil science; Robert Dawkins, munitions expert; Scott Kraska, the guru of New England military antiques; Dr. Sally Howard for psychological insights; Angela Rinaldi, for literary expertise.

In Verdun, I could not have had more knowledgeable guides than Tony Noyes and Christina Holstein, who provided an eye-opening tour of the battlefields, and introduced me to the extraordinary Jean-Paul de Vries, proprietor of the Romagne '14–'18 museum, which houses a personal collection of relics that tell the story of the lives of ordinary soldiers during World War I. Joseph P. Rivers, Superintendent of the Meuse-

Argonne American Cemetery and Memorial, provided valuable insight into the organization of the Gold Star Mothers tours of the 1930s.

Ten years ago I reached out to a group of Navy moms to find out what it is like to live day-to-day when your son is at war overseas. To these proud mothers who shared their experiences I owe the deepest gratitude of all: Cyndi Benjamin, Karen Brammer, Robin Faz, Donna Gilley, Terri Kido, Cyndi Marler, and Anne McCaffrey. Fair winds and following seas!

Over the past twenty-five years, supporters of this project have come and gone. What sustains in the end is the love of dear friends and treasured family—especially my children, Benjamin and Emma, and my husband, Douglas Brayfield, a creative partner in this book from the beginning, whose perceptions illuminate every page. Thank you to all for the joy of living this life with you.

A.S.
Santa Monica, California

A Note About the Author

April Smith is the author of the FBI Special Agent Ana Grey novels. She is also a television writer and producer. She lives in Santa Monica with her husband.

Center Point Large Print
600 Brooks Road / PO Box 1
Thorndike ME 04986-0001 USA

(207) 568-3717

US & Canada:
1 800 929-9108
www.centerpointlargeprint.com